Praise for KI

"*From action, espionage, military styled narrative, romance, all the way to the awesome science-fiction elements—a great out-of-the-box action thriller!*"

— Kashif Hussain
Best Thriller Books

"*This is an outstanding read and I rate it 5 stars! Kay serves in the military and the storylines reflect her deep understanding of the command structure and just how things are done the 'military way.' I look forward to her future productions. She's a great storyteller, especially in the 'what if's.'*"

— Julie Watson
Julie Watson Reviews

"*Provides some of the most fun and terrifying scenes I have ever read. Paul delivers a futuristic soldier sci-fi thriller that is absolutely fantastic!*"

— Chris Miller
Best Thriller Books

Also by KR Paul

PANTHEON

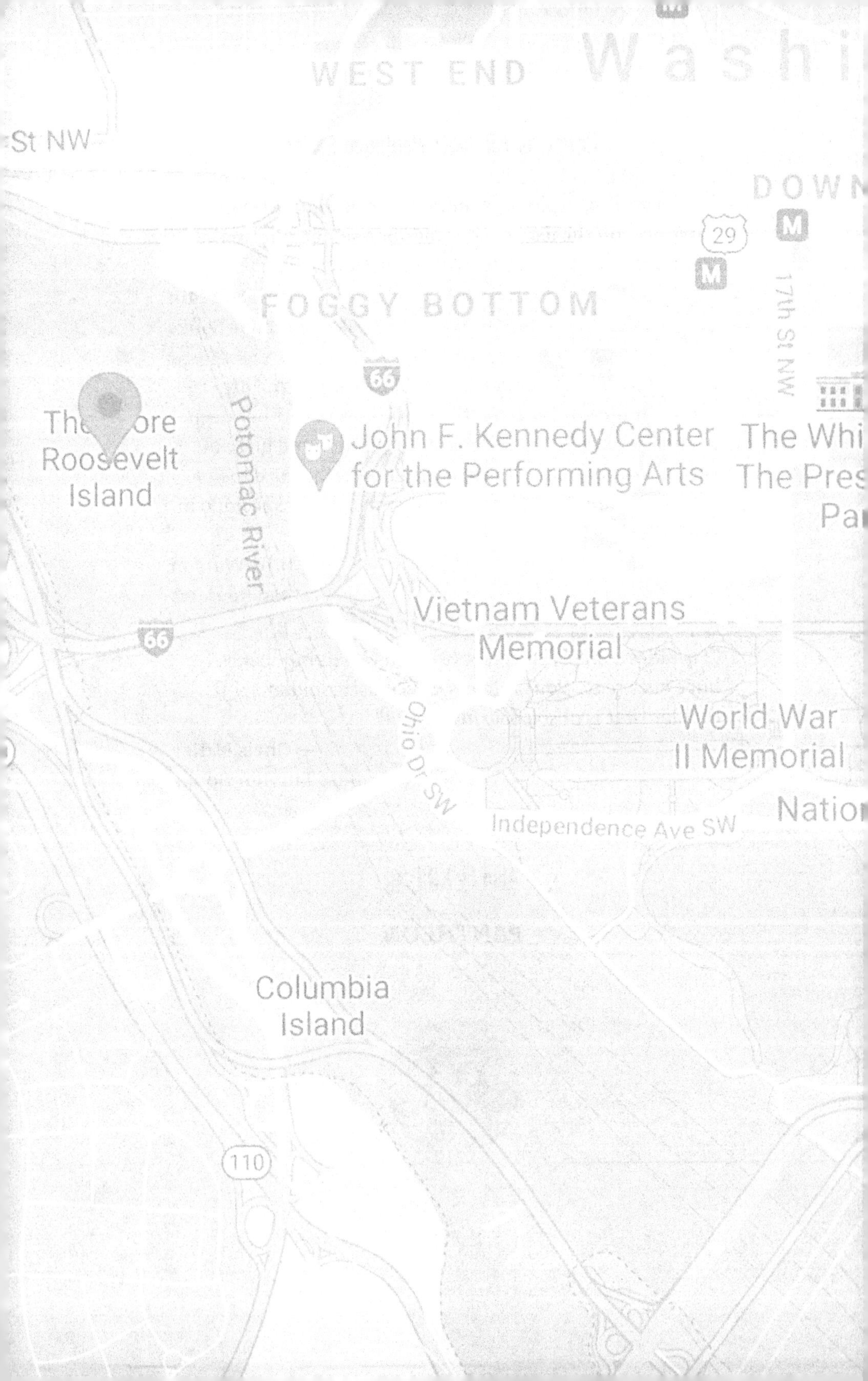

WEST END
Washi
St NW
DOWN
29
M
FOGGY BOTTOM
17th St NW
66
Theodore Roosevelt Island
Potomac River
John F. Kennedy Center for the Performing Arts
The Whi
The Pres
Pa
Vietnam Veterans Memorial
Ohio Dr SW
World War II Memorial
Natio
Independence Ave SW
Columbia Island
110

KR PAUL

PANTHEON 2

ARES & ATHENA

A TENCAP SPECIAL OPERATIONS ACTIVITY THRILLER

"Great results can be achieved with small forces."

Sun Tzu

FORCE POSEIDON
DETROIT

MILITIBUS SINE TERMINUS

FORCE POSEIDON

Published in the United States of America by Force Poseidon
forceposeidon.com

This book is a work of fiction. Except where noted, the characters, names, places, and any real people and places are fictitious or are used fictitiously. Any resemblance to people living or dead, or to places or activities is purely coincidental and the sole product of the author's imagination.

Library of Congress Control Number: 2021938464

Force Poseidon eBook edition – September 2021 ISBN-13 978-1-7366214-4-8

Force Poseidon trade paperback – September 2021 ISBN-13 978-1-7366214-3-1

This book was produced in Adobe InDesign CC 2021 using
Literata Book 10/16 for body copy and Bad Grunge for chapter headings.

For information about special discount bulk purchases of paper or ebooks,
please contact Force Poseidon Direct Sales via email at
reachout@forceposeidon.com

Front map courtesy Google Maps – Map data ©2021 Google

Manufactured in the United States of America

@ForcePoseidon · ForcePoseidon.com

Life is to be lived to its fullest so that death is just another chapter. Memories of our lives, of our works and our deeds will continue in others.

—Rosa Parks in Life *magazine, 1988*

KR PAUL

PANTHEON 2

ARES & ATHENA

A TENCAP SPECIAL OPERATIONS ACTIVITY THRILLER

CHAPTER 1
MURPHY HAWKINS
0130Z 0430L, 20 APR

US Marine Corps Staff Sergeant Murphy Hawkins rolled over in his narrow rack, snuggling up to the warm body next to him and relishing her comfort. Not too many moments of tranquility like this out here.

"Good morning, Zora," he mumbled with a smile. He ignored the gnawing hunger in his belly and his hand lazily patted his dog's face, scratching under her fuzzy chin.

Zora sat up, her weight depressing the center of the canvas cot. She gave him a smile, tongue lolling out in a happy doggy grin.

"Aww, come on, pupper, don't get up yet." He glanced at his Ares watch and groaned. "We got fifteen more minutes before we need to be up for patrol."

Zora stared back at him, one ear pointing straight up, the other flopping down. Belgian Malinois breed standards dictated that both ears should be "stiff, erect, and an equilateral triangle." Her slightly drooping ear had almost been enough to disqualify her from the Military Working Dog puppy program. Murphy thought it gave her a roguish look.

Sitting on the side of the cot where she barely fit, the dog did a sort of head toss and soundless bark, all open mouth and *hey-get-up*, then she licked Hawkins' face like he was made of Spam.

"Okay girl, okay. If you insist," Hawkins said, sitting up and rubbing his face. He wrapped both muscular arms around the dog's neck and hugged her. "We can get up."

Zora hopped off the cot as her master rose. She circled the tiny room, nose whuffling and sneezing at the piles of dust on the floor.

Hawkins gave the floor a disgusted look. The insidious moon dust grit drifted in despite how often he swept. After his many deployments, his hatred of sand had grown to epic proportions. He shook it out of nooks and crevices of his clothing as he dressed.

Hawkins and his fire team had been in Syria for months and he was still struggling to adjust to the change from his home in north-central Florida. Florida had a sultry, humid spring and sandy clay dirt, but this part of Syria was hot, dry, and coated in the damned moon dust that got in literally everywhere. Hawkins finished dressing, closing the last Velcro tab on his body armor and grabbing Zora's armor.

"Here, girl," he said quietly. Zora sat obediently in front of him. He lowered the canine flak vest onto her back. Hands swift and sure from long practice, he secured the buckles and gave a final scratch of Zora's ear before he snagged his weapons, checked both magazines were full and sand-free, and opened his door.

Zora sneezed and Hawkins squinted into the predawn gloom. The smells and sounds of the Al Assad suburb of Damascus assaulted both man and dog, although the stench wasn't as bad in the early morning hours as it would be in the peak heat of the afternoon. Around him, other doors in their makeshift urban camp were opening, and his security team members gathered for their patrol briefing.

Hawkins eyed the dirty courtyard where they gathered. Sunrise was at least an hour away and dim lamps still illuminated cobblestone roads. The door beside his hooch opened and the last two members of his team stumbled out, yawning and fastening body armor buckles.

They were short of Marines lately. His fire team's composition and order was disrupted by the dearth of replacements as the war tempo wound down, so roles and ranks didn't conform to the fondest assignment requirements of Marine Corps doctrine.

"Okay, team. Keep the radio discipline strong. My team is Red and you're Blue today, Gonzo."

Gonzales gave him a gap-toothed grin.

"Same deal as yesterday," Hawkins continued with a wry smile. "The LT is Red One. He wants us patrolling the eastern blocks while Blue Team goes west."

The new second lieutenant nominally led Hawkins' platoon, at least that's what the manning roster said on paper. Everyone knew Staff Sergeant Murphy Hawkins had been living the customary NCO tradition of gently guiding the new lieutenant to proficiency.

The young officer had arrived only three weeks before, his body armor still pristine and smelling like the plastic bags it came in. Second Lieutenant Alex Anderson was a model graduate of the United States Marine Corps Officer Basic School, gung ho and full of fresh book learning, but no combat time at all. Plus, he was a whiny, entitled pissant. The team had been forced to politely allow the young man to believe he was in charge while Hawkins systematically field-trained him to be a good officer.

The men bent to double-check guns and gear pouches full of ammo. Hawkins' second in command, Sergeant Manny Gonzalez, unclipped the lead from his own dog, Bali, preparing for departure.

Hawkins gave him a quick fist bump. "Good hunting, Gonzo."

Gonzalez said, "Cheers, bro," with a smile that displayed the new gap in his grin where he'd lost a tooth the week before.

The loss wasn't from enemy contact, but after a patrol where he'd gotten accidentally clocked in the face with a rifle butt trying to record a video for social media. Rather than allowing himself and Bali to be removed from the team and sent to the rear and a dentist, Gonzalez had pulled out the severely loosened tooth himself with his multi-tool and gone back on patrol the next day. The gap occasionally produced a comical lisp when he spoke.

Bali joined Zora and the two frisked across the sandy alley before returning to their handlers.

He ached for a cigarette, but his two-week stash, stretched thin over the month, had run out the week before. Hawkins reminded himself that his life in the Corps was only two more months. Then he would transfer to the Navy.

"Questions, comments, concerns?" Hawkins asked when they'd finished settling their gear.

The squad grenadier, Lance Corporal Sam Stratton, and automatic rifleman Lance Corporal Monty Ramirez, said nothing. Ramirez had asked his battle buddies not to use his full first name—Montezuma—as it would be disrespectful to a long-line descendant of Mayan royalty. No one knew or cared whether the claim was real. It was cool.

Heads shook in the negative. "All right, let's move out. And I swear to God, if any of you fuckers forgot your MREs again, you will fucking starve. I'm not sharing with stupid people again."

"Sorry, Murph," Rawlins called from his right. The team exchanged their traditional quick round of high fives and headed out. Their eight-man squad, comprised of two condensed fire teams, moved into the streets of suburban Damascus, Gonzo's Blue team going left and Hawkins' Red team turning right.

Each fire team consisted of a grenadier, an automatic rifleman, a rifleman, a designated marksman, and the team leader. In the case of his group, Hawkins and Sergeant Gonzalez were both canine handlers and team leads. The fire teams didn't usually have a K9 partner, or "fifth man," but for their mission in Syria, Hawkins' teams did.

Zora and Bali were charged with sniffing out bombs and various bomb-making supplies, as well as taking down suspected terrorists when they fled. They also provided a powerful intimidation factor. The terrorists hated the military dogs that, on command, would chew them up for fun. There often were such commands.

While the insurgents Hawkins and his team sought were usually fearless, something about two fierce Malinois scared the shit out of the Syrian jihadis. Additionally, Hawkins was a trained Arabic speaker, able to interpret and interact with the local community. Between his Arabic and Zora, he was the ideal team lead.

The first hour of their patrol was simple. Theoretically, they were hunting suspected terrorists hiding in and around the outskirts of Damascus, but so far, their daily searches had been fruitless. Hawkins was vigilant but he let his mind multitask as Zora loped ahead, sniffing the courtyards and alleys ahead of the team.

Only a few months ago, he'd been in the office of the Commandant of the U.S. Marine Corps. General Baker Sterling had interviewed him personally on his pending award of the Navy Cross. Hawkins had been both pleased and embarrassed to find out he was being awarded the Navy and Marine Corps' second-highest honor for action during his last deployment to Afghanistan.

He had sat stiffly in the chair offered to him, body nearly rigid and uncomfortable during the whole interview. While he knew the interview was merely a formality, a chance for the Commandant to get to know him before the eventual medal ceremony, he had been nervous. The Commandant had asked him about his time in the Corps as well as what Hawkins thought of his future.

Hawkins knew damned well the Commandant had expected him to say he was staying in the Corps.

The general officer couldn't have looked more shocked had Hawkins slapped him in the face when he said he was transferring to the United States Navy.

Irked because that tidbit hadn't been included in the general's briefing book on the young staff sergeant, he'd demanded of Hawkins to know why would leave when he was so obviously needed in the Corps. As calmly as he could, Hawkins told the general he had always wanted to be a Navy SEAL.

The Commandant had a murderous look for a fleeting second before acknowledging that a man who'd earned the Navy Cross was surely excellent material for the SEAL program. By the end of the conversation, he'd even offered to write a letter on Hawkins' behalf to the acceptance board.

Hawkins had smiled politely and thanked him, fully expecting the offer to be a polite formality—until the General called in his aide to take Hawkins' name, home phone number, and the date of the in-service SEAL selection board. A genuine smile had broken across the Commandant's face before Hawkins departed with a handshake.

Hawkins and his team walked slowly down each side of the street, scanning the dark, trash-filled street with an unsettled feeling. Roughly fifty meters down Hawkins could see movement behind a stack of crates. He whistled softly and Zora heeled, pressing against his leg. He signaled for his team to stop, listening intently and the hair on the back of his neck prickling. He caught voices speaking in hushed English, a rarity in the outskirts of Damascus.

"No, Ya'qūb, it must be in *less* than two months," a voice said. "If the bombs do not go off inside your nation of infidels, then the plan will not work." No one spoke back to the man, suggesting the one-sided conversation was on a cellphone.

Hawkins motioned his team forward and gave Zora the sign to search out the voice. They had been looking for high pay-off targets for five weeks and this sounded like a bomb-maker speaking. It was the most promising lead the team had thus far.

"No, three months is not soon enough," the man said. His tone was urgent and uncompromising. "If we are to show our strength, it must be two weeks or less." The voice paused, listening. "Yes. Good then. *Al-Wala wal-Bara*."

Hawkins recognized the term, which meant total loyalty to Islam and total disavowal of anything else.

"Until tomorrow, may Allah bless you and your wife and children. Allahu Akbar!"

Hawkins' team flanked the walls of the cobblestone street, hardly more than an alley. They moved forward without making a sound louder than their rising heartbeats.

"Damned American infidels!" Hawkins heard the voice say in Arabic. He had dialed another phone call. "They still believe we are on the same side but agree to their half of the destruction. By coordinating bombs in both their nation and ours, we can show how far reaching is the power of the New Caliphate."

Cold fear dropped heavy into Hawkins' belly. Terrorists in Syria coordinating with an allied terrorist group on American soil? The thought horrified him.

He signaled to his team. On his count, they would break down the small wooden door they had surrounded. Hawkins tapped his throat mic, calling his lieutenant, by now at least three miles in the opposite direction.

"Red One, Red Four. Probable contact. Req coordination for an extraction to interrogation in approximately twenty mikes."

"Copy. Standby," the young man's voice replied. The lieutenant might not be a seasoned veteran, but he was good at coordinating.

Hawkins nodded to his team and counted down with his fingers.

Three.

Two.

One.

A press of bodies burst through the flimsy wooden door, Zora hot on their heels. Hawkins followed, moving with a practiced gait that minimized the rattle of his gear, the butt of his rifle held tight to his shoulder and in the ready position. Before he crossed the threshold, chaos erupted.

Angry shouts in Arabic came through the door as the Americans entered. Hawkins flicked his ballistic glasses off his nose. Two men in long traditional kaftans and loose pants held guns but they were pointed at the floor and the team had their weapons up and ready to rock and roll.

Both sides were tense. Zora stood her ground and growled at the Syrians, who were more terrified of her than his men. They were pleading for the Americans not to shoot them.

"Put down your weapons!" Hawkins barked out in Arabic. Slowly, deliberately, the men complied. Hawkins felt a loosening of his tension, but the hair at the back of his neck still prickled. "Hands in the air," he ordered them. Their quick compliance seemed suspicious.

Hawkins' eyes flicked over the room. There were bomb-making supplies scattered across makeshift worktables. He gave a sharp nod to Rawlins, who breathed hard at his right. This was exactly the thing they'd been sent to catch. He wanted to relax, but something in the speedy compliance nagged at him.

"Cuff them and take them to the courtyard. LT has an extraction inbound in fifteen," Hawkins said. Their landing zone was only a few blocks away in a town square. Strake and Ramirez restrained the two men and marched them out the door.

Gunfire erupted in the dark, narrow alley. Rawlins and Stratton fired in opposite directions down the street.

Hawkins' mind went into overdrive as he watched the two Marines controlling the terrorists drop, bullets tearing into their bodies. He tapped his mic. "Red One, Red Four, contact three miles east of base, two are down," he shouted. Without waiting for a response, he pressed forward to look for shooters from the doorway. Before he could get his rifle barrel through the opening, Zora leapt forward.

"No!" he yelled at her. The moment the dog entered the narrow street she was struck by an enemy bullet. She emitted a pitiful yelp as she rolled across the cobblestones. "NO!" Hawkins roared.

He'd been scared and angry to see his men ambushed, and seeing Zora now also felled by a bullet drove the emotion from a cold fury in his belly directly into his heart.

Hawkins saw Zora laying on the ground next to his two Marines and the two restrained terrorists. He heard Rawlins and Stratton at his back providing withering suppressing fire for the injured Marines, but the enemy's return fire still kicked up deadly dust devils all around the Marines crouched in the street. Heedless of the hail of bullets, Hawkins darted forward into a baseball slide and slid into Ramirez. He took the drag handle on the body armor and pulled him into the building. He repeated the move with Strake while Rawlins and Stratton continued to provide crushing cover fire. Then Hawkins went back out for Zora.

He lay his body over hers as low as he could and scanned the street at both ends. At one the end of the alley, he could see a group of armed men rushing toward them with weapons drawn and pointed at him.

The swarm of oncoming men outnumbered and out-gunned them.

With only Rawlins and Stratton able to fight with Hawkins, the big gaggle of armed men approaching them would be a match, even for three well-armed Marines. He eyed the room they seemed to be trapped in. It wasn't perfect but it would provide a measure of cover, of safety, for his team while they unscrewed this mess.

"Red One, Red Four, I say again, contact three miles east of base, two are down." Hawkins raised his own M4, squeezing off a burst of gunfire. "Request immediate air support for ECAS."

Getting emergency close air support was going to be danger close. It risked the team's lives as much as it offered support.

Rawlins yelled and Hawkins looked back. At the opposite end of the alley, another hostile group was running toward Hawkins and his men, sprayin' and prayin' at random. Chips of the stony street and mud wall dust rained down on Hawkins as the attackers opened fire with no regard for aiming.

Pushing down his fear, Hawkins rallied his thoughts. He knew he and his men might soon be overrun and would likely be killed. He needed a safe place from which to fight and, hopefully, get warheads on foreheads rained down in the narrow Syrian street five hundred pounds at a time.

"Red Four, ECAS is inbound—I say again, ECAS is inbound. You keep those big water heads down, mister." The lieutenant's voice was calm as it crackled through his radio.

"Copy," Hawkins growled. He initiated a Larsen Electronics infrared emitter and tossed it down the street toward the advancing terrorists. Its heavy rubber base ensured it would land solidly and face the sky where the F-15 pilots could see it. The device would help the American aircraft find, fix, and eliminate the hostile forces now flooding the street.

He dragged Zora back inside the building by her body armor, crouching low. He was happy the hostiles were terrible shots and he could make it to even this small measure of safety unharmed. With Zora safe, Hawkins slapped a self-adhesive QuikClot gauze on the dog to stop the bleeding, but with her fur the seal was imperfect and it didn't work very well.

Hawkins rejoined Rawlins and Stratton, who crouched over their two injured Marines dressing bullet holes. The Syrian captives, still in plastic cuffs, lay low out in the street. They hadn't been shot at by their rescuers, but they weren't risking a run into the squat building sheltering the Marines.

"Cover me, I'll escort our guests inside," Hawkins said. He nodded to the two terrorists still in the alley. "I assume they won't shoot their own."

"I wouldn't bet the title of my car on that," Rawlins said. He stood near the door and Hawkins gave him a quick high-five as he settled against the door frame to provide cover. Stratton kept bandaging Strake and Ramirez and, in the street, the two FlexiCuffed insurgents were screaming for help to their jihadi brothers, now bearing down on them from both ends of the lane.

At Rawlins' nod, Hawkins crawled into the street and grabbed each Syrian by the scruff of their kaftans, pulling them inside the door while Rawlins' sprayed a blast of covering fire, first right, then left. Once back inside the mud building, Hawkins shoved the prisoners into a corner and shouted in Arabic, *Stay!* They each vigorously nodded their understanding of the order.

Ramirez was out and Stratton worked on his wounds. Strake was lucid but bleeding profusely from both legs. Hawkins tossed him a medical kit and made sure the man's gun was at hand.

"Put pressure on that and wrap it tight, then be ready," Hawkins said. "Rawlins, Strake, pull back in here, pull back."

Hawkins knelt next to his dog to assess her injuries. What a fucking shitshow.

He glanced around the small room, taking in each man and the dog. The building's meager walls would provide only a small measure of protection from a bomb run that all but guaranteed the weapons would land inside of the minimum safe distance.

He needed to pause this fight long enough to get them to safety, but they were out of options.

Out of nowhere, Hawkins' mind went back to the USMC Commandant's office once more.

Clean. Safe. Quiet.

Frightened and in pain, Zora whined in the rising gunfire and shattering of concrete around them. Hawkins couldn't hear the Air Force F-15E Strike Eagles orbiting in a CAS wheel overhead on their bomb runs for the rapid-fire explosions as 500-pound GBU-38 GPS-guided bombs dropped on the terrorists in the narrow street. The powerful explosions rapidly marched up the cobblestones toward the team's hole.

Hawkins' mind sought safety and, in his mind, he saw his men and his dog. It was Hawkins' responsibility to protect them and they faced probable death—whether from the overwhelming enemy force or their own U.S. Air Force—and all Hawkins could think of was the last time he'd truly been happy and safe. He visualized it perfectly and his mind reached for it instinctively. Desperately.

Then Hawkins, Zora, and the entire squad vanished just as a 500-pound weight-class warhead detonated in the doorway, destroying the building they were hiding in.

At his desk in the office, U.S. Marine Corps Commandant General Baker Sterling reviewed paperwork late into the night. His first wife had hated when he worked late, his second had used it to drunkenly sleep her way through half of the Quantico Officers' Club, and the third merely accepted it as the life and love she'd chosen.

Regardless of the havoc it created in his personal life, he enjoyed the peace and focus it gave him to work without the constant din of ringing telephones and congressional visitors, and his ever-present aide in the outer office intercepted the occasional telephone call.

When a gaggle of sweaty, combat-dressed men and a dog materialized in his large, darkened office, the general stood so fast he knocked over his chair. As the group arrived out of nowhere it too knocked a chair across the room when the air expanded forcefully in the office.

A career spanning thirty years in the Marine Corps had taught General Sterling to expect the unexpected, but the sudden arrivals strained his serenity. He gave the bloody, dirty heap a fast glance and recognized one of the dust-covered men.

"Staff Sergeant Hawkins?" the Commandant asked, cooler than he felt.

Hawkins heard a voice calling him but ignored the out-of-context moment. He was running on adrenaline now and focused on what was in front of him, but he could feel his body tensing up like never before. He ignored mounting muscle cramps. *What the hell is going on with me?* he thought.

Breathing hard, he searched Zora's chest with shaking hands, seeking a bullet hole but finding only a deep stripe of scarlet and the remnants of a QuikClot bandage where the bullet had grazed her flank. Hawkins ignored the sudden and unnerving quiet that had replaced the chattering of gunfire and exploding bombs as he pulled more gauze from his pack and pushed the wad onto the wound, securing it with a second roll.

He turned to his men and rocked back in confusion. Adrenaline allowed him to ignore the sudden fatigue weighing him down, but it didn't diminish his disorientation. Where was the building they had just been in? Still ignoring the voice calling to him, assuming it was the lieutenant in his earpiece, he took in his men.

His heart rate, already racing from the adrenaline, ratcheted up another notch when he saw the blood seeping across their uniforms.

"Sergeant Hawkins!" a voice bellowed, finally pulling his attention away from his team.

"LT, I need just another goddamn minute to sort this cluster out and we can talk about extraction," Hawkins said into his mic.

"No, Sergeant, I don't think you need an extraction. I think you have it under control," the voice said.

A gentle hand clasped his shoulder and Hawkins tensed. His skin still burned with adrenaline, his breath was harsh, and his hands moved over his dog without conscious thought.

Sudden realization sunk into him. *Carpet. Quiet. Clean.* Things that meant he was safe. His head turned toward the hand that had clamped on his shoulder, following the uniformed arm up to the face that hovered above it.

"General ... General *Sterling*?" He could hardly get the words out.

He felt like his blood was on fire and he was wracked with the most terrible muscle pain he'd ever experienced.

Hawkins expelled a ragged breath and looked around. The commandant's office was just as he had seen it last. And as he'd seen it in his mind only moments ago. He looked around to his men whose faces wore just as much shock and surprise as Hawkins'.

The Commandant's plush office surrounded him and his battered team but he could still feel the grit of Syrian sand digging into his knees where it pressed into carpeting next to Zora. Darkness crowded in as Hawkins pulled the frightened dog close.

I know, girl—me too ... Then Hawkins, his body wracked with agony, depleted and ravenous, fell sideways to the carpeting.

"Colonel Martin!" General Sterling called to his aide in the outer office, knowing full well the officer was there despite dismissing him hours ago. "Call Marco Martinez at Limitless Logistics. Tell him I need him in my office, *right now.*"

General Sterling paused a moment and smiled paternally at Hawkins. *How your young life is about to change, Marine.*

"Tell him the Pantheon is expanding."

CHAPTER 2
MURPHY HAWKINS
0645Z 0254L, 20 APR

Hawkins awakened in a sterile sick bay, an IV in each arm. Panic lanced through him and he bolted upright, looking for Zora and his men. He squinted against the fluorescent lights, searching the room. His overwhelming perception was that he was weak as a kitten and starving.

"Rawlins! Zora!" he bellowed. Some part of his mind registered how harsh his voice sounded.

Two orderlies ran into his room to find him trying to remove multiple lines of IVs.

"Let me go! Where am I, goddamnit? Let me go, man!" Hawkins howled in fury as the men wrestled him back onto his bed. He felt a sharp jab in his arm and the world faded to black again.

The second time Hawkins awoke more slowly. His first complete thought was that someone had cut his clothes off and he was no longer in his uniform. The heavy, gritty feel of a combat-weathered uniform, too long exposed to sand and sun, had been replaced with a warm heaviness on his legs and torso.

When he was able to crack his eyelids open enough to peer into a dim room, some part of him noted a hospital gown covered by a thin blanket. The antiseptic hospital smell permeated his mind along with an acrid tang in his mouth.

He realized he was still under sedation and he must have been hit when—well, whatever happened in Syria happened. He would have been out a long time if he'd made it out of a field hospital and into a full hospital. His thoughts moved with glacial speed. Did he and his team make it to Landstuhl in Germany? Or were they still in Iraq, too injured to risk a longer flight into Germany?

Hawkins remembered Ramirez and Strake being hit. And Zora. He mentally prodded his fuzzy memory for the sound of a helicopter, a sure indicator they had been MEDEVAC'd.

The aggravating hunger in his belly said that, wherever he was, he'd been out for a long time.

He looked up at the IV flowing into his left wrist. The clear plastic pouch had a big black-on-white label that read PANTHEON DIET N1b2. He couldn't make out much of the fine print, but it looked to be a high-speed nutrient drip of some kind.

M. *Guffin Blend. This custom infusion supports repair and building of muscle, balanced hormones, skin health, mood, athletic performance, detoxification, leaky gut, malabsorption, and extreme protein deficiency. This drip contains trace minerals of zinc, copper, manganese, chromium, selenium, and essential amino acids.*

There was much more information on the oversized label, but Hawkins couldn't read it without getting out of the hospital bed. And he didn't want to do that yet.

He remembered calling in the danger-close air strike on their attackers. He remembered Rawlins and Stratton providing cover fire while he rescued his Marines and his dog from the kill zone in the street. And there were wisps of a dream he'd had about being on the floor in the Commandant of the Marine Corps' office.

Then excruciating pain and darkness.

Hawkins' mind worked against the sedation but failed. He tried to move a hand to wipe his brow but his was arm stopped short, chained to the rail of the bed. No, wait. Not chained. *Handcuffed.*

Not Iraq or Germany, then, the thought bubbled up slowly. Had he been captured and brought to a Syrian hospital? Unlikely. He squinted at his wrist, trying to determine if he could slip the cuff.

"Hey-hey-hey, sergeant, hold on a sec," a woman's voice floated to him through his opiate haze. The woman's voice was soft. Honeyed. It wrapped him in a feeling of warmth that may have also been the hospital blanket and the sedative.

A soft fluorescent light flicked on overhead light and was turned down further, but it was still bright on his tired eyes. Hawkins winced and his eyelids slammed shut of their own accord.

"Sorry," she said in a soft voice. "We didn't want to wake you prematurely."

The woman's voice had only the tiniest hint of southern drawl, Hawkins noted. The tone and light accent made a slow smile scroll across his face.

The woman smiled and added, "You know you're still under sedation, right?"

Hawkins cracked an eyelid open again to see the hazy shape of a young woman leaning over his arm and unlocking the cuff. When her red-gold hair brushed against his arm the silken feeling was a stark contrast to the rough, grimy, deployed life he'd been living the last several months.

"Girl, I don't even know your name and I'd marry you right now," he croaked. Long hair and a slight Southern drawl, the woman must be an angel.

The woman straightened sharply and he saw her limp awkwardly to a chair near him.

"Yup, still under the sedation," she said with a laugh. "Do you know where you are right now?"

"Well, I've seen a few fine Syrian women, but none with hair your color. So, not Syria?" he slurred, sedation thick in him.

"No, definitely not. You're in Washington, DC. The sick bay of Limitless Logistics, and you're safe. What do you remember last?" Her voice was rich with quiet intensity.

Hawkins inhaled through his nose and tried to pull his scattered thoughts together. "Patrol with my fire team. Ambushed. No, wait.

Overheard terrorists discussing an attack on U.S. soil. There was a fire fight. Bombs. My Marines and my dog shot."

Hawkins' vision focused enough to see a frown on her pretty face, red-gold eyebrows creasing over bright hazel eyes. "Then we must have been picked up by QRF—thank God for the quick reaction force. Zora and two of my guys shot, I think. Did I say that out loud already or just in my head? Then weird dreams."

Hawkins noted the hum of the room's air conditioning. He floated in the morphine haze.

"Dreams?" she prompted.

"Huh? Yeah. I mean, I'd called the LT for an extraction. I assume we got hit with something bad and that's why I've been out all the way from Syria to here. Did we even stop in Landstuhl?"

Hawkins managed to get both eyes open and he studied her. She looked a little peeved.

When the silence stretched on too long he asked, "Come on, nurse. *Are* you a nurse? What did you say your name was?"

"I didn't say."

Hawkins focused on a Common Access Card hanging from a lanyard imprinted LIMITLESS LOGISTICS. It had her color photograph, an ID number over a bar code, and in large blue letters the name VALERIE HALL, PANTHEON. Two small gold stars appeared at the bottom.

"Okay, ah, spill. You can tell me. Did the docs take a leg or something? And where the hell is Zora?"

He missed the dog's reassuring weight and warmth.

"That beautiful dog you brought with you? That's Zora?" she asked. "That's a fine-looking doggo."

He nodded, not trusting himself to talk.

"I'll ask our docs." She leaned over with a slight wince and patted his hand. He felt the briefest flicker of calm at her touch. "She'll be all right, sergeant." She sat back in her chair. "Think again. Can you remember anything else about what happened?"

"Where is she, Zora?" Hawkins demanded.

"About two rooms over, being treated by the medics who initially patched up you and your men."

"Not a vet?"

"Not right now. Our medics are very good and the fewer people who see you both right now, the better."

"The fuck does that mean?" Hawkins barked. Anger was boiling away the morphine haze and he was starting to string coherent thoughts together.

She ignored Hawkins' outburst. "What else do you remember?"

"Nothing," he said, steel coming back into his voice. "A dumb fucking daydream." Hawkins struggled in the bed, pushing himself up onto his elbows. "Look, lady. I want to see my dog."

"Did this daydream perhaps involve landing in the Commandant of the Marine Corps office with your entire team?" she asked, a trace of humor in her tone.

Hawkins stared at her, jaw hanging open.

"Close your mouth, Sergeant Hawkins. I can explain," she held up a placating hand and smiled. "He's a little pissed about the carpet, by the way. Five dirty men, two of them bleeding, and a bleeding dog leave a hell of a mess."

"That shit was real? Are you fucking with me?"

She cocked her head and gave him an impish grin, obviously pleased to have surprised him.

"No. Should I be?"

Hawkins got one look at the wicked grin on her face and dropped back on his pillow, staring at the far wall.

The woman gave another of those rich, honeyed laughs and slapped his arm. "Don't worry about it. I'm fucking with you."

He turned to her and raised an eyebrow. "You know, I hear a lot of grunts swear, but rarely the chicks."

Her face sobered and she gave a quick *humph*. She studied him as if looking through a microscope.

"I'm tougher than I look and not unaccustomed to swearing." She cocked her head as she considered him. "First things first. Let's reassure you about Zora."

The woman stood slowly, using the crutch for support, and unlocked his handcuffs.

"Think you can walk? They had a couple hours' worth of work patching up your two men first and they just started working on her. I can take you over there."

Hawkins sat up and nodded. "Yes, let me see my girl."

He rose, careful not to entangle the IVs running into both arms and moved the poles around the bed where a duty nurse removed the needles and taped up the holes. The Marine towered unsteadily over the woman.

"I'm Major General Valerie Hall, US Air Force, by the way." She held out her hand.

Hawkins stared at her open-mouthed for seconds before recovering. *The two gold stars on her CAC ...*

"Staff Sergeant Murphy Hawkins, USMC, but most everyone calls me Murph." He shook her hand lightly, afraid to crush her. She gripped his hand far more firmly than he expected. Hawkins felt a momentary sense of trepidation at her touch.

"Man, those are some calluses. Guns, CrossFit, or both?" Val asked as she limped her way forward on her crutch.

"Uh, both, ma'am."

"Please don't *ma'am* me again, Murph. We seldom do rank around here," she said as they moved down the hall. Val flashed him a quick grin to strip the harshness from her words.

"Where or what is 'here'?" Hawkins asked. They walked down the passageway only a few doors and stopped before one.

"We'll get to that in a bit," she said. "Go on in."

Hawkins stifled a gasp as he entered the darkened space. On the other side of the slanted window looking into an operating theater, Zora lay under bright LED lights draped in a green sheet covering all but her chest and muzzle. Hawkins walked forward to the big window, transfixed as a man in full-body surgical garb delicately stitched a long, shallow wound together.

Bloodied gauze lay strewn about and Hawkins recognized one as the dressing he slapped on Zora's chest after he landed in the Commandant's office. He staggered back a step and turned to look at Val.

She pressed an intercom button mounted on the wall next to the window and the squawk box came alive.

"Mike, I've got Sergeant Hawkins here. Zora's his doggo." The doc looked up to the observation room and raised a thumb at them, then bent back to his task.

"She's doing very well, sergeant," Dr. Mike Tempest said as he worked. He was an Air Force colonel and flight surgeon. "I've got lots of combat medicine in my logbook and we've dressed wounds worse than these many times."

He cocked his head toward Zora's exposed muzzle encased in an oxygen mask.

"We had to guess at her body weight for anesthesia, but we went slightly lighter and she's tolerating it well."

The anesthetist scanned Zora's digital monitor and pointed a finger at a veterinary chart called up on a tablet. Then she reached forward and adjusted a valve and raised a thumb at the window.

"Her vitals are really good," she said. Hawkins could tell she was smiling behind her surgical mask.

"So, yeah," Val said. "You really went straight to the Commandant's office from Syria," she said to Hawkins. "No, I can't really read your mind, but I'm fairly new to all this too and I know how overwhelming it can be. The confusion. The pain," her voice hitched slightly. She spun on her crutches. "Stay with her, Hawkins. We can talk in a few." Val turned toward the door.

Hawkins watched her hobble out of the room. He turned back to the window and pressed the intercom button.

"Is she going to be okay?"

"Zora, or General Hall?" the doctor asked him, eyes not lifting from Zora's chest.

Hawkins spluttered, "She's really a general?" He still couldn't believe it.

"Yeah, they all are," the doctor said absently, his eyes focused on his hands working Zora's wound. "They'll both be fine though. Zora here," he said, patting the dog's covered head gently, "just needs a few more stitches. General Hall will be up and running circles around us soon enough. Small caliber round, through and through," he went on, HIPPA rules clearly far from his mind. "Val, not Zora. It didn't take much flesh and I expect her to be back on duty in a week or two."

"She really got shot?" Hawkins asked. He was astounded. That tiny little chick? "What the fuck—" Hawkins reconsidered, not knowing the doctor's rank but knowing military doctors are officers. "—that is, what the hell happens around here?"

"My man, are you in for a shock," the doctor chuckled.

Hawkins watched him work in silence for a few more minutes.

"Okay, last suture. Zora will be out for at least another two hours." He removed his mask and looked up to Hawkins with a steady gaze. "You can come back in an hour and a half to be there when she wakes if it's permitted. I suggest finding General Hall and finishing your debrief in the meantime."

"Yes sir, roger that," Hawkins said. Brows furrowed in thought, he retraced his steps back to his room. He found Val—General Hall—in a chair, idly thumbing through her phone.

"Satisfied that she's being well cared for?" she asked.

"Yes ma'am. General. I mean, Val ..." he said, flummoxed.

"Just Val is fine. Sit down, Murph." When he'd settled himself back on the bed she continued. "Let's go big to small first. I'll explain a little about what's going on, then you can ask questions. Good enough?"

Hawkins nodded.

"This place is Limitless Logistics, a cover for the Air Force TENCAP Special Operations Activity, a top secret, black-world program of the Department of Defense. We," she pointed at him then tapped her own chest, "possess certain skills that allow us to move people and things instantaneously around the globe or even into space, with a few limitations. You and I, along with seven others, are the only people known at this time in the United States capable of doing what we do. All but one is military. One is civilian, but she may get absorbed into the Air Force too." She paused to gauge his reaction. Even those whose discovered their skills traumatically often had hints of it earlier in their lives. Hawkins didn't so much as blink.

Good, she thought.

"When you Jumped your team out of Syria, you experienced what we call a spontaneous traumatic trigger. What happened to you unlocked an ability you already possessed and you Jumped."

Hawkins frowned.

"You teleported. We call it Jumping here."

He nodded, his brows furrowed. "Say what now?"

"You teleported your entire team to safety and into General Sterling's office because your mind unconsciously reached out to a point, a location, where you felt safe. It could have been your mother's house, or a bar, or Mrs. Pranion's 3rd Grade classroom." Hawkins started. "Yes, we have your background already in progress. Your squad and the dog didn't have to touch you to go along because so were very spun up and they were already present vividly in your mind. When you went, so did everyone else."

Val offered a sincere smile. She knew Hawkins must be reeling at all this.

"Now that you know what you're capable of, we would like to offer you a position here at Limitless Logistics."

Hawkins stared at her. He heard her words but they had simply washed over him.

"Sergeant Hawkins? Murph? Too much info or not enough?" she asked.

He shook his head and blinked, trying to fit what he'd heard with his memories of the last forty-eight hours. He held up a hand.

"Where are my guys now?"

"Ramirez and Strake are fine, though Strake's leg wounds may get him a medical discharge if he wants it. I imagine he won't. Lots of shot-up people go back on active duty once they're discharged from Walter Reed. Ramirez, Stratton, and Rawlins are back at Pendleton and pending new assignments."

Hawkins pondered the updates for a moment. He was a good steward of his people and he didn't like not being instrumental in their welfare, but that's the Marine Corps. He was relieved that none of the squad had been killed.

"Okay. Let me get this straight. I can—what did you call it, Jump?—anywhere, with anything?"

Val nodded. "With some restraints, but yeah, pretty much. You must have been in a place before or you have to take the image of the location from the mind of someone who's been there; you do that with a touch, usually just a handhold. And there's no such thing as a free lunch. You can go, but it's about a calorie-plus per mile and you have to allow for any weight you're moving other than yourself. Roughly, one additional calorie per five hundred pounds, plus what we burn for the distance." She smiled at him. "So, every one of us is physically limited to how much instantaneous calorie loss we can stand."

Hawkins eyed her slender frame. "So, you can go to, like, the end of the block?"

"I'm tougher than I look. I told you that already." Her face was carefully blank. He nodded, digesting that.

"Man, date nights are going to be a helluva lot more interesting." Val winced at that. *Mine was*, she thought,

"No, probably not. Like I said, top secret," she stressed. "Black. Unacknowledged. Men-in-Black levels of 'we don't exist.' You will be trained in all this in the coming weeks, starting with NDAs and as much of what not to do as the things you are permitted to do."

"So, no dragging my ladies to Paris for a date?" He watched her mouth tighten and her brows raise.

"No." Val smiled. "But in any case, you wouldn't be the first."

Val smiled at the memory of being in Paris at the *Musee d'Orsay* with CIA officer Brandon Powell and fighting for her life with the Russian Leon Orlov. She'd clawed out one of his eyes with her own hands in that battle and he'd vowed to avenge that. Nevertheless, the information she'd gleaned from Orlov's mind was enough to locate rogue Russian General Demyan Borya and his outlaw *Svoboda* group—

the Russian military equivalent of the Pantheon.

Borya had been trying to foment a proxy war between Russia and America to take the country from Putin's rule. Except that Borya was well-known to be even worse than Putin and he wanted his thumb on the nuclear button for all the wrong reasons.

Val had captured Borya for the Pantheon and she got her leg shot Jumping back to Limitless with the rogue Russian general in tow.

Borya was out of circulation now and no longer a danger to Russia or the U.S., and Val would be on a crutch for another few weeks as a result.

"There are some very nice perks with this assignment," she said with slightly forced brightness. "You'll get a very decent promotion. Limitless Logistics owns contracts with the government, so you'll be paid as a contractor by them on top of your military paygrade of O-8. That's a major general's pay."

"Wait, *what*?" Hawkins sputtered. "I'll be a general too?"

"Yes, technically. It's pretty cool the first few times you have to wear a uniform with your new rank, so don't get all Marine and spill soup on your tie. But we don't much go in for ranks here. It's just an advanced way for our service branches to pay us. And there are bonuses and allowances and all kinds of other good stuff."

"Wow, lady," the Marine staff sergeant laughed, "have you got the wrong guy for a general's stars."

"Nah. Like I said, we don't throw rank around here. And you will earn every dime, I promise you. We also have a handful of genuine generals in our universe who will quickly put you in your place if you get feisty with them, so don't do that. It's mostly just to keep overzealous commanders from trying to pull rank on you out in the field. If we let some bird colonel try to ride herd on us, they would waste the whole team on a low-priority Jump, risking the operators' health and our ability to execute an urgent or emergency mission."

Hawkins could see tension etched in her tight shoulders and the hand that locked in a death grip on her chair's arm.

"Continuing, I was an Air Force captain before I got here. Dee—Damarcus, you'll meet him—was enlisted like you before he went to OTS. He joined us not too long after he commissioned."

Hawkins accepted her herding him back on topic.

"And what is it we do, exactly, with these superpowers?"

"Superpowers?" Val asked with a laugh. "I can't wait to see your first full-gear distance Jump with Hank Gardner's boys. He's our usual mission boss, colonel-type, down at Hurlburt in Florida. He and his team are our primary mission trainers. We'll see if you feel like a superhero when you're bent over on your knees in the middle of a desert puking your guts out because you didn't eat properly."

"Hey ma'am, I CrossFit five days a week. Look at this!" Hawkins raised both arms, his muscles flexing. "Two hundred and twenty pounds of pure Marine muscle here!"

She regarded him steadily.

"Uh huh. Nice." Val grabbed his chart from a hook on his hospital bed and flipped through the pages. "Maybe you were two-twenty before, but you were two-oh-six when you got checked in here." The look on Hawkins' face was confusion and a little disappointment. "Yeah, not to worry. I told you Jumping was taxing, and you brought five Marines and a dog a helluva long way."

She waved a hand for him to sit down again. "Well, Super Marine, we spend most of our time moving stuff and people into and out of places fast. Some are preplanned Jumps to get supplies or people in or out of a mission space, but sometimes it's emergency Jumps for personnel recovery, supply runs, you name it."

"No patrols, no standing watch, and no getting screwed by the Big Green Weenie of the Marine Corps?"

"Not as such," she said, her mouth forming a wry grin. "We put the 'special' in 'special operations.' When you're on mission or planning for one, that's all you do. When you're off the Jump roster, you're working out, training, and prepping for the next mission. And eating—always eating." She smiled at him. "I'm going to take a wild guess and say your stomach is rumbling right now."

Before he could reply, Hawkins' stomach growled audibly. He realized he had, as usual, been ignoring his hunger.

"Let me grab you some real clothes and we'll go get some chow." Val rose again and hobbled to the door.

"Where are my clothes?"

"Spare scrubs are in the closet." She jerked her chin in that direction. "I'll wait out here while you change."

Once Hawkins had rinsed the last of the Syrian dust off in the shower and was decently clothed in the largest scrubs he could find, he followed Val's sedate pace to the elevator.

"So, you mentioned a promotion?"

"Yeah, you don't notice much more than the money, but you'll be a very comfortable dude."

Hawkins laughed, the sound booming around the elevator as they entered. "I never thought I'd hear me referred to as a 'rich dude,' not while still in the Corps."

Though he still found the financial news incredible, Hawkins was already planning for the mid-engine Chevy Corvette he lusted after.

Val looked up at him with a smile. "I think this is why Marco called me in to get you settled, to remind me what it was like to be the new guy. Remember the joy, and occasional embarrassment, of being the new guy. Someday you will be the one doing the initial Indoc."

The doors rolled open into a cheerfully bright hallway. Hawkins was taken aback by the bright, welcoming décor. "This is, what did you say, Limitless Logistics?"

"Yes, modeled after Fortune 500 companies. We poached their decorators. I doubt you care but, yes, we're supposed to look like a normal civilian logistics company to a casual observer."

"Hell yeah. I would never know this place was run by the military if I didn't know better."

"Well, run by military members. Technically, Limitless Logistics is its own business entity, working as a military contractor. Like—" Val searched her mind. "—uhm, Blackwater ... XE Services or Academi, whatever smokescreen they call themselves now."

"Contract mercenaries?"

"Oh, hell no. Logistics. Uh, I guess we're more of a FedEx to the U.S. postal service," Val said, her face a cloud of emotions.

"Right," Hawkins said, sounding dejected. He could have easily dealt with switching to a mercenary group. Being a glorified UPS pogue was not high on his to-do list.

Val stopped, leaning on her crutches. "Look, if it was up to me, I'd make changes. But I'm not running this gig for a few more years."

"What?"

"General Marco Martinez, he's our boss, promoted me to executive officer recently, so I haven't been able to affect changes yet. Right now, we're mailmen. If I have my way, we're going to branch out into more, ah, dynamic areas. Even if I have to break skulls on the Hill," she said quietly. She despised the political aspects of her job, like most military people often do.

"You don't look like the skull-breaking type, ma'am," Hawkins said with a discreet sideways glance. He had spent his career subtly poking senior officers as a sport, but he was unprepared when she dropped one crutch, snagged his scrub top, and slammed him into the wall.

"First, asshole, this is the last time I tell you not to underestimate me. Second, you call me *ma'am* one more time and I'll break your damned thick skull. Finally? The last person to call me a name I didn't like shot at me about twenty feet from here." She pulled him in close by the strained fabric of his scrub top. "I shot back. He's dead now and I'm not. Underestimate me again at your fucking peril, Marine. And if you want it in military terms, I will outrank you even after you're promoted, so consider this a lawful order—*don't fuck with me*." She released him and took a pained step back.

"Okay, Val. Got it. Sorry," Hawkins nodded, looking down at the tiny chick threatening his life.

Normally, he'd assume she was flirting. Chicks did that sometimes. But there was something in the way she carried herself, the look in her eyes. He'd seen the same edgy look before on young men fresh from their first enemy contact, a kind of feral animal rage restrained by only the thinnest thread of control. His inner Neanderthal took a back seat while the evolved part of his brain took over. Hawkins realized she wasn't kidding and definitely wasn't flirting.

She really had put a bullet in the last man who pissed her off. Moreover, she wasn't happy about having done it.

Hawkins studied her face. Something in her slightly furrowed brow, the set of her mouth, and the hard glint in her eye said that she knew she'd done the right thing, but that she regretted the necessity.

Hawkins fought a smile born of respect. These just might be his people after all.

CHAPTER 3
VALERIE HALL
1345Z 0945L, 20 APR

Val released Hawkins' scrub top and leaned back onto the crutches he respectfully bent to retrieve for her. She steeled herself, blanking her face into a neutral mask that hid the pain her calf was giving her. It had been only days since a bullet had torn a hole through her lower leg and the pain has only subsided from a fresh agony down to a deep, throbbing ache. She usually went light on her prescribed pain meds because she thought they made her dull.

But now, the pain from lunging at Hawkins was spiking through the medicine she'd hastily gulped down after Marco called. Before they sat down for brunch, she would discreetly excuse herself to the head to make sure she hadn't torn out her stitches.

She still didn't like the sight of blood. Especially her own.

Val said, "Okay, thus endeth the lesson. Come on, let's grab chow. Then you get to help me spring my best friend from G-Dub," she said.

Hawkins looked impressed. "She's in school over at George Washington?"

"Oh, no," Val said and frowned. "Sorry, she's at GW Hospital. She was shot the same time I was." She shifted awkwardly, making her crutches creak. "She needed more care than me. The clinic here is good, but they had to farm her out to GW for more intensive care. She should be ready to transfer back to our clinic to finish her inpatient time."

Val felt a stab of shame followed by a wash of guilt. Yesterday she had been so sure of her actions, but now? Now she was paying the prices for thirty years of someone else's subterfuge.

"Okay, that's good to go. Did she get shot by the same guy as you?" Hawkins asked as Val started to the elevators.

His question, delivered solicitously, still felt like a punch to the guts. Val's frown deepened. "No," she said hastily. "And if you don't mind, we can talk about that later. It's a pretty tough subject around here right now." She felt acid churning in her stomach, and she swallowed hard.

Surely, Mandy would see that Val's actions had been necessary. Surely, she would find it in her heart to forgive Val. Val swallowed hard again and scrubbed her suddenly sweaty hands on her khaki casual uniform pants as soon as they stopped inside the elevator.

"Yeah, I mean, sure. Later," Hawkins agreed. They rode the two flights up in silence.

Val caught the worried look he gave her. "Hey, I told you we got the guy. It's all right."

"Uh, sure, yeah."

"Oh, big bad Marine scared of a gunman?" Val teased.

"No," Hawkins said, his voice serious. "Big, smart, and savvy Marine wonders what the fuck he's getting into if there are active shooter situations in a secure top-secret facility."

"Ah," Val said as they exited the elevator into another bright and well-decorated hallway. "As I told you, this facility isn't secure, *per se*. The ground floor is porous to allow in anyone who thinks they need to conduct business with us. And we do legitimate but conventional, non-special logistics jobs for the general public to keep up with appearances. The basement and everything from the second floor up are secure. However, as you may have guessed, once one of us," she pointed to herself and then him, "learns a location, there's nothing you can do to secure it from them." She paused, frowning again. "The shooter was a retired member of the Pantheon, so he was intimately familiar with our office spaces since he'd worked here for decades."

Val watched Hawkins' eyebrows shoot up. "The what?"

"Oh," she laughed, "that's what they started calling themselves, 'The Pantheon,' like they were Greek gods or something. The founders were a married couple, so they were Zeus and Hera. The naming conventions stuck, and now we call all the folks with our skills The Pantheon. No other Greek god names yet, though." She pointed to the TENCAP SOA patch embroidered on her casual navy blue uniform polo, with two black galloping horses and one red one. "Or sometimes just Red Horse, from the logo."

"Zeus, huh?" Hawkins asked. "I'd like to meet the guy with enough balls to call himself Zeus and get away with it." He gave her a big grin.

Val sucked in a quick breath then let it out. "Too late. Zeus died during our little in-house battle."

"Holy shit ..." Hawkins glanced at her crutches. "Sorry. Was he shot?"

"No. He heard what was happening and he tried to Jump in to help. When he arrived and saw what happened to Mandy and me, his heart just quit on the spot. He was older and had cardiac issues, but it didn't stop him from trying to help us. He was a ..." she hesitated, seeking the right word, "... grand old guy." She frowned. Losing Zeus would affect everyone at Limitless for a long time. "Like I said, it's a pretty touchy subject right now. Ah, here's the cafeteria."

The automatic door slid left and right as they approached. "While you were knocked out, our docs assessed your baseline metabolics and took a guess at your daily calorie expenditure. They took a stab at an initial Pantheon diet for you."

"I gotta eat hospital food the rest of my life? That's even worse than field chow."

"No, you'll see. It's specially designed for your caloric needs, but it's really good stuff and you'll enjoy it. And it's a shit-ton."

Val and Hawkins moved through the line, Val nodding and murmuring thanks to the cafeteria staff doling out food as she shuffled awkwardly through.

"Alexa, this is our new accession, Sergeant Murphy Hawkins," she rocked a thumb at him. "His nutritional spec sheet was sent up this morning."

"We've got it, ma'am," the woman in a crisp white smock said. "Good to meet you, Sergeant Hawkins." She reached over the glass counter and fist-bumped him. "Welcome aboard."

"Just Murphy, ma'am, please, if you don't mind, or Murph," Hawkins replied.

He waited for Val to protest the *ma'am* but was disappointed when Val only smiled at the courtesy. The food handler ladled various foods onto two trays and passed them across the counter. Val frowned when she realized she couldn't handle a tray and crutches.

Before she could ask Hawkins for some help, a deep, familiar voice rumbled behind her.

"Allow me."

She turned with a smile.

"Well, hey, dork," Val called out to the tall man who had approached them. "Staff Sergeant Murphy Hawkins, USMC, meet Brandon Powell, CIA. Bran, Hawkins is the one Marco told you about. We're adding him to the roster."

Powell raised one dark brown eyebrow at Hawkins as they sized one another up. Powell held his hand out. "Jumped straight into the Commandant's office at midnight, I heard? Good one."

Val watched Hawkins smile and take the hand.

"Call me Murph, sir, if you don't mind."

Powell smiled, nodded in the affirmative and said, "*Ooorah.*"

Val contained her smirk as Hawkins' shoulders relaxed visibly. Powell must have given him a little dose of his transferable calming power when they exchanged handshakes. Even the CIA didn't know Powell could do that.

"What are you doing at Limitless today? I didn't think I'd see you until dinner," Val asked Powell.

"Marco wanted another round of debriefing for our new friend you dragged in, and I obliged." He grabbed an apple juice from the drink cooler for himself and took Val's heavily laden tray to an open table. "We're getting useful intelligence from him, surprisingly enough, but I suspect he's going to stop being useful in the next week or so."

Val asked, "What will you do with him then?"

Powell shrugged.

Val regarded his neutral expression and let the silence stretch.

"So, you two are a thing or whatever?" Hawkins asked after the silence stretched uncomfortably long. He pointed at them with a laden fork.

"Yes, I guess you could say that." Powell laughed, an expression that transformed his neutral mask into a warm visage.

Hawkins eyed him again, considering. Val wished she could find a casual excuse to touch Hawkins' hand as she watched several expressions cross his face in rapid succession.

Val reached out for Powell's hand and she could feel the tension leaving him. She tried not to laugh. He'd been worried she was attracted to the big, strapping Marine. She flicked a glance at him, catching his eyes, and a renewed feeling of calm flowed into her. She jerked her head in a quick nod.

"So, how's the first day in the zoo treating you?" Powell asked.

"Not terrible, I guess. I'm not really sure what to expect." Hawkins looked pointedly at Val.

"Your daily schedule will vary, but usually we, the Pantheon, arrive around zero-eight to work out with our trainers daily. After that, it's training on specific skills or what's useful for a specific upcoming mission. Self-defense, range, precision Jumping. Field medicine. Things like that."

"You use personal trainers?"

"Yes, Limitless keeps a team on staff. We have emergency Jumps that come up frequently, so the Pantheon strives to always maintain peak fitness. Obviously," Val said with a rueful grin. "I'm on LIMDU right now and not cleared for mission Jumps while on limited duty, but I can probably talk Marco into letting me come along on your short training Jumps in a few weeks."

"Roger. So, like CrossFit and stuff?" Hawkins asked and Val struggled to keep from grinning at his almost childlike eagerness.

"Oh, you do CrossFit, Hawkins? I never would have known since you didn't mention it more than ten or twenty times," she said with a laugh. "Yes, you and your trainer will design the program that's best for you. Training isn't any good if you hate it and won't do it, so there is plenty of latitude. There's no annual PT test or anything, either. We are expected to be good to go on literally a moment's notice as a condition of employment."

She smiled evilly. "But we can disable the Jump center of your brain if you fall off our programming," she lied. "A big laser is involved, and I'm told recovery isn't more than six, seven months. You'll relearn how to walk, but Walter Reed has a good program for that. So, you can go back to the fleet anytime you don't like it here."

Hawkins' eyes went wide. "You're bullshitting me."

Val just tilted her head with a goofy grin and shrugged.

"I already feel like there's no chance of that happening, ma—uh, Val," Hawkins said, laughing.

"I know you mentioned a CrossFit regime," she said with a light smile, "and I'm pretty sure our guys'll be happy to push you to your limits with that."

Hawkins gave her a rueful look. "Yeah, sorry. I know CrossFitters never shut up about it."

She returned his smile.

"It's all right, we can get into more later. Now that brunch is done, we need to get a move on to transfer Mandy back here from the G-Dub."

"You aren't driving are you, Val?" Powell asked her.

She leaned over and gave him a light kiss on the cheek.

"Nope, Hawkins is my wheel man today. See you tonight, dork."

Powell grabbed all three trays. Val nodded thanks as he strode off.

"Let's go get you changed into real clothes and then we'll go," she told Hawkins.

"Is it always going to be like this?" he asked, pressing the elevator button to go back to his clinic room."Me just following you around?" he said. The uncertainty in his voice was clear.

"Gods and stars above, no," she said with a laugh, entering the elevator. "I needed a wheel man for this trip and someone who can help with Mandy's bag. I'd love to do this alone, but I physically can't right now," she said, tapping her crutches against the ground.

"Can't just Jump in there, huh?" Hawkins asked.

"Yeah, no. Not into most regular civilian locations, and never into an unknown one. You don't want to materialize inside a file cabinet, or halfway into a wall in the nursery. Scares the children and it plays holy hell with your flesh."

She paused a moment, thinking about their earlier conversations. "All the other Pantheon types are busy piecing things back together, so you're literally the only one I can spare. Besides, it gives me a chance to assess you more and answer any questions you have."

Hawkins was quiet as they walked down to the Limitless Logistics garage to grab a company car. Hawkins opened the front passenger door and Val even let him help her into the seat. He placed the crutches in the second row and mounted up behind the wheel.

The sleek black Cadillac Escalade ESV roared to life when Hawkins hit the ignition button.

"This personifies sweetness," he said, his eyes roving across the elaborate digital instrument panel and reaching out to touch various controls. "This is Mad Men-in-Black-type mojo. If this monster could rocket up the tunnel walls I would not be surprised."

Val watched Hawkins caress the grippy leather-wrapped steering wheel in appreciation as she settled herself in and fastened her seat belt. She understood his joy.

"Yeah, our rides are all pretty nice, and be careful driving out of here. Our engines have been massaged by Pratt & Miller in Detroit. They build all the Corvette racing cars in IMSA sports car racing and for the LeMans 24-Hour, and for a few government agencies with occasional needs for more go power."

Val had preprogrammed the onboard Nav for the George Washington Hospital. "Press that Go Now button on the screen and just follow the prompts," she said. "It isn't too far, but it's complicated."

Hawkins fastened his seat belt, pulled the console shifter into Drive, and they exited the parking structure.

Val's tension rose and the knot in her belly twisted tighter. Fear that Mandy would reject her outright rose. She still felt skittish and shaky, and she couldn't imagine how Mandy would feel about losing her father—even an estranged, criminal, rogue father—at the end of Val's gun.

"So, what do you tell my old unit?" Hawkins asked, breaking the silence while he maneuvered the big vehicle into DC traffic.

Val watched his eyes darting down every side street they passed, constantly scanning his mirrors, the instruments, and most importantly, the road ahead. Looking for bad guys and IEDs.

"These are the streets of the Nation's Capital, Hawkins. They're rough like any big city, but there isn't any ambush waiting. Relax."

"Oh, uh yeah. You know. Old habits," he said. Despite her reassurance, his eyes resumed their constant scanning.

Val nodded. "The rest of your fire team gets a very basic explanation of the program, a stack of non-disclosure agreements to sign, and dire warnings about revealing what they experienced for when they go back to the unit. Your unit leadership is told your injuries were grave and that you're stateside for treatment."

"And Zora?"

"She'll likely get another handler and be sent back out." Val saw Hawkins frown. "You're attached to her?"

"Any canine handler worth a shit is attached to their dog," he barked at her.

"Okay, okay," Val said, hands raised in a calming gesture. "Sorry, I've never had a dog. I don't really know what it's like." She thought for a moment. "We obviously have some pull with the movers and shakers in DOD, and I can see what we can do to stop her from being transferred back. No promises, though."

Hawkins nodded. "So, what's my status, personnel-wise? I'm a US Marine. I really don't care to join no damned Air Force."

Val laughed. "Not to worry, big boy. We're as Joint as can be now and you get to inaugurate that as our token Jarhead. You will be assigned as a military liaison to Limitless Logistics, but Limitless also hires you on separately as its contractor." She gave him a level look. "Once you aren't driving, I'll tell you about the pay."

"You can tell me now," he eased into a turn, eyes still scanning.

"Nope. I passed out when Mandy told me. And since you also had a traumatic trigger, I don't want to risk you crashing the car."

Hawkins snorted. "I'm made of strong stuff. I really doubt I'll have a fainting spell," he said dismissively.

Val crossed her arms and stared at him.

"Did I offend you?" he asked, surprised.

"A little, yes, but I'll chalk it up to your ignorance of all this." She took a calming breath. "Strength and willpower have almost nothing to do with it. Your body is adapting to a massive change, one you have zero conscious control over. Trust me when I tell you, this shit is fucking hard." She gestured to indicate the whole Limitless Logistics experience.

"Jesus. Okay. Sorry," Hawkins said and gunned the car forward as soon as the light changed.

"Anyway," Val said, pushing on, "we have housing available at no cost to you. You'll get a handler assigned. I have one in mind already. They will help you find quarters, get some business clothes, uniforms, diets, and generally help you get settled in." Val gave him a tight smile. "Mandy Squires was my handler until a few days ago when she demonstrated her ability to Jump."

"Wait, let me get this straight. I thought all you Pantheon guys were military?"

"Yes. Mandy is our one exception right now, but traditionally everyone in the Pantheon is military."

"There aren't civilians that can Jump?" Hawkins was skeptical.

"Probably ..." Val sighed, "... but, well, there are several theories on why we don't get them here. Suffice it to say, I've got to figure out what to do with Mandy—if she even wants to join us."

Val's tension shot higher as she said that. What if Mandy decided she wouldn't join Limitless? It wasn't like Val had the authority to order her to join. At least she held some sway over Hawkins.

"If the money is as good as it sounds, why wouldn't she?"

"To start, she's just been through some pretty serious trauma centered around this group. Second, she's my best friend and I love her to pieces, but she's not exactly GI Jane." Val rubbed her temples, glad they'd arrived at the hospital. "Yeah. Like I said, things are a little complicated right now."

Hawkins nodded as he parked. "Want me to wait down here?"

Val eyed the entrance to the ER. "No, come in with me."

Hawkins shut off the big truck and they made their way inside. Val swept inside as gracefully and commandingly as someone could while on a pair of crutches. She stopped inside the entrance to the emergency department and gestured imperiously to a nurse. She flashed her Limitless Logistics badge.

"Picking up Mandy Squires, please," she said to the nurse, then turned to address Hawkins. "How much do you make as an E-5?"

"E-6," Hawkins corrected.

"What?"

"In the Marines, Staff Sergeant is an E-6."

"Oh, my bad. I'm still learning the joint service stuff."

"So, uh," he thought, "with base pay, hazardous duty pay, and BAH? Maybe five grand a month? So, sixty-ish a year, gross?"

"You will make a little more than half of that here per month," she said calmly.

Val watched him open his mouth to respond. He paled, blinked hard twice, and sunk in slow motion into the waiting room chair.

"Hawkins? Murph?" she called and, bending awkwardly on the crutches, tapped him lightly on the cheek.

"Yeah. Still here," he slurred.

Val stood upright again and gestured to the nurse. "Would you please get him into a bed? Check for shock, dehydration, and I'd be appreciative if you gave him a light snack."

She caught Hawkins' look of amusement from the floor. "You've got some pull here, huh?" he whispered to her.

Val nodded. "We donate some pretty hefty bags of cash to ensure we can get the help we need in a pinch. This is one of the few times they've had to call on GW for help. I'm glad to see Marco's scheme paid off," Val said.

A pair of orderlies assisted Hawkins onto a nearby gurney with some difficulty and wheeled him into a draped examination area. Val watched them without comment.

"Is this where you say, 'I told you so'?" Hawkins asked, eyes drooping. He chewed idly on an energy bar.

"No, not at all. I would have expected you to go out cold. I'm fairly surprised you're even semi-conscious." She gave him a wry grin. "I'm going to fetch my friend. Hang out here until you're recovered and we'll come back and get you."

Hawkins nodded and she left him. After another flash of her badge, an orderly led her to Mandy's room two floors up.

"Ma'am, this is her room, but I'm sorry, only family are permitted for visitation," the orderly said.

Val's voice took on some steel. "I'm here to pick my sister up. She's being transferred back to our clinic at Limitless."

"All right. Let me get the paperwork and we will release her."

"No, I'll be taking her now. Paperwork should be sent to Nurse Sarah Meyers at Limitless. Please ready a wheelchair and a set of crutches."

"Very good, ma'am. Right away." The orderly nodded smartly and hustled off.

All of Val's bravado faded as she opened the door to Mandy's room. She shut it gently behind her. Mandy lay in the big hospital bed propped up by pillows. Her usually neat blonde hair looked thin as it hung over her shoulders and her face was drawn and pale.

Not unusual for a woman who had been shot only a few days ago.

Mandy's eyes had flown open at the sound of the door and slowly closed again when she saw Val.

Val hobbled forward to sit silently in the chair beside Mandy's bed.

Fear knotted her stomach. Fear of rejection. Fear that her best friend was unable to look her in the eye. Fear that Mandy would hate her for killing her father in defense of them both. Silence stretched long, a chasm of pain and fear yawning open.

Finally, Mandy's voice bridged the silent abyss between them.

"Marco always told me that the Pantheon could sense the first layer of a person's thoughts and emotions through touch." Mandy held out her hand.

Val hesitated for a moment afraid of what she would feel, believing her own shame, guilt, and sadness would cloud the underlying foundation of grief and love she felt for her friend. She reached out for Mandy's slender hand, clasping it lightly.

Through their touch, Mandy transmitted that she felt a peaceful acceptance of Val's actions against Mandy's father. Val collapsed into tears at the detection of Mandy's acceptance.

"I'm sorry. I am so sorry, Mandy," Val whispered. She clung to Mandy's hand with both of hers as she was racked by sobs, leaning on her hospital bed.

"I know, Val. I know you had to do it," Mandy said and ran the fingers of her free hand through Val's red-gold hair. "I mean, he'd already shot me. You didn't have a choice. I'm not sure I would have done anything differently if I'd been in your place."

They stayed in that embrace, bypassing clumsy words that ill conveyed what they really felt in favor of reading each other's emotions through touch. Unlike Powell, Val couldn't push an emotion to someone, but she and Mandy could both receive the top layer of emotion each of them felt. The shame, fear, and guilt Val felt ebbed into relief and gratitude at Mandy's acceptance. Slowly, Val's sobs eased.

"Thank you," Val said.

"So, what now?" Mandy asked her. She took her hand back as Val sat up, brushing her long blond hair off her face.

"Well, first things first, I'm moving you into our clinic."

Mandy's mouth tightened. "Do I have to?"

"Well, no," Val said hesitantly. "I suppose you could stay here until you can go home, but I figured you'd rather be with us, with—" she stopped herself. She was about to say your family when she paused. "I know Marco and Dee would be happier with you nearby. I would too, and I'm sure Pete would like to see you."

At the mention of Mandy's boyfriend, she turned her head away. "He's already been by. He's ... conflicted about my ability to Jump."

Val's eyes darted around. "Let's talk about it back at Limitless. We aren't secure here."

Mandy nodded wearily.

"Yeah, okay." Her new realities were already weighing on her. Unlike Hawkins, Mandy knew what their future held from her stints as a Limitless admin and then handler to Val.

Knowing the challenges before her didn't make them any smaller—such as the struggle to get her heavily bandaged leg into oversize men's' sweatpants and a sweatshirt for the trip back to Limitless. The left leg of the sweatpants had been cut off cleanly at the hip to allow her thick wound dressings to pass through without constriction.

Val wanted to clasp hands again, to reassure herself that Mandy was okay with her, but that could wait. She stood instead.

"We're getting everything you need ready to be moved now, if you're up to it?"

"We?" Mandy asked.

"Yeah," she glanced at the closed door. "Embarrassment of riches. First you, and now it looks like we have another somebody to add to Limitless Logistics management," Val said.

She looked at Mandy significantly. That meant *Pantheon*.

"He's here helping me out. I'm still not cleared to drive with these aluminum sticks." She shook the dreaded crutches.

There was a tap on the door and Hawkins, now recovered from his financial windfall swoon, leaned in.

"They have everything they need to get you out of here."

He smiled when he saw Mandy.

"Miss, I'd be very happy to escort you to the vehicle," he said with enthusiasm.

Remembering how he'd treated her when they first met all of an hour ago, Val smirked.

"Is he for real?" Mandy griped. Despite her tone, Val saw a smile tug at Mandy's mouth.

Val introduced them.

"Mandy, this is the soon-to-be-former Sergeant Murphy Hawkins, USMC, our new teammate, and as far as I can tell from the last hour or so, there is nothing in this world that stops him from flirting with pretty girls."

Hawkins entered the room pushing a wheelchair and held out his hand to help Mandy down from the bed.

She looked at Val, then to Hawkins. Val gave Hawkins steadiness points at the sight of the heavily bandaged thigh, but with his combat pedigree, he'd seen lots worse, fresh and unwrapped.

"I could carry you if that would make you feel better?"

Mandy blushed. "Thank you, no," she said as she accepted his hand. "I think the hospital rather insists I go out in the wheelchair." Val had pulled rank to get the hospital sign off on discharging Mandy to her "sister" instead of transporting her in an ambulance.

As was the routine with injured Pantheon, Mandy already was healing at an accelerated pace.

Val saw reactions cross both faces faster than she could identify them. Both looked slightly stunned by the effect of their hand-to-hand contact.

Val thought Mandy was receiving Hawkins' obvious interest in her, and at the same time, he was likely a willing receiver for the hormonal surge of interest now radiating from Mandy. Neither of them would understand it perfectly, but Hawkins the least of the two. Hawkins settled Mandy into the wheelchair and grabbed the small plastic bag the nurses had stuffed Mandy's bloodied street clothes into.

With equal care, Hawkins had settled Mandy into the SUV's back seat once they reached the Escalade. He opened the rear hatch with a wave of his foot under the bumper and it swung open, allowing him to put the crutches and the folded wheelchair out of the way.

Val was amused at how soon-to-be-former Staff Sergeant Murphy Hawkins, USMC, could be the *muy macho* snake-eater one moment and a softly caring gentleman the next.

CHAPTER 4
MURPHY HAWKINS
1803Z 1403L, 20 APR

Hawkins had been mildly put out at being Val's chauffeur all afternoon, although meeting Mandy Squires had been interesting and he hoped to see her again soon.

Now, as his brain and body were still in the Damascus Eastern European time zone, he was struggling to assimilate Val's most recent verbal torrent. He hoped she wasn't a chatterbox like this all the time.

"So, just keep an open mind. I'm sure you and Joe will get along great," Val said with a smile.

"Huh? Joe?" he grunted. His mind had wandered back to meeting Val's stunning blonde friend in the hospital and the lightning bolt of attraction that had struck him when he had touched her hand. His impressions had been further stoked in the process of getting her out of the vehicle and pushed in the wheelchair up to the Limitless clinic, where she would be well cared for. And now Hawkins knew where to find her if he felt like just drifting in for a welfare check.

They returned the Escalade to the Limitless motor pool and headed back to the offices. Hawkins shook his head and tried to sort out the last three minutes of conversation in his mind. Something about psychological assessments, training Jumps, and needing a handler who would square away his gear and find him a place to crash. He rubbed a spot over his right eyebrow and winced. His head hurt. His brain hurt. His entire body was burning with fatigue. And he was hungry again. Really hungry.

"I'm assigning Joe Pax as your Handler, at least for the time being. He's been trained and he was next in the handler queue when I came online, but I went with Mandy instead." She shrugged. "Girl power. I think you two'll get along well and Ryan will be pleased to know Joe's been picked up."

"Who is Ryan again? Have I met him yet?" Hawkins asked, trying to keep up with her rapid-fire delivery. Ever since they had deposited Mandy at the clinic, Val had been much more upbeat and her mouth had been moving a mile a minute. He was too tired and grumpy to ask what had accounted for her mood enhancement.

"Ryan is Joe's boyfriend. Or partner. I'm not really sure what they call each other," Val said in a rush and waved a hand. "Keep an open mind, please."

"Are you serious?" Hawkins asked. Incredulity was etched in every line of his face.

"About which part? Yes. Almost always," Val said.

Hawkins grunted, dropping his head and rolling it from side to side. He was becoming unsure about all this Pantheon stuff.

"Look, Hawkins, let him help you get set up with an apartment so you can go get some rest. If you don't like him for some reason, you get the last word—but you do not get to pass judgment on his personal life. Key word there? Personal. I'll get someone else trained up if we must. However," she stressed, "I know a little about Joe and I think you guys'll work out."

Hawkins looked at her with a blank face.

"You savvy, Murph?"

Hawkins looked at her face and watched her upbeat manner fade into a mild scowl. He grunted again and crossed his arms. This battle of wills thing was going to get old fast. Did she seriously think she was going to ride herd on him like this?

Val stared at him, scowl deepening, waiting for a response.

Hawkins envisioned some prancing, slender young man hovering around him, cooing over how lovely his rigger's belt was with his combat boots. He let his silence be answer to her.

"You can't make this easy, can you? Fine. Just get your damn apartment and work with Joe until I say otherwise. I'll consider getting another handler after you log some time with him. Until then, you're with Joe Pax."

"Fine," Hawkins grunted.

"You are a surly son-of-a-bitch you know that?" Val snapped. Her temporary good cheer gone.

"Look lady, I'm tired as fuck. I'm, like, seven time zones off right now. I want to see my dog. And I'm not used to dealing with females who think they're stronger than me."

Val's eyes flared with an intensity that was almost painful to look at. She whipped an iPhone out of her pocket and dialed a number. Hawkins realized he'd offended her again, but he was too tired of her bullshit to care.

"Hey, Hank!" she said warmly into the phone. "Nah, I'm recovering well, thanks for asking. Surprised you heard about it already." There was a pause. "Aww, you're sweet to say that, thanks. Nope. We've got a new accession."

Hawkins understood that outside of the building "contractor" or "accession" were code for "Pantheon."

"I think he would benefit from seeing how you and the team operate, y'know? Get his head in the game early. I think he'd be a good fit. Got any training coming up?"

Hawkins could just barely hear the voice on the other end of Val's phone in a staticky Charlie Brown jumble of words.

"Perfect! One Hollywood and a half-gear Jump to WSMR? No, I'm on light duty. I can Jump you, but I can't run with you. Not that I ever do! Great. We'll be there tomorrow at zero-seven. Cheers!" Hawkins watched her punch off the phone with satisfaction.

"You and I are doing your first training Jump tomorrow at seven. Get your apartment, get some sleep—and get your fucking shit together before you report. Truth is, you have a bad attitude and lack an ounce of respect for people and process you know nothing about, but your tired badass Hollywood Marine act is over, big boy."

Val pointed an index finger at his face, a full head-plus taller than hers. "I'll see you back here at seven. Joe will ensure you aren't late."

She evaluated his borrowed hospital scrubs. "Oh, and I think Joe can get you some more appropriate clothes by then."

Hawkins watched her stalk away with as much dignity as she could muster on crutches. As she crutched down the hall, another man approached. She greeted him quietly then pointed at Hawkins. Hawkins ground his teeth. Despite his initial positive opinion of her, he was starting to dislike the woman. She was bossy and acted as if his masculinity was some kind of disease.

He watched the man who approached him with a critical eye. Tall, almost his own height of six-four, with a broad chest and shoulders to match his own. Hawkins guessed the guy could have held his own in a CrossFit competition and greeted him with a half-smile.

"You Hawkins?" the man asked. He had green eyes that seemed to be holding back a laugh.

"Yeah," Hawkins answered warily.

"Nice to meet you, I'm Joe Pax," he said. Joe held out his hand and smiled.

Hawkins stared at him in surprise for a moment. He hadn't caught everything Val had said, but he'd at least caught that "Joe" was the name of his potential handler and that Joe had a boyfriend. Hawkins had pictured some slender, diminutive man with a faint lisp, not a jacked, shaved-head man who could be his workout clone.

"Hey, I'm Murphy Hawkins. I go by Murph, usually."

"Nice to meet you," Joe said. Hawkins shook Joe's hand, and his grip was unequivocal but not aggressive. Hawkins was smart enough to know that truly powerful men didn't need to crush another man's grip to prove it. He nodded approvingly.

"So, Val says we need to get you a fast crash pad ASAP and some clothes that don't make you look like a nurse?"

Joe gave Hawkins an appraising once-over, taking in the deep circles under his eyes and borrowed hospital apparel.

"Look, Murph. If Val had her way, I'd drag you around to the five different apartment buildings Limitless owns this afternoon. But if it's good with you, I'll get you settled in the vacant penthouse level of my building. Damarcus and a couple of the other guys already live there, so I know it's good enough for the Pantheon. It's already tastefully furnished—by me, of course. If you don't like it after a few days, we can shift you back into a sandy CONEX with a worn canvas cot and an unshaded light—" Hawkins laughed. "—but right now, you look like shit and like you could use about a hundred hours of sleep."

Joe glanced at his Rolex Submariner watch.

"Unfortunately, you only have a little over twelve or so. We better get going."

Hawkins mustered up a halfhearted smile and nodded.

"Thank you, Joe."

"No problem, man." Joe eyed Hawkins with a thoughtful expression. "Uh, thirty ... four waist? Forty-eight-inch chest? And I'd guess you're a little taller than me, so maybe six-four?"

Hawkins nodded. "Spot on."

"Got it. I think I can find some utility clothes in uniform storage for you. You got any foods you don't eat?"

"Grains," Hawkins grunted. He rubbed his eyes, feeling the dry, gritty feeling he knew came with being too long awake.

"CrossFitter? Paleo diet?"

"Yes, CrossFit but not Paleo, I do Primal Blueprint," Hawkins confirmed, scrubbing his face. "I like alcohol and cheese too much to go full Paleo."

"Wine and cheese? You're a fucking girl!" Joe had an amused smile that took the sting out of his words.

Hawkins grinned. He might actually get along with this Joe guy after all.

Right now, he'd get along with anyone who was promising him sleep soon.

CHAPTER 5
MURPHY HAWKINS
0949Z 0549L, 21 APR

Hawkins had expected to wake with the Syrian sunrise, but he was pleased to sleep until almost zero-six local time. He rolled over in bed and patted Zora's head. He'd talked his way into picking her up before going to his new apartment building with Joe.

Joe offered to walk the two of them to the high rise, describing how close it was to work, but the recovering Zora did better in the back of an Escalade.

Joe reminded him that appearances were important and that under no circumstances was he to get to work "the fast way." Hawkins had simply nodded his acquiescence, ready to hit the hay. After getting him into the oversize penthouse apartment and handing him the keys, Joe had offered to pick up dinner. Hawkins declined, but Joe had reappeared a half hour later with a tub of Thai shrimp curry anyway. Hawkins thanked him, declined an offer to hang with him and Ryan in their apartment downstairs, and wished him a goodnight. Hawkins and Zora, a spectacular garbage disposal, had split the tub of Thai before passing out.

"Hey, Zora-girl! Where do you think we can find some good eats in this town?" Hawkins grumbled to Zora the next morning. He had just started wondering where he could wrangle up breakfast for the two of them when there was a knock at the door. Hawkins stumbled to it in his boxers, Zora alert and padding alongside carefully. Hawkins had quickly fallen out of his Marine Corps practice of early morning hours.

"Good morning, Murph! Here's breakfast and your clothes for today," Joe said brightly when Hawkins opened the door.

"Huh?" Hawkins grunted. He sagged against the door frame rubbing the sleep from his eyes.

"Food," Joe held up the smaller paper bag, "and clothes." He held up the second, larger brown paper bag. When Hawkins didn't move Joe asked, "Can I come in?"

Hawkins lurched off the door frame. Four and a half years in the Corps and if he wasn't a morning person by now, he never would be.

Joe followed him in and set the bags on the kitchen's immaculate and unused countertop.

"I stopped at the local greasy spoon on the way back from my workout. CrossFit's online calendar showed 'Fran' as the workout of the day today, in case you're wondering," he said as an aside, "but you don't have time for that today." He pointed to the bag of food. "Breakfast is bacon, eggs, hash browns if you'll eat them, and sausage. Plus, coffee, black as God and the U.S. Navy intended it to be."

"Bless you," Hawkins grunted.

"I'm told the cafeteria has your diet sheet and will have something ready if you head up there before your Jump."

Hawkins tore the lid off the Styrofoam food container and scraped half the sausage and all the hash browns onto it. He set it on the floor for Zora, who almost danced around his feet.

"Thanks, Joe," he said around a mouthful of eggs.

"No worries, Murph. I grabbed clothes while I was there, as promised. You'll need your own boots, but I got everything else from our uniform store. I also made you a really basic bag, not that I think you'll need much based on what Val told me."

"What the fuck am I doing today?" Hawkins asked. "She was less than articulate about it." The caffeine was warming his system.

"Yeah. Hoo-boy, I think you pissed her off," Joe said.

Hawkins grunted again and continued eating his breakfast.

"Anyway, you're off to train with my old unit at Hurlburt Field."

"You were military?"

"Yeah, six years as an Air Force pararescueman. The Air Force world was improving for same-sex relationships, but I left in 2006 because I was tired of hiding my personal life."

Joe scratched his shaved pate, waiting for a comment. When Hawkins didn't comment, he went on.

"I had already worked with the Pantheon in the training pipeline, so I applied to work here when I got out. I was hoping to be a handler, but they had a drought of new Jumpers for a time. I've been working supply for the last few years waiting for the next Jumper."

"Why didn't you work for Val? Wasn't she the most recent Jumper to join up?"

"Yes, she was, but she decided she wanted a female handler. Something about not wanting a male to fetch tampons and shit like that for her," he shrugged. "I got that. Handler gigs are designed to be intimate for best efficiency."

Hawkins looked at him and raised one eyebrow, like Mr. Spock in Star Trek.

Realizing how it sounded, Joe held up his hands in entreaty. "Not like that, moron. But I'll call Make-A-Wish for you if you like."

They both laughed comfortably.

Hawkins asked, "So what exactly does a handler do? Other than bringing me breakfast and uniforms?"

"Whatever you need to get the mission accomplished. We prep your mission go-bag, track you while you're out, and receive you when you return."

"Receive me?" Hawkins asked as he scraped the last crumb into his mouth.

"Val talked about how much Jumping takes out of you?" When Hawkins nodded, he continued. "We get you food, IVs if you're too nauseated to eat, or hustle your butt to the clinic as needed."

Hawkins looked at him blankly, still chewing.

"Remember, longer the trip, heavier the load, the more calories you burn. Big missions, people sometimes fall out on arrival. It happens often, in fact. The longer you do this, the better your body will adapt to the instantaneous calorie deficits."

"Is there any way to help that recovery process along?"

Joe shrugged a broad shoulder. "I have a theory. If you do paleo, primal, or a ketogenic diet, the goal is to get fat-adapted, right?"

"Yeah."

"Well, since the Jumping burns fat, I suspect that people who are already fat-adapted are better suited to it. Val said something about pushing you at the ER yesterday?" he prompted.

"Yeah, she figured I'd faint when she told me my new salary."

"And did you?" Joe asked.

"Fuck no! Well, I mighta got a little woozy, but I managed to stay conscious," he said, frowning.

"Okay, cool. So, I think when you had that shock, since you're already fat-adapted, your body could pull from your fat stores. Val, on the other hand, was a chubby carb lover when she joined us. When Mandy said the new salary, she was out for a couple hours. Her body had the fuel stores, but it didn't know how to use them."

"So, I'm stronger than her?" Hawkins asked.

"No, I wouldn't say that. And even powerful shock events like that are completely unlike what Jumping does to the body, but the process is similar. Your military body is already trained to burn calories more efficiently for what you do. It means your transition period should be much smoother."

"Wow, you've put some real thought into this," Hawkins said, impressed.

Joe gave a rueful laugh. "Yeah, well. Working in supply isn't as mentally stimulating as you might think," Joe said.

"So other than pack my bags, haul my ass to the clinic, and solve nutritional dilemmas, is there anything else?"

Joe gave another shrug and crossed his arms. "Each handler to Pantheon pairing is different. Some pairs are really formal and the handler only does mission-related stuff. Val and Mandy became best friends and are practically sisters. I think Mandy even bought Val's furniture for her."

Hawkins' eyebrow shot up. "Seriously? As friends or, you know, gals being pals?"

Joe's laugh echoed through Hawkins' empty apartment. "As far as I know, just friends. But I think a few of the guys and maybe some of the ladies might be hoping they're more. And yes, I'm pretty sure she bought every piece of furniture in Val's apartment. According to Ryan, Val is fashion-challenged."

He smiled and gave Hawkins a level look.

"Dude, if you're cool with me as a Handler, I will do what you need did, but I will also give you the personal space you need."

Hawkins nodded. "You're chill and seem competent so far." He waved a hand vaguely at the empty Styrofoam box and the clothes. "I'm good with you as my Handler. Let's keep it mission-oriented for now and see where it goes."

"I can handle that. I need to get some info on your gear preferences later. Simple things, like handgun pref, and whatever," he said and checked his watch. "Murph, you gotta scoot. Val expects you in fifteen and it's a ten-minute walk."

"Mmm, 'k. Shower, shave, clothes. I'll be back in seven minutes," Hawkins said.

True to his word, in less than seven minutes Hawkins reappeared in the apartment's living room dressed in Pantheon khaki pants topped with a navy blue, long-sleeve golf-type shirt bearing the Red Horse logo silk-screened onto the left chest. He stopped briefly before a full-length mirror and approved his look.

Zora padded up and looked into the mirror at herself, then sat and gazed adoringly up at him. Hawkins reached down and fluffed her ears and looked around, finally registering the apartment.

"This place is fucking huge."

"Standard quarters for the Pantheon guys," Joe said. He handed the keyring to Hawkins. "This set is yours."

Hawkins fastened a lead to her collar and said to Zora, "C'mon girl."

Her injury was healing fast due to the high-test Pantheon IVs the dog had been infused with and her old perk and friskiness was returning. She trotted proudly next to her master. Hawkins turned to Joe. "'Pantheon guys,' huh?"

"You put on a couple of stars and people start treating you differently, fercrissakes."

Hawkins gave a non-committal grunt and frowned.

Joe looked at him, never breaking his brisk stride.

"Seriously, man, about the stresses. Anyone who has a traumatic introduction to Jumping, which is most of them, passes out at least once the first training week. Inexperience. Tryin' too hard."

"I'm not used to being the weak one."

"Weakness has nothing to do with it—bravado does, though. We have the Type A's and the wallflowers here, and everyone adapts differently. It's all about how fast your body can acclimatize to a massive change." Joe chuckled. "And the pain is comin', oh my brother. I know you're a badass and *blah blah blah*. Just leave all your bad attitudes on the beach and you'll do fine."

"You sound like her," Hawkins said sharply. He felt a growing sense of resentment for Val.

"Once we get you fleeted up, you'll sound like her too." Joe's eyes narrowed. "Just what is it you don't like about Val?"

"Everyone treats her like the second-fucking-coming and despite how hot she is, and I can't fathom why. In my business, you earn your stripes. You don't get by on good looks."

"So, you're upset that a good-looking female is in charge of you? Oh man, now I know why she's going on the training mission today," Joe said, laughing.

"What?" Hawkins growled.

"Watch for it. She is going to knock you down a couple pegs. Look, Murph, I think we're going to get along great, but you need to get over yourself, mister. Not even kidding. This macho-man bullshit may have given you an edge in the Marine Corps, but read the room, dude. You are no longer in the Marine Corps, and you most definitely are not in charge. Here, we value the people who can make the tough calls under pressure. Val does."

Hawkins looked down at Zora, trotting along happily beside him. "And you think I don't know about some pressure? You know I pulled an entire team out of Syria under fire, right?" They walked through the front doors of Limitless Logistics toward the field house and the Pantheon compound.

"I do. But did you do it as a conscious action—or in unconscious terror?" Joe asked as they passed through security. Hawkins felt his handler's stare bore into him and he didn't answer.

"Either answer would be correct, by the way." Once in the elevator heading up to the Jump Room, Joe asked, "Do you know what happened here?"

Hawkins shook his head. "Not really." He frowned in disapproval and shook his head dismissively. "Some kinda shoot-out, I gathered. Big deal. I been in plenty."

Joe stabbed the elevator's Hold button, halting their ascent. This occurred frequently in these elevators and no alarm was triggered by the stationary car.

Hawkins rolled his eyes and moved to hit the button. Joe grabbed his hand and Hawkins felt anger, pain, betrayal, and pride trickling through. He tried to pull his hand back, but Joe held on.

"What the fuck is this, bro?" Hawkins demanded.

Joe's face was angry and frustrated. Foreign emotions suddenly swept through Hawkins and he weakened, moving back a step until his back was pressed against the wall of the elevator.

Joe met his eyes, his voice steely. "I'm going to tell you some things that are out of your current need to know, fuckhead, because you're evidently an asshole who can't figure out shit on his own."

Hawkins wanted to break free, but he felt his will being sapped.

"A retired Pantheon member—I don't say his name—betrayed us while on a freelance mission for a foreign power. He pulled five of our Jumpers into his trick. Four Jumpers were suckered into a deceitful Jump supporting the capture of a rogue Russian general trying to start a goddamned war between our country and his, and Val was lured into an ambush. While under fire, she grabbed our principal and Jumped him to the only place she knew was secure—here. Unfortunately, she was shot escaping. Lost a shit-ton of blood and she's lucky to be alive. Our retiree, the traitor," Joe spit the word out, "Jumped here after her. She defended our principal against attack and didn't engage the retiree until he shot his own daughter."

"Mandy?" Hawkins asked.

"The same. Then Val put a bullet in him, saving the lives of both Mandy and our principal. Marco, Powell, and two other handlers who came to her rescue said she was cool as a cucumber when they found her even though she had a bullet hole in her calf and was watching her best friend bleed out. So, if you think she's overrated, go ahead. You're in a minority of one. But underestimate or disrespect General Valerie Hall at your peril."

Hawkins started at him, stunned. A feeling of lightheadedness swept over him, but he ruthlessly suppressed it. "Wait, Val shot Mandy's father?" The foreign emotions shifted and Hawkins felt a wash of sadness and pity override the anger and betrayal.

"He had just shot his own daughter and was bent on shooting our founder, Zeus, as well as anyone who got in the way. Val shot him to keep more people from being killed."

"Jesus," Hawkins whispered, "no wonder she was edgy."

"Yeah, I'm surprised she went to see Mandy alone. I wouldn't have had the courage to walk in there by myself."

Joe dropped Hawkins' hand and the foreign emotions vanished as quickly as they'd come on.

Hawkins thought back to the ride to the hospital and realized Val knew what would happen when she told Hawkins about his pay bump. She'd even goaded him into reacting and waited until they were inside the ER to tell him. She'd planned the whole scene from start to finish to keep him occupied with ER nurses and orderlies while she talked to Mandy for the first time since killing her father.

"Whoa," Hawkins said simply.

"Underestimate at your own peril," Joe repeated. "And those feelings you got just now? Those are mine. I take it no one explained that casual skin-to-skin contact will transfer top-level emotions."

Hawkins nodded and touched the Hold button. The elevator resumed its climb.

"No one has told me much so far."

Joe gave a one shoulder shrug. "It only works one way. You get what I feel, but I don't get what you feel. I've got to read your shocked and outraged face like everyone else." He gave a light laugh.

Realizing his jaw was hanging open, Hawkins shut it with a small chuckle of his own. They arrived at the Jump Room's Point Zero only a minute past seven. Murphy eyed the benign beige décor and tried to ignore the strong smell of cleaning solvents.

"Good morning," Val greeted them as they walked in. "Did you sleep well?" Val bent down to pat Zora lightly on the head. "Hey, Zora—who's a good girl?"

Zora accepted the head pat with simple canine dignity and leaned into Val's good leg slightly.

"Like a rock," Hawkins said. "I didn't have any sheets on the bed, but I'm kinda used to sleeping rough these days. Plus," he patted Zora's head as well, "she makes enough heat for both of us."

"She sleeps in your bed?" Val asked with a hint of disbelief in her voice.

"Yeah, where else would she sleep?" Hawkins said. Zora sat down next to him, tongue lolling out as she watched Hawkins and Val spar.

Val looked at him thoughtfully for a moment, then continued. "We're going to practice Jumping today. You've proven that you can do it, but we need to work on our core skills. You need to learn how to accept a location from another person's mental image, Jump other people to a landing zone, and precision landing. I know you've Jumped while toting others once before, but this is the first time you do it as a conscious action. It's going to take a lot out of you, so prepare yourself mentally. You will also need to see how we do calorie replenishment. Are you squeamish about needles?"

"Uh, no. Why?" Hawkins' mouth compressed into a line and he glanced at Joe to see if she was kidding. Joe gave another one shoulder shrug.

"We're going to expend some calories today. It will be more than you can consume in a single sitting so our standard procedure is to pop you with IV nutrients."

"Saline and stuff?"

"Saline, nutrients, and the Limitless Logistics proprietary blend of vitamins, minerals, sugar, sugar, and more sugar."

Hawkins' eyebrows shot up.

"It also helps for those of us," she pointed at herself, "that feel nauseated after even a medium Jump. And it's an absolute requirement after the big Jumps for when you pass out."

"I think you mean 'if,'" he said.

"I think," Val gave a laugh, "I might have said the same thing when I was new. I was lucky enough to stay awake a whole two minutes on my first full-gear Jump before I hit the dirt. We'll see how long you last." She flashed him a friendly, but slightly challenging, smile. "Fortunately, the PJs in Hank's group are all eminently qualified to place a line in you."

"Geez, anything else I need to know before this truly terrifying training Jump?" he asked dryly.

"Yes, glad you asked," she smiled again but Murphy saw her eyes dart to one corner of the room as she leaned against one of the boring beige desks that decorated the Jump Room. Hawkins also noted she'd traded her crutches in for a cane today. "First off, this delightfully boring space is our Jump Room."

She gestured to a series of concentric black and yellow rings painted on the floor a dozen steps away.

"Point Zero is where we all Jump from and return to the building. There are others like it all over the world. It's our assured clear zone for coming back without worrying we'll materialize inside a desk or a car or some other unpleasant thing. Don't stand directly on it unless you're scheduled to Jump, because even if you aren't killed by an inbound Jumper, the arrival concussion can be pretty stout as the air is displaced and it can knock your ass over."

She pointed to a large sign over her head that read in large black letters DO NOT STAND DIRECTLY ON POINT ZERO UNLESS SCHEDULED TO JUMP.

He gave her a sheepish look and took a couple steps back.

"Also, you will have a fallback guy assigned to you. He places the IV replenishment line and defends you from attack, as needed, until you regain consciousness."

"Seriously? And why doesn't Joe come with me?"

"Joe stays back here to receive you after a mission. Trust me, it's a good thing to have an experienced fallback man when you make a Jump."

Hawkins digested what she had said.

"Okay, taking a placement and Jumping others. Both require a brief physical contact before Jumping. The physical contact will get you acquainted with the mental signature of the people you're Jumping. Each is different. Know the mind and the body will follow. A word of caution though—even the briefest contact will let you see their very top layer of thoughts and emotion. It's not exactly mind reading, but close. More like mind skimming. You can't dig below the top layer, but if they're actively thinking or feeling something, you'll feel it." Val remembered her shock at what Brandon Powell was feeling the first she gripped his hand.

"Yeah, so I've learned," he glanced at Joe. "I only get the top layer?" He recalled Joe's emotions in the elevator. All of that was just the top layer? He was going to have to watch who and how he came into contact with people.

Hawkins watched Val bite her lower lip, catching the corner of her mouth in her teeth as she thought. That got his mind whirling as he imagined possibilities. But as his mind wandered, Val's red-gold hair was replaced with Mandy's blonde. He shook his head and pushed aside thoughts of either woman as they would feel everything he felt.

"Yes, that contact," Val said. "It's why all the Pantheon people have that funny handshake. They're deliberately grabbing your cloth-covered forearm and not making skin to skin contact."

"Ahh, I haven't seen that yet, but now I know."

"Finally, the contact is how you get the image for your Jump."

"I can't just look at a picture?"

"Nope. A picture only gives a two-dimensional image. A mental contact will give you three dimensions as well as smells, sounds, the feel of the wind on your skin. You get the picture. Literally."

Hawkins absorbed that for a minute. As he thought, Joe brought out two bags. Hawkins recognized the sand-colored tactical go-bags. The exterior had multiple nylon loops for attaching additional gear while the interior had handy dividers to keep his stuff organized.

"Here Val," Joe said, hanging a bag to her. "Since Mandy's out and you don't have a replacement yet, I made up your bag for you."

"Aww ... thanks, Joe," she said with appreciation. Hawkins saw a genuine smile cross her face, her eyes crinkling at the corners. "My usual stuff?"

"Yeah. Mandy's notes are very detailed," he grinned at Mandy's level of OCD. "I gave you everything she would have packed."

Hawkins saw a brief flash of uncertainty on Val's face. Now that Joe had filled him in on what had happened so recently, he realized it was guilt. Her eyes darted to the corner again. Murphy had the sudden realization that this was where she had shot Mandy's father and both women had nearly bled to death. The lingering smell of cleaners and solvents made sense now—they must have spent hours scrubbing the blood off Point Zero.

"Thank you," Val told Joe. "Murph, if you're ready, you can take our first Jump destination from me. I'll give you the countdown and we'll go." She held out a hand.

Zora stood expectantly and Hawkins looked up to Val.

"No, she stays for now until we see how you do. We can have someone bring her and Joe down later."

Hawkins handed Zora's leash to Joe.

Mentally bracing himself, Hawkins placed his hand on Val's. Her hand was soft, but the feeling he got was resolve layered over guilt.

Shaking his head, he focused on the image he got of a hangar: concrete floors, corrugated metal roof, the loud *whoosh* of the industrial HVAC system. Smells of metal, gun oil, and dust on cold concrete.

A large pair of feet were painted in green and dominated the main wall of the hangar. He saw on the floor concentric rings of black and yellow—Point Zero at Hurlburt Air Force Base in Florida.

"Do you feel like you know where you're going?" Val asked.

"Yes," he said and patted Zora's head. "I'll be back soon, girl." Zora's tail thumped excitedly against the cheap metal desks.

"Okay, I go on one, then you." She nodded. "Three. Two. *One*."

Hawkins watched Val disappear. No wink. No blink. No slow dissolve of a Star Trek transporter. One second, she was there and the next she wasn't. The suddenly vacated place she had occupied in the room popped hard as the air rushed in to fill her void.

"Shit," was all he could get out. Concentrating on the image he'd gotten from Val, he Jumped.

He arrived in Florida an instant later with a strong feeling of déjà vu. Around him, men with packing lists laid out gear in orderly rows while an Air Force staff sergeant growled orders at subordinates scurrying around.

Hawkins grinned, recognizing a predeployment inspection.

"Nice Jump, Murph. How do you feel?" Val's voice asked from beside him.

"Fuh-fuh, fi ... fine," he stammered. As the words left his mouth, Hawkins realized he wasn't fine at all. He blinked hard to clear his double vision and swayed slightly until the dizziness passed. He felt like he'd just finished a CrossFit workout after a twenty-five-mile ruck, and he was depleted. Hawkins ruthlessly pushed aside the feeling of intense hunger.

Val placed a hand lightly on his clothed upper bicep. "It's all right to feel worn out. You just burned about eight hundred calories, and you may not be fully recovered from your first Jump."

She made a subtle hand gesture and two Air Force medics started taking steps toward Hawkins.

Val's calm, quiet voice didn't carry past the two of them in the bustle of the hangar. "Let me help get you restored." She reached into a cargo pocket and retrieved a powerful Pantheon energy bar. Most of the men loved then because they were drenched in a high-calorie coating that was a good simulation of chocolate.

She waved away the medics.

"I'm all right," Hawkins growled as his vision began clearing. But he took the bar, ripped off the wrapper and eagerly bit into it.

She gave him a searching look, then nodded with a calculating look on her face. Hawkins frowned, not liking that look.

He saw a man across the hangar come striding over with only the faintest hitch in his gate. The man wasn't tall, about Val's height, but he radiated a strength and vitality that made it easy to tell he was the unit's commanding officer, Colonel Hank Gardner. His dark hair was graying at the temples and matched the impressive gunmetal gray mustache that Hawkins suspected pushed the limits of even the Air Force's relaxed grooming standards.

Hawkins watched the man's face transform from the almost hostile face of a Marine Corps gunnery sergeant to the grin of a doting father. The man's eyes crinkled at the edges as he swept Val into a bear hug. Val accepted the hug, fiercely clinging to him, her cane dangling at her side almost forgotten.

"Gods and stars above, Hank, yes—I'm still alive. You've seen it for yourself. Now put me down before someone cries," she insisted.

"We heard about Belarus. The Ukraine. All that followed," Hawkins heard the man whisper. "I'm glad to see you're okay." The man searched her face. "Are you sure you're okay?" He set her down and Val smoothed her shirt.

"Things aren't perfect," she said quickly, shifting her weight to her good leg. "But they're getting there. The Limitless nutrition helps a lot with its healing characteristics."

Val stepped away and looked to Hawkins. "Colonel Hank Gardner, this is Murphy Hawkins, United States Marine Corps, and our newbie.

Hawk, this is Hank, commander of the TENCAP Special Operations Activity here at Hurlburt."

Hawkins offered his hand and received the strange "Pantheon handshake" Val had warned him about earlier, a firm grip on his forearm insulated by the shirt's long sleeve.

"Hey sir, I'm Murph," he said.

"So, this will be your first training Jump?" Hank asked.

"Yeah," Hawkins said. If he'd really been promoted to major general, a simple colonel should have offered the use of his first name by now.

"Very well. Just do as Val instructs," Hank said, his face expressionless, and turned back to his men.

Hawkins rocked back as if slapped. Hank's coldness was almost calculated. After Val had introduced him as a Marine, he'd expected to be greeted as a brother in arms.

"Don't worry. They take time to warm up to new people," Val said in a tight whisper.

"No kidding," he half growled, half whispered back.

Hank turned back to them. "The plan for today is to practice short-distance team insertion and extraction. I'd like to start everyone Hollywood style, and then build up to full gear."

"Hollywood style?" Hawkins asked. He remembered Val saying something about that on the phone.

"Uniforms and sidearms, no other gear," Hank said. The training team gathered around them in preparation for the Jump, and three armorers rolled out carts laden with 9mm Sig Sauer M18 issue handguns with extra mag pouches on the gear belt with the holster. The teammates all strapped on the weapons and an armorer issued Hawkins an M4 carbine that he slung.

Finally, here was an activity Hawkins understood. These was the same familiar weapons he'd carried in Syria.

"Expecting trouble?" Hawkins asked as he checked the action and load of the M18. It was pristine and the slide was smooth.

"No," Gardner said. "But train like you fight and you'll fight like you train, right?"

"Oh yeah," he said. "Heard that a few times before, sir."

Hank looked at Val, quirked an eyebrow and grinned.

Hank cleared his throat and offered a sly grin. "I believe you don't need to call me 'sir,' sir."

Hawkins ground his teeth in frustration. He knew they were needling him. "Thanks. Yeah, let's make that Jump." He looked sharply at Val.

"Sounds good," she said brightly. "We're Jumping to the far side of the base. The away team will do a hot lap around the training course in light gear, then we Jump them back. While on the ground, you and I grab nutrients as they prepare the Jump with our prepositioned gear. We'll head back here for lunch, then on out to our own training area at White Sands Missile Range in New Mexico."

"Fine," Hawkins said, peeved. As a senior NCO in the Marine Corps—and now a general officer—he'd expected to be treated with a little deference, at least. But he was being treated like a raw recruit.

Which, of course, is what he was.

"Right, then. Teams split, tag up, we depart on my countdown," Hank told them. "Val, you're Jumping yourself plus five. Hawkins, you have yourself plus five as well."

Val said, "Standard Jump teams. Two pairs, a fallback man, and a Pantheon operator. Looks like Sergeant Martin is your fallback man, Murph. He's a good dude. Good catcher if you fall out, and he slips the line in smooth as butter." A tall, slender man nodded to him and raised a thumb. "I, on the other hand, have Sergeant King, who is a walking disaster," she said with a huge grin. The short, stocky young man she nodded to grinned back at her.

"Hey, I'm on light duty too," he said, pointing at the plastic boot on his foot. "But at least I don't have a cane like an old lady," King challenged with a smirk. Hawkins watched Val give him a fierce scowl which dissolved into a smile.

"Jumping in five!" Hank hollered. "Tag up!"

Martin and the other four men assigned to him tapped Hawkins hand lightly. Each man's touch passed him the feeling of excited anticipation and a low thrum of restlessness associated with him as a new Jumper. He pushed aside their emotions and saw a picture of a sandy clearing, surrounded by scrubby, wind-wrought Southern pine trees.

"Three," Hank hollered.

"You're more than welcome to follow them on their run," Val said. "They hold about a 6:40 pace without gear."

"Two."

"Yeah, I think I will," Hawkins said fiercely. His pride had been stung and it was past time to show these people who he was.

Hank shook his head at Hawkins.

"*One!*"

Hawkins sought the five minds he'd touched and visualized a sandy clearing. In an instant, they arrived. Four of the men on his team started moving out almost immediately. Martin gave him a searching look.

"I'm fine, damn it," Hawkins said irritably. Martin shrugged and took off after the others.

"I'll be staying here," Val told Hawkins and gestured to her cane. "By all means, go prove how big your dick is. Just don't forget to eat your replenishment bars."

He didn't bother replying, but simply ran off after the others. When unhampered by twenty-seven pounds of protective gear plus the weight of extra gear, weapons, and ammo, a 6:40 pace was easy for Hawkins to hold.

He easily tore off through the sand and short scrub for a whole five, maybe six steps, then exhaustion struck him like a lightning bolt but his pride and determination kept him moving forward instead of back. It was everything he could do to even keep upright after that. Only sheer pigheaded willpower kept him staggering after the others.

Almost twenty minutes later he was back, trailing the main group, and wheezing like he'd just had a double lung transplant.

Of course, he'd forgotten all about eating the special Pantheon energy replenishment bars.

Hank moved directly into the next phase of the training evolution without missing a beat.

"All right groups, form up around your Jumpers. Short hop back to the hangar for lunch, then we'll do the full-gear Jump to Wizzmer," Hank hollered in his best parade ground voice.

Hawkins sucked in a breath and stood upright. He nodded to Val and Hank and his five men surrounded him. *Good to go.*

"Okay, steady up. Three ... two ... *one!*" Hank called out, and the teams disappeared.

Hawkins Jumped his small team back to Point Zero in the Hurlburt hangar. As soon as his feet touched the painted concrete, he staggered to one knee. A hand caught his arm and kept him from rocking forward on his face. Hawkins gazed up with unfocused eyes at Martin, who held him firmly while escorting him to a gurney that had been positioned safely adjacent to Point Zero.

"Okay, lay down, He-Man," Martin commanded.

Hawkins did as he was told, unable to keep standing. He blinked hard, trying to bring his vision into focus. It wasn't working.

He saw a soft-focus person loom over him but he couldn't resolve the image well enough to recognize it. But he recognized its voice.

"You didn't eat anything, *did you?*" Val's voice was a sharp whip-crack above him. "And you still ran off on your stupid little dick-measuring trip, *didn't you?*"

Hawkins realized he was lying on the gurney with his pack under his head. Someone had removed his gear belt and weapons. In his delirium, Hawkins wasn't sure what Val was asking him, but he was certain she was angry.

"Jesus, Hawkins. These rules are not for your amusement. They are for your protection, and the protection of your teammates and mission. I brought you here to give you a chance to see what a real Jump does to your body and I expected you to do some kind of bull-headed Marine crap, but I didn't think you'd just be plain *stupid.*"

She placed her strong hands firmly on Hawkins' shoulders.

"*This shit will fucking kill you, goddamnit.*"

Now Hawkins didn't think Val was angry. She was scared.

She turned to Martin and King, who had been hovering at her

shoulder, and spoke in her command voice.

"Gents, if you would, please get him his IVs. He should also have a real lunch in that bag. Make him eat it. I'll go tell Hank we're on a logistics hold until this rookie is repaired."

CHAPTER 6
MURPHY HAWKINS
1143Z 0643L, 21 APR

Hawkins groaned as Val stomped off to find Hank, her cane clacking loudly on the concrete. He wanted to reply, to snap back at her, and tell her to quit her bitching, but he couldn't lift his head. He felt like a gigantic piece of granite sat firmly on his chest, holding him to the gurney.

He fervently wished his dog was there.

"Fuh ... fuck me. How do you all dee-deal with her?" Hawkins asked once King and Martin had the powerful Pantheon IV nutrients flowing into him. He was slow to replenish due to the consecutive caloric drain and he was still stammering a little. But he felt like his mind was clear.

"General V?" King said. "We don't have to 'deal with her.' She's not usually like this."

Hawkins looked at King, reading the man's anger and the reproach in the set of his jaw.

"I don't usually have this effect on women," Hawkins muttered under his breath.

King seemed to relax a degree with the weak display of humor. His stocky shoulders dropped.

"It's not you, man. Not all you, anyway. She's been through a lot lately," Martin said.

"Yeah, my handler told me about Belarus and shooting her best friend's father."

"Man, that's not even all of it," King chided him. "That woman is as tough as my Momma's combat boots," he said with sincerity. "We'd all go to war with her tomorrow."

Martin nodded in agreement.

Hawkins flinched at King's comment. "Fuckin' Momma's boys," he muttered.

King had been bent over Hawkins' left arm checking the IV, and his head slowly swiveled up.

"What did you just say?" King asked.

"You guys are all Valerie Hall fan bois, ain't ya?" Hawkins asked mockingly "God, she's not even like us. Don't you know that?"

Martin and King just stared at Hawkins. They feverishly hoped he was still delirious.

"That chick can't understand what it's like for us ground pounders," he told them. Hawkins realized his hands had tightened into fists at his side and he forced himself to relax.

"Sir, if you'll excuse my breach of decorum, you don't know what the actual fuck you're talking about," King said testy as he loomed over Hawkins.

Martin grabbed King's bicep to pull him back and shook his head. *Don't do it.*

He stared down at Hawkins. "This was your first training Jump and you're talkin' shit like it was your fiftieth."

"Fine! You wanna fill me in on her genius, then?" Hawkins snapped back. The super-nutrients were taking hold now.

"You know how it is," King replied, mocking Hawkins' earlier tone. "We," indicating Martin and the rest of Hank's team, "don't accept and respect just anyone." His tone heavily implied that Hawkins was not included in that group. "You earn respect here, you don't command it."

"And she has?" Hawkins' voice held scorn. "That skinny-ass chick holds her own against you guys?"

"Man, you are some kinda terminally fucked up," King said and looked away, mouth set in a firm line.

Hawkins stared at him, but King didn't speak.

Finally, Martin spoke into the silence. "It isn't whether she's as strong or fast as us." Martin paused, thoughtfully. "The Pantheon does something damned few others on Earth can do and that saves lives—and they all do it with more class than you. Even though she knows she's not as strong or fast, she still uses her considerable skills to put her life on the line to save others. It just isn't about push-ups here, you sad bastard. It's about character. You can do a thousand push-ups, I suppose ... but you're still an asshole."

Martin stared at a point over Hawkins' shoulder, a sorrowful and pensive look on his face. After a moment, he spoke again.

"A few months ago, General V was doing her first training evolutions with us, much like you're doing today. General Dee had said she'd had a traumatic transition and we could see how hard she was fighting just to keep up with the initial Jumps, let alone trying to follow us around."

Hawkins caught the quiet intensity with which Martin spoke. He knew it all too well. It was an intensity used when telling a story over beers, late at night, when the harsh truth you told could later be excused as the beer talking, not the soul-baring cry of a deeply affected man. Hawkins swallowed hard and listened harder.

"We were out at WSMR, patching up this dumbass's broken ankle," Martin pointed at King who was staring fixedly in another direction. "We got an emergency recall. So, she and General Dee Jumped us all back. Now, they'd already dragged us there and back, plus a training Hollywood Jump earlier in the day, just like you did this morning. Sit up."

Martin and King both took Hawkins' shoulders and rotated him up, adjusting the back of the gurney to support him upright. Martin extracted Hawkins' lunch from the small go-bag and dropped it into his lap.

"Eat that."

Across the hanger, Joe Pax and Rich Dunn arrived with Zora. When Hawkins saw his dog, Joe let her off the leash and she bolted across the concrete floor, jumping up to put her paws on Hawkins' chest. She licked his face in happiness to see him again. He ruffled her head and scratched her ears and left one arm wrapped around her furry neck.

"So, our recall. Out and back, that's about eight-thousand calories and the associated fatigue," he said sharply. "We'd been called back for a personnel recovery in Syria. Heard of it, Syria? An F-15E had been shot down near Damascus and we had to get out there ASAP or risk losing both aviators to ISIS."

"When? A couple months ago?" Hawkins asked.

"Yeah, why?"

"Damascus? An F-15 over Damascus?" Hawkins asked, the bravado gone from his voice.

"Yes," King said.

"That was my squad. I called in that original personnel recovery," Hawkins said quietly. He and his platoon had been in Syria only a week, but they already knew what would happen to any American serviceman ISIS got ahold of. He shuddered, the cold seeping into his core.

Martin continued, unimpressed. "Wow, small world after all, right? So, Val immediately volunteered to Jump a rescue mission. Knowing what was at stake. Knowing that we couldn't do it without her. Knowing it could kill her."

Martin's words punched into Hawkins as strongly as if Martin had struck his chest with a five-pound sledgehammer. Zora's head cocked to the right while she took in the tension she received from both her master and this other.

"General V led that mission without hesitation, even knowing how much damage it would do to her because she was already heavily depleted from the first two Jumps. I listened to her screams when we inserted. That Jump put her in a kind of agony we seldom see here. She endured that, willingly, to save others." He stopped and cleared his throat.

"So, Mr. Hardcore Snake-Eater *whatthefuckever*, yes, we respect the hell out her. You may have accidentally dragged your team out of Syria to save them, but she willingly Jumped into Syria to save others. When you show that commitment, we'll respect you, too."

Hawkins stared at them, stunned. Zora, sensing his disquiet, gave his cheek a lick. He patted her flank.

"Your bags are almost empty, Hawkins," King said, his voice less hostile now. "You ready for a real lunch now?" Zora yipped at that. She understood all food references.

Hawkins nodded and dug into the lunch in his lap and cooperated as Martin removed the IVs. Hawkins chewed the food silently and shared bites with Zora as his mind churned.

Val arrived a few minutes after he finished eating.

"You ready to go, slug?"

Hawkins felt like a million bucks now. The Pantheon nutrition was the best, and the liquid food didn't stick between his teeth. He rose to his feet, shouldered his bag, and nodded once.

"If you feel up to it, He-Man, you can make the ground run with them at WSMR," she said. She pronounced it *Wizzmer.*

At that point Hank wandered up. He gave Hawkins a hard look but said nothing.

"Are they going Hollywood or full packs?" Val asked Hank.

"Half load for most, thirty pounds," he said, "and King is Hollywood until he's fully recovered." Hank eyed his young sergeant. King grinned sheepishly.

Val nodded. "Well, it's heavy enough to make work for him and heavy enough to slow you boys down enough to let him catch up."

Hawkins felt a flare of outrage but held his tongue, only blinking at her. "*Ooorah*. I'll ruck it out with them either way," he said as blandly as he could.

"It's your first long Jump. You've had two IVs and a bag lunch, but you'll need to ingest fluids again via IV at Wizzmer. Do you think you can you eat and run this time?"

"I'll try to keep up," he said with only a small drip of sarcasm.

"Okay, mix the protein powder with your water and eat a damn granola bar or something," she said. "You did okay on your maiden voyage solo, so this time let's see how you do with Zora—and how she does. We've never Jumped with a canine before. Are you up for testing that?"

Hawkins reached down and scratched the head of his quiet dog sitting obediently at his side. "Yeah, we'll be good to go."

Val gave him one last appraising look before addressing Hank. "I think we're ready."

Bone-wracking fatigue tormented Hawkins as soon as they landed at the WSMR training area, but he suppressed it. He'd been tired before and the Pantheon brand was nothing special so far. In fact, Hawkins was starting to feel like he was getting the hang of this gig already.

Zora seemed no worse for the trip—it was no more traumatic than an eye-blink to her. Since Hawkins had towed her with his team the dog sacrificed no energy to the experience. She sensed his discomfort, though, and pawed lightly at his leg with concern.

"No sweat, girl," Hawkins to the dog. He bent and hugged her neck. "We got this, right?"

He squinted as the blazing sun reflecting at him across the white sand for which the range was named. He fumbled to put his Oakley Flak sunglasses on.

"Ruck up, fellas," Hank hollered out to the team.

"You sure you're okay?" Val asked Hawkins quietly.

"Yes, I'm fine," he said without attitude. He was still processing the heroism King and Martin had relayed to him about their boss. He was starting to see why they worshiped the ground she walked on. If people unironically referred to the Limitless Logistics team as The Pantheon, it was because people like Val personified the goddess of strategic war, Athena.

"Okay, then. Have fun," she gave him a little smirk. "Martin, I bet you're itching for a good run?"

He raised his pack to his shoulders. In addition to the standard Jump load of extra ammo and medical supplies he carried for the operators, today he also carried additional nutrition for Hawkins if he fell out of the run.

"I am indeed, ma'am," Martin said, raising a thumb with a grin.

Hawkins, Zora, and Martin raced off after the two teams. As their landing spot receded behind him, Hawkins heard Val speak to King.

"Two IVs this trip, King. I feel like I'm going to need it."

The three caught the running group soon enough and eased into their pace. Hawkins reveled in the feel of hard-packed sand beneath his boots, the sun baking the landscape, and heat cooking everything around them. There was comfort for him in the discomfort of physical exertion, a kind of peace. Unexpectedly, he staggered a step and Zora short-stepped thinking her master might be stopping.

Musta tripped.

Hawkins caught himself and pushed on.

The group rounded a turn in the trail and the flat sand gave way to free sand dotted with scrubby, squat bushes. Hawkins kept his head down and his eyes on the trail in front of him. His view of it wavered as he ran and the shimmering sun made him squint, especially through the orange sunglass lenses. Hawkins shook his head, ejecting sweat drops from under his Kevlar, and the spots in his vision stayed and grew.

Hawkins' steps slowed until he was stopped, doubled over, hands on knees. Zora automatically halted and sat down on the sand, awaiting Hawkins' commands, but the spots in his vision expanded to gray around the edges, then darkness. Hawkins toppled over, the fatigue and pain he'd spent a lifetime training himself to ignore crushing him flat.

The last thing he recognized as he passed out was a single alert bark from Zora.

When Hawkins came to, the cool of the polished concrete hangar floor pressed against his back about thirty meters off Point Zero. Zora's warmth was pressed along the length of his side and he had an IV in each arm. His eyes fluttered open and he recognized his surroundings with a bit of difficulty.

"Well, hey there, devil dog. Welcome back." Val's cheery voice came from his right. Her voice was the smooth, honeyed tone he had heard when he first woke up in the Limitless clinic.

Hawkins turned his head to her voice. "Hey. Hey, Val," he whispered and waited for her to speak. When she didn't, he remarked, "You know, this would be a really great time for you to say 'I told you so'."

"Why? What purpose would that serve?"

"I dunno. I guess I figure I'm due," he said.

"How are you feelin'?" The question came out with a hint of Southern inflection, just noticeable enough for him to hear it. He realized she was trying to be as soothing as possible, which meant he was probably in a bad way.

"Better," he said. He reached over and patted Zora's flank. "What, uh, what exactly happened?"

"You passed out on the run. Martin radioed me. He stayed with you and sent Airman Perkins back to give me your location. I Jumped you and Zora back to the LZ, where King got you all set up while we waited for Hank and the guys to get back. Then we hauled you back here."

"They didn't break off when I went out?"

"Oh, hell no, we were all expecting it," she gave a light laugh. "We were watching for it. You were fine, just fatigued," she said.

Mortification churned the acid in his stomach. "So, I guess this is a little harder than I imagined," he said self-consciously. "You really knew this would happen?"

She nodded. "Yeah, I figured it would. You needed to get it out of your system." She patted his shoulder and checked the IV drip. "This is why it's called training, after all."

"I'm sorry I underestimated you. And this," he gestured around to indicate Jumping the team. "I should have listened." Frustration and embarrassment tightened his voice.

"And if you had, you would only have been told. You wouldn't really know," she said calmly. "Lots of this gig is going to be hands-on, on-the-job training. We teach some broad concepts in the Indoc phase, but there is no real classroom for what we do. You will learn it by doing it, by experience."

Hawkins thought that over. "And now I see."

"And now you see," she echoed. "I needed you to know this is more than a glorified delivery service. You need to respect what we do here so you don't hurt yourself or your teammates."

"And now I do," Hawkins said. He saw her think, look at her phone, then nod. It was only then he saw she also had a replenishing IV in each arm. “Shit. You had to Jump both teams back—I was dead fucking weight,” he let his head fall back on his pack, annoyed.

Val laid a gentle hand on his. He felt her calm reassurance and acceptance. “It’s why I asked King for two bags as soon as we landed at Wizzmer. I knew what was coming.”

Val’s phone chirped. He watched her thumb through her messages, smiling.

“How ya doing there, Murph?” Hank asked as he came over to squat by Hawkins’ head, weight shifted only slightly to favor his one flesh and blood foot.

“Like an idiot, but physically? Better.”

“Don’t worry about it too much. Damarcus and Walker both went through a similar introduction,” he said. Hawkins heard chuckles of recognition from some longer-serving team members.

“Well,” Val said in a louder voice, “everyone listen up. It looks like we’ve got some good news.”

“What?” Hawkins asked. He pushed himself upright, sitting to face her.

She read an email from her combat tablet. “The Secretary of the Navy is pleased to announce that Staff Sergeant Murphy Elijah Hawkins will be awarded his Navy Cross on Tuesday.”

Hawkins stared at her. He vaguely remembered interviewing with the Commandant, but it had been shoved out of his mind by everything else that had happened in the last few days.

“Hank, I’m sorry to say that with the ceremony coming so soon, you’re unlikely to make it,” Val said.

“I’ll be sad to miss that,” Hank said.

Hawkins could see just a hint of a grin as he caught on to Val’s train of thought.

“Hey Murph, do you mind if Val reads your citation for us, since we’ll miss the award ceremony?”

All Hawkins could do was nod, his mind jolting back to a freezing night in Afghanistan.

Val cleared her throat and spoke in a rich voice that carried across the hangar.

"Attention to orders!" she commanded. Everyone in the hanger stopped what they were doing and stood at attention. Hawkins rose to his feet as quickly as he could with help from Martin. Even Zora rose from the floor to all four paws.

"The Navy Cross is presented to Staff Sergeant Murphy Elijah Hawkins for distinguished service in the line of duty as commander of a patrol operating in the Laghman Province of Afghanistan. Staff Sergeant Hawkins and his squad came under heavy fire while on the patrol mission. They were ambushed by numerically superior forces, splitting the squad."

Hawkins shuddered but kept his face blank as he listened to her silken voice describe that night.

"Staff Sergeant Hawkins was alerted to the fact that the other fire team had taken significant injuries and was unable to return fire. He ordered his fire team to maintain position and provide covering fire."

Hawkins stared across the hangar. He felt oddly disconnected. The memory of Afghan dust and gunpowder returned to his nose.

"Without regard for his own life and while taking heavy small-arms and mortar fire, Staff Sergeant Hawkins moved to the other fire team's position and rendered first aid. From his position, he reorganized his squad and led a charge to suppress the enemy forces, including a courageous call for a danger-close attack on the enemy by supporting aircraft. With enemy forces nullified, he efficiently called for extraction, thereby saving the lives of his wounded squad mates. By his decisive actions, bold initiative, and unconquerable spirit and his skill, initiative, and courage in the face of enemy fire, Staff Sergeant Hawkins reflected great credit upon himself and upheld the highest traditions of the Marine Corps and the United States Naval Service."

Val's voice faded into silence and Hawkins blinked hard. His heart pounded as he remembered the night of the battle. Slowly, the sound of gunfire chipping rock faded and he began to register clapping. He looked up to see Hank holding out his hand as he approached. Hawkins stepped forward to take it and felt Hank's genuine respect at the contact.

"You'll do okay here, kid," Hank said as he clapped Hawkins on the back. "A real Ares in the Pantheon, huh Val?" He gestured to Hawkins and bellowed to the assembly in his best command voice. "Behold Ares, our god of war!"

Around them, the members of Hank's team clapped and hollered even louder and more boisterous for him, shouting *Air-rees! Air-rees! Air-rees!*

Hawkins ducked his head, pulling himself together to the here and now. The realization struck him that Val had somehow engineered this entire scene. She knew he'd be a pigheaded grunt and not cooperate if she'd alerted him to the presentation. Without his permission, she had extolled his virtues and redeemed him in the eyes of this extraordinary group of warriors.

"Okay, okay," Val said with a grin, waving down the applause. "SuperMarine and I are due back in DC." She turned to Hank. "We'll be back in a few days."

"You're both welcome in our house anytime, Val," Hank said. Hawkins watched him hug her tightly. "In fact, all three!" He ruffled Zora's ears.

Hank released her and offered his hand to Hawkins again. They shook hands in farewell—a traditional handshake—and Hawkins was heartened to feel Hank's respect flow across the grip.

Hawkins and Val walked the few steps to Point Zero. Val caught his eye and smiled. "Okay, standby. We go in three ... two ... *one*."

A split-second later the three landed in the Limitless Jump Room and Hawkins turned to Val.

"You didn't have to do that, you know. The citation thing." He was still dismayed by her impromptu award ceremony intended to impress the Hurlburt training team with its newest Pantheon member.

Val smiled and bent to pat Zora. "I need you to respect our work, but I also need them to respect you. I have a feeling you'll be assigned to them a lot and you need to be a member of a team."

Hawkins shook his head and bent to pat Zora as well. "You planned this whole thing, start to finish, didn't you?"

Val shrugged. She straightened and leaned against the desk.

"What did you expect from your time in the Marine Corps? Retirement?"

Hawkins looked at her, surprised, "Uh, actually, I was scheduled to cross over into the Navy in a few months."

"Why?" She tilted her head up at him, reddish gold ponytail swaying behind her.

"Marines can't be SEALs."

"Why did you want to be a SEAL? What drove you to it?"

"I wanted that mission. I think I'd be good at it," he said.

"That's it? No other reason?" Hawkins saw her tilt her head slightly in question.

He scratched the back of his head and thought. "The prestige, too. I mean, Navy SEALs! Everyone knows they're the biggest bad asses on the planet."

"Did you want the notoriety, or did you want to be elite?" Val asked carefully.

Hawkins considered her question. "I guess I never thought of it that way. I think I wanted to be elite. I don't know if I really cared who knew. It was more important for me to know, to see, and accept a big challenge, and then apply my skills to protecting the country."

Val smiled at him, a genuine smile that crinkled her eyes at the corners. "You are one of only thirteen Americans so far ever known to be able to do this mission. I think that's about as elite as it gets."

The door opened and Joe entered. He'd been tracking the trip in Mission Control. "Hey, I saw your dots come back."

"Hey, Joe," Val greeted him with a smile. "Murph's had a rough day. Get him some chow and then he's off duty. Take Friday and the weekend off," she directed Hawkins. "Rest and recover." She looked back to Joe. "Take Friday to get his housing finalized. You know, maybe some sheets for the bed, dishes in the cupboards, and food in the fridge?"

"Sure thing, Val," Joe said.

"Oh, and he'll need business clothes. Take him to our house guy and square him away?"

Hawkins watched Val limp out, staring after her.

"You okay, man?" Joe asked him.

"Yeah. Yeah, I think I am."

CHAPTER 7
VALERIE HALL
1130Z 0730L, 02 MAY

Val woke to the sound of her cell phone and her boyfriend's voice beside her in bed.

"If you don't shut that thing off, I'm murdering you here and now," Brandon Powell said, his voice heavy with sleep.

Val slapped at her phone, silencing it, and rolled over to face Powell.

"You know, if you were anyone else, I could laugh that off as a joke. However, I never know with you CIA guys," she said, a hint of question in her voice.

"I have two guns, a knife, and a belt that I can reach from here," he muttered into his pillow.

Val lifted an eyebrow at his naked back and smiled. Words like that should scare her, but under the blankets, her leg was pressed into his, and she could feel his emotions. He wasn't mad, far from it. *In fact*, she thought with a smile, *he might make me late for the office again*. Val smiled. *Damn the luck*.

"Have you ever been diving off the island of Guam?" she asked lightly and ran her hand over his shoulder. When he grunted she continued. "Beautiful scuba diving. Right next to the Marianas Trench, incidentally." Val leaned over Powell's ear and whispered. "I'd Jump you to the edge of the Trench and drop you before the hammer fell, Bran."

Without warning, Powell flipped her to her back and pinned her arms beside her head. Val squealed and yelled, "*Oww*—my leg, damn it!" But the protest was more hollow than it sounded.

Powell swooped down for a kiss, pressing her hands into the mattress. "Should I go get that belt?" he whispered with a grin on his face.

She gave him a tight smile.

"Mmm. As much as I'd like to explore your kinky side, that alarm was telling me to get my ass to work," Val said. "Much to my great regret." She gave him a quick kiss and he released her.

"You want breakfast here?" Powell asked as he rolled out of bed.

Val watched him walk naked through his bedroom. He was more heavily muscled than could be seen when he wore his usual business suit, and she enjoyed the view as he grabbed clothes for the day from hangers in his large closet.

"Are you going to cook naked?" she asked.

"Eggs I could, but if you want bacon, then no," he said.

"Pass, then. I won't trouble you. I'm sure the cafeteria has a huge, calorically dense monstrosity for me," she said, making a face of distaste.

"All right. You showering here or there?"

"I'm working out with Pete first. I'll shower after." She began dressing and gathering her things.

"How's Pete doing with Mandy still in the clinic?"

"Fine, I think," she answered. A moment's thought had her frowning. "You know, I saw Mandy every day this weekend, but it didn't seem like Pete had been there."

Powell, sensing her distress again, caught her in a hug from behind. This didn't trigger the romantic response he expected.

Instantly, the mood in the room altered when Val could not stop herself from remembering a night not many months before. She could feel the grit of a damp alley beneath her feet, a broken bottle in her hand, and smell the pungent, coppery odor of blood seeping onto wet concrete.

Her heart rate surged and she felt constrictions in her chest. A terrible recollection possessed her mind, controlled her thoughts, and kept her from shutting out the terror of a sudden vivid memory.

"Whoa—whoa, Val!" Powell's voice was barely a buzz in her ear as she struggled to escape his arms.

Against the flashback.

Against his embrace.

Against one too many traumas, too close together, too close to the surface, and covered by only the thinnest veneer of normalcy.

Powell dodged her failing arms and spun her in his grip trying to catch her gaze. Her unfocused eyes stared beyond him, seeing nothing in the present.

"Val. Val, talk to me." Powell gave her a little shake.

Val could feel him pumping calm across their physical contact but nothing, not even his considerable talent, could stem the flashback.

She was back in the wet alley behind the restaurant. She was being assaulted. A bitter taste filled her mouth.

Powell held her at arms length. "It's him, isn't it? You're remembering him again?" he asked as gently as he could.

At the mention of her attacker, Val finally snapped back into the present, the smell of blood on concrete disappearing. She nodded. Powell ran a hand down her arm. The feeling of calm washed over her now that the flashback had faded.

"It's like that sometimes. I experienced it the first time I had to ki–" he stopped himself. His mouth went thin and Val felt the barest flash of anger and resolve in their touch. Powell cleared his throat. "Anyway, it gets easier with time. You might want to see someone about it, though. Don't let it mutate into full-dress PTSD."

Val nodded. "I know. I just—" she bit the corner of her lip. "I'm just not sure whether I'm ready yet."

Powell nodded and released her. "Let me know if there's anything I can do to help." His face was set in its usual impassive mask.

Val waited for more but he didn't elaborate. She knew she needed help to get past her sexual assault, but she needed to be ready for that. For now, she wasn't.

"Yeah, okay Bran."

They each finished getting ready for the day and then offered a mechanical kiss goodbye, a trace of irritation and resolve seeping through it. Val was still rattled by her episode and moved in a daze. She hid her shaking hands from Powell.

Val Jumped to her apartment, landing neatly in her bedroom. She knew she probably shouldn't be Jumping back and forth between Powell's apartment and her own, but both had cleared landing areas; he had a spot in the living room that was always kept unobstructed for her arrivals, her own small Point Zero there. Plus, even at six in the morning, she'd never make it from Chantilly to downtown DC in time for work.

She limped through her bedroom gathering things for the day and tried to keep her mind as blank as possible. Every time a feeling of panic rose, she ruthlessly squashed it down. She didn't need to probe what had just happened too deeply. She understood the root cause intimately, of course, and though she wasn't sure what sparked the flashback, but she wasn't going to risk triggering it again.

Her head snapped up. *Bran*. Not only had she had to relive the worst night of her life, but she'd also dragged Bran along for the ride. With his secret intuitive power there was no way he didn't feel every second of Val's pain, anguish, helplessness, rage, and fury. She grimaced. They'd have to talk about it later. For the time being, she ruthlessly shoved the thoughts and emotions out of her mind until a comfortable detachment settled on her.

Minutes later, Val was through Limitless Logistics front doors and limping her way to the gym.

"Good morning, Val," Pete's voice called out to her as she stepped into the Iron Palace of Limitless Logistics.

"Hey, Pete," she called back with a tight smile. Only a few months ago, Val wouldn't be caught dead in a gym. Now, under Pete's tutelage, she appreciated what it did for her. As Val put her hand out to shake Pete's, he could see a little bit of muscle had been added to her newly trim frame. Pete eyed her bare arm, turned without taking her hand, and started toward the weight racks.

"You've still got a couple weeks before we can work legs again," he said, waving a hand at her leg. "We'll focus on upper body today."

Val nodded, ignoring the snub. *He knows I'm Mandy's friend.* "Maybe I can finally build up enough muscle to get faster on the rock wall."

"You'd been breaking your PRs on that before your setback, so I wouldn't worry too much. But we'll see what we can do down the road when we get back to legs. Meantime, keep walking and exercising those legs for me," Pete said. He stopped at the bench press.

They worked through her sets without much comment, the only sound coming from three other Pantheon members in the gym. Rich Dunn, Wilson Armstrong, and James Lee worked out with their own trainers. The rest were on missions, Val knew. Being the new deputy meant she usually knew who was doing what with whom.

In between low-weight familiarization lifts on the bench press, Val finally asked, "You've been to see Mandy now that she's back in the clinic?"

Pete helped her guide the bar back onto the rack as she finished the set, but he looked away.

"Pete?"

"No. I haven't."

"Are you going to?"

When he didn't answer, she sat up, looking hard at him.

"Pete?"

"I'm not sure," he said quietly.

"Pete!" Val stood up, snagging her cane, and her angry stare boring a hole in him until he finally looked her in the eye. "You've been together for six months. She counts on you. She trusts you to be there for her and she needs you. After all that happened, she needs support from everyone who loves her."

"But, that's the thing, right?" he said. "I don't."

Val stared in surprise. "But you—wait, what? You don't what?"

"I don't love her, Val. It's been four months and I like her, but I don't love her. And now ..." he trailed off.

"Now?" Val prompted, an ugly feeling rising in her chest.

"Val, don't get me wrong. I like you and I respect you, but—"

"But you don't want your girlfriend doing it?"

"You and them," he pointed to the other Pantheon in the room, who were obviously trying hard not to be caught listening to the conversation. "You're the types who run toward the gunfire. Mandy isn't. And she was what I wanted: a good girl, who would have made a great wife. But now? Now she's one of *you people*." He spat out the last words.

Val's eyes widened. "One of *us*?" she asked. "What the hell does that even mean?" Her voice wasn't devoid of anger, and inside a sense of outrage was building.

Pete saw her expression and his back stiffened. "You know what I mean."

"No, Pete," Val said. "I don't think I do."

"Look, I told you I respect what you do, but you've got to admit, you are all freaks of nature," Pete said.

Any cool he had maintained was boiling away. His voice was rising in anger too, and all activity in the gym halted as the word *freaks* echoed across the walls. Armstrong, Lee, and Dunn stopped their workouts and stared openly, all pretense of detachment gone.

"Pete, I think you need to consider your next words very, very carefully," Val said in a cold whisper. Out of the corner of her eye she could see the other men approaching.

"It's unnatural, Val—and now you've dragged Mandy into this. Jesus save me, she's already been shot by her own freak father and now you're going to drag her further into this nonsense?"

Val's rage, simmering unnoticed since she had returned to her apartment, exploded. Her cane creaked as her grip tightened on it.

"Get out," she snarled. "Get out or I *swear* I will beat you to death here and now."

She raised her cane like a broadsword but a firm hand clamped over hers and held her arm in place before she could strike. Rich Dunn had walked up from behind and grabbed her before she could take a swing at Pete. He wrapped another arm around her ribcage, holding her back as her rage grew.

"Leave—*now* would be good," Dunn's deep, calm voice ordered.

Val couldn't see his face, but she knew Rich would have the same unflappable look he usually had.

Pete gave Rich a dark look and sneered. Wilson and James, both much taller than both Val and Rich, stepped closer.

"*Now*, mister," Rich commanded, "or I'll let her go and you can get your bigoted-ass beat-down by a cripple." Rich's voice turned hard and the calm that had flowed across their hands turned to anger and a deep weariness.

At that, Pete turned and stalked out. Rich released her and Val had a brief desire to hobble after him.

"No, Val" Rich said quietly. "No. It doesn't help."

Val looked up at his face, graced by a few lines but more youthful than his fifty-one years should show. Only a faint white scar through his upper lip, faded by time, and a bare sprinkling of gray at his temples suggested his real age.

Val sagged, leaning heavily on her cane.

"Do things like that crop up here very often?" she asked, the rage fading to disappointment.

"A few times in my thirty years. It stings every time."

A feeling of awkward guilt hit her then. Marco had promoted her into Rich's job. Ideally, it gave Marco the opportunity to train her to take his own position as head of Limitless when he retired in four years. With a guilty looked on her face, Val opened her mouth to speak, but Rich cut her off.

"I think I know what you're going to say, Val, but disregard it. Really, truly. Thirty years is long enough for me," he said. "The politics of it wears. The close-minded intolerance of a few people who know. The long, difficult, and dangerous missions," he shook his head. "I'm relieved Marco put you in my role. The idea of staying on in that capacity, even for the two years until I could retire? It would have been too much. I'm happy to finish my two years in peace, helping out emeritus while the vitality of youth carries us forward into the future."

Val smiled, relieved he wasn't angry with her. "Thank you, Rich. That helps a lot."

Rich shook his head. "Don't thank me. This is a tough role you're taking on. I don't envy you." He gave Val's hand a gentle squeeze. Through the touch, Val could feel his worry for her mingled with relief that he no longer had to deal with these things.

Val nodded.

Rich said, "Go hit the showers. I'm sure Marco has plenty of work for you lined up already."

His prediction was correct. As soon as Val got the deputy commander's office Rich had surrendered to her, Anna found her. Marco's secretary was tall, with skin the color of milk chocolate and an official-business face that masked her deep love for her Limitless family. Years of working for military officers and battling the incessant pushy calls of politicians and generals alike had seasoned her against both charm and tedious rank pulling. While she had no supernatural powers, even Marco swore the woman was at least a minor deity amongst the Pantheon for "her ability to put up with our bullshit."

"Good morning, ma'am. General Martinez would like a moment of your time," Anna said briskly from the doorway.

"Okay. Thank you, Anna." Val settled her suit coat across the back of her chair before limping across the hall to Marco's office. "Morning, boss."

"Good morning. I hope you had a pleasant weekend," Marco said briskly.

"Yes, thanks. You?" Without waiting for Marco's invitation, she eased herself into one of the dark leather chairs across from his large mahogany desk.

"Fine." Marco gave her a quick smile. "I mostly spent time with my family. Got in to see Mandy twice."

"Good. She needs everyone she can get these days," Val said with a frown.

Marco studied her. "I heard about Pete." His face was a professional mask, giving away nothing of his emotions.

"Bad news travels fast, huh?" Val said, slumping into the thickly padded chair.

"Indeed. He's asked to be released from his employment contract and I've agreed to let him go. His terms will call for a healthy severance check, but it's money well spent."

"You're paying that asshole to *leave*?" She sat bolt upright. "I mean, I should have fired him on the spot for cause—the cause being rampant assholery."

She paused and thought. "Am I even authorized to fire people?"

Marco waved a hand. "Val, he signed a non-disclosure agreement with us, but I find that a healthy severance package is often an effective salve to wounded pride and the glue to keeping mouths firmly shut."

Val took a deep breath in through her nose and let it out slowly, counting to ten.

Marco said, "I'm going to need you to break it to Mandy."

"Aw, geez, Marco–" Val started, but Marco cut her off.

"According to Rich, you verbally threatened Pete and would have brained him with your cane if he had not interceded." His eyebrows rose in question.

"Yes, I probably would have," Val said firmly and without a hint of remorse.

Marco drew in a slow breath. "You have anger issues."

"I do not."

"Paris?"

"I—" she stopped. She looked away from Marco. "I may be overly sensitive to some things."

"You beat a man senseless," he chided. "You destroyed one of his eyes and almost killed him."

"Fuck him. He assaulted me. He intended to rape me."

"I know that," Marco said, "but are you a member of the Pantheon or not? Could you not have just escaped his grasp and Jumped out?"

Val drew in a breath to retort but let it out again. "Maybe I could work on being less sensitive to certain things."

"By all means, be She-Hulk when you need to defend yourself, but I ask you to use better judgment when you have other avenues for defusing a situation."

"Yes, Marco," she said and stared at the polished wood of his desk.

Marco leaned across his desk and offered an open hand, palm up. Val grasped it lightly.

Pride and a fatherly affection warred with worry in his touch.

"You've grown on me, Chair Force girl," he said.

"Squid," she said with a smile.

Marco's worry faded slightly. "It's been a tough couple of weeks, but know that I'm rooting for you, Val."

Val nodded and released his hand. "Hey, that reminds me. You were Navy, right? Why in the hell are you a general and not an admiral?"

Marco's grin held a trace of sadness.

"Blame Zeus. He was insistent that American politicians were wholly uneducated about military ranks and wouldn't be able to mentally sort it out if some of us were admirals and some generals, especially in a discipline that typically requires no sea-going assets." He grimaced. "So, as much as it pained me to don ground-pounder ranks, he wouldn't budge."

Val nodded and smiled, leaning back into the chair once more.

"Stars is stars. Now, on to today's business," Marco continued, looking down at a stack of files. "Do you have a suit coat with you?"

"Yeah, it's on my chair in the deputy's office. And I've got other changes of clothes here, of course. Why?"

"You're office, Val. It's your office now," Marco said, glancing up from the stack. "And to your questions, we're going to the Hill," he said simply. "My second in command and I. And I need her to look the part. I also need you to keep your temper in check, no matter what occurs there."

"Understood. I'll get my jacket," Val said, quietly.

"You have a few minutes before we need to be in the car," he said. He handed her four folders. "Heads and deputies of both the House Armed Services Committee and Senate Armed Services Committee."

She took them, flipping one open. "Both sides? And they're in on the program?"

"Yes, to both. They know because they fund us. Jack Covington, the head of HASC, and John Holmes, the deputy of SASC, are for us and get us the money we need. Rich pulled Senator Holmes out of the line of fire a few years back, so he's about as solid a support as you can ask for. Conversely, Maureen Mitchell, the head of SASC, and Jacob Belton, the deputy on HASC, are both against us as a group, but don't stand in the way of our funding."

"Who's on first and what's on second?" Val quipped.

"It'll be easier once you've met them. They're, ahh ..." he paused, thinking, "... distinctive."

Val and Marco rode in separate cars, for much the same reason as the president and vice president of the United States didn't travel together. She spent the next twenty minutes studying congressional dossiers as the two black Chevy Suburbans separated by a couple miles wound through thick DC traffic to Capitol Hill.

Maureen Mitchell was a Senator, a Southern Baptist from Missouri, and she was known for voting her religion, even if it transcended party line. Her deputy on the committee, John Holmes, was pro-military, known for consistently voting for military spending and supporting military action around the globe.

In the House, Jack Covington was a middle-of-the-road liberal sympathetic to military spending. His deputy, Jacob Belton, had a positive track record, too. Looking at these histories of military support, Val was surprised by Marco's assessment that they wouldn't support the Limitless budget.

Her car stopped just as Val closed the last folder. Marco opened her door and leaned in. "Ready?"

"I think so," Val said as she shrugged into her suit coat.

They walked in silence for a few minutes before Val finally said, "So, do we not have a secure room on the Hill? Wouldn't Jumping in make more of an entrance? A business case, even?"

"There is a room. In fact, there are secure Points Zero all over town in case a major evacuation is ordered someday," Marco said. "If DC falls under nuclear attack, for example, the president won't be waiting around for any Air Force One."

He leaned in and raised his eyebrows meaningfully. Val got the inference—the president would be evacuated courtesy of "Pantheon One."

"But with this group I find things go more smoothly when we make the normal type of entrance. I try to keep our," he paused to find the right word, "*differences* to a minimum. I aim for a soft touch." His eyes met hers and he gave her a significant look, "I always have. I can't change now." He laughed then. "Speaking of making an entrance, politicians are all about showboating, in case you haven't seen cable news in thirty years. They'll probably use little tricks to assert their dominance. Be ready for it. Forewarned is forearmed, so don't get upset. It's no different than the mind games the instructors play in boot camp or SERE. It's a show, it isn't personal, and these people have TV cameras to posture for."

Val gave one nod for confirmation, staring up at the long marble stairs and wondering what could possibly go wrong.

Thirty minutes later Val was contemplating stabbing the next person who uttered the words "synergy," "cost-saving measures," or "sequestration." She let her eyes drift around the well-appointed room, with its oiled oak wall panels and marble accents, judging it to be the most elegant and luxurious secure facility she'd ever seen.

As a former intelligence officer, she had seen her fair share of secure rooms and felt herself a connoisseur of secure facilities. This one was trophy-class.

The top-secret joint Senate-House committee meeting droned on. Val looked around once or twice, but she was certain no C-Span television cameras recorded these sensitive proceedings.

"No, Maureen, once again you're not listening to me," said Jack Covington, the senior Congressman from Florida and deputy chair of the House Armed Services Committee. He'd spent his allotted five minutes in heated defense of Limited Logistics' proposed twelve percent increase in the budget rather than a fifty percent reduction. He had spent the five minutes before that furiously arguing that Limited Logistics needed to be further militarized. "With an additional Jumper on board, now they need the twelve percent increase at minimum."

"Why do they need a bigger budget when they're not even necessary?" Committee Chairperson Senator Maureen Mitchell glared at him furiously. "We have an entire Pentagon," she drawled, "filled with patriotic service members and civilians for whom we already pay a pretty penny." She looked at Covington over her half-eye glasses. "A pretty penny, I tell you."

Covington pinched the bridge of his nose, bringing his unruly salt-and-pepper eyebrows together like a Muppet's, Val thought with a grin.

"I could list the unique attributes that the Pantheon bring to the extended fight, Maureen, but the Senator knows their many skills as well as anyone here."

He didn't even crack a smile, but Congressman Covington was making a snide and indiscreet reference to an alleged affair Senator Mitchell reportedly had with an unnamed Pantheon operator some years ago. The operator had never been identified publicly and the affair never made it all the way to the Washington Post.

But Marco, in the best interest of his deputy, had discreetly told her that the unnamed operative was none other than his previous deputy, Rich Dunn. Mitchell had ascended to her position following her husband's death in 1982, filling in the ticket at what would have been his first midterm election. Not long after, she met a charming and brand-new Pantheon operative and had elected to sublimate her grief in the young man's arms.

Senator Mitchell rocked back in her seat, dark eyebrows rising into her gunmetal gray hair. "The congressman's time has expired." Her expression didn't change, but Val got the impression that Congressman Covington's remark had reached its target.

Val suppressed a frown and leaned back in her chair. She wondered why Marco had even brought her along since they were rarely called upon for information. Struggling mightily, she reined her temper in and sat upright. Val considered leaving the table to see if the little darkened nook she'd spotted earlier was, in fact, a coffee corner. She spent a few minutes peering into the corner and fantasizing about coffee.

Jacob Belton cut in smoothly. "Madam Chairperson?"

Mitchell responded, "The gentleman is recognized."

"Madam Chairperson, motion to postpone the question to our next regularly scheduled committee meeting and move on to the question of equipment Limited Logistics has requested for next year."

"Without objection," Mitchell said automatically.

Val sighed, leaned back in her chair, and listened for another twenty minutes as a further round of squabbling ensued with apparently no progress.

The debate swam back into Val's consciousness.

"Now, I'm not the first one to leap to Limitless Logistics' defense but I'm not the last one, either. It's clearly undeniable that they have a positive mission impact," Congressman Jacob Belton said with a charming smile on his handsome face. "We live in a time of uncertainty. Asymmetric threats, nuclear-capable rogue states, nuclear-armed non-nation states, and quite simply put the Department of Defense is not as good at counterinsurgency against terrorists. Limitless Logistics provides services that allow us to counter those threats in a timely manner, potentially halting attacks before we might otherwise be able to get a traditional team in. Without a doubt, Limitless Logistics needs this equipment request approved for the next fiscal year. I yield back the balance of my time."

Val glanced searchingly at Marco, who just nodded, his face blank.

"Madam Chairperson?" said Senator Winston Holmes. It was the first time he'd spoken in a while and Val had presumed his mind had checked out ten minutes prior.

"The gentleman is recognized."

"Like it or not, we need them. The Pantheon." He fixed every member of the committee in a hard, unblinking stare. "Like it or not, they have more people and God bless 'em for it. They need a budget consistent with their capabilities."

He took in a deep breath. He'd said his piece. That was the speech.

"I yield back."

Heads turned in Holmes' direction. His oratory was legendary on the Hill, and for him to speak so powerfully and briefly grabbed the attention of everyone in the chamber.

Senator Mitchell's face suffused with blood and to Val, she looked like a bullfrog about to croak. Mitchell decided to cut her committee short rather than risk looking foolish.

"I will hear a motion to adjourn."

Val's temper flared and she looked to Marco. His usually placid face gave another significant look, it finally clicked. 'I aim for a soft touch and always have, I can't change now,' he had said in the car. She gave him a wolfish smile that he returned, but he shook his head.

No.

Val placing both hands flat on the table in front of her and leaned in.

"Madam Chairperson, I think I'd like to be heard, please," she said with deadly calm. She could feel her temper starting to flare and she seized the anger. She was no longer the calm before the storm. She was the storm.

"The witness will suspend unless called upon," she said dryly without looking up. "A motion is on the table."

"Ma'am?" Val said, a bit more urgently than she'd intended.

Mitchell did look up then and her voice dripped with condescension. "You are simply a deputy, young woman. You have no need to speak in these proceedings." She waved her hand with a sneer. Winston and Jacob, the deputies for their respective branches, shifted irritably in their chairs.

"Is there ..."

"Oh, but I have considerable need, Madam Chair," Val continued, her voice a tranquil contrast to the tempest within.

"You are sorely testing this committee and are at risk of contempt of Congress!" Mitchell barked. She pulled off her glasses and they hung from her neck on a golden chain. "But you're feisty, and I like feisty. I'm often considered rather feisty myself." Mitchell smiled. "If you have anything you would like to say in camera, my staff will give you an appointment, as necessary."

She looked to her deputy, who quickly said, "I move that the committee do adjourn."

Val leaned further over the table, the old wood creaking under her hands. "Because if you want a fight, Madam Chairperson, I'll give you one." She sunk every ounce of frustration and anger she'd been suppressing that day into her words.

"You other three, you've acknowledged the necessity. You've acknowledged the budget required. You outnumber her three to one, vote for the budget with a ten percent increase." Val turned to Jacob Belton and addressed him blandly, "If I remember correctly, you have the ability to reallocate military assets?" She gave Marco a small smile, "I have a military working dog, kennel name Zora, I need to be transferred to Limitless Logistics today. Can you make it happen?"

Belton looked once quickly at Marco, then turned back to her, and nodded. "You'll have the paperwork by the end of the business day."

"Thank you. Lady and gentlemen, please understand that from henceforth you will be dealing with me. I know some of you think that we are aberrations or freaks." Pete's comment earlier that morning still stung. "And let me tell you, I simply do not give a fuck. Whatever your personal feelings may be, you will work with us and you will be polite about it. Because, as Congressman Covington pointed out, Limitless Logistics could easily be weaponized. Do you want to be my friend? Or do you want to be something else?"

Without another word, Val took Marco's hand and jumped them back to his office.

CHAPTER 8
MURPHY HAWKINS
1302Z 0902L, 19 MAY

Hawkins sat in the cafeteria slumped beside his breakfast. He picked at the last few forkfuls of hash browns.

"Good morning," Rich Dunn greeted him and sat down across from Hawkins with a steaming cup of coffee.

"Sir," Hawkins grunted, but sat up a little straighter in the chair out of deference for the second oldest Pantheon member.

"Hmm, hope you didn't work out too hard. You're getting your first live Jump today."

Hawkins straightened further. "No, sir. I'm good to go."

"Drop the 'sir' stuff, Hawkins. I know Valerie and Damarcus have spent the last few weeks harassing you about that."

"Sorry, Rich. Hard habit to kill." Hawkins grabbed his own coffee mug and downed the last few inches, glad it had cooled as he ate. "So, live mission, huh?" An expectant grin spread across his face.

"Don't get your hopes up. It's a milk run at best, but it is a long haul. Several long hauls, in fact, strung together. And you just might help us avert war with Iran."

Hawkins jerked fully erect at the mention of war with Iran. "Say again?"

Dunn smiled. "C'mon, let's go to the briefing room."

The quick walk to the briefing room plus Hawkins' pot of coffee finished waking him up. He nodded pleasantly at Damarcus Washington, who stood just inside with Staff Sergeants King and Martin from Hurlburt. Nearby lay two full go-bags, M4 carbines, and M18 handguns in utility belt holsters ready for use.

"Washington," Hawkins said in greeting. "King. Martin." He gave each man a nod, wondering if they were still sore over his comments about Val.

"Good morning, Rich," Damarcus said, ignoring Hawkins. "I've briefed King and Martin on today's mission. They're all yours. I'll be waiting to take them back to Hurlburt tomorrow when you're mission complete."

"Thanks, Dee." Dunn gave him a light slap on the shoulder as he left. "Hawkins, today we're taking helicopter parts to a stranded Air Force HH-60G, downed just inside the Iranian border."

Hawkins looked around, briefly searching for the parts.

"We don't have them here, bubb," Dunn said with a laugh. "We're meeting with the helo crew's team on the good side of the Iranian border for the piece, then Jumping in to deliver it once we get the placement from the man who has been to their location before."

"Which unit?" Even as a Marine, Hawkins recognized the HH-60G Pave Hawk was used by the Air Force for the insertion and recovery of special operators, including combat search and rescue.

"A helicopter unit."

Hawkins gave Rich a look. "Explain."

"Don't ask so many questions," Dunn said with a hard look.

"Okay, it's special operations, probably?" Hawkins said. "Someplace somebody probably shouldn't be? And we're helping them get out of town before they get caught where they shouldn't be and inadvertently start a war."

"Son, don't pick at this." Dunn's voice had a note of warning.

"Rich, do you know how many times I have definitely not crossed the border from Turkey and definitely not been in Iran just for laughs? Let's say I'm not shocked and I'm not gonna call The Washington Post." Hawkins laughed.

Hawkins realized Rich was trying to hold back a laugh. "Very well, then. This will be Sergeant King's first mission back after his accident and this will be your first live mission. Fortunately for both of you, this is a milk run. It doesn't require precision, which you are still learning, Hawkins. And it doesn't take much more than a few IVs consumed and food eaten, which should keep King from being his usual walking disaster." Dunn gave the young sergeant a smile to show he was joking.

"Iran's a long way away, Rich," Hawkins said.

"It sure is. That's why we've got multiple logistics holds set up. You remember what those are?"

"We Jump a few thousand miles and stop for snacks. Real food plus the IV boost."

Rich was skeptical. "The technical manual and the docs say you can expend up to five thousand calories on a single mission leg without dying, but it doesn't recommend more than three thousand." He gave Hawkins a wry smile, reminiscent of a certain 80s archaeologist. "It's not so much the miles, it's the load. The weight."

"Yeah, calories per mile plus extra for each five hundred pounds, right?"

"Good man, that's right. The Jump sequence is DC to St John's Bay, Canada; to Lisbon, Portugal; to Nicosia, Cyprus," Rich ticked off the spots on his fingers, "where we will meet with someone who knows the FARP—the Forward Aerial Refueling Point. This guy was brought in from Iraq because he's previously operated at the FARP. His local imagery will be old, but still functional. We kinda roll the dice on obstacles by inserting blind, but that's why we make the big bucks. Once you get his data, we will Jump directly to the FARP where one of their team members will give us the visual for the helo's location."

"Ah, now I see why we're getting the helicopter parts just before the last leg of the trip."

"Right," Rich said. "Even that lesser weight, plus our two fallback men, is a haul across the Atlantic. That, and we don't exactly have a tool crib and maintenance shed for Black Hawk parts here in DC."

"How long are the stops?" Hawkins asked.

"Anything under two thousand miles we can recover in under an hour," Rich told him. "The long haul across the Atlantic and then to Cypress will require almost two hours to get all the IVs and food. Plus, your head may spin a little after that."

"Not exactly a fast trip." Hawkins considered what Rich had laid out. "Can the team in Iran stay in place that long?"

"Son, we're still faster than they could get another covert operation together to get them the part. That helicopter cannot stay in Iran. Can you imagine what the Iranians would do if they had it in their possession? Even if it was destroyed, they would claim a shoot-down and it would dominate the news cycles for weeks."

Hawkins nodded in agreement. "Saving the world, one helicopter at a time. I guess we'd better get started."

The first Jump to St. John's felt easy to Hawkins. It was slightly shorter than the Jump from Hurlburt to WSMR. King eased his pack from his shoulders, helped him sit, and placed his IV while Hawkins dug for his second breakfast with the other hand.

Nearby, Martin did the same for Dunn.

They sat easy in their own thoughts as they absorbed their food and IVs.

"Ready for the long haul?" Dunn asked as King and Martin tidied up the empty nutrient bags. Hawkins shrugged.

"I guess." But inside, his stomach roiled with anticipation.

"Okay then. Let's go." Everyone stood and tagged in. "Ready, in three ... two ... *one*."

In a safe house at the Lisbon waypoint, Hawkins staggered, dropped to a knee, and was caught by King. Beside him, Dunn dropped like a stone. Martin rolled him to his back and swiftly worked to place IVs.

Hawkins had just enough consciousness left to see Dunn was already passed out as Martin inserted the needle, then he too slipped into blackness.

"Hawkins?" Replenished, Rich Dunn's voice called to him.

Hawkins grunted a response.

"I'll have them update your charts. Martin and King say you were conscious as we arrived, so I think you've got a little more strength than me, but your recovery time is slower."

"What does that matter?" Hawkins groaned. Beside him, King was swapping his nutrient bags and placed a protein bar by his other hand.

Dunn, already sitting up, shrugged. "It doesn't matter much, really. But if we have the flexibility, Limitless tries to match our strengths to the missions." He gave a rueful smile. "I'm not strong anymore. Docs think that we wear down after decades, like a rechargeable battery that won't hold a full charge when it's old. Arguably I'm the weakest active Jumper, but even after doing this about thirty years, I recover faster than anyone and I'm the most accurate. They tend to put me on mission profiles with short, light Jumps that require speed and precision."

"Hmph, I guess that makes sense." Hawkins groaned as he sat up. King moved with him, keeping his IV elevated by the simple expediency of throwing the bag on his shoulder and standing up.

"You haven't worked on precision targeting yet, but once you do, we can establish your limits. I'd hazard a guess you'll have raw strength but be a sloppy Jumper."

"Hey!" Hawkins bristled.

"No offense intended. It just seems to be how these things go." Dunn was unapologetic.

Hawkins grunted as he chewed his bar.

"Are you about ready? This Jump to Cyprus will be a lot like this one was."

"Sure."

Hawkins landed in Cyprus somewhat awkwardly, dropping to a knee again just after Dunn's three-count died away. He had a moment to register a few people waiting for them before his lights went out.

"NRO has re-purposed a satellite to follow the Islamic Revolutionary Guard Corps ground team headed to the downed chopper's location. They've got two hours, at most," a voice drifted into Hawkins' consciousness. He opened his eyes to see King staring across the room. Hawkins followed his gaze to see Rich, an IV in each arm, studying a digital map displayed on a hi-res 12.9-inch iPad Pro encased in a thick rubber combat case.

"Hawkins? Come take a look at this. We need to move."

Hawkins pushed himself upright, stumbling as he walked to look over Rich's shoulder at the map.

Rich stabbed a finger just east of the Iraq/Iran border where a red pin marked a location. The area was desolate.

"The helo team is here." He dragged his finger a very short distance away. "The Iranians are aware of the helicopter but not its precise location, and that contingent of IRGC troops are headed there now to see what's what. We need to move in a hurry. You about ready, mister?"

Hawkins took a deep breath and grinned. "Just a milk run, huh Rich?"

Rich smiled. "The only constant in life is change, son."

The man by the table tapped it briefly and Hawkins laughed and held his hand out. He saw the Forward Aerial Refueling Point through the man's eyes. It wasn't much more than a collection of plywood shacks clustered around large, semi-rigid fuel bladders.

"A little more than six hundred miles. I got this," Hawkins told Dunn.

"Let's go then. It's a short logistics hold once we get there. Then we grab the replacement parts, tag up for the end point, and then we have to bug outta there."

Hawkins nodded. "From three then."

"Going in three ... two ... *one*."

Hawkins' boots landed on a dark sandy spot, surrounded by small flags barely visible under the full moon. "Holy hell, UXO?" he barked out. "Did you land us in a damn mine field?"

"Oh shit, no, sir. We just didn't know a better way to mark your landing spot to keep it clear."

"*Jay*-zus, man!"

"Sorry, sir," the man said. He came forward, hand out. "Welcome! We've got the helo repair parts prepped and my man has all the visual you people need to get there."

There was a hint of question in the man's voice that indicated he wasn't used to working with Pantheon personnel.

Hawkins noted the man was dressed in a desert uniform and didn't introduce himself. The man's OCPs showed no rank, name, or unit designation. Hawkins just smiled. He knew.

The man moved out at a jog toward one of the plywood buildings. "Parts are in here," he said as he ran. Hawkins and Dunn followed him with Martin and King already digging through their bags for food.

Inside the shack was dimly lit but effectively chilled with high-efficiency air conditioning. A fuel boost pump and new fuel lines sat atop a long wooden worktable. Scraps of plastic shrink wrap littered the floor like transparent snow drifts.

"They said to lighten your load as much as possible, so we stripped the deliverables down to just the two parts. Sorry, you'll probably get some grease on you."

The man gestured to a second man in the shed, also dressed in unmarked fatigues.

"Our guys reported number-one and number-two fuel pressure lights, which are *land-right-now* priorities. Never happens in a good place, right? They might be able to just replace the line to the fuel boost pump, but we're sending the boost pump too just in case." He gestured to a compact plastic toolbox. "We're also sending along the special tools they'll need, in case they don't have them onboard. Airman here has your destination."

The man nodded and stepped forward with his hand out.

"Just picture the site, son," Rich told him in a fatherly, supportive tone. "We respect your privacy and if you think of anything other than the site, we'll get that too, but no worries."

The young man's face went pale and he glanced at his superior, who nodded. His hand remained out for Hawkins and Dunn to tag.

The young man's visualization was strong and clear, giving Hawkins the feel of a light, gritty wind on his face, the smell of hydraulic fluid and avgas lightly scenting the air. The helicopter sat on a small, sandy rise, easily visible for miles.

"How far do you think it is from here?" Hawkins asked.

"A hundred miles, maybe less," the crewman told him.

Hawkins nodded at Dunn. "You take the pump, King, and Martin. I'll take the lines, tools, and our escort. Easy money."

Dunn nodded to Hawkins and addressed the two other men. "We'll stay until the repairs are made and they're off the ground. Can you call them and let them know we're inbound?"

"We're radio silent right now, sir, but they know you're coming."

"Okay. Well then, hope they don't shoot on sight," Dunn said easily. "Ready Hawkins? Clock's running."

"We estimate twenty minutes to repair the bird and the IRGC is about twenty-five minutes out."

"Oh, that's an easy window," Dunn said. His humor was as dry as the sand around them. "King, Martin, stick close. We'll replenish while they make the fix." He gave the weapon holstered at his hip a pat to ensure it was in place. Hawkins did the same, but he frowned. An issue handgun wasn't going to be much use if the IRGC rolled in heavy.

"Okay, steady up. Going in three ... two ... *one*."

A chorus of expletives greeted them on the other side when they appeared out of thin air and atmosphere was forcefully displaced across the desert sand with a loud pop. King and Martin held their hands up to the startled helo crew, palms visible, while Hawkins and Dunn held the helo parts aloft. The unidentified escort just waved.

"Took long enough," the pilot said.

"Someone order an engine?" Hawkins asked with a smile.

"It's a fuel pump," someone answered.

"Whatever. But you need to get it installed right now," Hawkins told him. "Company's coming for tea."

"Yeah, we see 'em," the airman said, jerking his head southeast. Standing a few feet away was another airman watching the IRGC's progress on a surveillance satellite feed to his combat tablet. On the horizon, vehicle lights were visible.

"They're about twenty minutes out now," Hawkins told the man.

"Shep! Jonesy! Let's go. You have less time than you need," the pilot hollered. Two men snagged the pump, lines, and tools and ran to the helicopter.

Dunn and Hawkins ate quickly and took in the IV nutrients that flowed into their arms.

"Fuck, I'm going to look like a heroin user or some shit," Hawkins growled as King taped the line down.

"Sorry Hawkins, you'll get time to recover from the mission when we get back. The bags are potent too—they'll help everything heal fast and neat," Dunn told him, but he looked at the dimpled surface of his own arms. Despite the miracle properties of Limitless products, he healed more slowly these days than before.

Hawkins watched the enemy's lights as they approached with obvious intention. The hair on the back of his neck was standing up as his eyes darted from the helicopter team to the lights.

It was going to be close.

"Man, you need to start setting up. They're going to be in range soon." Hawkins pointed to the .50-caliber door gun. "That ma-deuce still work?"

"Yeah, but—"

"No 'buts'—man it up and get two of your folks in overlapping fields of fire off that guns line. Anyone with a gun who isn't turning a wrench or getting the bird ready to fly needs to get ready to fight."

"Jonesy?" The man bellowed up to his mechanic.

"Five minutes, Frank," echoed out from the helicopter.

"You don't have five minutes, Frank," Hawkins told him.

"Mitch, man your gun. Everyone else, clear the line of fire."

As the words left him, a sudden burst of gunfire erupted from the distance and Frank crumpled.

"Fuck! They sent scouts ahead," Hawkins yelled. He caught the airman as he slumped, easing him to the sand and looking for a bullet hole. A single hole oozed blood from the man's belly.

"Everyone get down!" Hawkins yelled. He grabbed the collar of Frank's fatigues and hauled him to the helicopter's side. "*You*," Hawkins pointed at a helicopter crewman, "get a kit and hold gauze to this wound. He won't die, but it's gonna bleed like a sonofabitch." Hawkins' eyes met Dunn's. "We gotta get them out of here right *now*."

Another burst of gunfire erupted, striking the tail of the helicopter.

"Gunner, commence firing!" Hawkins bellowed over the staccato of the enemy machine gun. The IRGC vehicles skidded to a halt and Iranian soldiers poured out of them.

"You two—" He pointed to the two men lying prone by the far wheel strut. "—one here and one here, aim downrange. Spray and pray. We can't do much more in the dark but we'll keep their damned heads down. Now, go!" He yelled when they didn't move.

"They need five or six more minutes to get the fuel pump installed, Hawkins," Rich Dunn yelled over the powerful blasts of the fifty-cal. "We could take the men with us now, but we can't leave the bird."

Hawkins snapped his M18 out of its holster, flicked the safety off, and aimed downrange. "I know that, but we don't have time. If you haven't noticed, we're taking what I would call direct fire." He pulled his trigger several times at Iranians who looked like they were attempting a flank. They fell heavily to the sand. "You really want to wait until someone else gets shot?" He fired two more times. "The little bastards are getting closer."

Dunn protested. "That helicopter is ten thousand pounds! I can't move that!"

"Sir, she's more like sixteen thousand or so right now with fuel and gear," the door gunner shouted down. "Here, sir, take this!" He nudged an M4 carbine to the edge of the door and Hawkins.

Hawkins grinned fiercely at Dunn and reached up for the rifle. "Now it's a party!" He checked the safety and it was already off. Lifting the weapon to his shoulder, he nailed three more Iranian soldiers foolish enough to break cover. The rest of the aggressors poured on the attack.

"Rich, you've taught me the load numbers." Hawkins sprayed a burst of return fire. "Long haul is bad because of the mileage, but the weight factor is roughly one calorie extra for each five hundred pounds."

Dunn ducked as a line of bullets tore into the tail again.

"Are they trying to shoot the tail off?" he yelped.

"Can't fly without it, sir," the airman to their left said.

Hawkins sprayed another burst of suppressing fire at the attackers, keeping their heads low and interrupting their shooting.

"Rich, sixteen thousand pounds—no, man, I need you on the exterior line. Yes, that guy!" Hawkins squeezed off another burst. "Sorry, sixteen thousand pounds by five hundred and add a calorie for me," he thought for a half-second as bullets sprayed sand a few feet away. "Thirty-three calories a mile. The last logistics hold is only a little over one hundred miles west. Three thousand calories, Rich."

"More like thirty-four hundred by my math," Rich replied, "but I'm a words guy."

"Whatever. I just did that going across to Lisbon. We're replenished, right? You can take the crew and I can move the damned helicopter a hundred miles."

Hawkins turned to the door gunner. "Nice work, man, but I'm gonna need you out now. Grab that other M4 rifle and lay down more suppressing fire—this fuckin' bus is leaving. Rich, tag them up. I've got the helo. You get the men."

"Hawkins ..."

"Do it, damnit!" Hawkins bellowed over the gunfire. "We leave a $40 million helo behind and the Iranians will have a field day with this, whether we blow it or not. You already said we get the bird out or risk war. It can't stay, goddamnit, and neither can we—tag up, and do it right fucking now."

Dunn gave him a hard look before shouting up into the helicopter. "Everyone out! Meet me on the far side. King! Martin! Get them in a daisy chain. We're counting down to Jump from three!"

"Cease fire on two. We Jump on one!" Hawkins bellowed. He turned to the door gunner on the fifty. "Sorry, man, you're doing good work, but time to get to the far side with Rich. Count of three!"

Hawkins laughed, turning back toward the attackers.

"Boy, are these assholes getting a big surprise ..." He put one hand on the helo's tire as he knelt beside it and yelled. "Three ... two ..."

"Cease fire, cease fire!" Dunn thundered.

There was one silent moment, then, "... *one!*"

Hawkins felt the heavy-lift fire enflame his bones and the depletion acid in his veins as he and the helicopter landed beside the fuel bladder a hundred miles away. He slumped forward on his knees and face-planted in the dirt, sprawling across the ground. His eyes stayed open only long enough to see Rich arrive with the helicopter pilots and crew, and their two fallback men a few feet away. Then the blackness.

"... Pantheon and they didn't have an Ares? They damned sure got one now! Hell yeah, that was some real god-of-war shit, dude!" King said.

"Shut up, King, he's wakin' up," Martin's voice was hushed.

Hawkins now lay flat on his back in the sand with replenishing IVs in his arm and a rock-crushing headache.

"Sir? How do you feel."

"Fuck," Hawkins grunted.

"You've taken two bags and we've got two more in you now. If you can, it would help if you could eat something solid too," King told him.

Hawkins looked up to see the man holding another Limitless Labs special-formula protein bar out for him, a look of reverence on his face.

"The hell, King?"

"I'm sorry, sir."

"For what?" Hawkins took the bar and tore the wrapper off. Chocolate-coated protein never tasted so good.

King looked at Martin then back to Hawkins.

"We misjudged you, sir. You *are* like her."

Hawkins didn't need to ask to know he meant Val.

"You made the big choices under fire. No hesitation," King smiled at him. "The Pantheon had a Zeus and Hera, and we think of General Hall as Athena. Do you ..." he hesitated. "I mean, can we call you Ares? You're both gods of war."

Somewhere beside him, Hawkins heard Rich Dunn groan an *Are you fucking kidding me?* groan.

"Ares. The other god of war. I think I like that. Yeah, King, I think that'd be okay by me." Hawkins gave a laugh. "I'm not changing my driver's license, though."

Six hours later, they returned to DC and Dunn presented their after-action mission report that consisted mostly of Hawkins organizing the team and coordinating a heavy return—towing a helicopter.

"Cool under fire again, Murph. Well done," Val said with an approving smile.

"The unfortunate news is that King and Martin refer to him as 'Ares' now," Dunn said.

Hawkins nodded, then got a wicked gleam in his eye. "Yeah, I like it. It's appropriate. You know they call you 'Athena' when you aren't around, don't you, Val?"

"Not a chance in hell," Val said, but she chuckled in disbelief.

"Hey, if you can call me Ares for pulling a team out under fire, then you certainly deserve to be Athena for pulling that downed F-15 crew out of Syria under fire."

Val frowned. Then smiled.

"Deal, Ares."

Hawkins nodded. "Athena."

"Ares and Athena?" Rich asked and rolled his eyes.

When they walked out of the Jump Room, laughing at their silly new names, they were met by the horrible news of terrorist bombs killing people in Montgomery, Alabama.

CHAPTER 9
MONTGOMERY, ALABAMA
1413Z 0913L, 20 MAY

Three men stood silently watching a building. The oldest, a tall and pale man whose shaved pate gleamed in the early morning light, leaned casually against the brick wall behind him. His arms rested easily across his chest as he took in the flurry of children streaming from a school bus into the building's parking lot.

In contrast, the men beside him were their own flurry of activity. Another pale man with a smoothly shaved head alternated between leaning against the same brick wall and standing slouched, his arms restless at his sides.

The third was a slim, swarthy man whose fingers twitched and fidgeted with his jacket. Despite the warmth of the sultry summer morning, his fingers danced between the zipper of a fleece jacket and its pockets, tugging, patting, and smoothing with each movement.

"Stop fidgeting, Amir," the eldest man said sharply. Dumb bastard was going to set something off prematurely.

Amir's hand paused briefly then went to his pants, wiping the sweat from them. "Sorry," he muttered, traces of his native tongue in the word.

The other two exchanged a glance.

"Can you handle this last task, Amir? Or not?"

"Yes—for the glory of Allah, I *can!*" he said with all the fervor of a recent convert. The elder suppressed a grimace. He hated the man. Hated him for the mere fact of who he was. But he was useful. A necessary tool. And he needed to be coddled a few minutes longer.

"Allah will be your reward. Seventy-two virgins are promised to martyrs."

A last school bus entered the parking lot and began disgorging school children. The cacophony of children delighting in a day away from school desks reached the three men.

The second man inhaled sharply to speak, but instead turned to give the eldest man a nod.

"It's time, Amir. Go with God and be loud about it." He gave the swarthy man's shoulder a squeeze and a small shove. The man's feet moved forward, taking tentative steps, then found their surety and were soon pounding down the brick sidewalk toward the sounds of high-pitched laughter.

"Dumb fucking *hajji*, he better be sure to proclaim or they won't know who did this," the youngest man muttered as he fumbled with the camera on his cellphone.

"Goddamn, it'll be good to get rid of him," the older man commented as they could hear the first shouts of *Allahu Akbar* drown out the laughter.

The man dashed through the crowd of children, some crying out in surprise as he knocked them down. He dodged past a bench and shouting his war cry as he ran. He pushed children and a young teacher out of the way to make it inside the doors of the Rosa Parks Museum. The two remaining men stood filming the scene, flinching only when the powerful detonation pushed a shock wave they felt in their chests even a half a block away.

By that evening, every television and news website showed a single image: one tiny shoe, caked in blood and dust, resting on the brick sidewalk exactly where Rosa Parks' bench once sat.

In the background, a tiny bloody body lay on the ground next to a fountain. It looked as though the child had merely settled his head against the fountain for a quick nap except for the pool of blood that had spread under his light brown curls. Over the fountain only a few steps away, the entire southwestern side of the museum building had been blown away, and the courtyard was littered with bricks and concrete debris among dozens of dead children and adults.

No news agency dared show the extensive imagery captured at the scene. The images of dead and mutilated children were too much for even jaded American sensitivities.

CHAPTER 10
AMANDA SQUIRES
1239Z 0839L, 26 MAY

The television monitor extended from the wall on a black articulated arm. It was tilted slightly so as not to reflect the soft ceiling lights from its screen. Mandy turned up the volume from her bed in the Limitless clinic.

"The White House has declined comment on statements from terrorist organizations taking credit for Tuesday's attack on the Rosa Parks Museum in Montgomery, Alabama. Anonymous spokesmen for the so-called Islamic Revolution in America and the white supremacist National Command Structure both have claimed responsibility for the blast through posts to social media, but the claims are unconfirmed at this time. The White House said the investigation into the bombing is ongoing."

Mandy sighed, dropping her head back against her pillow. The news had been the same for days. She pinched her lips together and looked back at the screen.

"After reports of protests and rioting extending from Montgomery to Selma and even into Birmingham, the Governor of Alabama has activated the National Guard to maintain order and has imposed a statewide curfew. He stated in a news conference yesterday that should the rioting continue, he will be forced to declare a state of emergency and institute martial law in the affected counties. The declaration touched off additional race-related protests and counter-protests in seven major cities nationwide ..."

Distantly, Mandy could hear the high tempo chirping of her heart rate monitor. Jaw clenched, she muted the TV and picked up the magazine Marco had left her during his last visit. As she was reaching the rag's latest round of sex positions "guaranteed to blow his mind," the door to her room opened. Athena limped in, grimacing as she leaned on her cane.

"Heeey Val—or I guess we're calling you Athena now," Mandy said softly as Athena settled heavily into the chair next to the bed.

"Hey, Mandy," Athena replied. "I'm still getting used to the new name myself." The smile on her face was marred by the way Athena's jaw tightened ever so slightly. Mandy recognized the tiny furrow in Athena's brow that appeared when she tried to suppress frustration.

"Not recovering as well as you thought, or are you using that to make me feel better?" Mandy asked, pointing at Athena's cane.

"It felt like I was flaunting my recovery to come in here without it," she said. "I don't really need it, I guess."

Mandy nodded. "Anything new?" she asked, gesturing to the TV with her magazine.

Athena looked relieved to move off the topic of her cane. "In news media? No. They're clueless," Athena said, her smile thinning into something brittle.

"And from our clients?"

"The Intelligence Community isn't much better off than the news media," she gave a small shrug. "But some better. Evidently social media and the dark web are alive with conspiracy theories, but also chatter being looked at very seriously as being authentically from possible bomber groups."

Mandy pushed a few buttons and raised the back of her bed to an upright position.

"Anything actionable coming out of that?"

"Not yet. Both the IRA and the NCS are claiming responsibility. Both have their reasons for blowing up the Rosa Parks Museum. One of them, possibly both, are lying."

"Where does that leave the investigation?"

"Well, the extremist right would love to see a monument to civil rights erased. Islamic extremists have no problem killing Christian children and it brings a lot of attention to them, especially in the Middle East. But there's crap probably headed for the fan elsewhere. Michigan sent National Guard to Dearborn to protect the big mosque there after it was firebombed." She shrugged again, face drawn. "I sure hope we'll get actionable intel soon."

"Are we actively working this?" Mandy asked.

"Do you really want to know the details? Are you—"

Athena opened her mouth once as if to speak, then closed it again. Athena looked at her for several seconds before answering. "I mean, if you want to be involved, I'm happy to bring you in with the rest of the team, but I can't authorize you to train, let alone be an active—"

"No," Mandy cut her off abruptly. "No, I don't want to be a part of it. I just—" She frowned. "—I guess it was more just curiosity."

Athena bit the corner of her lip, a small gesture Mandy might not have caught a month ago. "We can talk about your role here when you're ready," Athena said gently.

"No. I won't be. I don't want a role here. Not like that. I want to stay as a Handler."

"I'm not sure I can do that. You know this place. We need every single body I can get," Athena said.

"I can't do it, Val—Athena. I just—" she stopped. Taking a deep breath, Mandy fought down the heaviness in her stomach. "I tried. I tried to do it again. I wanted out of here so badly yesterday, but I couldn't make the Jump."

Athena stared at her, mouth open slightly.

"Maybe I'm not like you. Maybe you didn't see what you thought you saw," Mandy suggested. Deep down, she knew it was a lie, but she couldn't face the responsibility that came with the job.

"Mandy, I'm sorry, but you Jumped. You did."

"I've watched this my whole life, Athena. Marco, Dee, Rich, my—"

she swallowed hard, trying to dispel the lump in her throat that cut off her words. "—my father. I've watched them stagger in, a haunted look in their eyes when they return from Jumps with teams. The stress that crushes them, body and soul. Every time I think about that and I try to Jump? I just can't do it."

"Okay. It's okay," Athena reached to pat her hand, but Mandy pulled it back.

Oh no you don't—no sneaking in emotion reads right now.

"We don't have to talk about this now."

"Thanks," Mandy said and let her head fall back on her pillow.

Mandy could almost see the chasm widening between them. It made her sad, and a little angry. Most of all, Mandy didn't want to lose Athena as a friend due to something Mandy had no control over. And Mandy knew Athena was juggling their friendship and Athena's new responsibilities as Marco's second in command.

Both just stared at the silent television for long, uncomfortable minutes and watched the mindless news broadcast without speaking. It was awkward.

"So, what do you hear from Pete?" Athena finally asked.

Mandy opened her mouth to speak, but tears choked her words. She gave Athena a teary shake of her head and pulled out her phone, unlocked it and handed it to Athena to read a message.

Athena read the few words and said simply, "Asshole. Who breaks up with someone via text? After six months! And when they're in a hospital?"

Mandy nodded and this time let Athena take her hand. Still choked up, she soaked in Athena's anger and indignation on her behalf. Mandy ran a thumb across the back of Athena's hand in thanks, reveling in the satin smooth feel under her thumb. The emotion coursing across the contact said that her friend supported her, but there was a curious hum of something else she couldn't quite place.

"He's just shocked, I think," Mandy offered. "I'm hoping to talk to him once I'm out of here. You know, actually sit down, face to face, and talk it out. I think if I can just talk to him maybe we can work it out," she told Athena earnestly. "He's freaked by my potential for Jumping, and if I can convince him I'm not going to be a Jumper after all and not joining the Pantheon, maybe he will reconsider, y'know?"

Mandy's plaintive voice squeaked with pain and fat tears rolled down her cheeks.

"Y'*know*?"

Athena nodded. "Well, he's no longer employed by Limitless Logistics, so I can't order him in here." Athena looked embarrassed. "Uh, but, let me know if you want to go meet with him. I'll drive you if you aren't allowed to yet. Or we can send you in a car. In fact, I like that better. Keep the stress off your boo-boo leg as much as we can, even after you're discharged."

A flash of fury raced through Mandy at Athena's words, anger that Athena had provoked Pete's departure. Logically, Mandy knew Pete would have left regardless; he'd shared his increasing discomfort with the Pantheon mission and operators. She snatched her hand back as fast as she could, but it was too late. Athena had gotten a full blast of Mandy's anger and what she'd been thinking.

Athena rocked back as if slapped by the powerful emotions that flowed across the touch.

"I'm sorry, that was—" Mandy started, but Athena cut her off.

"I should go," Athena said, rising awkwardly. She looked at Mandy, face blank. "I'll let you have some more time to recover."

Mandy watched her limp out, unsure if Athena meant she should recover from the gunshot or the breakup. She brushed aside a tear, then another. In a moment she was curled painfully on her side, tears silently sliding into her pillow.

The next morning, Nurse Sarah found her watching the news again. Sarah assessed her patient with kind eyes.

"How did you sleep last night?" Sarah asked briskly.

Mandy shrugged. Her eyes stayed locked on the television.

"I see you didn't finish breakfast." She tidied the dishes sitting on a wheeled table beside the bed.

Mandy's hand gripped the remote tighter, but she didn't answer.

"Mandy?" Sarah called. She pushed lightly on Mandy's shoulder.

Mandy turned to her with a scowl and went back to the TV. Sarah snatched the remote from her hand and turned the TV off. "You don't get to leave here until I'm satisfied you can care for yourself. Which means," she jabbed Mandy in the ribs with two fingers, "if you aren't eating, I don't let you out."

"I wasn't hungry," Mandy muttered.

Sarah flipped through Mandy's chart. "Well, you have physical therapy now, so let's hope you work up an appetite by lunchtime that convinces me you're ready to leave."

Mandy groaned as Sarah pulled back her sheet and gently tugged her feet over the edge of the bed. Mandy shifted awkwardly, her injured leg was still wrapped to the knee, causing it to stick straight out.

"The therapist will unwrap your dressing and get that leg moving. Now, take your crutches," she handed Mandy the sticks, "and get out of this room. You've already stewed in here too long today."

Mandy found scant sympathy from the physical therapist. She'd crutched into the gym and flopped down onto the padded, blue vinyl therapy bed lining the far wall only to be rousted up a moment later.

"Let's get things started. Before I unwrap you, let's see you put some weight on that foot," her therapist, Bill, said as he sat on the rolling stool beside her.

His pleasant, almost chipper tone grated on her. Mandy swallowed down a retort and rose again. Without conscious thought her eyes darted around seeking Pete. It took her a half second to realize what she'd done, and she felt a sick sensation rise in her stomach. Sighing, she did as Bill asked. With most of her weight on the crutches she slowly transferred weight to her right foot. Pain scorched through her leg, burning a line from her mid-thigh to her spine. She inhaled sharply.

"There was some nerve damage along with the soft tissue, so you can expect a little pain," Bill said.

"Gee, Bill, you think?" she ground out sarcastically.

Bill looked at her calmly. "Most of the damage will heal, but until the nerve damage repairs itself, you'll have pain that will seem odd. Didn't they brief your condition at George Washington?"

"Probably, but I was drugged to the teeth then snatched here to finish recovering," she said as she tried putting weight on the foot again. Pain bloomed from inside her thigh to the skin around the bullet's entry. She sucked in another breath.

"Well, since you might have missed it, here's the run down." He began unwrapping the dressing from Mandy's leg. "It was a small-caliber bullet with clean entry and exit wounds, so you're lucky there. There were some veins that had to be repaired but nothing terrible. There is minimal nerve damage from them digging around in your leg, but that's what happens when you have to go into muscle. You can expect that sensation around the entry and exit wounds will be ... oh ..." He paused in thought. "... odd? Pressing on an area may feel numb while skimming your finger along another area will be hypersensitive, painful even. It takes time for your body to sort all that back out, but it'll come."

"And walking again?" she asked. "How long before it stops hurting to put weight on my leg?" She gasped when she put weight on it.

Bill was quiet for a moment, watching her transfer weight on and off the foot.

"Bill?"

He looked up at her, face now somber. "Mandy, it might not. The bullet plowed a hole in your leg. Small, yes, but the nerve damage may inhibit walking and may keep you from running for a while."

A buzzing filled her ears. She looked at Bill, trying to process what he'd said. A jolt of pain made her realize she'd sat down abruptly. Her stomach churned looking at him, trying to process.

"Say that again?"

"I'm sorry, the surgeons did what they could, but they had a hell of a time cleaning the wound out and stopping the bleeding. You may walk with a limp for an extended period. That's why we're here now. I have to start you working the leg now to save as much mobility as we can." He reached out to pat her forearm, but she jerked back not wanting to feel the pity she could see in his eyes.

She took a deep breath, steadying herself and choking down the angry replies that threatened to spill out. She turned her head and wiped away the hint of moisture at the corner of her eyes.

"All right, how do we start?"

Mandy spent the weekend working with Bill. Her days were filled with intense physical therapy twice a day. At each visit he would unwrap the dressing on her leg, inspect the healing wound, then begin her therapy. At the end of the session he would re-wrap her leg with fresh dressings.

Mandy came to hate every minute of it.

Athena showed up at the end of the third day with clothing in hand and, despite how their last visit had ended, she looked like an angel of mercy standing in Mandy's door.

"Come in," Mandy said when Athena tapped hesitantly on the door frame.

"I heard you're getting out today, so I brought some of your clothes," she said and handed over the bundle.

"Thank God. I'm so sick of hospital gowns. They make everyone think I'm sick. What I am is sick of being treated like a china doll."

Athena wobbled to the door she'd left partially open and closed it while Mandy shimmied awkwardly into her clothes.

"I'm so done with this place. Not to go all basic bitch, but I need a latte!" Mandy said, words coming out in a rush. She felt a nagging pang of guilt for driving Athena out on her previous visit. "Starbucks on the way home?"

Athena said, "We're walking, not Jumping. You up for it?"

"Yes—anything for some real coffee and sunlight."

Athena smiled at her. "Okay, Starbucks, then back to your apartment. And, if you're off the industrial pain killers we can continue the basic bitch trend and get white-girl wasted tonight. I think you're overdue," Athena said with a smile.

"I love you so much right now," Mandy said.

They made as dignified a wander as two women with gunshot wounds in their legs could make toward their caffeine salvation. Mandy observed that Athena kept their conversation light, veering away from current events or Limitless' role in it. Mandy also noted that Athena neglected to mention Powell at all.

"I'm sorry about earlier," Mandy finally said as they settled at a tiny table in the late April sunshine.

"It's okay, I shouldn't have—" Athena cut herself off. Her fingers tightened on the white and green cup.

Mandy became wistful and resigned. "I know you fought for me, but I also recognize that Pete probably would have left regardless. I plan on texting him tonight, see if he'll talk to me now that he's had a few days to calm down." Mandy brushed an errant strand of hair from her face. "I mean, surely he'll understand, right?"

Athena made a noncommittal murmur and sipped her tea.

Mandy's stomach was in knots and the coffee wasn't helping.

"All right, enough navel gazing for now. We should get back. Do you need to go back to work? I think there's wine trapped in a bottle somewhere. We could go rescue it."

Athena laughed, head tilting back as she giggled.

"Nope! Your Tio Marco and my boss gave me the afternoon to get you settled. He was definitely thinking in Tio mode and not boss mode. I'm almost certain he expects me to be hungover tomorrow."

Athena put her hand out and Mandy took it, basking in the warmth that flowed between them. They rose and limped their way toward their apartment building.

"We should see Madame Volaire this week," Athena said from nowhere.

"You need new clothes again? I can get us an appointment," Mandy said. She gave Athena's outfit an appraising look. The dark jacket fit well in the shoulders and bust but had unflattering bagging at the waist. The trousers sat lower than they should and bagged at Athena's pert rump. "Yeah, you need to go down a size again."

"Come with me?"

"Sure, you know I can't pass up an opportunity to see Madame's latest," Mandy said with a smile.

The doorman opened the large glass doors for them and they continued their hobble to the elevators.

"However," Mandy said with a wince, "let's take one of the cars. I'm not sure I could crutch my way from here to her salon."

Athena nodded and gave her a smile. She punched the Penthouse button and held her finger over the scanner to activate the elevator.

Mandy reached across to jab the button for her floor, a few below the Pantheon's lavish apartments, but Athena intercepted her.

"Athena, I'm fine coming up to drink, but I need a shower first. And these are nice clothes, but honestly I think I'm going to lounge around in my PJs if that's cool with you?"

"Sure, but you aren't on that floor anymore," Athena said carefully as the elevator started to rise.

Mandy looked at her, brows furrowed. "What?"

"After you said you were having problems Jumping, I knew we couldn't have you use moving as a training exercise like I had. I had your things transferred to the open penthouse so you wouldn't have to worry about it."

Mandy stared at her, hands gripping her crutches tightly, "You what?" She could feel a flush race across her body.

"I didn't want you to have to worry about it, I thought—"

"You moved my stuff? You just took all my stuff and moved it!" Mandy demanded, shaking her head in denial and disbelief. Her crutches creaked as she leaned toward Athena.

"I'm sorry, I wanted you up on the penthouse floor. Safe. With the rest of us," Athena said with a bewildered look.

"I'm not one of you. I'm not doing this. I can't," she told Athena, eyes pleading. She shook her head, her long blonde hair swinging. "I don't belong up there. I'll arrange to have it moved back tomorrow."

The elevator dinged and the doors opened. Athena stepped out, holding her hand against the door to keep it open as Mandy hobbled out. Athena touched her hand as she passed. Fear, agitation, and determination flowed across the touch. Mandy took a step back, glaring at Athena.

"You are one of us," Athena said, voice holding a quiet surety. "Like it or not. I'm sorry if that upsets you or you disagree with it, but you belong up here and in this apartment." Athena's mouth was set in a determined line. "You don't have to work for Limitless. You don't have to do the job. But you've earned the right and I want—" she paused. Mandy saw her jaw clench once, then she continued. "—I need to know you're on the most secure floor."

They eyed each other for several seconds. Mandy wanted to yell. Wanted to scream at Athena. It was high handed. It was unnecessary. She wanted to scream, but she just couldn't find the energy.

"Fine. Which one?" she said, slumping onto her crutches.

"Across from me," Athena said.

"Fine. I think I'm tired. I'm just going to stay in tonight," Mandy said.

Athena nodded once and handed her a key, "There's food in the fridge. I asked Joe to snag Thai for you since he was headed there anyway. I expect he'll drop it off when he drops Murph's food off."

Mandy nodded but didn't answer as she unlocked the door and slipped in. Pleased that Athena would remember her favorite restaurant but still chaffing at her high handedness, she closed the door to her penthouse apartment without a backward glance.

CHAPTER 11
MURPHY 'ARES' HAWKINS
1208Z 0808L, 08 AUG

"You know," Joe panted, "if I had known you were going to bitch this much, I'd have made you get a personal trainer like everyone else." His voice was laden with as much humor as he could muster at 0800 and an hour into their workout.

Ares grunted and hefted a loaded barbell overhead, glaring at Joe.

"All I'm saying is that you do the workout of the day as it's scheduled. There's no need to add to it," he groaned as he completed another thruster. "'Hildy' is seventy-five thrusters with a forty-five-pound barbell, not ninety-five. And, you jerk, I'm already wearing body armor!"

They raced toward the rack of medicine balls, ready to throw them at the wall. Twenty steps in, each man slowed to a trot, then a staggering walk, as the effects of the thrusters lit a fire in their quads. They finished the remainder of the workout wordlessly, grunts of effort their only communication.

"My God, why did anyone think it was a good idea to do strength training before the WOD?" Joe gasped as he all but fell off his rowing machine.

Ares, sprawled next to his own rowing machine, simply raised his hand, fist balled, and held it out. Joe bumped Ares' fist with his own.

"Good work, Murph. Or should I call you 'Ares' like your fan boi club down in Hurlburt?" Joe laughed. "I'm not really going to make you get a personal trainer. I love Ryan to death, but his lazy ass would never do CrossFit. I'm glad to have someone to share this pain with."

Ares grinned back, realizing how much Joe had grown on him despite his initial reservations. Out of the corner of his eye, he saw a small blonde figure limp in on crutches. He watched her, Athena's best friend Mandy, settle on the physical therapy table on the far side of the room.

"Okay, slug. Stretch and foam roll, or don't blame me when you can't keep up in training this afternoon," Joe said.

"Huh? Oh, yeah," Ares said, taking his eyes off the blonde. He whistled sharply and sixty pounds of fur and fury came bolting toward him from where she had patiently waited on the sidelines. "Hey girl!" Ares said, his voice going soft as he tussled with the dog. "Ready to run?"

Zora gave a single loud bark and leaned into his knee.

"You're going to run after that workout?" Joe asked, incredulous.

"Man, if I don't, Zora will be nuts all day. You ever work with military working dogs when you were in?"

"Nah. Saw a couple guys jump with K-9s. Skydive, that is, not capital-J Jump," he clarified, circling his finger to indicate Limitless Logistics. "But no, I didn't work with them myself."

"Well, in the words of my buddy, PC, 'a German Shepard is a thinker, happy to lie around and contemplate world conquest, but the Malinois is a fur-coated chainsaw on meth.' If I don't run her batteries down this morning, you will see the chainsaw on meth by afternoon."

Joe raised his hands and shook his head. "Okay then. I'll see you two girls in a bit."

Ares flipped him a good-natured bird and jogged toward the door.

A half hour later, his quads screamed for relief and he hobbled back into the Limitless gym. Joe was slumped against the wall, pretending to stretch. At the back of the room, he saw Mandy struggling through her physical therapy. Ares' mouth compressed and his brow furrowed as he dropped down beside Joe, considering.

"So, what's her deal?" he asked.

"Who? Mandy?"

"Yeah, she got a boyfriend? I mean, I'd like to go say hey when she's done, but I don't want to intrude on something."

"Man, you must be the only person here who doesn't know," Joe said, suppressing a laugh. "She was dating Pete, a trainer here, but the dumbass dumped her. Oh, and he got fired. Unrelated to Mandy."

"Idiot. Who lets a woman like that go?" Ares asked.

They both watched her struggle through her therapy, her brows knit in concentration the occasional grimace crossing her face.

Joe shrugged a shoulder. "You like that type? Blondes?" he asked.

"I love all types. There is not a woman I don't see as beautiful. But she's something special."

Joe frowned.

"Look man, I don't wanna harsh your war plan, but she's not over Pete. I think she believes she can work it out with him. Additionally," Joe said sternly, "she's, like, everyone's little sister here. I think a lot of dudes here would take it personally if you hurt her by flirting with her for sport."

"Whoa, not it's not like that," Ares said, hands going up in defense. "I said she was something special. I only thought I'd say hello, so call off the extended family."

They watched her struggling with her therapy.

"Look at that determination. I mean, I heard a little about what happened. Getting shot? Like that? By her own father?" Ares shook his head. "The *cojones* on her, to even walk back in here after everything that happened. She could have gotten physical therapy anywhere."

When Joe nodded, he continued. "But she's here. She's fighting the demons, one day at a time. That's a woman I can respect. If I flirt with her, I promise it won't be for sport."

Ares watched Joe nod once, rise, and offer a hand up. They made their way to the men's locker room with Zora in tow.

"You'll be working on precision Jumps with Dee this morning," Joe said later as they chowed down on breakfast.

"Define 'precision,'" Ares said around a mouthful of eggs. He was hunched over his plate, wrists resting on the edge of the table, fork in one hand and knife held ready in the other.

"Gross!" Joe told him and threw a napkin at him.

Murphy caught it, dabbed primly at his mouth, and nodded at Joe to answer.

Joe sliced a bit of steak from his platter of steak and eggs, popped it into his mouth, and chewed thoughtfully.

"Ideally, you'll want to be able to land inside a circle with a five-foot radius. That means you should always land inside the room you're aiming for. When we're hauling cargo, you can be as sloppy as you want."

"Like the helicopter?"

"Like the helicopter. Although, to be fair, Rich Dunn strung his group out further than he should have. But, cargo usually ends up in an open area or large warehouse where there's room to maneuver it afterwards. You know, someplace where things can surreptitiously show up without anyone seeing or noticing," he gave a sly grin. "However, when you're paired up with the three letters—"

"Three letters?" Ares' fork, which had been on automatic, paused in mid-air.

"CIA, FBI, NSA, et cetera," Joe said, waving his fork with a roll of the wrist.

"Got it." Ares focused on his plate once again.

"They tend to need to be close to a specific target. We assist in their ability to gather HUMINT, human intelligence."

"Yeah, I'm a Marine, not a dumbass. I know what HUMINT is," Ares said with a wry grin.

"Usually, it's a snatch and grab scenario. We get the target's pattern of life, snag them close to locations they are known to frequent at times they typically arrive. The black bag goes on, you Jump them out, and they sing like the proverbial canary until they stop being useful."

"Neat and tidy I suppose." Ares took another bite of eggs and considered what Joe had said. "No assassinations? Grab a guy, Jump out into open air, release, Jump yourself back, target goes splat?"

"No, they're pretty strict. We move cargo, we don't dirty our hands," Joe said with a stern face.

Ares frowned. "I'm not 'dirtying my hands,' as you so elegantly put it. I'm the man willing and able to do violence on behalf of those who aren't—'god of war' and shit, right? You should know that. You lived it." He smiled. "I mean, you were in a lesser service branch, but the concepts are the same."

Joe frowned, but Ares could see him considering what he'd said.

"Imagine what would happen if we were exposed. Imagine how scared, frightened, and angry the American masses would be if they knew what you could do."

Ares nodded, considering. His own mother considered herself a conservative Christian, despite a slew of broken marriages and neglected children. He had yet to tell her anything about his current job.

Even had he not been bound by a stack of non-disclosure agreements and threat of jail time for exposing secrets, he wouldn't tell her because he could imagine her fear. And the greed that would flare in her eyes if she ever got wind of how well he was being paid now.

"Now imagine their outrage if they knew what you were truly capable of doing. You aren't a coldblooded killer, but the fact that you can put yourself into a frame of mind capable of taking a human life? It scares civilians. If you had that carnivore's mindset and could enter their homes without them being able to stop you?"

"I take your point," Murphy told him, "but in the end, what's the difference? They'd be at the doors with shotguns and pitchforks either way." He inhaled deeply and let it out slowly. "All I'm saying is that we could do a lot more."

They finished their breakfast in a companionable silence that stretched until Damarcus came to get Ares for his morning training. Ares gave Joe a distracted wave as he and Damarcus walked to the Jump Room with Zora in trail.

"So, 'Ares,' how's it going, slug?" Damarcus asked in his deep, calming voice.

"Oh, you know, just trying to learn the ropes. Dragging helicopters out of hostile nations and livin' right. Typical day at the office, you know?" Ares said with a wry grin.

"Athena been working you over the coals, huh?" Damarcus said with a laugh.

"You heard?"

"Nah, I figured you two would butt heads. An enlisted Marine and an Air Force officer? I thought the two of you would be fighting by the end of the first week." Damarcus laughed. "Ares and Athena, indeed!"

Ares laughed. "With such a low opinion of our professionalism, I can only guess you were Army?"

"Guilty as charged," Damarcus said with a nod. "Logistics officer. Only got about a year of it though. I did my first Jump not much more than a year after I commissioned. I learned just enough to speak 'logi' and make it sound like I know what real logisticians do when I have to talk to those who aren't on the inside of the program."

Ares nodded. "So, precision Jumping today?"

Damarcus held the door to the Jump Room open for him, "Yeah. You need to—"

"Land my ass and my team inside a hula hoop or something like that," Ares answered with a surly tone.

"Or gear. Either way, you gotta be close enough to the target to keep from breaking the goods or losing them."

They spent the morning Jumping around various points in DC. Damarcus would give Ares the location of a space that Limitless owned and held clear for Jumps, then transferred the destination imagery by a touch that allowed him to attempt landing as close as possible to the target. By lunchtime Ares was starving but already landing within the desired five-foot radius.

"So why precision, not speed?" Ares asked Damarcus as they walked back to the cafeteria for lunch.

Damarcus gave a little shrug. "You saw how it worked with moving Hank's guys, as well as the helo mission. We're set up for logistics holds to get calories in. You tap your resources too fast and you'll be on the floor. Can't help anyone or move anything like that."

They joined the short line of Pantheon employees for food, shuffling along with their trays as they talked. Ares had a small sense of relieved familiarity at the normalcy of standing in a chow line; doubled because he thought it meant the members of the Pantheon ate the same grub as everyone else. But every Pantheon member was noted by facial recognition software as he or she entered the food line, and a computer automatically served up the nutrition designed specifically for that member.

"But, if I could sort of," he scrunched his nose up trying to think of the right word, "skip ahead as I moved, I could move fast. Unpredictable. Less likely to be a target."

Damarcus gave another little shrug. "I like where you're going with that, but we're logistics men. We're the back-end supply chain—with teeth, mind you; we don't go out naked—but we're not front-line trigger pullers."

Ares sighed and fought to keep from grinding his teeth. The white-coated attendants assembled his approved lunch and a quiet groan escaped him.

"What?" Damarcus asked.

"Nothing." Ares took the plate, setting it gingerly on his tray. The pinching hunger in his stomach faded as he swallowed hard. "I was kinda hoping for, you know, actual food."

"Not a fan of mac and cheese?" Damarcus asked.

"Not since I was seven," Ares said as they settled at a table. He poked disconsolately at the orangey pasta then turned his fork on a bowl of broccoli.

"You can tell them," Damarcus said. "They'll get you something else with equal calories and macros and shit. I mean, if you specified 'no grains' they shouldn't have given it to you in the first place."

"Nah, I can't—" Ares halted. Inhaling through his nose, he forced himself to unclench his jaw. "It's fine. I'll let them know tomorrow."

He ate everything on his plate, including the heaping pile of macaroni. Even after putting away a substantial amount of food, his stomach rumbled and ached for more. He gritted his teeth and eyed the food line.

Damarcus watched the flow of his expressions, considering. Finally, he put his hand out. "May I?" he asked gently. Before Ares could answer, Damarcus took his hand in a firm grip. He held it for a long moment then released his grip. Ares felt curiosity, then sadness, and an old anger flow across his touch.

"Yeah, I got you. I know that look, brother. I lived it. You grew up hungry too, huh?" Damarcus asked quietly. His usual cheerful expression was replaced by a somber look, tinged with old anger and vivid unpleasant memories. "Can't let food go to waste, no matter how much you don't want to eat it."

Ares' head rocked back slightly. "My, uh, my Mom. She's not, uh ... not a great Mom. I love her, but ..." He fought a grimace at the white lie. "But she always had something more important in her life than me and four brothers."

He stared at his plate, unwilling to look up and risk seeing pity in the other man's eyes. Damarcus gave him the moment to pull his emotions back together.

"When it was just me and Zeke, it was okay," Ares told Damarcus once he'd tightened down on the anger writhing in his stomach. "Zeke's older and made sure we had food. I didn't ask questions about where it came from. But he was out of the house by the time Charlie and the twins came along, so I had to feed us."

Ares looked at Damarcus, a child's fear and pain haunting his eyes.

Damarcus nodded. Something passed between them, even without the curious empathic link of touch.

"And now, you can't pass up food. Hunger is fear and uncertainty. Being full is safety. Comfort. A knowledge that you'll make it one more day."

Ares could tell Damarcus was talking to him, but he knew Damarcus was also reminding himself.

"Someone near my house worked at a local processing plant, and one year they donated pallets of mac and cheese boxes to the local food pantry. I got as much as I could and carried it all back on my bike. It's all we ate for nearly a month. At the end of three weeks, we were so sick of it, but I hadn't seen Mom since before I got it. She was off in search of ex-husband number four, or maybe it was five by then. Anyway, she hadn't been home."

Ares pushed his tray forward, ignoring the rumbling in his guts.

"Foster care in Philly," Damarcus said, thumb in his chest. "Not kind, not an easy upbringing. I can't eat chocolate pudding for similar reasons. Come on man," Damarcus said, rising. "We'll go let them know. You don't have to eat it ever again."

Ares followed him to retrieve a plate of chicken and potato casserole. He still hadn't told his mother about his change in status. She'd been "traveling with friends" last time they spoke on the phone, which he knew meant she was couch surfing again, or worse. As far as she knew, he was still in Syria. He dreaded her ever finding out what kind of income he really made now, knowing she would demand her "fair share" as recompense for raising him.

Back at their table and desperate for another avenue of conversation, he returned to their earlier discussion. "So, logistics only? Why? Where did that come from?"

"It's been that way since the beginning. Zeus and Hera always kept it that way."

"Who and who? You guys really take this whole 'Pantheon of Gods' theme way too far, you know that, right?"

Damarcus laughed. "Yeah, but some folks are starting to call you Ares when you aren't around, for your Navy Cross and that helicopter stunt. You know that, right? But, yeah, not my naming scheme. Zeus and Hera Ward founded Limitless. Zeus is—" he stopped, frowning. "Zeus was adamant that we kept it as far from combat as we could. I think he knew that transitioning to combat would make us vulnerable to the naysayers, and there are plenty. The politicians who fund us wouldn't be able to swallow that."

"But we're not really a full logistics company either, right? I mean, think of everything we could do if people knew."

"But they don't. And the American public would have a fucking fit if they did. Can you even imagine? Religious freaks would be camping outside our door waiting to burn us at the stake." Damarcus shook his head. “You’re right, we’re not really one side or the other, but it’s the safest way for us to continue existing.”

“Much to my vexation and disappointment,” a deep voice said behind them.

Ares turned to see Athena and a tall man with dark brown hair approaching. He recognized the guy but couldn’t place him.

“Hey, Powell,” Damarcus waved. “Athena. How’s the leg?”

“Bitchin’,” Athena said.

“Murph, you remember Powell? Everyone’s favorite CIA ghost.”

“Yeah,” Ares said, rising to shake his hand. “Athena’s boyfriend, right?” he asked, looking at Athena.

“Yes, that’s me,” Powell looked at Ares’ hand for a moment before seizing it.

Belatedly, Ares remembered the odd Pantheon handshake he’d seen. Powell’s handshake was the same firm but not crushing grip he remembered from the week before. There was an odd feeling of calm over a hint of guilt when they made contact. Ares saw the corner of Powell’s eye tighten briefly before his polite smile returned.

Athena and Powell took seats at the lunch table. “Since Athena can’t take missions until she’s off limited duty, I’m here to see if you’d be available for a mission.”

“Me?” Ares said.

“Well, both of you, actually.” Powell wagged a finger Ares and Damarcus, stopping on Ares. “You’re not trained yet, but hot missions successfully executed get you qualified and signed off faster. You’ve seen the news?”

“Yeah. Can’t exactly avoid it these days.”

“I’ve got a snatch and grab on a potential intelligence source and I’d like your help.”

“Why me?” Ares asked. Not a naturally suspicious person, he didn’t like the odd undertone of guilt he felt trading grips with Powell.

“Most recent combat experience and greatest depth of knowledge,” Powell answered easily.

“Surely one or more of the other Pantheon guys has more experience. I have less time here than the guy who buffs the floors at night," Ares replied, shifting in his seat. He wanted to reach out for Powell's hand again to feel his emotions as he answered.

Ares idly wondered if all new Jumpers wanted to play with their powers when they first discovered them.

CHAPTER 12
MURPHY 'ARES' HAWKINS
1653Z 1253L, 08 AUG

So, snatch and grab, huh?" Ares asked him.

Powell looked back at him and crossed his arms. "Yes, sort of. We've got someone who might give us a lead on the bombing."

"Cool. Give me the standard five W's."

"Excuse me?"

"Who, what, where, when, why, and how?" Ares said and ticked off on his fingers. "Okay, five W's and an H, but I'm a Marine and we don't talk so good."

Powell's expression never altered and that gave Ares the creeps.

"Let's find a briefing room. We can't talk here."

"You're a weird dude, you know that?" Ares said. He shot Damarcus an *Are you kidding me?* look.

Damarcus gave a shrug, his face unreadable. "Mysterious man, our Mr. Powell." They both rose and followed Powell to the Secure Compartmented Information Facility.

Powell started off down the hall and Ares and Damarcus followed.

"I hear you were awarded the Navy Cross," Powell said.

Ares faltered a step. "Uh, yeah. I mean, on paper. The ceremony was supposed to be a few months ago, but you know ... with the bombing and all. Maybe another time."

Powell nodded and stopped before an unmarked door.

"Probably for the best. Considering your new job and its, uh ... demands." Powell swiped his ID card through the wall-mounted reader and punched in a six-digit code, then pulled open the vault-like door to the SCIF.

In contrast to the modern and bright interior design in the hallway beyond, the interior of the SCIF dull and government perfunctory. Beige walls were broken only by whiteboards and large monitors. On one whiteboard a rough diagram was sketched out. The drawing illustrated a single building with rough-sketched terrain and annotated call-outs like "point of entry," "assumed point of egress," and "PoL indicates stop here."

Damarcus and Ares walked to the whiteboard and studied it. Ares stood with his arms crossed over his chest and considered the illustration. Behind them, Joe Pax quietly entered the space with Ares' go-bag and Zora. *Evidently he knows more about my travel plans than I do*, Ares thought.

A subtle cough finally pulled his attention back.

"Well?" Something in Powell's voice said this was a test.

Ares elbowed Damarcus and gestured to the plot.

"Just a simple 'snatch and grab,' huh?"

Powell ignored his barb.

"You know, Powell, seeing this, I'd be nervous too."

Ares almost laughed when, for a fleeting instant, Powell's blank mask broke and anxiety flashed across his face. Ares held the laugh in with an effort and bent to the task of fixing Powell's inexpert tactics.

"Be nice," Damarcus stage whispered.

Ares tilted his head and fluttered his eyelashes.

"Look, you have us Jumping us into a blind valley. Single entry, no exit." Ares pointed at the white board. "I assume it's to minimize the possibility we're seen?"

When Powell nodded, he continued.

"But if I do that, here is where I'm getting ambushed from." He tapped three points where snipers could catch them out. "I presume you chose this location because you haven't been able to get closer?

Like, this was designed from a satellite view, at best."

Powell nodded silently again and shifted his weight against the drab institutional desk.

Ares raised an eyebrow. "No? Well, you have 'PoL' here, which I can only assume is 'pattern of life.' So, it's someone you can track fairly closely, but the subject or their security detail are smart enough to sniff out a tail."

He cocked his head at Powell and gave him a grin.

"Alternatively, you assume this is the only place to catch them alone?"

Powell shifted against the desk, his agitation now plain to see.

Ares saw the fabric at his sides ripple and guessed the man was clenching his fists under his crossed arms. He almost wished Powell would take a swing at him because he suspected it was going to happen eventually. Better to get it out of the way early and move on.

"Oh, big bad Mr. CIA-man, are you mad that you're this transparent?" Ares mocked Powell in a sing-song voice. "You afraid I'm going to figure out all your dark CIA secrets with one touch?" Ares took a step toward Powell with his hand out, a wry smile on his face.

Powell's reaction was immediate, his face dark.

"Don't."

They locked eyes. Ares stared him down, trying to see beyond the public mask. Nothing about the man's behavior over the last hour made Ares feel at ease. He assumed a CIA agent would have plenty of things to hide, but the level of paranoia Powell had failed to hide meant he was nervous. A nervous CIA agent just plain worried him, even if it had nothing to do with him or the mission he was being asked to undertake. Powell blinked and looked away.

"I don't know you enough to give a shit about whatever it is you're hiding right now so long as it won't endanger me on this mission. Can you tell me that it won't impact my mission?"

"Yes," Powell said, a hint of relief in his voice. "Just don't dig in here without permission." He pointed to his head.

"Fine. I'm right, though? And if so, which scenario?"

"Yes, second scenario. We need you to grab the target without being seen. As you have already guessed, this is a remote wilderness location. Small hunting cabin outside Kenai Fjords National Park. A lobbyist for the American Family Values League."

Ares grunted. "Far right wingers. In Alaska?"

Powell shrugged. "Not as much as the name might suggest. They're thinly veiled white supremacists who are trying to buy up Congress. He owns a hunting cabin on the outskirts of the national park and our information is that he takes time up there before the summer tourist season gets into full swing."

"What do you want from him?" Damarcus asked.

Powell gave him a blank look.

"Good question," Ares said. "Hey, I'm grabbing the guy. I gotta know what to look for."

"Links to homegrown terrorism."

"Like 'write my manifesto from a shack in Montana'-type terrorism or 'I just blew up a museum full of kids'? I heard those Daesh pricks claimed that one."

Powell shrugged again.

"Really, dude? Museum full of dead kids a week ago and you ain't talking to your own teammates?" Ares choked down his irritation at the man's obstinance. "Fine, just a plain ol' homegrown terrorist then. What's his name and are you going to give me the cabin location?"

"His name is Abe Dunphy—and you'll get it when I'm ready to give it to you." Powell gave him a searching look. "Does that irritate you?"

"Yes, you tight-lipped prick." Ares felt his irritation bubble up into anger. He was really starting to wish Powell would just take a swing. Ares suspected Powell was hoping the same.

"You've been through a lot recently, haven't you?" Powell's voice was calm, soothing even.

The question and its easy tone surprised him, but Ares realized just how tightly he'd gotten wound up. A feeling of calm washed over him.

"Yeah, I guess so," he answered, surprising himself with an honest reply. He wouldn't admit it even to himself how much the last few weeks had taken out of him. A deployment was difficult enough but the sudden and large revisions in his life had made him feel like the foundation of his life had cracked.

"Look, Jump in. Hike to the stand coordinates, snag the man, bring him back here. I'll take it from there and then we'll see Athena about giving you some time off. You look like you could use some decompression."

Ares nodded. "Yeah, I suppose." He made himself calm down and gave the drawing a long look. "Wait, hike to the stand?" He considered the drawing and frowned. "You don't hunt, do you?"

Powell looked down at his sophisticated bespoke suit, then back up at Ares with one eyebrow raised and a cynical grin.

"Not in the conventional sense."

"Fine, you don't hunt," Ares said. "But picture this: You're in your deer stand, moose stand, whatever. You hear a noise rustling the bush. You realize how thick the forest in Alaska can be, right? As the sound approaches, what do you think their first action is going to be?"

"Shoot?"

"Shoot," Ares agreed. "How about this: I Jump. I wait in the cozy warm cabin, and I grab this Abe guy when he comes in for the night. Better, I Jump us both in, you do your thing, we leave him thinking he's been attacked by a wild animal, and we leave. You got anything in the CIA toolkit that alters memory?"

"Maybe. I think I like your plan better. How good is your precision Jump training?"

"Pretty good. Accurate destination source material is the decider." Ares eyed Powell.

"We land on the porch, leave no footprints, and help ourselves to his cozy, warm cabin before he returns."

"Fair." Ares held out his hand. "You got the point in your head there or do we need to meet up with someone else?"

Powell eyed his hand. "I've got it. Get your gear first, then we'll go. And bring your weapons, just in case," he added. "I'm bringing mine."

Ares did as asked, gathering his go-bag and an issue 9mm Sig Sauer

M18 and holster rig drawn from the arms room by ever-ready Joe. An excited Zora danced around everyone's feet as they prepared.

"Hey girl, you gonna be quiet while we work?" At the question, she sat down, staring up at him with a doggy grin on her face.

"The dog stays," Powell said.

Ares gave Powell a *that's bullshit* look. "Zora doesn't stay, man, Zora *goes*. She's better than most guns."

"I can't have a dog barking at the suspect, giving us away."

"Asshole," Ares said in a hard voice, "she's better trained than *you* are. She'll be fine."

"Negative," Powell's voice was unyielding. "Are you hard of hearing? The answer is a hard no."

His mask of calm started to crack, a hint of anger oozing through.

Ares offered a smug I got you look. "Then we don't go."

They glared at one another. A moment passed. Another. Then Powell pulled a Glock 19 from a shoulder holster and pressed the muzzle against the top of Zora's head.

Damarcus and Joe jumped back as if electrocuted. Ares automatically went for his own weapon but stopped short when Powell pressed his gun harder against Zora and shook his head.

Don't even think about it.

"Bitch, listen up," Powell said evenly. "Let me express it in terms you understand—you are an asshole rookie numbnuts who does not call the shots here or anywhere else, understand? If this fucking dog stands in the way of national security, I promise you I will end it and sleep like a fucking baby."

Ares thought furiously about what to do, but nothing he came up with could get Powell's gun away from his dog's head before she was killed.

"I didn't give a fuck about this dog when you got here and I give less than that now," Powell said. "What the fuck are you even thinking, diva-ass boy? Jesus. 'God of War'—Ares, my ass. You run nothing here. You take orders, understand? You do not give them. Fuck with me about this and you won't be taking any calls either."

Ares' face was red with anger, but he feared anything less than an agreement would jeopardize his beloved Zora. He took a few deep breaths to calm down, but they didn't work.

"Fine," Ares spat out. "She stays. But you ever hurt my dog and I will fucking kill you."

Powell nodded once, pulling his weapon away from the dog and returning it to its holster. Rubbing it in, he said, "Okay, tough guy. But you really need to see someone about your attachment issues."

"*Fuck you*. This isn't over." He raised the leather lead. "Joe, please?"

Joe stepped gingerly forward under Powell's steely gaze and took the lead attached to Zora's collar.

"She needs a walk now," Ares said, "so she doesn't see me leave without her."

"You got it, Murph. Be safe in the world." Ares ruffled Zora's head and scratched her ears, and she and Joe trotted off for a jog.

"Jesus, Powell," Damarcus said. "You go black hat on us and I'm out. I'm pretty sure Murph can handle you and this grab on his own." Damarcus stalked off without waiting for Powell's answer.

Angry, Ares still held out a hand to get the destination from Powell. "I don't know how Athena deals with you."

"Fortunately, dipshit, none of that is any of your fucking business either." The words lingered in the air as Powell's fingers connected with Ares' hand.

He was stunned by what he felt in Powell's touch. Anger, resentment, and guilt flashed across their touch along with the image of a small cabin, lightly covered in snow. A second image swam across with emotion—a large, broad concrete building, surrounded accordions of razor wire. In a flash as quick as the sound of Athena's name a wave of images and emotions skittered across the bond.

"What did you do?" Ares whispered. He stared at Powell.

"Nothing." Powell stepped back, tucking his arms across his chest again. "You ready?"

"I'm damn well not ready. What did you do?" he repeated. The touch had been benign until Ares has mentioned Athena. It was her name that had triggered the avalanche of emotion.

"Nothing that concerns you. Let's go," Powell commanded.

"If you've done something that will hurt Athena, I will leave you in Alaska."

"What I did is helping Val—Athena, whatever—and it's none of your damned business."

"Helping? Then why do you feel so guilty?"

Powell's eyes narrowed and he frowned at Ares.

"Leave it alone. Just Jump us. We need to get there while Dunphy is still out."

"You and I are going to talk about this when we get back."

"No," Powell said with certainty. "We are not."

Ares eyed him again, jaw clenched. He wanted to grab Powell, dig deeper into whatever it was he was trying to hide. Finally, he gave up trying to bore into Powell's head with his eyes.

"Ready to Jump in three, two, *one*."

CHAPTER 13
MURPHY 'ARES' HAWKINS
1748Z 0948L, 08 AUG

Ares' feet landed neatly on the cabin's narrow porch. Powell, who was standing a stride's length away, landed at Ares' level, over the stairs. He dropped the few inches and started to fall back. Ares snatched his suit collar and pulled him in.

"Jesus!" Powell swore quietly, a small puff of breath escaping his lips into the crisp morning air.

"You're fine, you big baby. I didn't even tear your fancy suit."

Powell climbed the steps and turned around.

"Good. We haven't disturbed the snow." He pointed to the light dusting on the lowest step. His feet had narrowly missed dropping to the bottom step and leaving footprints.

Powell eyed the rough-hewn wooden door. "I don't suppose you have a lock-picking kit?"

Ares gave the iron handle a twist and pushed the door open. "Or we could just, like, open it."

Powell glared at him but walked inside.

Ares looked around at the snowy landscape and smiled. Alaska was a far cry from his home in north Florida. Where northern Florida was all flat, sandy soil with patches of pine, Alaska boasted rugged hills, rocky outcroppings, and thick stands of trees as far as his eyes looked. He took another deep breath of the bracing morning air and followed Powell into the cabin.

The classic scents of cold and pine followed them in and mingled with the lingering aroma of wood smoke from the fireplace. Ares walked to the embers, holding his hands out for what little warmth remained. There wasn't much. The chill in the cabin made him long to stir the embers and feed the fire with some of the wood stacked on the hearth, but he knew the smoke from the chimney would be a dead giveaway to their target that his hideout had been penetrated.

Behind him, Powell prowled the cabin, touching everything only with his eyes. Ares took in the incongruity of Powell's designer suit against the rugged backdrop of the cabin. Finally, Powell stopped prowling and set his small bag down on the table. Ares turned, putting his back to the embers, and watched Powell pull various items from the bag. A small vial, a syringe, and duct tape printed with a mac-and-cheese image were laid across the cabin's single table.

"You must be fun at parties," Ares muttered. He picked up the duct tape. "Mac and cheese?"

Powell glared up from his small pile of tools. "It was all the hardware store had and I was in a hurry."

"Are all missions with you like this?"

"No. Some are fun."

Ares clamped down on his irritation. "So, what's up with you and Athena?" The sound of a small knife dropping onto the pile rattled loudly. "Seriously, that's a lot of guilt you're carrying around."

"Drop it."

"I'm just saying, women hate it when you're hiding something. And that one knows more than other women. They know, man. I don't know how, but they always know."

"Yes, I'm aware," was Powell's icy reply. "My first wife left me for exactly that reason."

Ares rocked back on his heels a bit. This was the most personal detail he'd ever gotten from the man. He realized he was starting to get under Powell's skin.

Unable to stop himself, he jabbed Powell in the pride.

"I guess you didn't learn your lesson then."

Powell jerked upright and Ares could see a seething anger in his eyes.

"Look, Ares, I don't know what your deal is, but drop it. This is between Athena and me."

"You might think so, but I've already seen her pissed off. That woman has more rage problems than many of the guys I saw just back from a deployment. And oh, I've seen her be mildly vindictive. I'd hate to see her in a full rage, even if it wasn't aimed at me. So, for the sake of everyone at Limitless, you'd better air out your shit with her when we get back."

"You don't know a fucking thing." Powell growled.

Ares said, "Look asshole, I already don't trust you, and whatever bullshit you two have going on is probably going to fuck us all. You can be a stone-cold CIA killer on your own missions, but I—"

Without warning, Powell drove his fist into Ares' side, nailing him in the floating ribs. He let out a surprised cry of pain but returned the punch to Powell's solar plexus. Ares had the satisfaction of watching Powell double over, gasping for breath.

He caught Powell's cheek with a fist as he went over. Powell rocked back with the blow, staggering back a half step. Powell caught his footing while still hunched over and swung at Ares' stomach. Ares caught Powell's arm, locking it with his own, and used Powell's momentum to drag them both to the ground.

Powell gasped as he hit the wooden floor. The two grappled, rolling into the battered leather couch as each tried to overpower the other. Before either could land another blow, a loud rattle outside caused Ares to still.

"Hold still, dumbass," Ares whispered directly into Powell's ear. He squirmed once and Ares wrenched his arm back harder. "*Shhh ...*"

Powell stilled. "What is it?"

"Did you hear that?" Ares whispered between heaving breaths.

"I don't know, I don't hear anything," Powell said, his voice as strained as his arm.

"You relax now," Ares whispered, and eased the pressure off Powell's arm.

They both waited then, breathing gradually returning to normal.

"You fight like an asshole, Powell," Ares finally ground out.

"I know."

Ares walked carefully to the window and looked out from the side. He saw nothing that might have made the noise he thought he'd heard. There was an old Inuit symbol made of rusty metal hanging on a nail outside the cabin, and Ares though it must have caught the breeze, accounted for the sound.

He turned back to Powell.

"We good now?" he asked.

Powell shrugged and nodded. Sure, whatever.

"I'd ask if it was something I said but, fuck it, I'm an asshole too and I baited you. What did I say to finally break through your shell?"

"All of it," Powell sighed deeply and sat up, letting his head fall to his chest. "Athena. Trust. Her rage issues. The fact that I am a stone-cold killer," his voice trailed off. "That is, the supposition that I'm a stone-cold killer."

Ares watched Powell's former bluster fade away. Sudden realization hit Ares: He realized he would never again have a normal relationship. When he could easily uncover a truth or emotion from anyone, they would never truly be at ease around him.

"I've seen it, the anger when it's unleashed" Powell said, voice low. "I saw what she can do in Paris. It's ugly. Scary. She's—" He swallowed hard and leaned his head against the battered couch. "She's a good woman, and she's been through a lot." Powell's face crinkled in a wry smile. "But she's different now. Changed. I suppose that's to be expected in your line of work."

Ares nodded.

Powell gave Ares a pained look. "She's having flashbacks. PTSD.

Some other shit maybe going on, I don't know. I can't watch her go through that anymore. I can feel ..." he trailed off again. Powell shook his head. "I've put some plans in motion to take care of the problem, but I think I might have made a mistake."

"What did you do?"

"Well, I have contacts everywhere. On my trip here to get the location, I stopped in at Fort Leavenworth and talked with my friends there; we'd been in, uhm, Iraq together. I, uh, I may have suggested that a certain individual incarcerated there was a problem. Told them what he'd done—the full story, not the bullshit that asshole would have admitted to."

Athena hadn't related her backstory to the new recruit, but Ares knew from scuttlebutt that Powell was talking about the former Air Force Major Brian Parker, who had sexually assaulted Athena on their first date. A subsequent investigation had disclosed many other victims from other duty stations. Parker had been convicted, busted to O-1, and given a Bad Conduct Discharge followed by most of the rest of his life in the federal penitentiary at Fort Leavenworth, the only maximum-security prison in the DOD.

Powell said, "I think they might have misjudged what I wanted."

"And what did you want?" Ares asked quietly.

Powell said, "I just wanted them to give him a hard time, make his life in prison a living hell. I think they may have taken it too far."

"Does Athena know?" Ares asked. He thought he already knew what was coming next.

"That he's dead?"

Ares shut his eyes. Oh, shit. He hadn't realized the man was dead from the Powell contact and Ares had just assumed something bad from the level of Powell's guilt.

"Yeah, that," Ares said.

"No. I wanted to be able to tell her, but we had the mission. I think Marco plans to tell her. I thought if I could tell her first, she might better understand why I might have played a role in it."

Ares looked at Powell and saw pain and fear in his eyes. "You are fucked." There was no need to lie or sugar-coat it.

"Yeah, probably. The joys of dating a telepath."

The silence stretched between them. Powell, still on the floor on his knees, picked up his tools scattered from the table during the fight, then Ares offered his hand and pulled him to his feet, politely ignoring the wash of emotions that flowed across the touch.

"Think she'll forgive you?" Ares asked quietly.

Powell shrugged. "If she doesn't, I hope she can at least understand. There are ... other things in play between us. Other reasons I needed to do it."

Ares didn't push for more answers. He realized that his earlier mistrust had evaporated now that he knew why Powell was agitated.

"Look," Ares said, "for what it's worth, I'm sorry. I wish you the best. You guys seem pretty good for each other."

"Thanks."

They settled into silence as they waited for Dunphy to show up. Thinking of Athena, Ares dutifully dug out a protein bar from his go-bag, slowly chewing it in the silence.

The cabin held a damp chill that the dying embers in the fireplace couldn't chase. Ares watched the shadows from the pine forest lengthen, and he wondered how Powell wasn't freezing in his thin suit coat. He glanced over at the man and saw a shudder run through him.

"You okay?"

"I've had worse. Didn't expect to be out this long today."

"You didn't think I'd drag you along?" Ares asked as he fished out two more bars. He held one out to Powell, who shook his head.

There was a thumping outside the cabin, the solid thump of metal on timber. Ares held up a closed fist then pointed two fingers at the door. Powell nodded.

As soon as the door opened, Ares was a blur of motion. He leapt for the man and had him on the ground with wrists zip-tied before he could react. Ares' swift action didn't prevent Abe Dunphy from crying out. The man was howling curses at them as Powell approached.

"Abe Dunphy?" he demanded over the stream of obscenities. When it became clear the man wasn't going to answer, Powell nodded to Ares to stand him up.

"Sit him up."

Ares sat the angry man on the chair next to the table.

Powell held a needle in front of Dunphy's face, now a shade of dark red.

"I'm not going to bother with any shit about you 'doing things the easy way,'" Powell said. "I'm simply going to shove this needle in your fucking arm and then get the answers I need. Then I'm going to drop you with a second shot and, far as you'll know, you were attacked by a wild animal. Sound good?" Powell asked with a cold smile.

The man's eyes went wide and he started screaming curses at them again.

"Yup, that's what I figured." Powell jabbed the needle into Dunphy's arm. The cursing gradually slowed as the drug took effect.

"Who are you?" Dunphy muttered.

"I ask the questions." Powell flicked on a small digital recorder. "What's your name?"

"Abraham Isaac Dunphy," he said quietly.

"Where are you from?"

"Biloxi, Mississippi."

"Are you now or have you ever been a member of a group known as the Ku Klux Klan?"

"Yes."

"Are you now or have you ever been a member of any neo-Nazi or white supremacist organization?"

"Yes."

"Did you have any part in the terror bombing in Alabama?"

"Yes."

"What was your role in the bombing?" Powell asked.

"I was tasked with recruitin' our bomber and sending him in."

Ares' eyebrows rose. He knew that Powell's CIA contacts had worked hard over the last few weeks, but he'd assumed this man was just a cog in the wheel, not the power behind the bombing.

"What else did you do?" Powell prompted.

"Nothing. I didn't plan the bombing or the location. The bombin' materials was given to me. I just had to find someone who fit the description, some fuckin' *hajji* willing to die for his shit."

The man's drugged stupor was joined by a hint of anger.

"Why was the bombing done?"

"Don' know. To pin it on the little shits. Make it look like they did it." His face took on an ugly expression, pride mixed with hate.

"Why not you? Seems like killing brown people is your thing," Ares asked, more than a hint of anger in his voice. Powell shot him a look.

"It is. But that wasn't his plan."

"Whose plan? "Powell asked.

Dunphy gave a small shrug. "Don' know. Didn't use no fuckin' names."

"Describe him."

"Tall bastard. Got politician hair."

"Politician hair?" Powell and Ares both looked at him, puzzled.

"I dunno. Good cut, prolly costs a week's pay. Blonde on top, going gray on the sides. And he has green eyes. Kinda yellowy green."

Ares looked questioningly at Powell.

Powell cut off the digital voice recorder. "Thank you, Abe." He looked at Ares and nodded. Ares swallowed hard and touched Dunphy's hand, and the image of the ringleader flowed to him shadowed and distorted.

Ares said, "I think he's too drugged. I can see the haircut he's describing but the face is shadowed and blurred. He's not thinking straight?" Ares' voice trailed off in question.

Powell shrugged. He reached into his bag for another preloaded syringe, pulled the cap from the needle and injected its contents into Dunphy's exposed upper arm. The little bit of consciousness remaining in the man fled and he lolled back in the chair.

"All right, you wanted to be more tactical. Have at it. He's got to look like an animal mauled him."

Ares frowned. "Just like that?"

"What?"

"You go from interrogation to 'okay, beat the shit out of him' just like that?"

Powell cocked his head. "The man is an actual member of the KKK. Ever met one before? They're *complete* assholes. He's also some kinda fascist or whatever, and he admitted to involvement in the Montgomery bombing that maimed and killed children—and you have a problem roughing him up for it?"

"I suppose not."

"I got what I needed, and he doesn't have anything else that advances my mission. Additionally, we both know I have other business to attend to. Now, make this asshole look like he's been mauled by a bear."

Ares' frown deepened. "Fine, but you're helping. As the Pantheon has been telling me, I'm not supposed to get my hands dirty." He rolled his eyes.

Powell shook his head but slowly removed his tailored suit coat, removed gold cufflinks bearing the images of eagles, and rolled up his sleeves. Then they each donned latex surgical gloves and methodically went to work.

Within minutes the man looked like he'd been attacked by an Alaskan black bear. Curiously, Powell had brought along a custom-made tool that left long, deep, bloody swipes on Dunphy that looked quite like they were made by a bear claw. Drugged as he was, Dunphy only grunted a few times as he was mauled by Powell and Ares, then he was carefully arranged on the floor. He'd wake up in a couple hours in bad shape, but he'd live. This time.

Powell scattered a small twist of bear fur around the room, then pulled a fully charged throw-away cellphone from his bag and tossed it on the table. Ares got the fireplace roaring, breaking up Dunphy's bloody chair to feed it.

They silently re-packed their respective bags and went to the porch, closing and scratching the front door with the bear claw. Ares put a plastic bootie on his boot and kicked the door free, leaving it hanging from the upper hinge. Powell took the last few bear hairs and lodged them in the cracked door.

Ares gazed out into the forest, blanketed in fading afternoon sunlight. He inhaled deeply to take in the scent of cold pine needles and melting snow.

"There's no bear prints in the snow," Ares said.

The pine forest scents calmed him after what they'd done. In his heart, he knew they'd done what was needed. A part of him, if he admitted it, had even enjoyed beating that racist to a bloody pulp, but he frowned. The whole thing had pushed against even his relaxed morals.

"Yeah, thought of that," Powell said. "We timed the trip to coincide with a big snowfall due here in an hour or three. Dunphy won't be rescued before then."

If Limitless Logistics was a rigid bureaucracy with black and white, codified rules, then the CIA was a daunting morass of gray morality Ares wasn't prepared to explore. He liked what he'd seen in Limitless so far, even if they were uptight and controlled—like the Marine Corps.

If he could just find a way to open Athena up to more military-type actions, he'd be a lot more comfortable with his new lot in life.

Ares inhaled the clean piney air again.

"Ready?" he asked Powell.

"Honestly? No."

"Not ready to face Athena?"

Powell gave a rueful laugh.

"I could Jump you directly back to CIA. I'm mean, surely you guys have a room or something there?" he offered Powell an out.

"Yeah, we do, but no thanks. I'll have to face it sooner or later. It might as well be now." He sighed. "Let's go back to Limitless."

Ares nodded. He held out a hand and Powell tapped it lightly for mental signature, only the smallest hint of emotion flowing across: guilt and resignation. Ares had the Point Zero at Limitless fixed in his mind.

"Okay, then. Here we go. In three ... two ... *one*."

CHAPTER 14
VALERIE 'ATHENA' HALL
1653Z 1253L, 08 AUG

"Valerie, may I have a moment?" Marco's voice from the doorway into the Jump Room had a quiet intensity that put Athena on guard.

She frowned at Marco's use of her full name. Athena usually only heard her full name when she was in trouble with her father.

"Yes, of course, Marco."

She gave Powell a small smile. "I'll see you later."

Marco walked slowly to his office, accommodating her limp.

"How much longer before you can get rid of the cane?" he asked politely.

"Probably another week or so," she said. Marco shot her a politely incredulous look. "Okay, fine. Probably two, and I'll limp for another month or so. It's responding well to OT." Athena attended occupational therapy sessions four times each week.

They entered Marco's spacious outer office.

"Anna, please hold my calls for the next twenty minutes or so," he asked his secretary. Anna nodded with a tight smile and Marco opened the door to the inner office for Athena, expecting an *I can do it* protest but not getting one. He gestured to the comfortable padded leather armchairs in the corner of his large executive space.

Athena limped to a chair and flopped down into it, concerned about why Marco was being uncharacteristically quiet. She watched him settle into the chair opposite her. His hand shook slightly as he unbuttoned his suit coat.

Athena inhaled deeply.

"So, what can I do for you, Marco? What's wrong?"

He gazed at her, his expression a mixture of worry and resignation. "Valerie, why do you automatically think something is wrong?"

"First off, you only call me Valerie when you're angry, which you don't seem to be at present. Second, I don't have to touch you to see how nervous you are right now," she said, ticking off her fingers as she answered. "And third, the look on Anna's face as we walked in means she knows what you're about to tell me and it's not good."

Marco nodded with a grimace.

Athena watched his face, looking for the tiny hints of emotion he was trying to suppress. She wanted to reach out, mentally, to pick thoughts from his mind. She briefly lamented that she didn't possess Powell's intuitive skills in that way. There was a slight tightening of Marco's eyes, and she was hit with a flash of insight: weariness, apprehension, and fear—of her. She frowned, unsure whether she was reading his face or his emotions.

"You need to tell me something and you're afraid of how I'll take it," she said.

"Yes," he said slowly. "You're a good officer, Athena, but you're—" He paused, searching for the right word. "—volatile. So, yes, I need to tell you something and I'm not sure how you're going to take it."

She nodded. "I'm pretty sure I can guarantee I won't explode into a rage, if that's what you're worried about."

"It actually is," he said so quietly she barely caught his words.

Athena shifted in her seat and wiggled her toes in her shoes. The swelling from the gunshot in her calf muscle extended to her foot and her right shoe pinched. She frowned with the discomfort.

"I'm not sure there's anything you can tell me right now that's going to throw me for a bigger loop than what's gone on in recent weeks."

Marco gave his head a little shake. "You did very well last Monday, Athena. I'm proud of how you picked up on my hints and I enjoyed the spectacle, but even with my warning, you stepped right up to the line, almost over it." Marco gave little laugh, but his smile faded. "Athena, you know you are volatile. I never know how you'll react emotionally, and we both know how Paris ended."

Athena sat upright, hurt that Marco would think she could harm him, then flushed thinking about how Paris actually ended—with Brandon Powell, and things that didn't make it into her trip report.

"Marco—" she started but he raised a hand and cut her off.

"Athena, listen, I'm just going to say it. Major Parker is dead."

Athena rocked back in the plush chair. Whatever she had expected Marco to say, that wasn't it.

A rush of emotions washed over her, from grief to relief to sickening revulsion, and guilt that she felt relieved the man who had assaulted her was dead. She opened her mouth to reply but no words came out. Images of Parker flashed across her memory: He had looked every inch the American Fighter Pilot Hero in his flight suit.

That memory was replaced by Parker's face twisted into a stomach-turning leer under the dim glow of low-pressure sodium-vapor streetlamps, and later his face crumbling in shame and fear as he was led from the courtroom in handcuffs, convicted of multiple counts of rape and sexual assault.

She remembered staring into the depths of his eyes as he was escorted out by Security Police, and seeing the rottenness of his soul was reflected in them.

She tried to speak a second time but her throat tightened, and she broke into a sob. She cried for him, for herself, and for the previous carefree life that had been taken from her. She felt relief at his death, but guilt stabbed sharply that she could be so hardened to the news.

She tried to tell Marco how she felt, explain why she was in tears over a man who had assaulted her and would have done worse if she hadn't stopped him, but her tears choked her. Instead, she held her hand out, letting Marco feel the complex swing of emotions. He touched her hand, taking it in. He came around his desk, pulling her up into a fatherly hug.

"It's okay, Athena. Your feelings are yours. There's no need to feel guilty over how you feel."

She nodded into his shoulder, her sobs leaving wet spots on Marco's suit coat.

Marco held Athena in a warm embrace until her breathing slowed again. When she calmed down, she sat back onto her seat.

"I'm sorry Marco. I think I got makeup on your coat."

He smiled and brushed at it. "No worries, Athena. If you knew the number of times Mandy and my daughters have cried on my shoulder, you wouldn't feel so bad."

Athena offered a thin smile. The smile faded as she formed the next question she had to ask. She swallowed hard. "How did it happen?"

"Prison fight. They might be criminals of one type or another, but the former servicemen in Fort Leavenworth take a dim view of rapists. They especially dislike serial rapists."

Athena closed her eyes, picturing a blank wall, trying to stave off a flashback. She took in three slow breaths, steadying herself.

"If it had been one of my daughters," Marco's said with chilling resolve, "they never would have found his body."

"I think my father felt the same way, but Parker was in custody then," Athena said with a little smile. "How are your kids, Marco?" She leapt at the opportunity to seize on any other topic for a moment's respite from the disturbing conversation.

"Fantastic, of course. Louisa finishes at Maryland in a week and has already been accepted into Duke's medical school."

"That's wonderful, Marco!" She smiled at his paternal pride.

"We had to talk last weekend though. After, uh, Mandy, I needed to see if anything had manifested in Lou. She's a little young still but, well ... all of us with older children have been doing judicious checking in light of what happened."

"You suspect it could be hereditary?"

"It obviously is to me, but who knows? Zeus and Hera never had children. They suspected—" he cut off and gave her a pained look.

"What?"

"They suspected something about Jumping may have caused Hera to miscarry. Several times." He frowned in sadness.

Athena absorbed that nugget of information. She'd never given much thought to children, but to have the choice possibly taken away was distressing.

"It could have been other issues," Marco said, "but they suspected it was the Jumping. Either way, there was no way of knowing whether they would have had children with the ability. That Mandy and her father—" Athena noted he was careful not to say the man's name. "—both can do it seems a bit too coincidental. So, we're all doing judicious checking."

"And if your daughter could Jump?" Athena asked him.

Marco's shoulders slumped. "I would be disappointed. I'm a second generation American. My father came here to live the American dream. For my family to have gotten a child into medical school in only three generations seems like quite the accomplishment. I would hate to see her have to give up her dream for this." He shook his head. "I'm proud to be able to support my nation in my way, but I'm prouder of how my children will help the world." He paused. "Without putting themselves in harm's way."

Athena nodded. She inhaled deeply. "You know it wasn't me."

"What? Oh, yes, I know," he said easily. "There is security footage of the whole fight from several angles. It was most decidedly a group of inmates, not you or anyone else we know."

She frowned at him. *Or anyone else we know*, she thought. *He means Powell.*

"Like I said, he definitely was killed at the hands of inmates in the yard. DOD will charge and prosecute the suspects, of course, but these people are already in prison, right? They obviously don't care." Marco's face was blank as he spoke.

Athena took in a deep breath and sat up in the chair. "Will that be all, skipper?"

Marco nodded. "Yes. I wanted you to get the news from me and not the newspaper. As far as I'm concerned, the official report on his death is accurate. Please don't do anything to complicate that. I need you, Athena. I need your head in the game here. We've got another fight on the Hill this week and you made more progress in one session than I have in years."

"Okay, Marco."

"Don't—" he stopped and gave her a searching look, his arms tight on the armrests. "Just don't go looking a gift horse in the mouth, Athena."

She looked as if she had more to say but nodded and took her leave.

Athena limped slowly to Communications. Her thoughts buzzed with what Marco had said and the things he had implied. To think there could be a link between genetics and their abilities made her head spin, though it made sense. She knew her father had no abilities other than the ability to make her laugh at his terrible Dad jokes, but what about her mother?

Athena limped forward, her cane clicking along the tiled floor of the Communications passageway. Despite having a near eidetic memory, Athena's memories of her mother were still fuzzy at best. A warm hug, the light scent of her perfume, and a general feeling of love. The day of her death was the only truly clear image, forever burned into her mind.

Athena stopped outside the door to Mission Control, leaning against the wall as she recalled that final morning. Athena, only five, had gotten out of bed as soon as she'd awakened. Her parents had discouraged her from getting up to watch Saturday morning cartoons, but they hadn't specifically stated she couldn't get up to play with her toys. Athena, happy with that loophole, had slipped from her bed, gone to the living room, and started quietly playing.

She remembered launching He-Man and She-Ra into a heroic battle for the fate of her My Little Ponies as her mother walked into their small suburban living room. Athena recalled a slight frown on her mother's narrow face followed by a warm smile. She remembered immediately running to her mother's embrace and her mother carrying her into the kitchen to make pancakes while her father slept in. It had seemed so normal, so mundane. Athena could almost feel the press of her mother's thin shoulders into her face, and she snuggled closer on the short walk to the kitchen.

Athena closed her eyes as a detail nagged at her. Her mother had made the pancakes, frowning as she poured out one scoop of flour, then a second. They had just finished cooking the last pancake as her father came in, him kissing her mother's neck and setting the plate down on the battered kitchen table. Her mother had started to turn back to the kitchen, probably to get the syrup, when she collapsed, her slender body sinking to the ground. For just a moment, neither she nor her father had assumed anything was so terribly wrong.

Athena blinked and suppressed the surge of grief that washed over her. She concentrated, wringing every detail she could from the memory. Her father's shouts of fear turning to grief as he clung to her mother. Athena remembered reaching for the house phone on the wall, tiny fingers only brushing the bottom of the unit so high on the wall, unable to call for help.

She bit her lip and pulled her mind back to the present. Had her mother always been thin? She'd been no more than twenty-six at her death. If she had been a Jumper, that was four years after she could have had the ability unlocked.

Athena shook her head, realizing she was trying to find clues where there were none in order to avoid what she really needed to concentrate on—the problem facing her right now. And that wasn't happening until Powell and Ares returned from the Alaska mission.

First things first.

She pushed through the door into the Mission Control & Communications Room. A glance at the screens tracking their movements showed both Ares and Powell were still in the Alaskan wilderness doing Powell's secret squirrel stuff.

Joe Pax monitored their dots. Zora sat at his feet with her head on her paws, eyes wide and swiveled up to watch Joe.

"How are they doing, Joe?"

"Hey Athena, didn't expect you in here today," he said with a smile. "They're fine. Landed a bit ago, haven't moved yet. I imagine they're waiting for their target."

"Okay if I wait here today and observe?"

Joe gave her a side glance and a smile. "No problem. You know I work for you, right?"

Athena waited with a growing sense of disquiet. She mulled over Marco's words, his implications. Major Parker was dead at the hands of fellow prison inmates because they knew what he had done. However, he had been at Leavenworth for over two months. Surely if they were going to attack him, it would have occurred earlier. *Why now—and who could have altered their opinions*?

She looked up at the screen that showed Ares' location in southern Alaska. She shut her eyes slowly, head falling forward. She knew who had altered the perceptions about Parker. And she knew why. She was lying to herself if she thought she didn't.

Time dragged on as she stewed, waiting for Ares' dot to move on the screen. Finally, Joe called her attention to the boards.

"They're moving around a bit more. I think they will probably be headed back soon."

"Thanks, Joe. This is a pretty big Jump for Ares so soon after he's started. I'm putting him on leave for the next three days. Try to make sure he lays low, okay?" She gave a half smile at his thumbs up.

Minutes later, she was sitting atop one of the beige Jump Room desks, hands resting easily on her cane. Joe stood next to Athena with Zora, who sat calmly.

There was a big puff of displaced air from Point Zero and Ares and Powell appeared from thin air.

"Ares, Powell," Athena said.

Not '*Brandon*,' Powell thought.

Her voice was ice cold and devoid of emotion. "Did everything go as planned?"

Ares nodded his head. "Yes, ma'am, it did."

She ignored the *ma'am*. "Thank you. Good to go. Grab some chow, write me up a short after-action, then you're on basket leave until Thursday."

He didn't have to be told twice.

"All right. Thanks. See you in three days." He took the worn dog lead offered by Joe. "Come, Zora."

Ares made for the door as quickly as seemed polite. Just when he went through the exit, he heard Val address Powell.

"Brandon, you and I need to talk."

Ares winced. No man ever wanted a conversation started by a woman to begin, *We need to talk.*

Powell stared at her, his usual impassive mask in place.

Athena leaned against the desk and waited. Seconds ticked by and she watched him, trying to keep her face neutral over the swirl of emotions inside. Finally, she closed her eyes, unable to look at him any longer.

"It's a good technique," he said quietly. "An interrogation technique I prefer myself when time isn't critical."

Athena kept her eyes closed, dropping her chin to her chest.

"What is?"

"Leveraging silence. People don't like long, uncomfortable silences. They seek to fill the void and it leads them to saying more than they should. I had a buddy once who was a radio DJ, and he called it 'dead air.' He couldn't stand the idea of dead air."

"Always the company man, huh Bran?" she asked, head still down. The question hung in the silence over them. Another minute ticked by.

"Yes, I suppose."

She suppressed her frustration, fully aware that he could feel everything she did, even from across the room. A thought hit her and she inhaled sharply, eyes flying open. She watched the subtle wave of emotions, almost too subtle to see, ripple across his face.

"That's what this is about," she said slowly. She felt like she was reaching out, mentally, to grab his thoughts and emotions as she observed the tiny changes in his expression. Athena felt their minds connect in a stunning moment of clarity.

To anyone watching them, the bland silence would have betrayed the mental war the waged in a fraction of a second.

Guilt.

Righteousness.

Relief.

"You might as well know, I already know," she said, blinking back tears. She watched his façade shatter, face crumbling into despair, hands going out for hers. The emotions she'd sensed without his touch were replaced with shame and guilt. "It was it you. Bran. You did it."

"You know the answer already, Athena," he said quietly.

"I need to hear you say the words."

"I contacted someone I know inside. I told them his real story. I—" he stopped, swallowing hard. "I suggested no one would be upset by his demise."

He wouldn't meet Athena's eyes.

"You did this thing for me?"

A wave of guilt flowed into her. She gasped and batted his hands away. Athena looked at him in growing horror.

"Val. Athena. *Whoever* ..." He pleaded. "I feel everything! Everything you feel. Every flashback. Every time you catch me moving out of the corner of your eye and jump. Every conflicted feeling you had over him. I couldn't let you suffer like that."

"So, you had him—" She stopped and stared up at him again. A feeling of subtle calm crept over her, insidious and alluring.

"Brandon, stop it!" she growled.

"Just take a damned breath."

Her horror at his actions gave way to simmering anger. Athena's mind reached out along the line of calm, like fingers seeking their way up a braid, feeling its weave, and flowing back to its source. She was in his mind, mired in the black morass of truth, and dug in.

Powell's eye widened. "Get out, Val!"

She felt the connection squirming under her control, writhing in an attempt to slip her touch. The insidious calm she'd felt snapped, and her own emotions came back from him in full force.

"*Liar!*" she hissed. Eyes narrowed in pain and anger, she looked up at him. "You didn't do it for me, you did it for *you*. Your own selfish reasons. You had a man mur—" she cut herself off, unwilling to say it aloud, not sure if it was for his protection or because she still couldn't believe him capable of it.

"And worse, you're trying to cover it up to me. I'm not some street thug, Bran—I'm supposed to be your girlfriend! You don't get to just alter my emotions to suit you."

Her hold on his mind flashed her guilt and pain, and a growing anger. Her conflicted feelings blended with Powell's own emotions in a whirlwind of fear and disappointment.

"Get out, I said!" Powell said through a clenched jaw, his balled fists tucked under his arms.

Disgusted, she released her hold on their connection, still staring up at him from her spot on the desk. Powell relaxed, clutching his head in both hands as if he had the world's biggest headache.

"How did you do that?" he asked quietly.

"I don't know," she whispered. Her anger faded and the ignored pain was returning to her injured leg. "Lately, it seems like," she paused, searching her memories, "like the closer I am to someone, the more I—" She paused to consider. "—the more I care, the closer I'm able to get."

He let go of his head, eyes meeting hers. "Are you in here now?"

"No."

Silence hung between them.

"I don't think ..." she started.

"Athena, look ..." Powell said at the same time. He stopped, gesturing for her to speak.

"I can't do this, Bran. I can't be with someone I don't trust. I expected some level of complication from you; it's your job. But this? And then trying to override my emotions? And not even override them for me, but so you can 'manage' me better." She drew air quotes in the air. "I can't trust you. I can't trust that what I feel around you is real, that you aren't manufacturing for me feelings you think I don't already have."

Powell nodded, swallowing hard. "And I can't be with someone who can get in my head like you can."

"Yeah, doesn't feel very good, does it?" she asked, her bitter words stinging him.

Powell's expression turned sour.

"No, I guess it doesn't." He swallowed hard. Hesitantly, he put his hand out for her.

She met his eyes, the lost expression on his face almost breaking her. Steeling herself, she took his hand. She gasped as he pulled her to her feet. Despite their sharp words, his feelings for her ran deep and the pain of loss flowed across the contact.

"Thank you," she murmured, acknowledging his feeling but unable to meet his eyes.

Moments passed before he replied.

"I'll work on finding a replacement liaison for the Agency."

Athena nodded and turned for the door.

"And," Marco said. Athena?"

She looked back to him, trying to hide her own pain yet knowing he felt everything she did.

"I know you have the 'key' to my apartment, but please, don't ... don't use it."

She nodded, first appalled he would think she'd invade his privacy that way, then ashamed knowing how she'd just invaded his mind.

She watched him walk out ahead of her. The door hesitated briefly as he closed it, as if there was something left to say. He looked at her once, then let the door swing closed.

She settled herself back down on the desk and broke into tears.

When she managed to regain a semblance of control, she snagged the desk's phone and dialed.

"Marco, Athena. I don't feel so great. Without objection, I'm taking the rest of the day off," she said, voice tight.

"Okay, Athena. No problem. Need anything?" his deep voice carried a fatherly concern.

"A couple gallons of ice cream and three bottles of wine? The big ones?" she said with a halfhearted laugh.

"Ahh, I thought it might go that way. Sorry."

"Had to happen, but we'll live. Thanks, Marco." She hung up.

The dull throb in her leg flared into a stab of pain as she stood. She leaned heavily on her cane, debating just Jumping home. With a twist of perverse self-hate, she elected to walk home and subject herself to the pain.

A man was dead because of her. Maybe not directly and maybe he deserved it, but it was different than a battle casualty. When soldiers died in combat, she mourned them, but their deaths weren't her fault. It was fortunes of war. They knew what they'd signed up for.

This wasn't the same. US Air Force Major Brian Parker hadn't gone to prison with any idea that he'd get dead there.

She gritted her teeth and limped home in the sultry late spring air.

As she unlocked the door to her apartment, mentally cursing herself for walking, the door across the hall to Mandy's new apartment opened and she crutched her way out.

"Oh, hey Athena," Mandy's voice was hesitant. She eyed Athena's own crutch. "We have to stop meeting like this."

"Hey," came Athena's despondent reply. "I'm gonna down at least a bottle of wine and a gallon of chocolate chip cookie dough ice cream. Care to join?"

Mandy's eyes widened. "You, uh, broke up with Brandon?"

Athena nodded, and looked at the floor.

Mandy's eyes darted to the apartment Athena had secured for her, then back to Athena.

"I'm sorry, I ... just can't right now."

Athena nodded, turning her key in its lock. "Yeah, okay. No worries at all."

"I'm sorry. I'm—" She hesitated. "—I'm about to head over to Pete's, see if I can't patch things up." Mandy gave a little shrug around her crutches.

Athena looked at her a moment, searching her friend's face. Frustration filled her but other emotions, alien to her, seemed to haunt the edges of her mind.

"Okay, hon. Good luck, I guess."

"Thanks."

Athena's anger and disapproval of Pete still lurked below the surface, despite trying to control it. She watched Mandy hobble down the hallway and the alien emotion faded.

Athena tried to shake the notion that she'd felt far more than Mandy had just said. She sighed and limped into her apartment.

Solo flight for you tonight, girl, Athena thought to herself.

Cursing herself over burned bridges, she snagged a wine glass, a bottle of red wine, a spoon, and a half gallon of ice cream held in a terrycloth dish towel to minimize the melting. She'd eat it right out of the carton.

Juggling them all and her cane, she plopped down onto her couch for an evening of self-pity. As the last of the sunset's light died in her living room windows, Athena crawled into bed. All the ice cream and the bottle of wine had befuddled her mind.

She couldn't decide if she was more upset that Mandy was trying to patch things up with her shitty boyfriend or because she wanted Mandy to stay in with her.

CHAPTER 15
AMANDA SQUIRES
1316Z 0916L, 08 AUG

Mandy gritted her teeth and struggled to move her leg. Motions that were once so easy, so automatic, confounded her now. She blinked back tears of pain and frustration as she struggled against a one-pound weight looped around her ankle.

"Keep diggin'! Engage the quadricep," Bill's voice directed.

"It is engaged and it fucking hurts!" she snapped. Bill gave her a calm look and she felt guilty. "Sorry," she mumbled. "I'm being a pissy baby."

"Verbal today, too." Bill patted her knee. "It's okay. I know how it goes and I know it's hard. I've been working with this lot for over a decade, and no one around here ever wants to be sidelined. They always want to push back into the fight as quick as possible."

Mandy had no intention of "getting back into the fight," even if she wanted to.

"Don't worry, Bill," she said. "I'm not that eager. I just want to walk without these damn crutches."

Bill nodded, adjusted her leg weight, and told her to start again.

Mandy struggled through the exercises, letting her mind wander as she pushed and pulled under Bill's supervision. She observed other Pantheon members, those who weren't out on assignment, as they arrived for their daily workouts. Ares and Joe had been hard at work when she arrived, with the rest of the Pantheon arriving for their workouts toward the end of her session. She glanced at Ares and Joe, smiling, then frowned. Ares was attractive, no doubt, but he was also full of himself, flirting with her shamelessly every time they encountered one another. She appreciated the attention, glad someone could interact with her so normally.

Ares, perhaps alerted to her scrutiny, looked up from his seat on the floor and she glanced away.

Mandy sighed, following Bill through another exercise.

I want to be with Pete, she said to herself. Or at least, I want Pete to understand what had happened wasn't my fault.

For them to spend six months together and then he pushed her away, as if she were diseased, rankled her. She wasn't sure she needed him back, but she wasn't sure she wanted to just let him go.

Teeth clenched; she pushed her shin against Bill's hand trying to sort out her conflicted emotions.

How can he be mad at me when I can't even really Jump?

She couldn't Jump and she wasn't Pantheon, no matter what Athena said. Mandy swallowed hard. She had tried again this morning to Jump into work, but no go.

Bill finally released her to her daily duties. She went about her morning ensuring Athena's equipment was ready for when she returned to duty. What normally took no more than half an hour took her the rest of the morning. She was slowed by her crutches and checking her phone every five minutes to see if Pete had texted. By lunch time she was starving and frustrated.

"Good morning, Mandy," Marco's voice cut through her mental turmoil as she stood in the lunch line.

She blinked at him. "Oh, hey boss."

"Wool gathering?"

"Yeah, sorry."

Marco's face was serious. Long association with Marco had taught her that the tightness around his eyes and mouth meant he was dismayed by something but wasn't about to share it with her.

"Here, let me help you," he said and gathered her tray.

It wasn't until he started carrying both their trays to a table that Mandy realized she hadn't had a plan for how she would have crutched her way to a table with the food tray.

"Thanks, Tio Marco," she said with a rueful grin.

He nodded. "*De nada*."

They ate in easy silence for a few minutes. Marco ate with speed, warrior-style, but still managed to get every morsel in his mouth with grace. Mandy picked slowly at her plate, not tasting what made it to her mouth.

"How's physical therapy going?" Marco asked after several quiet moments.

Mandy shrugged and pushed her long, blonde hair back over her shoulder. "It's going."

"And?"

"And what, Tio? Bill isn't sure I'll ever walk normally again. It's frustrating as hell and I don't feel like I'm making progress." She sat back, letting her hands fall to her lap.

Marco frowned. "Keep working at it. Make all the progress as you can, but don't hurt yourself trying."

She nodded. "I know. I will, and I won't."

"Making any progress with Jumping?" he asked gently.

She eyed him, trying not to glare. "No," she said carefully.

"Have you been trying?"

A long silence followed his simple question. Marco regarded her, his face an expression of soft patience. Mandy briefly considered lying, telling him she hadn't spent all morning trying to Jump from room to room, but her pause gave her away. Marco held out a hand.

"Yes," she finally said, looking away as she placed her slim hand in his.

She could feel Marco searching her face. Mandy closed her eyes, letting her fear, frustration, relief, and guilt flow into him. A moment passed as he absorbed her touch.

"*Bueno, mija*. As long as you're trying," he said finally. Love and understanding flowing across their touch.

"Are you saying that as my boss or as my Tio?" She looked at him with haunted eyes.

"Both," he said, a gentle, fatherly smile tugging at the corners of his mouth. He released her hand and cleared his throat. "I need every Jumper I can get, but I also need you happy and healthy," he said.

"I don't fit in with this, Tio. This isn't my place. This isn't what I do."

"This absolutely is your place, *mija*. You grew up here, this is your family. You are my family, no matter what. And we need you, to be perfectly honest."

"Thanks."

Mandy's guilt lingered and she was torn. She had never been envious of the Pantheon who were able to Jump, so when her own ability surfaced traumatically when she was shot, it disturbed her. She didn't want to face what it would pull her into. But at the same time, she knew Marco needed all the reliable Jumpers he could find and she wanted to support the Pantheon family at Limitless.

At the thought of family, Mandy swallowed hard.

"How are your girls, Marco?"

The question seemed to catch Marco off guard.

"Reading my thoughts, *mija*?" At her small shrug, he leaned back in his chair. "They're well. Louisa graduates next month, and Ana will finish her freshman year at Georgetown. They both send their love and best wishes for a speedy recovery."

Mandy rocked back in her chair. "They know?"

Marco eyed her over his fingers. "Yes. I—" he took in a deep breath. "After everything that happened, I told them your whole story. I needed to know."

Mandy gave a small nod. "You needed to know if it was genetic."

Marco brushed his hands through his wavy chocolate hair. "Yes. But we don't have to talk about this if you aren't ready."

Mandy thought for a moment. "Yeah, I'd rather not. Not right now." She swallowed her pain and regret. "And the others?"

"The others with children?"

She nodded, not making eye contact.

"We decided that since the age Jumping ability manifests is around twenty-two to twenty-four, it would be best to only discuss it with adult children." He frowned. "Everyone with children over eighteen broached the subject, but there were no surprises. Well, none for us." He gave a small laugh. "Lou and Ana fully believed I was a paper pusher for a transnational logistics company. I had to Jump them both to our cabin in Tahoe to prove it."

Mandy gave him a small grin at the thought of his wonderful but naïve girls having the illusion stripped that their father was just another middle-aged man wasting away in an office.

"Did they never wonder why you were always fitter than their friends' dads?"

"Nope, they just assumed it was because I was a health nut. That was a hell of a conversation." He laughed.

Mandy said, "I'm glad you were able to tell them. Of course, you told *Tia* Mina?"

"Yes," Marco said soberly. "My wife, though ... well, she's not talking to me right now." Marco looked away, his full lips pursed in frustration.

"That's a big secret to keep."

"And for more than twenty years," he agreed.

When Mandy reached out to give Marco's hand a light squeeze, he detected her physical and emotional energy was nearly depleted. Her condition matched his own.

"You should go home, Mandy."

Mandy's leg ached terribly by the time she got home. She could have asked any one of the Pantheon in the office to Jump her back, but she called Limitless motor transport and had a black SUV take her back to her apartment, saving her from having an emotional breakdown from the pain on a DC sidewalk. She had just thrown the bolt on the door of her new apartment when the tears started. She staggered to the couch, leaving a trail from her door to her brand-new sofa.

She abandoned herself to the sobs. The grief closed in and she gasped, her whole body convulsing in anguish. The pain of losing her father flooded through her and she couldn't halt the tidal wave of emotion that crashed down. She lay on the couch bawling until her pain subsided and she was spent. Her arms and legs a tumble across the couch, her nose and eyes red, she fought to regain the control she'd lost. Time passed and her sobs eased, and Mandy fell into a doze.

The quiet *ding* and vibration of her phone jarred her awake. She picked up the device and her stomach lurched when she read the short message.

M, I'm moving out today. Have your stuff in a box. Come get it, I know I can't stop you from coming in. Pete's terse message was a study in indifference.

Mandy fumbled with the phone and she typed a reply, biting her lip. *I'll be down in a moment. Can we talk while I'm there?*

She waited a moment for a response, but when he didn't reply, she limped to her guest bathroom to splash water on her face. The face that met her in the mirror was haggard, her eyes puffy and red-rimmed, her nose a beacon that shouted she'd spent the last few hours crying. She splashed cold water on her face and paused. Waiting a few more minutes would serve two purposes: First, keep her from looking like she was as desperate to talk to Pete as she really was, and second, to ensure she didn't look like she'd spent the last hour bawling over him.

She hobbled back to her living area, frustrated that she couldn't spend the time pacing to relieve nervous energy building up within.

Mandy wondered about Pete. How could he be so dismissive? He treated this whole thing like she'd made a conscious decision to Jump. She snatched up her phone, rereading his terse text. She tried not to read into why he wouldn't have answered her request to talk. Her nails tapped out a rapid tattoo as she tried to craft the perfect response. Several moments passed as she wrote and rewrote texts. Finally, she gave up and headed for the door.

She crutched out into the hallway and to find Athena opening the door to her own apartment.

"Oh, hey Athena," Mandy's voice was hesitant.

"Hey," was Athena's dejected reply. "I'm gonna down a bottle of wine and a gallon of chocolate chip cookie dough ice cream—with chocolate syrup. Care to join?"

Mandy took in Athena's appearance, the puffy eyes that matched her own and her eyes widened.

Athena looked at the floor.

"You, uh, broke up with Brandon?" Mandy asked gently.

Athena nodded, looking back up at Mandy.

"I'm sorry, I ... I just can't right now."

Athena nodded, turning her key in its lock. "Yeah, okay. I understand."

"I'm sorry. I'm–" She hesitated. "—I'm actually about to head over to Pete's, see if I can't patch things up." She gave a little shrug.

Athena looked at her a moment, searching her friend's face.

"Okay. Good luck, I guess."

Mandy could almost feel the disapproval radiating from Athena. Not just from the expression on her face, but deep in her core. There was a feeling of sadness and longing that hadn't been there moments before. Mandy blinked hard, at a loss for what to say.

"Thanks," she said. She closed her apartment door and headed down the hallway to the elevators.

Mandy arrived at Pete's apartment several floors below her new apartment to find the door propped open by a stack of boxes. Pete's text had said he couldn't stop her from coming in and she hoped this is what he meant.

"Pete?" she called into the apartment. She hobbled in, moving with care to angle around half-packed boxes and stacks of paper.

"Your stuff's in the box on the table," he called from the depths of the apartment.

Mandy shuffled back to his bedroom. She found him carefully wrapping the small wooden cross that had hung over his bed, neatly tucking it into a box on his bed.

"Hey Pete," she said. She tried to push down the flutter in her stomach when she looked at him. He was the same Pete, dark hair tousled slightly from packing all day, strong jaw set in a determined line. He looked older than he had when he'd visited her at the hospital just a week before.

"Pete?"

"What?" The single word held daggers of ice.

"Can we talk?"

"There's not much to talk about. I can't be with you, and you sent your enforcer after me to ensure I didn't have a job or—" He gestured around. "—a home."

"What? Wait, what?" She'd heard how his employment had terminated from both Athena and Rich and this wasn't what they'd said.

"Pete, you left me. You were, uh, fired before you left me," her voice trailed off, confused.

"Fine, but I have no home or job because of you!" he snarled.

"What are you talking about?" Mandy's voice cracked, full of confusion and concern.

"Look, I can't be with someone like you. What you do is unnatural."

"But I can't do it. I mean, once, but I can't now. That isn't me, that isn't who I am," she pleaded for him to understand. "Please, Pete, I didn't want this. Any of this," she gestured to the half-packed room. "Can we please just sit and talk, please? I need ... I just want you to know this isn't me."

Pete closed his eyes at the pleading in her voice.

"Fine. I have a few minutes before the movers get here anyway." He gestured for her to lead the way to his small living room. She turned with difficulty and went to his couch, landing heavily on its overstuffed cushions.

Mandy's heart gave a little flutter when he pulled a stack of paper out of the way and helped her to sit comfortably on the couch.

As mad as he might be, she thought, he's still a gentleman. Her belly tightened as she looked at him, the feeling of longing rising again but warring with a strange feeling of dread.

Pete settled stiffly on the other end of the couch, waiting for her to start talking.

Mandy tried to find a neutral way to start what she knew would be a painful conversation.

"Have you got another apartment lined up?"

"Maybe," was his terse retort.

She looked at him for a moment, then nodded. "You're afraid I'll have access to your new apartment if you say anything about it."

"The only plus side of leaving this place is that I get the security of knowing you can't just show up."

"I'm not—" she stopped herself. "Pete, I told you, I can't."

"I liked you, Mandy. You were everything I wanted in a woman and maybe even a wife."

Mandy felt a twisting stab of pain at his words. She opened her mouth, but he continued.

"But I'm a good Christian, I can't be taking up with a witch. What you do is unnatural."

Mandy choked down her reaction to the absurdity of being called a witch, focusing on his words. "I'm still the same woman I was last month. I can still be that woman. No matter what I can or, at this point, can't do, I'm still a good person. Jesus, Pete, I've been to church with you! We could work through this." She reached out for his hand, but he stayed stiffly pressed against his end of the couch, his handsome face closed.

Mandy sat back, at a loss.

"I'm not a monster."

"No," he said after a long moment, "I suppose you aren't. But I can't be with someone who is outside God's laws."

"Pete, please, I'm telling you, I can't."

"How do you know?"

"I tried. I wanted to be sure I wasn't one of them. I can't do it." Mandy's eyes dropped to her lap. "That's why I haven't been scheduled for Indoc or put on the training roster. I'm getting the super heal-faster drugs the Pantheon get, but that's because of my Uncle Marco. And that's all."

Pete shifted on the couch and she looked up at him. Even his dry smile lit a fire in her.

"Well, if that's true, then maybe we could make it work. Promise me to my face that it'll never happen again."

Hope and lust flared inside her, and she reached forward, ready to promise him anything to have his smile on her again.

"If that's what you want, I'll—" her hand touched his and she snapped her mouth shut in shock.

Mandy felt Pete's deception through their touch. His disarming smile was nothing but a porcelain façade over a seething cesspool of hate. She snatched her hand back, almost gagging at the abject feel of him. Pete's eyes narrowed and she realized he knew what she'd felt.

"Witch!" he shouted, hands roughly grabbing her upper arms to pin her to the couch.

"Pete, stop!" she struggled to stand, hard enough with her injured leg, but wanting to be nowhere near the hate and disgust that roiled off him. Frantic, she tried to squirm away but he clung to her, rising anger flowing across their contact.

"You're nothing more than a heathen and filthy *whore* like the rest of them!" he raged. "Sent by the Devil to tempt me into Hell!"

Horror flooded into Mandy as she struggled against him, trying to escape his grasp. She felt his anger turn ugly, and she gasped at the sudden twist of his mind.

"Or maybe," he snarled, "I'm here to beat the evil out of you. One way or another." His hands slid up her arms, pulling her closer.

"No, Pete. No!" Mandy tried to break his grasp, to get free and escape. The cruel irony occurred to her then, that the thing that would save her—Jumping—was a thing she couldn't do. Tears of frustration and pain spilled down her cheeks that the thing he hated about herself wasn't even available to save her. The trauma suppressing her ability was only leading to more trauma, just as it had for Athena.

Mandy could tell Pete was also confused about his harmful feelings toward her, but she also felt his resolve was hardening.

"Athena!" she called out in desperation. It was useless, Mandy knew. Athena was several floors away and probably soaked in wine and her own problems, but Mandy still screamed for the one person in the world who would understand.

Athena! This time she screamed in her mind.

Mandy? What's wrong?

Mandy's head jerked up as she thought she heard Athena's sleepy voice respond. Pete's eyes narrowed as his grip on Mandy tightened.

"*Athena—help me!*" Mandy shrieked again, calling out with her voice and her mind at the same time.

Mandy!

Mandy's mind was flooded with an image of Athena sitting bolt upright in a king-sized bed, covers pooled at her waist. Mandy seized the image, her mind latching on to it with an iron grip.

Pete's face, twisted in rage, slid into an expression of shock.

How could I have been so wrong about him?

"The devil be damned," Mandy screamed. "And *you* too, asshole!"

Without another second of hesitation, she Jumped.

CHAPTER 16
AMANDA SQUIRES
0003Z 2003L, 08 AUG

Mandy landed in the middle of Athena's bed, sprawled across her one uninjured leg.

"Mandy? Mandy!" Athena yelled and pulled her into a fierce hug. "Oh, gods and stars above, what happened?"

Mandy clung to Athena fiercely, head in the crook of her neck, and unable to speak. Easier and faster than explaining, Mandy let her memories of the last hour flow across their touch. She felt Athena stiffen in anger and the emotion echoed across the connection.

"Hell, Mandy. I'll kill him myself," Athena murmured.

Mandy felt Athena's anger die as the words she had said registered in her own mind. "No, Athena. He's not worth it."

Athena nodded, face suddenly still as she remembered Brian Parker's death in prison at the hands of inmates.

"I know. No one is worth that."

Mandy looked at her then felt the last few hours of Athena's day, slightly hazy with wine, flow across. "Oh, Athena. Oh, oh, honey. I'm so sorry. I didn't know." She pulled her best friend in tighter.

"What a mess," Athena whispered quietly, cheek pressed to Mandy's, lips brushing her neck as she spoke.

Mandy gave a delicate shudder and sighed. The light touch felt better than she might have expected it would. She leaned back on one elbow, carefully moving her injured leg out of the way.

"I'm sorry. I didn't mean to wake you—or drag you into my problems. I wasn't even aware that I could wake you that way." She hesitated. "I knew about Powell. I mean, Marco had said something vague, but I didn't know how bad it was. I didn't mean to pull you into my problems too."

Athena nodded. "It's okay, that's what friends are for. Burdens shared and all that. Especially the shitty burdens."

Mandy regarded Athena and it was only then that she realized her friend was nude from the waist up. Mandy blushed and was glad the dimly lit room hid it. Athena's sudden laugh reminded her that despite the lack of illumination, there was nothing stopping her from feeling Mandy's thoughts.

"Geez, okay, I'll put some clothes on. But as many times as you've seen me change at Madame Volaire's, it's not like this is the first time you've seen my amazing boobs," she said with a comfortable laugh. Athena gave her shoulders a playful shake that made her firm breasts sway impressively.

"Stop that," Mandy said, and laughed. "Yes, I've seen them—but this is the first time my face has been this close to them."

"It's okay, you're among friends, hon." But Athena reached to the floor and retrieved the T-shirt she'd stripped off in the night, pulling it over her head.

Mandy said, "Stay comfy if you want. I'll head back to my apartment." She swung her legs over the edge of the bed but cried out in pain as the sudden change in blood pressure slammed against the inflamed nerves in her leg.

Athena's hand rested on her shoulder, stopping her. "Easy, easy! Your crutches didn't follow you when you snapshot-Jumped. Which event, by the way, we will need to talk about."

Mandy bit her lip. Athena was right on both counts.

"I don't know what happened. I–" she hesitated, "I tried to Jump this morning and nothing."

"Trauma," Athena said quietly, compassion and understanding

flowing across their touch. "What Pete did to you broke the emotional block that was holding you back."

Mandy reached up, covering the hand on her shoulder with hers. She sighed. "I know."

"Yes, you do."

"And now? What now?" Mandy asked. Frustration and pain colored her voice.

"Now? Well, now you need to get some sleep. We can talk about the rest of it tomorrow."

Mandy nodded. "I could sleep. Guess I can Jump back to my apartment, huh? Who needs stupid crutches?"

"Probably you can now, but you are more than welcome to stay here. I'm a pretty good nursemaid when needed." Athena's voice was full of warmth and compassion, concern flowing through strong via their touch. "There are T-shirt sleepin' shirts in that top drawer." She pointed to the dresser.

Mandy hesitated only for a moment. "You know, yeah. I think that's a grand idea if that's okay?" She didn't relish the idea of either Jumping to her apartment or trying to hop around without her crutches. Plus, it was nice to have a friend at hand just now.

"Absolutely it's okay," Athena said and settled back into her several pillows.

Mandy stood slowly and turned away from the bed. She pulled her athletic shorts over the leg dressing and pulled off her top, removing her bra. She put on a Taylor Swift T-shirt from the dresser drawer and sat back down on the bed, rotating her body carefully so as not to enrage the injured leg. Truth was, though, she thought it was getting a lot better.

Mandy lay down on her good side facing Athena, who curled up facing her. Athena reached out, taking her hand.

"Everything in my life has been turned upside down," Mandy said. "I mean, you know it as well as me. Pete dumps me ... and I get shot by my own father, who then is killed in front of me." Her eyes welled up. "Sometimes I just don't see my place on this planet, you know?"

"Everything will be okay, Mandy. I don't care what Marco or the politicians push for, I won't put you on the Pantheon roster if you aren't ready." She leaned in, pressing a sisterly kiss to Mandy's forehead.

The spark Mandy had felt in Pete's apartment returned at the touch and she heard Athena's soft gasp as it ricocheted back, also catching Athena by surprise. Mandy pressed her forehead against Athena's, the tips of their noses just touching. Mandy inhaled and luxuriated in the soft vanilla smell of Athena's shampoo.

Something fluttered deep within her.

I have never felt closer to a human being in my life than I do right now, Mandy thought. And she knew the sentiment was being broadcast back to Athena in real time.

She opened her eyes to meet Athena's. When their eyes met Mandy could feel Athena's echoing flutter roll between their touches. She inhaled sharply. This was all so new and utterly familiar all at once, and desperately exciting.

"Athena, I ..."

Athena leaned in, kissing Mandy hesitantly on her full lips. The kiss was soft and only lightly laced with wine, her lips softer than any man's Mandy had ever kissed. An instant spark of heat and desire bloomed deep in Mandy's belly, and she was shocked to feel it returned and enhanced from Athena. She could feel Athena's desire as well as her own reflecting back at her.

"Athena, what the—"

Athena reached up and swept a length of blonde hair off Mandy's face. "Don't speak," Athena whispered, and pressed a passionate kiss laced with wet tongue on Mandy's neck.

"I've never, uhm ... *ooohh!*" Mandy gasped when Athena's hand traced down her back. Athena's mouth descended onto Mandy's and probed hungrily with her tongue. The effect was a strange burning hypnotism and Mandy was instantly enflamed. She could feel Athena's pleasure at touching her, and their mutual desire.

The thinnest thread of bewilderment mingled with their roaring passion, and the overall effect left Mandy gasping. Never in her life had a touch been so erotic.

Mandy responded to the strangely echoing sensations rolling between them and abandoned herself to it. She pulled up the T-shirt, freeing her breasts first for Athena's hand and then her energetic mouth. Hesitantly, she stroked Athena's bare back. Athena arched into her in response, firm breasts pushing into Mandy's own. Mandy abandoned herself to sensation, hands skimming, nails raking, fingers twining within Athena's hair. Athena's hands traced fire over every inch of her. Mandy let go of every inhibition.

"Oh, *gods*—" Athena gasped. She grabbed Mandy's hand and crushed it harder into her breast. "Please don't stop that ..."

Mandy felt Athena's every quiver as well as her own, amplifying the shared feelings by orders of magnitude. Each stroke and twist and squeeze sent a twin sensation through her own body—made even more electric when the first woman's hand to touch her slid between Mandy's taut legs and the fingers produced shuddering magic after shuddering magic.

"Oh my god, Athena, what's going on?" Mandy whispered. "It's not like this ..."

The sensation built until she almost couldn't stand it, echoing to her core.

Exquisite pleasure was turning to fear that it would truly never end. Vibrations zoomed through Mandy's hands and realization finally broke through the overpowering craving. Sensations flew up through her hand, up her arm and realization dawned on her.

She snatched her hand away and the connection broke.

Both women laid back on the big bed, drew in heaving breaths and pulled sweaty hair off their faces. The energies subsided and their breathing slowed.

Spent, Mandy faded into blackness.

CHAPTER 17
VALERIE 'ATHENA' HALL
1224Z 0824L 09 AUG

The next morning, Athena awoke to Mandy sprawled across her. Startled, she started to shift away, only then realizing they were separated by a sheet. She sighed in relief, afraid she would get locked into some kind of neural feedback loop again.

"Athena?" Mandy's sleepy voice called.

"Yes?" Athena answered hesitantly.

"That wasn't a dream, was it?" Mandy sat upright, clutching the sheet to her chest and her cheeks reddened.

"So, I—" Athena started.

"Uh, Athena—" Mandy said at the same time. She gave a small, nervous laugh. "Uh, you go first."

Athena took a deep breath and started to speak. Her mouth hung open for a moment and she shook her head. "Hoo boy," she said and let out the breath.

"Yeah."

Athena leaned against her plush, padded headboard, trying not to think about Mandy last night. She pressed her fist to her mouth and wrapped her other arm across her bare torso.

Where did that even come from last night? Athena thought.

"What ... what was *that*?" Mandy asked, her voice quiet but unafraid.

"Well, it definitely wasn't a mistake, if that's what you're worried about," Athena said. "It was ... a release. A much-needed release," she said. "For us both. With all the boy drama we've had to deal with, my view is we just became one person last night, with one brain and identical needs."

Athena reached over and placed her hand atop Mandy's, allowing her truth to flow between them.

"We were close before, or last night wouldn't have happened. We're obviously attracted to each other, personally and emotionally, so comforting each other in a time of mutual hurt is just natural. I'm pretty solidly hetero, though I had a one-off fling with a woman in college. I take it last night was your first with a woman, but I felt your energy. Neither of us was faking it."

She batted her eyes comically. "And it was fun."

Mandy smiled and nodded in agreement on all counts. "Are we... I mean, what happens next?"

"Oh, geez, are you asking if we're dating now?" Athena laughed, cutting her off.

Mandy laughed then too, dispelling the awkward tension that was smothering the room. "No! Geez, no. That was fun but, uh, I guess I never really got into girls before. I mean, yeah. That was a first for me."

Athena hadn't been looking to jump into a relationship, especially something that was well outside her norm. But hearing Mandy discard the idea so quickly stung more than she would have thought it would.

"No, what I was going to ask is, are we the only ones who know about—I don't know what to call it. A feedback loop? A sensory overload? Every time I touched you or you touched me, I felt the electricity bounce back and forth between us."

Athena felt a twinge of guilt. She knew from firsthand experience that the feedback loop was genuine and could happen, though she was still surprised to have felt it so intensely. But she wasn't ready to get into the details with Mandy this morning. She looked at her watch.

"Shit—we're late. We need to get into work."

Mandy glanced up at the clock on Athena's dresser.

"Crap." She winced. "Can I shower here? I don't know if I can get up to my place without my crutches."

"Yeah. I'll text Joe to grab a new pair and meet us in the Jump Room. I'll take us both in," she glanced at Mandy. "Unless you think you can get yourself in?"

Mandy shook her head vigorously. "No. I mean, maybe, but I'm not sure I'm ready to try today."

Athena wanted to fight her on it, force her to realize she was over her mental block but didn't push. "Okay, but when you're ready to join us, we're here for you."

Mandy stared at her a moment. "And do what, Athena?" Mandy shook her head. "I'm not in the military, I have no desire to be in the military. I have less a place here now than when I was just a handler."

Athena closed her eyes against the dismay in Mandy's voice. "You're a part of this Pantheon, even if you aren't in the military."

"Athena," Mandy said sharply.

"The original Pantheon was more than the warrior gods and goddesses. There was a god of wine, even."

"Athena ..." Mandy warned.

"Hestia," Athena said. "Goddess of the hearth and home. That's you. You'll be what holds us together."

Mandy sighed and didn't answer.

"Fine." Athena limped into her shower, texting Joe as she moved. Even having to work around their injured legs, they were showered and dressed and had Jumped to Limitless Logistics within twenty-five minutes of waking.

Joe greeted them in the Jump Room on arrival.

"Morning Athena, Mandy. Here you go, girl." He handed Mandy a set of lightweight carbon fiber crutches and then pointed to two steaming cups on the nearby table.

"Bless you, Joe." Athena said and grabbed her cup of tea. "Uh, if you don't mind. We're going to finish them in here. We'll catch up with you in a few." Joe nodded and left them. Athena watched Mandy sip her coffee and crafted her next discussion with care.

"Can we do this?" she asked.

"What? Do what?" Mandy's brow furrowed over the cup.

"Be coworkers who've slept with each other?" She crossed her arms, one hand at her mouth.

"Of course. Like you said, we were friends who cared about each other before last night. Nothing in that has changed for me, honestly, except to deepen the friendship—we have just put the 'friends' in 'friends with benefits'."

Athena's face creased in a grin that underscored her relief.

"Not that I think we're a thing now or anything like that, but half the office wants to think we've moved beyond 'gals being pals' anyway." Mandy gave a small laugh and a little one-shoulder shrug and smiled. "If I ever had pictured this conversation, in my wildest dreams, I would not have pictured you as the hesitant, emotional one and me as the composed one."

"I'm not emotional," Athena said. She grimaced. "Okay, some. I will concede that I might be a bit more, uhm ... passionate—"

"Heated."

"—about things," she mock glared at Mandy, "but I'm not emotional about this." She looked down at her tea and wrinkled her nose. "I need more caffeine," Mandy said. Together, they limped toward the cafeteria.

Athena wondered aloud. "So, do you think all Jumper to Jumper relationships are like this?"

"Who knows? I mean, it's not like we can ask Zeus and Hera."

"Oh geez. I wonder if it was like that for them every time?"

"God, I don't think I could handle that." Mandy said.

"Maybe they didn't. I mean, they didn't have children, right?"

"Loveless marriage?" Mandy asked.

"Maybe," Athena thought on it as they entered the cafeteria. "It does kinda makes sense. I mean, they started Limitless in the late Sixties?"

It wasn't too early in the morning for more complications.

"Mr. Powell," Mandy said as they passed a table.

"Valerie," Powell said. Ares stood beside him.

A flurry of feelings crossed through Athena, and she could see Mandy stiffen beside her. If she was receiving Athena's emotional tidal surge, surely Powell was too.

"Mr. Powell, I believe you said you would find a replacement," she said coldly.

"Oh, it's 'Mr. Powell' now?"

"Cut the crap, Bran. I cannot continue working with you. And as I can't trust your judgment, I don't think I can let you keep working with Limitless."

"First off, Athena, we are the customer by law, so unless you start hauling sweaty French asses around, I'm gonna be here whether you like it or not. I can't get a replacement read into your program in under a day—and I'm not replacing me here, I'm replacing you, as liaison." He rocked a thumb back at Ares. "This new newbie has a lot of potential."

"Thanks, man, I've got that from here," Ares told the kitchen staffer holding Mandy's breakfast tray. "Mandy," he said as he pulled out a chair for her, "would you care to join us for breakfast?"

Athena broke her stare with Powell to watch Ares set the tray down. She swallowed the irritation, telling herself that it was unreasonable to completely cut Powell out of her life so fast, especially when he was correct—Limitless couldn't cancel the CIA relationship, and the personnel couldn't be rejiggered overnight. She set her tray down across from where Ares settled Mandy and avoided both Mandy and Powell's eye.

It was difficult, because every time she marshaled her thoughts back to work topics, her subconscious would sneak in an image of Powell, dark eyes flashing as she hovered over him, or Mandy, hair strewn across her pillow. She could see Mandy's cheeks flush as she too felt Athena's emotions. It was dangerous to even think of such secrets in front of powerful intuits like Powell and Ares.

"Sorry," Athena whispered to her then turned her face back to Powell where they traded glares.

Ares looked up from his breakfast then with a sudden realization dawning on his face. He leaned back in his chair and scrubbed at his face with both hands.

"Okay, so wait. Let me get this straight. You," he pointed at Athena, "were sleeping with him?" He pointed at Powell. "But now you're sleeping with her?" He pointed at Mandy's stunned face. "And you," he pointed back at Powell, "somehow knew that without being told?"

He pushed back from the table, eyes wide. "And now I can do it, too? Jesus, Mary, and Chesty. People shooting coworkers. People screwing coworkers. People reading each others' minds. This is a professional organization? How does anything get done around here with this much fucking drama?"

There was a half second of stunned silence as everyone realized no one was fifteen years old and in a first serious relationship. All this could be worked out, and there was more important work to do. The feeling of *All this will be okay* rippled through all four.

Ares broke the trance.

"So—*aaannyyway*, Powell is here because he has some things we'd like to try out," Ares told the group, dragging them back to the here and now.

"Yeah?" Athena said, still unwilling to meet Powell's eyes.

"Yes. New insertion technique we're going to try with some actionable intel he has regarding the Montgomery bomber."

"New technique?" Athena dug into her breakfast but was clearly listening. "How's that work?"

"Yeah, it's a sort of—" Ares looked at Powell. "—skipping?"

"It's a way to move rapidly within a short distance. Keeps your movements unpredictable, but without the huge deficit created by long Jumps," Powell chimed in.

"And why is that useful?"

"Harder to hit a moving target?" Ares said with a shrug. "Plus, Colonel Gardner down at Hurlburt Operations has some interesting data on lower energy consumption for consecutive short hops to target vice one long one."

Athena's mind latched on to the word *target*. She sat up and dabbed her napkin at the corners of her mouth with care, trying to hide a smile. Ares was what Limitless needed, now and in the future, and he didn't even know it.

"You know that, as the Deputy Director of Limitless Logistics, a noncombatant company, I cannot condone the use of offensive tactical maneuvers," she said blandly.

"And you know that I'm a CIA field officer who has been with you on such missions, right? Or have you forgotten how many bad guys were killed on that CSAR rescue action in Syria?" Athena held up a hand to cut him off.

"I'm going to the Hill today," she stressed, "to discuss the somewhat limited Limitless budget."

"This is not an overtly tactical maneuver?" Ares offered.

She worked to keep from laughing out loud at his carefully phrased statement.

"I will be testifying today to members of the House Armed Services Committee and, if asked, I need to be able to tell them—" Athena looked Ares directly in the eye. "—that we have never engaged in direct combat offensives. As the deputy director, I stand with Marco in our primary logistical mission, regardless of any personal opinions I might have in where the future of Limitless Logistics may lie."

She quirked a red-gold eyebrow at him, expression otherwise neutral. Across the table, Powell leaned slightly forward and Mandy looked away.

Ares said with a wide grin, "If we happen to make, say, a whole lot of stops on the way to or from a place, I wouldn't be obliged to tell you about that, right? So long as I manage not to hurt myself?"

Athena brought her drink to her lips and sipped primly. "As long as you remain available for assigned missions, if/when, whatever you do with your personal training time is self-directed. We've never required travel logs for your Jumps," Athena said with feigned shock. "But Mr. Powell here might take along a couple extra Nutrium bags, just in case his new acolyte wears himself out with puppy-dog enthusiasm."

Powell gave her a nod. He and Ares stood and took everyone's food trays as they departed for who knew where.

Once the men were out of earshot, Val put her hand out to Mandy.

"You okay?"

Mandy gave Athena's hand a squeeze and sat back.

"That was ..." she paused, searching, "... not how I imagined my day would start."

"At least it's all out in the open, I guess."

Mandy nodded.

Athena scrutinized her face. "I can't feel you anymore."

"I know. I lost the link too when Murphy called us out. Maybe earlier."

"What happened?" Athena asked. She watched Mandy's face, trying to read her thoughts from the shift of her expression. Mandy frowned slightly then composed her features, aware she was being scanned.

"I'm not sure. But I think," she paused, searching her thoughts, "I think it's when you said you could kill Pete."

"I didn't say that."

"No, maybe you didn't—but you thought it. I think it cut when I realized not only what you were thinking but that you really, truly felt it." She looked at Athena with a new tightness at the corner of her eyes. "You have a problem, Athena. I'm not siding with Powell," she held up a hand to forestall Athena's comment, "but I felt it too. I felt the flashback start, the turmoil that radiates off you whenever your attempted rape memory comes up and you spiral down into anger and regret. It's out of your control. I hate to call it this because it perpetuates a stereotype, but I think you have PTSD. It's not combat driven, it's from the attack. But it affects you. Deeply."

Athena sat amazed as Mandy's words rushed past her. After the closeness they'd felt only a few hours ago, this felt like a betrayal.

"I'm fine. It's okay. Now that's he's dead I have it under control," Athena ground out. Even as the words passed her lips, she knew it wasn't true. The look on Mandy's face said that even if she wasn't reading Athena's emotions, they both knew she was lying.

"Fine then," Mandy said. "Keep having blow-ups. Keep driving people away. You can deal with it now when it's just starting to affect your personal and professional life, or you can wait until ..." She stopped and swallowed hard. "You can wait until you've destroyed everything in your life and are raving on the Jump Room floor."

Mandy stood abruptly, clumsily got her crutches under her and stalked out.

"Crap," Athena said to the empty table.

But now was not the time or place for navel gazing.

CHAPTER 18
VALERIE 'ATHENA' HALL
1329Z 0929L 09 AUG

Good morning, Marco," Athena called into his office a few minutes later as she limped into their shared waiting area.

"Good morning," he said with a happy face.

"You're in a good mood," she said.

"Mina is speaking to me again and and she may let me sleep in our bed again tonight. I am overjoyed to know I might not spend tonight on my couch," he said with a remorseful grin.

"I'm glad she's understanding."

"Eh, it may not be understanding but she knows me and knows I didn't do it out of malice. And when do you tell a secret that big? After a year of marriage? Two? Ten? Twenty? When do you just accept that it is a secret that will never come out or that it's too late to tell it now?"

Athena shrugged. "My—" she faltered. She swallowed the lump in her throat and continued. "My fiancé and I knew that there would be things we couldn't tell each other about our work. He understood because he knew the job. I guess when your spouse isn't on the inside, it's tough to really explain it to them."

"Sir, ma'am, it's time. Your cars are here," Anna told them briskly.

"Are you ready for another round?" Marco asked Athena as they made their way to the motor pool.

"As ready as I can be, I guess."

"Are you sure? You don't look it." He hesitated, a hand on the passenger side door. "Athena, dear, you look rattled. Anything you want to talk about?"

She bit her lip. She had a perfect opportunity to ask for time off, time to get counseling, anything to help ease her burden. Mandy's words echoed through her head and yet she couldn't make herself say the words.

"No, it's nothing."

Marco's laugh startled her and he held the car door for her as he laughed. Once she was seated, he held out his hand in a tacit request for hers. "Bonita, I have a wife and two daughters, three if you count Mandy, which I do. Maybe four if I start adding you to the mix. I know when women are hiding pain."

Athena gave him a tight smile, pleased that he would consider adding her to his rather loosely defined family. She dropped her head and held out a hand. When he clasped it within his warm hands she spoke.

"It's a whole lot of childish drama that concludes with Mandy, of all people, claiming I have PTSD," Athena finished in a rush. She dragged in a deep breath and met Marco's warm honey brown eyes.

Marco had absorbed her entire statement without batting an eyelash. "You do have PTSD," he said, voice calm and matter of fact.

Athena yanked her hand back and glared at him, her ever present temper flaring.

Marco held up a hand to forestall an outburst. "Don't give me that look. I can feel it when you said it. You know it. She knows it. You know damn well Powell knows it. Don't get mad at me, or anyone else for that matter, for pointing out what is extremely obvious and," he stressed, "extremely understandable."

"You were attacked. Recently. Then your entire life was flipped upside down. You haven't had time to process that or half of the other shit that's gone on here." He cupped her cheek. "After we finish out our work on the Montgomery bombing, you're going on leave. A long leave. I'm not out of here yet, I can run things in your absence. Go visit your father. I will get Anna to find you a therapist. You will work through this and come back stronger."

"We're going to be late," she told him.

"I know. They'll live." When she nodded, they each went around to the rear passenger doors of their Suburbans and mounted up. The drivers departed to the committee meeting, taking different routes.

In the congressional committee room, the usual political ping-pong went back and forth with spirit and not a little rancor. Limitless Logistics had its congressional detractors, but it also had its supporters.

Jacob Belton, the congressman from Colorado's Second Congressional District and committee chairman, tried to gavel the blather back to order with increasingly powerful strikes of the wooden mallet.

"Lady and gentlemen, if you please. The sole matter at hand is funding the Limitless Logistics budget for the next fiscal year, not—" he glared at Winston Holms and Jack Covington, "anything else. That is a separate discussion for another meeting. Now, if you please." He shuffled his papers. "The three options are decrease funding, approve last year's numbers, or increase funding. Around the room?"

"Decrease," Marleen Mitchell huffed.

"Increase," Jack Covington countered.

"Increase!" Winston Holms seconded.

"And I vote for approving last year's budget," Belton told them. "Marco, based on our votes, we will figure out a slight increase in your budget. Please have your line items finalized and sent to my office. The usual memos will do for your cover story."

Marco nodded sharply. "Thank you for your consideration, lady and gentlemen."

The committee dispersed instantly, some, no doubt, to go posture before television cameras and reporters in the passageway. Athena struggled to rise and had trouble pushing back the heavy wooden chair with her one good leg in the deep carpeting.

"Allow me," Jacob Belton's calm voice said from over her shoulder. She slid back and he offered his forearm for her to rise.

"Thank you, Mr. Belton," Athena said with a smile. "If I didn't know you were the senior representative from Colorado, I would have thought your manners perfectly Southern," she said, letting a hint of her Carolina drawl flow in.

"And from your delicate accent and perfect manners, I can tell your Southern mother raised you well," he returned her smile.

"Father, actually."

"Oh? My apologies."

Athena kept the smile plastered across her face. "No offense taken, Mr. Belton. My mother died when I was very young."

"Please, call me Jake. I was wondering, may I accompany you and Marco back to Limitless? Last meeting, you requested the transfer of a military working dog into Limitless' inventory, and I confess I'd like to meet this special canine," he said with a boyish grin.

Athena gave a bark of laughter and looked at Marco.

"Certainly," she said after catching Marco's nod. "Dog lover, are you?"

He offered his forearm again. "Yes. It's almost embarrassing," he said with a conspiratorial smile as they made their way to the black Chevy Suburban.

Marco insisted on Suburbans when meeting government officials instead of the frequent government-standard Cadillac Escalades, he said, "Because if we roll up in an Escalade, everybody thinks they're paying us too much money."

Belton helped Athena into the big SUV and follow her in, automatically snapping on his seat belt.

"No matter how many times I see military and police working dogs or how old I get, my reaction when I see them is still the same: It's all I can do to refrain from shouting 'Puppy!' and dashing over to scratch their chins."

They chatted amiably about childhood pets on the short drive back to Limitless, but it turned to work as soon as they were in Marco's office.

"I'm sorry for a bit of subterfuge. I do want to meet your canine, but I needed a moment of time and didn't need noses of the rest of the committee poking in."

Marco nodded as if expecting it.

"I needed you both to know that I support you even more than it comes off in the meetings."

"Do tell," Marco said. His face was a mask, but Athena sensed his growing anxiety.

"America should be setting the standard and primacy for international security. The poor and rich nations of the world alike look to us to help maintain peace and order against thugs and extremists. That is done by many levers of national power, of course, such as diplomatic, economic, and so on."

In her chair across next to Belton, Athena studied him as he spoke. Her recent dive into military education had illuminated some of the levers of power available to all nations. She followed Belton's words and watched his face as he spoke.

"While I believe in the function of diplomatic power, I would like to focus more on the military aspects of international relations." He gave a light laugh. "I'm on the committee that helps call some of these shots, after all. I have some sway over many aspects of the military, especially funding."

Athena took a deep breath and reached out to Belton, mentally grasping for the tendrils of connection. Belton was a blank slate.

As a "pure civilian," in Limitless terms, he should not have been unreadable.

"Look, there are bad groups of people in the world," Belton said, "I think we can all agree on that. Groups that, through religion or a lack of education, hate America and what she stands for. This nation has a glorious history and prosperous future, but those people seek to harm our proud American way of life, as we saw only weeks ago in Montgomery. That brought American security at home to the forefront in a way that hasn't been seen since the Islamic terrorist attacks of 9/11. I think Americans are realizing that they need a strong military presence to ensure they are secure both at home and abroad from those people. That will come from better funding, that will ensure the best-trained and best-equipped military personnel keep defending America. A strong military means a strong America. And a strong America can lead these backward, ill-educated, and poor nations to security and prosperity."

Athena couldn't feel Belton, probably because she only barely knew him, she thought, but she could just barely feel Marco as Belton spoke. She only saw the micro-expressions that flitted across his face, but he had bristled at Jacob's description of the attacks.

"We cannot allow American prestige to slip. Not when we're facing groups like those people. As a part of the American military," Jacob continued, "albeit a silent part, I feel you can benefit from this. Previously, I haven't taken a stronger stance on your funding as I have had some questions about the morality of your work, but the recent events have shown me that your abilities could be better utilized if we considered expanding your role and funding commensurate with an expansion."

"Those people?" Marco asked quietly.

"Islamic fundamentalists, obviously," Belton assured them.

"I'm sure there are more threats than just Daesh to worry about in the world."

"Certainly, there are plenty of those types of people out there. The kind that needs American leadership to pull them out of their hovels and capture hearts and minds."

Athena watched Marco closely, but his expression remained neutral despite a low simmering tension emanating from him.

"What exactly would our expanded role entail?" she asked when Marco didn't speak.

"I think a good first step would be to arm you for more than just self-protection and then consider expanding your mission profile from there. I mean, imagine your impact as an implementation of foreign policy anywhere on Earth, literally at a moment's notice."

Marco took in a deep breath. "We will certainly consider your thoughts, which have paralleled discussions we've had here from time to time." He rose and offered his hand. "Thank you, Mr. Belton. I'm pleased to see more of the Committee starting to back us."

Belton smiled and clasped Marco's forearm in the traditional Limitless handshake. Athena did likewise.

"Before I go, I understand you work with the CIA. Do they have any leads on the terrorist bombing?"

"Well—" Athena started, but Marco cut her off.

"Mr. Belton, you will understand that we don't speak for the CIA. I'm sure you can get the latest updates on that via your committee." He opened the door to his office, signaling the meeting was over. "Anna," Marco said to his admin, "please have our car take the congressman back to the Hill."

"Thank you, Mr. Martinez. You're probably right. Good meeting. We'll talk again soon."

Belton strode from Marco's office to be greeted by Anna, who escorted him to the Suburban idling in the Limitless Logistics circular driveway out front.

Athena watched Belton walk past Powell and Ares in Marco's lobby, and she wondered why they were clearly waiting for either her or Marco.

"That man is a racist," Marco whispered.

"Marco ..." Athena said.

"'Those people.' You can always tell." He shook his head. "I'll gladly take his money and influence, but watch him. Both will come at a price." Athena saw an intensity in Marco's face she'd never seen before. She nodded.

At her nod, Marco called to Powell and Ares. "What's up gents? You need me or Athena?"

Athena looked back to them and saw a look of horror on Ares' face and a look of shock on Powell's.

CHAPTER 19
MURPHY 'ARES' HAWKINS
0801Z 0401L, 09 AUG

A chirping text message woke Ares from a deep sleep. No daylight leaked into the room through closed mini blinds. Seriously contemplating homicide against the unfortunate soul who dared to text him at zero-dark-thirty, he rolled on to his back and groped blindly at his bedside table. Zora gave a quiet whine beside him. She didn't want to get up yet either.

Ares, need your help on a project. Are you available to discuss a former business associate and potential future venture this morning at 0800? — Mr. Black

The text came from an unfamiliar number with a DC area code. Ares smashed the power button with one callused thumb.

"Who the fuck is 'Mr. Black'?" he grunted and rolled back over. After a few months back on U.S. soil he had finally reset his circadian rhythm, but he was unready to face cryptic text messages at four in the morning.

Ares nearly levitated out of bed when his phone chirped again an hour later; still unused to being ordered around by dings, clicks, chirps, and bells. In the Corps, if someone ordered to you do something, they did it to your face, probably rousing you from your bed, sleeping bag, or patch of dirt by banging on a trashcan or its lid first. He snatched the phone up and had to exert the most extreme levels of self-control to keep from throwing the tiny device against the bedroom wall.

Murph, need an answer. —Powell the text read. It had come from a different phone number, which left Ares scratching his stubble in confusion. *Why didn't he say so in the first place?* He tapped a few buttons and listened to the phone ring.

"Powell," came a terse answer.

"The fuck you want?" Ares grunted out.

"Figured it was obvious from the first text. This isn't a clear line, by the way."

"Fuck you."

There was a long pause.

"So, I'll see you at eight?"

"Bring coffee and explanations."

"Fine. I thought you Marines were morning people."

"Again, fuck you." Ares hung up.

Ares flopped onto his side and squinted at his clock. At a few minutes past five, he didn't have enough time to fall asleep again before he needed to be up to meet Joe for PT. Groaning, he rolled over to Zora and she raised one paw and dropped it on his shoulder.

"Sometimes I hate humans, girl," he muttered. Zora's tail thumped against the bed. "Fine. Maybe I'm okay with female-type humans waking me up this early, but only," he paused dramatically, "if they have debauchery in mind."

When Zora declined to comment on his pronouncement Ares gave her one last quick squeeze and a scratch behind her flopping ear, then got up from the bed.

Almost three hours later, Zora safely left doggie daycare at Limitless, Powell found Ares hunched over a tray of food large enough to feed a family of four. Ares watched Powell glance quickly around the cafeteria before sitting down.

"Aren't you CIA guys supposed to be subtle?" Ares asked.

"What?" Powell's hand froze over his own plate.

"She's not in here if you're scared of getting run out."

"Oh. Yeah," Powell said. He slapped some butter on his toast and cleared his throat. "You know about that then?"

"You broke up, right?"

Powell gave a quick nod, not looking up from his breakfast.

"Figured. I mean, I did think she'd chuck you when she found out you—"

"Don't!" Powell's eyes snapped up to Ares' as he cut him off. "We both know, don't say it."

Ares nodded. "Fine." He consumed half his platter and two cups of coffee before speaking again while Powell slowly ate his own breakfast. "You going to explain your text messages this morning?"

Powell glanced around quickly before answering. "Yes. The first was a burner number. I use 'Mr. Black' on that one and in the field, if necessary. The second was from my personal number."

Ares raised an eyebrow in question, but remained hunched over his meal, forearms resting around his tray as if Powell might take it.

"Look, I'm not explaining either the CIA's or my own personal methods right now. I've got a mission but, uh, I think Val kind of handicapped me at Limitless when she kicked my ass to the curb."

"Can you blame her?" Ares shot back.

Powell glared at him. When Ares didn't flinch under the baleful stare, he sighed. "I guess not." Powell scrubbed his chin. "Look, I will respect Athena's wishes, but I can't get someone read into this program and trained overnight. That said, you are well placed and well equipped to serve as the new CIA liaison. Something's come up and I need the skill set you possess."

Ares made a circling get on with it gesture with his fork and then shoved another mouthful of eggs in.

"The asshole we dragged on Tuesday? He had good intel. Gave us a string of leads."

When Ares kept eating without commenting, Powell frowned. He was unused to anyone being better at silent interrogation than him. It wasn't even a sullen silence, they type Powell usually employed, it was a simple silence that said he could wait all day long to be told something. Powell suspected being an enlisted Marine had something to do with it. They often were a stony bunch.

"Fine. Long story short, we've mapped the cells and probably have the number two guy. I have actionable intel that should get us that number two who, if you can pull it, should have seen or met with the head of this whole shit pile." He took a deep breath and continued. "I need you to get hands on him and grab the leader's image. A clear image, not distorted by drugs, so I can put you with a sketch artist. Then we circulate the image and we'll find a way to snag him."

"And of course, you need me, because ..." He made air quotes and offered a cynical grin. "... I'm 'operator as fuck' and possibly the only member of the Pantheon still speaking to you?" The fingers of Ares' right hand tightened on his knife as it hovered over his plate. He didn't necessarily trust Powell, but he understood him.

"Yes, to all that, and I have that tactic we discussed briefly, but I'm fairly certain Marco would decline it."

"Too tactical?" was Ares' sour retort.

"Maybe," Powell said with a snort. "Probably."

The ghost of a smile tugged at the corner of Ares' mouth. "Enlighten me. For entertainment purposes."

"So," Powell said, leaning back in his chair, "your training explained how each Jump burns a bunch of calories? Something about weight times distance, whatever. But what if you only hopped a series of short distances? Sort of just skipping ahead, about as far as you can see? You'll still burn the calories for your body weight, but since the distance is so short it's almost negligible—and the burn isn't cumulative, somehow. You still burn calories, but Colonel Gardner has tested it and he thinks the burn is less intensive. I think it has potential."

Ares frowned. "How is that useful again?"

"Oh, c'mon. Now I know you're just testing me," Powell said, slightly exasperated. "Gunfights? Close quarters or urban movements? Inside buildings? Your movements would be fast and unpredictable. Athena did about the same thing when she captured General Borya. She ran from a forest to snatch him from behind, but that's when Mandy's father and the Russian Svoboda 'Pantheon' Jumped in to get him themselves. She snapshot Jumped the last twenty feet, wrapped him up, and instantly snapshot Jumped his butt back here to Limitless." Powell crossed his arms. "My tactic is the basically the same principle."

Ares grinned then sobered. "Yeah, and it didn't save her from being shot in the leg and almost dying because you thought she was covered in Mandy's blood instead of her own."

Powell's mouth pressed into a tight slit, but he didn't protest. What was true was true.

Ares shoveled a big bite of hash browns into his mouth, and mumbled as he chewed, "Why haven't they tried this before?"

Powell shrugged and gave him a rueful grin as he sensed Ares' willingness to try the plan.

"As you said, too tactical, and considered out of scope. The super-powered stevedores here really only plan for long haul, heavy Jumps, carrying the real warriors and their crap. All the Pantheon has been up to now is a fleet of high-strung military trucks. And like a jet fighter or any other high-strung military equipment, it needs frequent, specific, and extensive maintenance when used. That's what your logistic holds are for: to dope you back up with energy to get a mission back home."

Ares had only been in the Pantheon fold a short time, but he'd breezed through indoctrination and his initial and advanced training cycles. He and the training cadre had also gotten Zora acclimated to Jumping, which she took to very well. Ares' training Jumps had clued him in to the Jumper's need to replenish in the field. The weight and distance determined the caloric burn, and the caloric burn determined the volume of fluids and length of time to replenish. Any operators towed along with his dog didn't need restoration because they traveled at Ares' expense.

"All the tactics I've seen employed so far are for massive, one-shot caloric loss and logistic holds for recovery," Ares said. "Why plan for skipping in close quarters when you can extract a team all the way out to a safe location?" He thought a moment. "Skipping won't be a perfect solution to all scenarios. Plus, you will have to pay the piper at some point. No matter what, as far as I understand, there's still a sunk cost per Jump."

"You aren't getting it. If short, consecutive Jumps use less energy overall than one long Jump, that speaks for itself. But what I'm getting at has nothing to do with towing along operators—I propose you and your teammates be the operators."

"But tactical ..." Ares began.

"Yeah, I know—Pantheon is logistics, not fighters," Powell said. "I and folks much higher in my food chain have a great desire for that to change, and I know that's been discussed not only here but in Congress. Everyone in the Pantheon is military except Mandy, and it's unclear to me that she will ever join as an operator. Where that leaves her is unknown and frankly not my concern. The bottom line is we need a reliable strike force that can get in, do a job, and get the hell out. And they need to be trigger pullers."

He eyed Ares.

"So, you willing to try it?"

Ares gave him a wolfish grin. "Athena said my training time was my own when I'm off the duty roster." He scraped up the last buttery remnants of fried potato and slurped it from his spoon, pushing his empty plate away.

"Clean plate club."

He looked over at a long glass-top freezer a few feet away filled with Klondike Bars, Nutty Buddies, pints of Ben & Jerry's, and more.

"I get dessert."

They were still there making preliminary plans for Ares and Powell to do a field trip three hours later when the cafeteria began filling up for lunch. Ares, leaning back in his chair and slowly sipping the dregs of black coffee gone room temperature, saw Powell sit upright and turn slightly aside. As if that subterfuge would conceal him.

Ares saw Athena and Mandy limping into the cafeteria. They were so engrossed in their conversation that they missed Powell and Ares sitting only a few meters away.

"So, are all Jumper-to-Jumper relationships are like this?" He heard Athena wonder aloud.

"Who knows? I mean, it's not like we can ask Zeus and Hera," Mandy responded. Her perplexed voice carried across the small cafeteria.

"Oh, geez. I wonder if it was like that for them every time?"

"God, I don't think I could handle that," Mandy said earnestly.

Ares watched Powell's face as his eyes followed them through the chow line.

The tone of their conversation had Powell's full, jealous attention. A kitchen staffer followed the two toward the table carrying their food trays.

One awkward conversation, some nasty accusations, and a few discrete comments from Athena later, Ares and a dumbstruck Powell found themselves with tacit permission to do exactly what they had planned.

"So," Ares said as he dropped his breakfast tray with the cleaning crew. "Cleared hot?"

"I'd say so," Powell said. "One stop first."

Ares looked at him sideways.

"I want you to meet Kelly-Anne Wilson. She's a recent hire with some interesting capabilities."

"Oh? Pantheon?"

"No," Powell said with a grin, "much more grounded than that."

They walked the Limitless halls to Wilson's office and Ares mulled over their earlier conversation. Clearly, Athena was had given them tacit permission to try out a new tactic; even subtly encouraged it.

"Powell, level with me. What did she mean about 'before'?"

"What?" Powell seemed taken aback.

"When she and Mandy were discussing Zeus and Hera as they walked in, she said something about a feeling she'd had before. Did she mean you?"

Powell looked sidelong at him and gave a quick shake on his head. "I will be honest with you one day, but not here or now."

Ares stopped walking. "Yes here, yes now. You hide more than I'm comfortable with and I'm sticking to Murph's Rule Number One: Don't risk your life with or for someone you don't trust. You don't tell me, and I don't take another mission with you."

Powell turned to face Ares. "You cut me off and neither I nor the CIA have an in here for a while. You value your own petty interests so highly that you would cut me off in the middle of a terrorist manhunt?"

Ares ground his teeth. "No, but neither do you." He narrowed his eyes at Powell and took a gamble, calling his bluff. "So, talk."

Powell's mouth tightened and his stare drilled into Ares, who crossed his arms and stood feet slightly more than shoulder width apart, his weight shifted slightly to his toes. Inside he was seething. Powell recognized the stance and took an involuntary half step back, hands up.

"Fine." He strode forward, yanking open the first hallway door they came to. They stood in the tiny janitorial closet, trying not to elbow each other. "You are going to be the second person I've told this to, which means if I hear it come back to me, I know who I'm going to first."

"Bring it on," Ares ground out, done with Powell's CIA intrigue bullshit.

"You're a Jumper, right? But it's not just the telekinesis. You can also, at a touch, read a very top level of thought. Pull an image, read an emotion, or get a flash of their steam of consciousness. You're stereo and I'm mono, but Hi-Fi mono."

"Huh?"

"I can read the emotions. And like you, I can sometimes do it without touch. I can't do images, which is why I need you. But yeah, I can pull the emotions without touch."

"Oh," Ares breathed as he took that in. "Everyone? Not just us?"

"Everyone. The stronger the emotional connection or the physical touch, the stronger I can pick up the emotions."

"So, Athena?"

"Everything. I can feel everything," he said quietly. "I can, uh, I can transmit emotion too. Make the person feel what I'm transmitting is their own emotion."

Ares tilted his head, considering Powell's words. "You prick! The other day, when you asked if I was irritated, you calmed me down? That's a bullshit move, Powell."

"I know. I'm sorry, but I needed you on top of your game."

"That's messing with me on a whole other level," Ares growled. He took in a deep breath, trying to calm himself down. "Show me."

"What?"

"Show me how you do it. Calm me down."

A cool, calm swept over him almost instantly. Ares blinked hard. It was like the rising tide of anger had simply ebbed away. He let out a breath. "Holy shit."

"Yeah, but noticeable once you know I can do it. Athena knows, so I can't use it on her."

"That can be a major violation of trust, too."

"Yes."

There was a moment of quiet while Ares processed things. "Athena's PTSD, you got that in full force," he whispered. It wasn't a question.

"Yes. No. It isn't PTSD. Don't call it that," Powell said in a rush.

"Why not? That's what it is. Occasional spikes of uncontrollable rage? Flashbacks to the attack where she's there, not the present? Let me guess—you've seen it, the whole attack?"

"Seen it? No. Remember, I'm mono," he pointed to his chest, "not stereo. But I felt it, which might be worse. Can you even imagine, feeling everything your girlfriend felt as she was about to be raped?"

"I'm not condoning murder, but ..." he trailed off. Powell nodded. "Look, I think I get it now. I get what you do and why you're so fucking good at this CIA thing. Just don't use that whammy on me without my permission and we'll be okay."

Powell nodded again. "Deal. Can we go on?"

"What was Athena talking about?"

"Oh, uh ..." Powell stammered.

"Holy shit, are you blushing? You fucking girl!"

"Okay, picture this: You and your lady of choice—"

"Which right now might be Mandy," Ares said with a wolf's grin.

"Well, TMI, but fine, whatever. Actually, very applicable." Powell scratched his chin. "It explains why they were talking about Zeus and Hera, too. So, you and Mandy, should you be so lucky, can both sense each other's emotions with a touch. You touch her, she's just burning up for you as you are for her. It rebounds between you. And rather than die as an echo, it builds. And every time it echoes, it builds more." He smiled.

"Oh," Ares said. "Oh, damn ..."

"Which, if my personal emotion detector is right, means that firstly, that's what Zeus and Hera felt, and second, Athena and Mandy ran into the phenomenon. Very recently."

"Oh, man! I would have loved to have been a fly on the wall that night."

Powell glared at him for half a second then smiled. "Yeah, okay, me too. But Athena and I had to figure it out a bit to keep from overwhelming each other. I imagine they ran into that as well."

"Well, ain't that some shit? I didn't know either of them was bisexual."

"Yeah, me neither. Given the undercurrents of their conversation, I'm not sure either of them knew it, either."

"Wow. This fucking place gets wilder and wilder."

"Only in the last few months," Powell said with a smile. "Before Athena arrived, things were quiet. Jump, move people, rest. Jump again."

"Okay, I think we should step out of this closet and go find your contact."

"And here I thought Athena and Mandy were the only ones coming out of a closet today," Powell said with an uncharacteristic smirk.

Ares' laugh echoed down the hall as they went in search of Powell's contact.

CHAPTER 20
MURPHY 'ARES' HAWKINS
1337Z 0937L, 09 AUG

Ares and Powell found Kelly-Anne Wilson in a plush office that could have rivaled anything in Silicon Valley. A plum-colored bean bag chair slouched in one corner and a colorful formed plastic chair in the other. Huge windows spilled light over a striking dark-haired woman in a form-fitting dark blue shift.

Ares scanned her tight, well-muscled form. She had a healthy all-American, girl-next-door look that radiated strength and self-assurance. She sat at a glass and steel desk, chin in hand, staring intently at her top-of-the-line computer.

"Kelly-Anne Wilson?" Powell asked.

"Yes," she said, narrowed eyes still focused on her computer.

"I'm Brandon Powell. Murphy Hawkins and I had a couple questions we wanted to ask you."

Kelly straightened immediately at the mention of Hawkins' name and stood, her office chair rolling back on wheels.

"General Hawkins—Ares, yes! Oh, please come in, sorry! I got so—" She paused when she saw them. "You're taller than I thought you'd be." She winced. "Sorry, sir. I have no filter."

She brushed down her dress to smooth invisible wrinkles and Hawkins was entranced. The woman was five-ten if she was an inch and ripped. Her arms, displayed by the sleeveless dress, displayed strong muscle development.

"Okay, much as I enjoy the whole general-officer charade, I'm just Ares, or Murph, okay?" He offered his hand and the light touch telegraphed that she'd be happy to show him her abs and glutes too if he asked. As a non-Pantheon person, she received nothing but Ares' warm hand.

"Major Kelly-Anne Wilson, U.S. Air Force, sir—uhm, Murph." Her grin widened. "Kelly, if you like."

Ares fought to keep his own grin from deepening. Her answering smirk suggested she knew exactly what she was doing.

He gestured at her, up and down. "Pantheon?" he asked, though he knew she wasn't. He just wanted to hear her response. The only people he'd met with physiques like hers were his over-hyped Pantheon teammates, lean from their Jumps, their custom nutrition, and their training.

"What? Oh, no. Not me." She smiled. "I do it the old-fashioned way: lifting weights, plenty of cardio, and eating right."

Her smile was warm and inviting.

"Major Wilson is our newest civ-mil liaison, but she's got a few hobbies I think we could be interested in," Powell said.

"Admin POG?" Ares asked her. Intrigued that a woman who so clearly lived an active life would be stuck in an office.

She winced. "Yes, sir. These days."

"Murph."

"Thanks, Murph." She blushed saying the words. She flicked her long brown hair back over her shoulder. "Athena found me a few years back writing air campaigns on a shithole base in the sandbox. Don't let these rippling muscles fool you, I'm a head-shed strategist, so I am the queen of the staff weenies." She gave him another disarming smile.

"Powell here mentioned you have some interesting hobbies?" he prompted.

"Well, interesting to me, anyway. Obviously, weightlifting. I also do some rock climbing, skydiving, and cave diving when I can get a chance. Athena only pulled me over here a month ago, so I'm trying to get my feet under me here before I get some leave time to head back out again."

Ares looked at Powell. Now that he had a greater understanding of how the man's mind worked, he had an idea where this was going.

"Kelly, the cave diving, what's that like?" Ares asked her. He caught Powell's subtle nod.

She gestured to the two chairs.

"Would you care to sit? I can't guarantee they're comfortable, they came with the room." Once they were seated, Ares slouched in the bean bag chair and Powell perched on the plastic chair, she continued. "Imagine you are in a pitch-black cave and a flashlight is your only source of light. It's silent except for the rush of the frigid current going past. Your gear fails, you die. You run out of air, you die. You get lost, you die."

"That sounds ... interesting and intense. Why would anyone want to do that?" Ares asked.

She looked to a picture on her wall. It showed a diver, festooned with gear, surrounded by rock formations, and back lit by beautiful blue light streaming in from an opening above.

"Some caves have ancient stalactites and stalagmites formed in the thousands of years when they were in open air, before rising aquifers submerged them. They make the whole room look like an underwater cathedral."

"That's you?" Powell asked and pointed at a photo on her wall.

She smiled and nodded. "Mexico in 2001. Not long before I joined the Air Force."

"I take it Big Air Force isn't a big fan of the risks involved?"

"Nope—they sure aren't, but as long as I fill out the appropriate paperwork and remind my bosses that I have, like, eleven certifications, they let me go."

"Who snapped the picture, your boyfriend?" Ares winced in his head, afraid he was being too transparent.

"Then. It's ancient history for a long time now."

Relieved that Wilson hadn't seemed to catch his underlying interest, Ares steered her back to the thread of conversation Powell had started. "Mexico seems pretty remote for a dive."

"Yeah, you aren't kidding! You fly into Cancun, then you have drive to Tulum in whatever rickety rental you can get. Don't even get me started on the 'roads.' Oh, and keep a few hundred pesos squirreled away, because if the *federales* see you driving they'll find a reason to pull you over for a shakedown."

"And the dives?"

She gave an indelicate snort. "Cake walk. Really. Compared to north central Florida, it's benign. The caves are shallow, so you don't worry about a ton of decompression, and they go on forever. And there are always dive groups to join for company."

Ares glanced at Powell who nodded again. "What's the deepest you've been back in those caves?"

"Oh, we got a good way back on scooters one year. I mean, you can only really reach that spot on a scooter or by rappelling in. But if you fast-roped in, you'd have a hell of a time hauling out yourself and maybe sixty pounds of gear."

"Can you show me?" Ares asked.

"Show you?" She looked confused for a moment. "Oh—yes, of course. Athena told me about the image transfer thing. Yeah, it's beautiful." She rose again and held out a hand. With a wicked grin, she grasped Ares' hand.

Ares caught the image of the cave, with dark stalactites clinging to the ceiling, the room illuminated by a single beam of sunlight from a shaft many feet overhead. He caught an image of her wrist computer showing she was only thirty-some feet underwater, but there was the slightest hint of anxiety. This was the farthest in she'd ever been, and she was nervous that if her scooter died on the way back, she wouldn't have enough air to make it out without being towed by another diver in the party. Even then, survival wasn't assured.

He breathed in, impressed by her courage and skill. He smiled at Kelly, who smiled back.

A second image crossed their touch and his grin broadened. The image must have been Kelly that morning, striding nude past her full-length mirror, presumably just out of the shower, her tall, well-formed body on full display. Ares caught her eye and saw a hinted smile, but a gleam in her eye.

"Thank you, Kelly, that was useful," he said. To his right, Powell coughed in a way that sounded suspiciously like a laugh.

Powell said, "Yes, thanks, Kelly. We might drop by again to talk to you about skydiving later."

"Great! See you around campus, I hope," she said, her terrific smile back in place.

As soon as they were back in the hallway and the door was closed, Powell turned to Ares. "I feel like she flashed you more than that cave image, didn't she?"

Ares smiled knowingly but said nothing. "An officer and a gentleman never tells."

Powell looked at him and laughed out loud.

"*Since when?*"

Joe wasn't waiting for them in the Jump Room but had obviously received Ares' hastily written text. An olive-green ripstop go-bag lay against the wall waiting for them when they entered the space. Ares checked the contents and he and Powell walked into the concentric circles of Point Zero.

"Where to first?"

Powell considered it then replied. "Take the image from my head. We can talk and work on skipping there." He held out a hand. "This is a Hollywood Jump. No weapons required."

Ares tapped Powell's hand and pulled an image with a swirl of emotions: anger, pain, loss, and fear. He focused on the image, a flat, bland, dun-colored landscape broken only by a narrow dirt road. He made a face. "Where the fuck is that?"

"Just outside of Parshall, North Dakota. It's about as close to nowhere as you can possibly get. It's also flat as can be, so you'll be able to see for miles in all directions."

"Copy. Okay, here we go. Going in three ... two ... *one*."

Their feet crunched on the rocky dirt road as they arrived and Ares took in the arid landscape. They stood at a T-intersection of two roads, each one stretching to the distant horizon. The dull brown grasslands stretched for miles around with only the slightest sloping of a hill along one road to break the tedious monotony. Hawkins' ears registered the almost staticky sound of scrub grass brushing against itself as it waved in the breeze.

"Welcome to the Fort Berthold Indian Reservation. One of many unremarkable places to which we shoved the original owners of this grand land."

Ares looked around. "Yeah, scenic. We're clearly not going to be overheard here."

Powell took the subtle hint.

"Yes. I want you to start building a library of places to hide a body."

"Moving from directing hits to conducting them yourself, Brandon?" Ares asked.

"Not to put too fine a point on it, but yes. Think about it this way. If we catch the man behind this bombing, he'll go to trial and probably end up on death row. It takes years—decades—to get through the legal hurdles and appeals before Alabama gives him the needle or the chair. So, maybe we let the trail finish there, you know? Maybe he 'breaks out,' disappears, or otherwise drops from view—possibly in a cave in Mexico that, at most, two hundred people in the world have the skill and gumption to reach."

Ares held up a hand. "Yeah, I don't know what rules the CIA operates on, but you are asking me to violate so many parts of the Constitution that I can't even begin to pick it all apart."

Even though the air was crisp with early spring chill, Ares could feel himself flush hot with anger.

"Christ, you're stupid. I thought you were a clearer thinker. If two hundred people in the world have the skill and gumption to reach that cave, a percentage of those one day will. I promise you if they find that guy's body down there, the list of potential suspects will be small but distinguished."

"You would let this guy live?" Powell was incredulous.

"Hey, dipshit, I swore to support and defend the Constitution, not tear it to shreds and wipe my ass with the remains because it suited me." Ares took a step toward Powell, shaking finger under the man's nose. "Don't, for one second, think that my willingness to do violence on behalf of my nation makes me ready for murder. I think I crossed a line the other day helping you beat that asshole to a pulp to cover our tracks. I'm not doing it again."

"Fine," Powell said, but held his ground.

Ares took a half step back and lowered his hand.

"It gets easier after the first time, doesn't it? That Parker asshole, who attacked Athena. Was he your first?" Hawkins pinned Powell with a hard, unblinking stare. "Oh, I understand. I had to kill my first once, and it freaked me some. But after the first few, they weren't people anymore. Just targets, no different that the pop-ups on the three-hundred-meter line at the range. You popped your cherry with Parker, and now it's easier to be that avenging angel."

Powell stood rigid and angry. He was no longer sure Hawkins was going to work out as his inside man.

"Yeah, righteousness can be a motherfucker. You have a moral ambiguity I'm not sure I'm comfortable with." Ares said.

"Yes, I do. The CIA calls it a job description. Anyone who can't see past it would never last. Just as you wouldn't last in this job." Powell took in a deep breath of the clean Dakota air. "We're each suited for the jobs we do best, I guess. I'm sorry to push you. I won't ask again for you to do what you can't do with a clear conscience."

"Thank you."

The steady Dakota wind rustled the grasses around them as both men thought.

"Do you want to try the skipping technique?" Powell asked.

"Yes."

"Good. First, I want you to just try taking in the area, say, fifty feet down the road, and Jump there."

"Fifty feet? That's all?"

Powell shrugged. "I figure in an open space like this, you can see where you're going, even if the perspective will be slightly different. It's the same as if you pulled the image from someone's mind."

Ares' mouth tightened. He closed his eyes and concentrated on a spot about fifty feet down the road. When he finally decided, he felt the slight pull that indicated a Jump and realized he'd departed without conscious thought. He whirled around to see Powell far behind him.

"Well, I guess that answers that," he called back to Powell. He concentrated slightly and Jumped back.

"How did it feel?" Powell asked.

"I just sort of ... went. It wasn't a conscious action, which seems weird."

"But how do you feel? Tired? Hungry? The usual exhaustion?"

"I'm not sure if I'm experienced enough to know what the usual exhaustion entails but I don't feel tired or hungry at all." Ares glanced down the road, thinking. "They told me I couldn't go anywhere I hadn't seen before and that's why we have to get personal images from people who had been where we go. Clearly, I've never been here before," he gestured to the gently waving brown grass, "nor have I been to that point fifty feet away—but I can see it from here. That's how was I able to Jump there. Yeah, it's not a huge difference but the visual was slightly different."

Powell looked pensive for a moment. "I'm not sure it's as cut and dried as not being able to go somewhere you haven't seen or been to before. You guys practice precision Jumping, right?"

"Yeah, I did that with Dee."

"So, if you could only go to a very exact spot in a mental image, why practice precision Jumping? I mean, if you can only go to that exact spot, then precision would be unnecessary, right?"

Ares gave a shrug, considering Powell's point. "So, maybe I'm traveling to where my mind thinks that spot is, especially if I've only pulled the image and not been there before?"

"Yes. I think your brain fills in the unknowns. It does that in other ways too. If I showed you a picture of a girl in a pretty dress standing by a painted door, your mind would start filling in context, even if you didn't have any. I think you're hardwired to fill in enough details to make the Jump on minimal information."

Ares considered that for a moment. "How much is enough information? What happens if I don't actually have enough?"

"I think you either know enough and you go, or you don't, and you don't. Athena once said she thought that was some fail-safe Limitless hasn't figured out yet. The skill set itself tries to keep you from hurting yourself while using it."

"Seems risky," Ares hedged.

"Probably. But if we could get useful information out of it, we could change how Limitless operates and broaden its portfolio."

"Fair enough." Ares scanned the horizon. The rustle of grass in a mild but constant wind surrounded them. "I'm going to try skipping up to that small ridge. What do you think that is, a mile, maybe less? Maybe that will help show how many blanks need to be filled in to do this."

Powell shrugged a shoulder. "Sure. We've got all afternoon to see what we can learn."

Ares studied the small dirt road that led up the hill. As before, the first time he decided he Jumped fifty feet ahead. He scanned ahead again, then had a thought. He Jumped back to Powell. "Hey, what happens if I Jump while running?"

Powell paled a little at the question.

"Powell?" Ares asked, concerned.

"I haven't seen the Jumper moving at a run, but I saw Athena Jump her team as the team ran up to her. As soon as she made physical contact, she snapshot Jumped." He paused. "The two men they were carrying ... they sort of threw at her, to make sure she had contact. She started falling back as she Jumped and kept falling on the other side." He scratched at his neck. "That was her first major Jump with the pararescue team," he said quietly. "Then, she was flying through the air at General Borya that time and snapshotted back on contact."

"Oh," Ares said. "Uh, yeah. They told me about it. She hauled them all after a bunch of training Jumps. I heard not everyone made it, right?"

"Yeah. It was impressive work, and she made a hell of a choice. Might have killed herself getting the team out," he whispered.

Ares put his hand out and stopped, not sure how Powell would take it. He looked at Powell, who's head hung as he thought about Athena, and put a hand on his shoulder. "I'm sorry man."

"I will literally never find another woman like her."

Ares bit his lip, not sure what to say. "Your relationship may not be dead. She might just need time to accept things."

"I fucked up pretty bad."

"True," Ares said. Powell's head snapped up. "But I've seen pretty bad fuck-ups and they still worked it out."

"Oh, yeah? Any 'Had her would-be rapist murdered because of her rage issues' kind of fuck-up?" he asked dryly.

"Well, no. You've got me there. But she's smart. Fuck. She's the most hyper-rational person I've ever met. There's a chance she'll logic her way through it."

Powell's face lightened ever so slightly. "You may not be wrong."

Ares smiled. "Okay, if we're done with our little bro-ment, shall we get back to the tactical shit?"

"Yeah, yeah, yeah. Go Jump over the moon, you cow,"

Powell said. He pulled two handset radios from the go-bag and handed one to Ares.

"Here. These both have locator chips in them in case you skip out of range. I need to reach you when you're out there." He waved his hands around. "Get a good fix on this location for your return."

Ares put a hand to his heart. "Aww, Powell, you almost sound like a Marine. I knew I'd find something about you I liked eventually." He clipped the handset to his gear belt.

Powell swatted at him and he Jumped down the road. Ares took a moment to dwell on Powell's words. He was almost right. There was one other woman like Athena, but if Ares had his way, she wouldn't be available to Powell. He shook his head sharply, wondering how that thought had slipped in. He tried to squash down the image of Mandy's bashful smile and blonde hair.

Ares started a light, easy jog as he concentrated on the hill in front of him. He decided, Jumped, stumbled, and fell flat on his face. Even sixteen hundred meters away he could still hear Powell's horse laugh clear as day.

"Pretty smooth, ace!" Powell voice crackled from the radio. Ares dusted himself off, shot Powell the bird, and started jogging again. He concentrated, decided, Jumped and stumbled again, but kept his feet under him and moving. Ares repeated the process until he was just below a meager ridge, maybe six miles away from Powell.

"A-OK there, mister?" Powell radioed.

"Good to go," Ares radioed back. "Getting the lay of the land and will keep going a bit more."

"Copy, that's good to go." He was following Ares' progress on a tablet displaying a digital military map. The location was indicated by a red dot that moved around when Ares did.

Now came the tricky part. He assumed the other side of the ridge would look almost identical to this side, with windblown brown grass, slight gravel surface, dull blue sky. He worried that even a minor difference would alter his Jump. Not knowing what would happen if he Jumped to a place he envisioned but that wasn't confirmed, he hesitated as he jogged.

Ares frowned. If he envisioned high, he would drop hard to the ground. In that case, he hoped it wasn't far. If he envisioned low, he might find himself a hundred feet underground and instantly crushed. Then he took a deep breath, pictured the other side of the ridge, and Jumped.

He let out a whoop of laughter when his feet landed firmly on the other side of the ridge, still moving at a light jog. He stopped running, pictured his spot by Powell and Jumped back.

"I can move where I can't see—and I can do it at a run."

"Sweet. That's what I was hoping for!" Powell said. "Try some more Jumps in a run."

"Fire-fight skipping?"

Powell nodded. "Stopping to Jump seems like it would have fairly negative consequences then."

"Okay, but let's not tell Athena." He gave Powell a smile and took off, eager to practice their new technique.

An hour and numerous short Jumps later, Ares was downing his second foil pack of nutrients as Powell watched the dry brown hills.

"You think this technique will work at combat speed?" Ares asked around a mouthful of food.

"I think it'll have its uses," Powell said.

"You have more in mind than dodging bullets, don't you?"

Powell nodded.

"Can we at least start with paintballs when we try to dodge bullets?"

Powell nodded silently, but the corner of his mouth twisted up.

Ares debated asking the follow-on question, but let it go.

"So, you mentioned a bag and grab?"

"Yeah. Although, we might be able to do it more subtly if you're uncomfortable with kidnapping."

Ares shuffled uncomfortably from his seat in the grass. He felt like Powell was taking subtle digs at his principles, but Ares didn't back down. He did what he always did in a fight—dig in and push back until he succeeded.

"Actually, I'd like to see this subtle other method," he told Powell. "What do you have in mind?"

Powell briefly described his secondary plan. When he was done, Ares held out his hand for Powell to tap and they Jumped.

Minutes later, he and Powell were snagging stools at the bar of a

Tex-Mex joint in a tiny town in North Carolina, thousands of miles from the dry, brown Dakota hills. Ares waved at the bartender, ordered them two shots of tequila, and placed a drink in front of Powell.

"Cheers," he said.

"You can't just shoot tequila. You need salt and a lime," Powell said irritably. He snagged the bartender's attention and requested the correct tequila accessories. "Philistine," he muttered under his breath.

"Marine," Ares corrected.

"Same-same," Powell said.

Each man licked his well-salted hand, downed the shot, and bit into the lime. This went on for several cycles.

"Yes!" Ares exclaimed in approval after the last one, his tongue extended as he grimaced. "That never gets old."

"All that and not a single patron looked at us," Powell whispered from behind his shot glass.

"Yeah, we aren't the first tequila drinkers this place has ever seen. And no one matches the image of your suspect, either," Ares whispered back, pushing his shot glass forward with an index finger. "Let's go grab some chow."

They marched back down a narrow stairwell into the main restaurant, a garish neon sign proclaiming it the "Armadillo Grill." The dive's orange and green décor should have made patrons cringe, but the modern design of the tables and signs balanced it, giving the room a far trendier look than they expected from a bar in a tiny Carolina town.

The two men settled down with burritos at a table covered with ceramic tiles. The table fell into silence broken only by the occasional happy groan.

"That's a fucking fantastic burrito," Ares said around a mouthful of food.

"Queso's good too," Powell said and looked down. "Target just entered the front door," he muttered.

Ares risked a quick glance. “Want another burrito?”

“Yeah, I think I actually do.”

“Cool,” Ares said and walked to the line. The restaurant had a long, chest-high counter with ordering pads under posted menus. He walked casually up to the counter and snagged a pad and stared at the menu a few moments before turning to his mark, now standing in line behind him.

Ares turned back to the man, acting tipsier than he was. “Hey man,” he said, slurring and making an exaggerated point to a menu item. “I just had a burrito that will knock your socks off.”

“Yeah, grub’s good here. You should try the queso.”

“I got a bowl of it still at the table. Any other suggestions?” Ares asked and glanced at the television mounted over the cashier.

“Uh, try the quesadillas if you’re still hungry after a burrito and queso,” the man answered.

“Cool, thanks. I’m Murph, by the way.” He held out his hand but glanced at the television again as it played some news update of the Montgomery bombing manhunt.

“Trey,” the other man said, following Ares’ gaze, but grasping his hand.

Ares tried to cover his sharp intake of breath he had as he grasped the man’s hand. He gave a tight smile. “You know, I think I might be full after all. Thanks though, I ‘preciate your help.”

As soon as he turned away, his smile dropped. He all but fell into his chair.

“Decided against another burrito?” Powell asked mildly.

“Not sure I could eat right now.”

“Should we head out?” Powell said briskly.

Ares shook his head. “Come outside.” They exited through the restaurant’s side door to the parking lot before he could speak again.

“He’s ... he’s just *sick*, man. The inside of that man’s head is nothing but dark rot.”

“Did you get the image we need?”

“No, it was too fuzzy. All I got was his hatred. The sick and twisted shit he wants to do to some people. I couldn't touch him long enough to get the image. I need another look in his head, as sick as that makes me feel."

"I think we can get that covered," Powell told him.

Ares stared at him hard. "We're not killing anyone here, Powell."

"You're right, we're not. But you need to get a deeper look and I might have an issue or two to work out. After one peek in his head, can you honestly tell me you don't want to pound in his face? Just a little bit?"

"I do," Ares told him. "That's what scares me. I can't lower myself to that level."

"Yeah, but I can. You just need to get the image."

Ares grunted, but didn't counter Powell's assessment.

"Most patrons go in the front door but come out the back. We can wait here. I'll grab, do my thing, then you do yours."

They waited by the side door on a patio facing a narrow street. Across from them, a handful of cars sat in a gravel lot. Ares fidgeted, wondering if associating with Powell was going to have a damaging effect on his morals. Before he could reach any conclusions, the side door opened, and their quarry stepped out.

Powell's hands were a blur of motion, grabbing the man and spinning him hard into the building's brick wall. The man's breath went out in a whoosh and he gave a choked gasp.

"Okay, shit stain. Tell us about your leader," Powell growled. He nodded to Ares.

Swallowing his revulsion, Ares grabbed the subject's hand. Images swam through the man's mind, unfocused and laced with pain. Ares shook his head.

Powell pulled the man into him then slammed him into the wall again. "Tell me about your leader or I'm going to crack your fucking skull open and leave you for the rats to eat your brains." Powell shook him again. "Everything you fear in life? That's what's about to happen."

A horrific cascade of images flowed to Ares. "Stop, man. It's fucking with his head. I can't get through the pain and bigotry."

At the word 'bigotry,' a single image solidified. Ares could see one man clearly among a crowd, speaking to them in a designer suit.

"Damn, Dunphy. He is a politician or something, and it's not just the hair," Ares growled. The images clarified and shifted at his words. He pulled more, building the face in his mind. It wasn't anyone he was familiar with. "What's his name?"

The man struggled against Powell and didn't answer. He managed to get one shoulder off the brick wall and twisted in Powell's grip. Ares shot one foot out, neatly hooking the subject's ankle and pushing him over his thigh. The man landed flat on his back.

"*What is the name?*"

The man made a shocked gasp again, the wind clearly knocked out of him.

"Hey now, what's goin' on here?" A man had exited the restaurant to see the interrogation and edged hesitantly back away from where Powell and Ares loomed over their captive.

"Shit—get behind the building," Ares told Powell. They ran left the man sprawled on the concrete and bolted.

"You get it?" Powell panted as he checked for pursuit.

"Yeah, same as the guy from three days ago, only clearer. No haze of drugs. I got a couple vignettes of him giving orders, explaining plans, that kind of stuff. His face, the 'politician hair' Dunphy talked about. Even down to the gray at his temples. I got the time and location of their next meeting. The rest ..." his voice trailed off and the only sound was their feet crunching on the restaurant's gravel parking lot.

"That bad?" Powell asked quietly.

"This guy was a gold mine of imagery. He's also some sick ideas of what he would do to certain politicians if it was legal." Ares shook his head. "And I feel sorry for his last few girlfriends."

Powell nodded. "Okay, let's head back. Athena's probably back from her meeting on the Hill. We can tell her about your new buddy and figure out what kind of effort she and Marco will allow us to mount to grab this guy."

They lightly tapped hands and Ares Jumped them back to Limitless. The drab black and red concentric circles of Point Zero and the Jump Room's beige walls were a sharp contrast to the riot of color in the Tex-Mex joint.

"Before we run this past our leadership, what are your thoughts for grabbing this guy?" Ares asked as they headed to Limitless Logistics front office.

"Depends on the location, but mass grab. We can try something like the Russia grab, purpose build rooms with no exits," he said. They paused at the secretary's desk. "Anna, is he in?"

"He came back with General Hall and a congressman after their meeting on the Hill. They're all still in there. Have a seat, I don't think they'll be much longer."

Ares flopped down into the sturdy leather chair as Powell eased into the chair beside him.

"I need another shot or twelve of tequila," Ares muttered and suppressed a belch laced with alcohol and Mexican food.

Powell nodded. "That help you calm down?"

Ares looked at him with an eyebrow raised. "The burp or the tequila? And if it's the tequila?"

"Not judging. Booze isn't the only way to calm down though."

"Geez, don't say it like that. You make us sound like a couple or something."

Ares laughed then too, his shoulders dropping as he relaxed a degree. Then Marco's heavy wooden office door opened and Ares sat bolt upright. Marco was ushering out a tall man with blonde hair, lightly sprinkled with nearly invisible gray at the temples. Athena limped behind.

"Thank you for your time, Congressman Belton. We'll consider your proposal." Marco told the man.

"Hey, your emotions just did a one-eighty on me. What the hell?" Powell whispered.

"That's him," Ares whispered fiercely. "*That's the ringleader.*"

CHAPTER 21
MURPHY 'ARES' HAWKINS
1550Z 1150L, 09 AUG

"*Saywhatnow?*" Powell's own whisper came out in a rush.

Ares' eyes followed Congressman Jacob Belton, then he looked at Powell. A cold chill washed over him.

"Stay here," he told Powell. Ares pushed out of his chair and caught up with the Congressman. "Sir?" he called.

Congressman Belton turned toward the voice and stuck out his hand, his automatic political response.

"I, uh ..." Ares' brain churned faster than it had in his entire life, trying to think several moves ahead. "... I'm Staff Sergeant Murphy Hawkins, sir. I heard you're the one who got my dog transferred here? Thank you for that."

"Oh ..." Belton seemed to hesitate before clasping hands with him. "Why yes, you are welcome, son. You're the one they call Ares, I believe. The nation appreciates you as well as your dog for your service."

Ares kept his face blank and made his eyes flick to the small TV next to Anna's desk, "Shame about Montgomery, huh? That's your district, right?"

Belton's face and handshake froze a fraction of a second before he replied. "No, my district is in Colorado. But yes, it's certainly a shame what those people did."

Ares forced his grin to widen and watched Belton's eyes flick over his shoulder and then back. “Oh, for sure. Okay, well, thanks again,” Ares said, his grin still plastered across his face.

“Glad to, son. Least I could do.” Belton followed Anna down to the front lobby and his ride back to Capitol Hill.

Ares walked back to Powell, internally screaming, and crashed into his overstuffed chair. The things he’d caught in Congressman Belton’s head would give him nightmares for the remainder of his days.

“Ares? Murph?” Athena’s voice cut through his thoughts.

Ares stood back up. “Yes, ma’am—Athena?”

“What just happened?” She searched his face and slowly stuck out her hand.

Ares took in Powell’s face, now a blank mask, Athena’s concern, and Marco’s consternation. He held out both hands. “Listen, this shit is fucked up. You’re going to have to read it, too. All of you.”

Athena and Marco put a hand on his immediately, but Powell hesitated.

“Dude, you need to at least get the basics,” Ares said. Athena shot a look at Powell, then to Marco, but everyone extended hands and connected with Ares.

The mélange of thoughts coalesced into a single image.

“How did you know we could do this? Meld thoughts together?” Marco asked, awed as the collective thoughts washed over him.

The patchwork of imagery squirmed and slipped in Ares’ mental grasp as they acclimated to the shared image.

“I didn’t. I just thought it’d be everyone reading my thoughts. I didn’t,” he paused, “I didn’t realize everyone would be an open party line.”

“Out with it, Murph,” Powell said.

“That guy is our bad guy. He’s the Montgomery bombing mastermind.”

“What?” Athena asked. “Who?”

“He’s the one, the congressman you were just talking to,” Ares said. “He organized the bombing attack on the Rosa Parks Museum.”

“Dude, that’s Congressman Jacob Belton, he’s on our—” she started but she jerked, wide-eyed, as the imagery captured by Ares was distributed through the group contact.

Ares thought of everything he'd seen and done over the last several months, letting it flow across the contact. Images of dusty Damascus, his impersonal room in the Limitless clinic, his empty new and sterile apartment, reuniting with Zora, following Hank's men across the country, and chasing a racist from Alaska to DC. The images and feelings associated with them all flowed across the contact.

Marco looped back a feeling of resigned anger, a quietly seething rage that mourned the injustices seen in a lifetime. Athena contributed her growing belief that Belton was a racist killer. It looped back on itself and fed self-doubt and anger.

"Athena?" Ares asked softly, but words didn't matter. Every person touching him could feel their emotions ricocheting through the group.

"Just say it, Ares. I think we all know it's go time now," Athena growled through clenched teeth.

"He's the guy," Ares said.

Ares reviewed the congressman's memories received, Belton's face twisted in hatred, enraging a group of men, shouting slurs, and whipping them into a frenzy. Then men were around a long table in a small room, bomb-making materials being assembled under a single cone of light.

"He's the kingpin. He recruited a group of white supremacists who then recruited Islamic fundamentalists to execute attacks on the U.S. homeland—a classic 'the enemy of my enemy is my friend.' He's told them Americans hate brown people. For him, it drives public outrage and calls for a stronger military, and he gets a political win."

"What's next?" Marco asked.

"The Mall." Ares closed his eyes, dragging up what he'd picked from Belton's brain. "Multiple school trips are converging on the National Mall tomorrow. He's planning some kind of big attack then." Ares frowned, trying to pull more details out of the brief contact. "Some of the shit bags you have in holding," he told Powell, "probably still have details. We can pull from them and work to counter it."

Powell said, "We should grab Belton now."

Marco, ever cautious, disagreed. "First, we have no demonstrable proof. Nothing tangible, anyway. Second, people would notice if a congressman from the Intel Committee came up missing."

"So, we get the real proof," Ares replied. "Powell, you have intuitive skills and you're subtle. Can you go see Belton on some ruse and see what you can dig up from him?" He could feel Powell's resistance across the touch. He wanted to stay at Limitless and help plan the response.

"I don't take orders from you, Ares," Powell said.

"But you take them from me, Powell. Go." Marco said. "Please. Only you can do what you can do, we all know that now, and we damned well need it ASAP."

Powell's anger sparked across the group touch. Instead of being made part of the team, he felt shunned.

"You don't trust me?"

"Of course, I do, but we'll need as much proof as we can muster. And," he looked Powell in the eyes, "you've got a lower moral standard than us and have better control of your temper."

They all felt a small flare of discomfort when Marco gave Athena's hand a hard squeeze.

"Listen to me," Marco said. He looked first at Athena and then back to Powell and his voice took on a harder tone. "Join him after we pull the Pantheon in. For once, I don't give a shit what's going on between the two of you. You check each other pretty damn well minus your current trust issues with each other. I can trust the pair of you to keep doing your jobs without regard to whatever your bullshit problems are."

He put a brotherly hand on Powell's shoulder.

"Go now. And get your shop to send me the names and locations of any known cell members at large. We'll need find and grab the ones not participating in the Mall attacks. Report back any helpful outcome of your Belton 'interview.'"

"Okay, Marco," Powell said. His previous angry and suspicious tone had fled. "I'm on this."

Athena and Powell stepped back and each released Ares' hand. Marco followed suit a moment later. In that last second, Ares could feel Marco's fear.

Marco paused while Powell departed, then he turned to Athena. "We'll need the whole team on this. Athena, I want you to call a Signal 200 and have all hands meet us in my secure conference room. I have to make a phone call." Marco looked at Ares. "When everyone is present, you can explain all this crap."

A Signal 200 was the Limitless Logistics equivalent to a Navy ship captain ordering a General Quarters—everyone drop everything and respond now.

Ares nodded and set off at a jog. Four minutes later, having collected Zora from the office they'd set up as her temporary doggy daycare, he sat at the long conference table while the rest of the Pantheon and staff hustled in and found chairs. Zora took a comfortable reclining position at Ares' feet and he scratched her furry ears.

Rich Dunn and Wilson Armstrong, at almost thirty years each, were the two longest-serving members after Marco. They filed in silently and took their usual places at the table with a simple nod to Ares. Damarcus followed in with a recognizing point of an index finger at Ares. His handler, Ryan, smiled at Zora and gave her a quick pat before sitting against the wall behind Damarcus with the other seconds.

Walker McCann and James Lee dragged in, both still in black shirts and cargo pants from their morning lift mission. Both still clearly felt the effects of their Jump work and gave Ares a quizzical look.

Marco, Athena, and Mandy were the last to enter. He pulled out Mandy's chair as she eased down from her crutches to her seat. Then he moved to the podium and the assembly immediately became quiet.

Marco's drawn face reflected the gravity of the situation. "In my time here, I've never issued a full team recall," he said, "but we have a situation which drives it. Our newest accession, Murphy Hawkins—Ares—will present."

Marco aimed a knife hand at him. *It's your show now.*

Hawkins' stomach clenched as he stood. Briefing his fire team had been easy. He was the highest ranking and most experienced, and they listened. But here he was junior to every man and woman in a briefing room.

"Good afternoon," he began. Mentally kicking himself for his nervousness, he went on. "You all know what happened in Montgomery. You know that it's pushed the nation toward a brink that's still developing, but one that skews toward a general erosion of freedoms."

No one spoke. The bombing of the Rosa Parks Museum was still fresh in everyone's minds, and it dominated cable news. Talk of martial law still reverberated on alt-right media.

"What you don't know is that as of this afternoon, we know who is behind the attack, why it occurred, and what's coming next."

A stunned silence reigned for a moment before the room exploded with questions.

Marco stood at his seat, raising his hands against the cacophony. "Hang on a moment, folks. He'll explain the background then we'll start talking about what we can do about it."

At Marco's nod, Ares walked them through what he and Powell had pulled from Abe Dunphy in Alaska and the imagery and information that was gleaned on their trip to North Carolina. And when he presented the terror connections to Jacob Belton—a sitting member of Congress—the room went cold.

"He's using Daesh and the friggin' neo-Nazis and whatnot?" Wilson asked.

"Yes, that's what I got," Ares said.

Wilson squinted at him, the smile lines at the corners of his eyes deepening. "His emotions told you that much?"

Ares scratched his jaw. "Not exactly. I could actually see the imagery. Shaking his hand, I could see his visual memories through his own eyes. Talking. Briefing. Giving orders."

"Son, we can't do that," Wilson said shaking his head in disbelief.

"Respectfully, sir, I can. More than the top-layer emotions, I can get whole conversations and focused images, like looking at a subject's

16mm movie about what he did on his summer vacation, only clearer."

Ares looked at Marco, who nodded. *Keep going.*

"There's more, too. At least for some of us newbies, the Pantheon skill set seems to be evolving. We discovered that, over time, some of us can read or send thoughts at a distance. Mandy and Athena," he swallowed back a chuckle, "uh, Mandy and Athena can send to and receive from each other. Full conversations, full range of emotions. I can pull images and memories without touching, but it's still more clear when touching. I suspect Athena can too."

"How?" Walker McCann asked, incredulous. "Can we others get that tune-up if we want it, too?" Other heads around the table nodded.

"Honestly? I don't fucking know," Ares grimaced. "Sorry. I just don't know."

Lee barked a laugh. "It's okay, man, we're all military here," Lee said when Ares winced at his own swearing. Mandy said nothing.

Ares grinned and continued. "I have a theory, though." He looked to Marco again.

"It's okay, Ares. It's all gotta come out."

"It's not just physical contact—it's emotional connection too." Ares squirmed.

Talking about emotions was not his strength, but he suspected it wasn't a strength for anyone in the room.

"The stronger an emotional connection, the stronger the ability to communicate across the new channels. That's how Athena and Mandy can do it. They're as close as sisters. But I also think some of it is just knowing it's possible."

Ares walked to Wilson Armstrong's chair.

"Help me out, brother. Think of an image or a memory with strong emotions associated with it. Something I could never guess," he asked of his teammate and extended a hand.

Armstrong frowned but held out his hand. Ares grasped it and concentrated. He took a deep breath and sought the connection he knew was there. An image formed in his mind: a child's drawing of a house, done in brown marker on yellow construction paper. A second memory lurked, almost hidden under the paper—a young woman with long brown hair, wearing a hospital gown and seated on a padded table. Her eyes filling with tears and a feeling of guilt, anger, and despair overlaid on top of it. Ares released Wilson's hand.

"I'm sorry," he said.

Armstrong shook his head.

"No," he said softly. "No, please. It's okay. Go."

"The drawing. Your daughter's?"

He nodded. "The first one she ever brought me."

"And the other matter? Long brown hair. Hospital gown."

Wilson shook his head wordlessly.

"Also, your daughter, but today, not when she was just little." Ares took a deep, uncertain breath before continuing. "Lymphoma, yes? Non-Hodgkin's?" Ares said softly, sadly, but everyone could hear.

The people in the room had known Armstrong for a very long time. Some of them had been to gatherings at the Armstrong's and knew Alicia, his daughter and only child. They gasped or cried out. Marco and several of Armstrong's closer friends leaped from their chairs to put their hands on his shoulders and say commiserating things.

"We found out on Monday," Armstrong whispered back, his voice choked with grief, his eyes welling with tears. "I ... I haven't told anyone here yet."

Armstrong nodded to the group, confirming Ares' assertion. Ares returned to the podium and everyone wished Armstrong their best wishes for a few more moments before the room again fell quiet.

Ares was confident in his delivery now. His anger was building. None of this was fair—not Alicia's cancer, not the horrific deaths at the Rosa Parks, not any of it. The time of timidity was over.

"We know that tomorrow they plan to attack the National Mall. There are start-of-school-year field trips planned for the Smithsonian and the Natural History Museum across the Mall. They're going to hit them."

Ares' anger rippled spread across the room and he raised his voice.

"The Pantheon is not letting that happen," Ares said. "We will mobilize against this."

Marco's head cocked to the side and he squinted at his subordinate, and then his face turned toward Athena.

"Let him go," she said with a sly smile. "Everyone knows you sign the paychecks. Ares is on a roll."

"They saw the 9/11-class reaction in the media their attack in Montgomery provoked. This Congressman Belton dipshit has organized the whole thing. He seems to think the Mall attacks will stoke enough national outrage that—like 9/11—he can get a huge new domestic security bill ramrodded through both houses and then signed by an angry president. And he's right. This will tip things over the edge. Then it's sayonara democracy."

The conference phones in the middle of the long table all rang at once. Marco had left specific orders for only one call to be rung through and he slapped the speakerphone button on the unit next to him. This opened the speakerphone feature on all the phones so the entire room could listen in.

"This is Marco Martinez speaking."

When the caller spoke, it sounded like he was in the room.

"Marco, it's Jim Hastings."

The Secretary of Defense.

"Mr. Secretary. I have you on speakerphone with the entire Pantheon group in my secure conference room. You have received my classified brief?"

"I have. Scary stuff. I've spoken to the DNI and the President. You're officially cleared for all operations necessary to halt this planned attack on the Mall. The level of threat is designated as High and the Pantheon is authorized to break its non-combatant prohibition. Call me with your plan once you have it."

"Understood, sir. Will do."

"Time is short, Marco," the SECDEF said, his voice somber. "You're working without a net here—and we need you and your team on your A-games." The phone clicked and went silent.

Marco took a deep breath. You could hear a pin drop in the room.

"You heard the man. We have the approval of the Secretary of Defense, the Director of National Intelligence, and the President, people. Now we need a plan."

Athena rose and went to a Limitless car waiting in the building's small circle driveway. She needed to catch up with Brandon Powell.

CHAPTER 22
VALERIE 'ATHENA' HALL
1633Z 1233L, 09 AUG

Athena had live-texted the meeting to Powell in his absence, and now she texted him to come back for her at the Starbuck's at 20th and L Street, only two blocks from the Limitless headquarters building near 20th and M Street. By the time her driver pulled the black Escalade to the curb in front of the coffee shop, Powell was already emerging with Athena's favorite tea, a venti vanilla tea latte. She thanked her driver and climbed into Powell's logan green 1970 Pontiac GTO.

"Well, this is cool," Athena said with admiration, looking around the pristine interior. The car looked like it had just rolled out of the showroom.

"Thanks," Powell said. "I've had it since high school. Keep the oil changed in almost anything and it will last forever."

She accepted the tea latte and Powell pulled the muscle car into traffic and headed for Capitol Hill.

Silence stretched as he wove through DC traffic, which sucked because of course it sucked. Athena leaned her head against the window and built a strategy, even as she fumed.

"So, what's the plan?" Powell asked around a sip of hot tea.

"I've got to get him to talk. Belton. At least, to think, so that we can intercept details. I'm sure he won't admit to anything outright, but I need him to corroborate what we have, at least in his head."

"How?"

"I dunno." She sighed. "He likes me. Maybe I can leverage that? I need more than that, though."

It was a short trip from Foggy Bottom to the RHOB—the Rayburn House Office Building where Belton kept his office hours. Athena had made phone calls and sent texts, fingers flying on her phone.

"I think I have an idea but, jeez, if it isn't going to be hard to pull off." She outlined her plan as Powell drove.

"Holy crap—you can't be serious. That's asking a ton from someone predisposed to be uncooperative," he said as he pulled the GTO into a parking spot for official-only visitors. Powell hated parking his baby so close to other vehicles, but this was the last close-in parking slot. He'd take his chances with door dings.

He flipped down his sun visor to display a placard that read UNIVERSAL EXPORTS. All the DC parking enforcement folks had been briefed that the sign indicated an official CIA car—in the movies, Universal Exports was the front company for James Bond. If the vehicle license plate was run, the record that returned was registered to police headquarters.

"I know," Athena admitted. "I don't know if I can convince her—she's a tough old babe. I'm going to lean on her patriotism and simply hope that one problem being bigger than another gets the agreement we need," Athena said, shimmying out of the car with the door narrowly open. "You think you could have parked any closer to this guy?"

"Only spot open," he said, and passed her the cane that she couldn't pull out with her.

Grinding her teeth, Athena nodded. "We're in the usual secure room for the meetings. First one's in five minutes and Belton will meet us in twenty-five."

"Cutting it a bit tight, aren't we?"

Athena's rubber-tipped cane made no noise on the floor as they walked into the official visitors' entrance, flashed their IDs, and were waved in through the metal detector.

"Yes. But it was all the time Anna and Marco could arrange on short notice. I'm glad we got any at all." Athena's face set in a grim frown. "We don't need much for this."

They hurried down the halls as fast as Athena could manage. Her brain raced, thinking through every step of how she needed the next thirty minutes to unfold.

"I don't want Ares to be right, Powell," she finally said.

"I know," he said. "Neither do I."

"He's so personable. It's hard to believe someone can have such a friendly exterior and hide such a rotten soul." She looked up at Powell. "I guess people are capable of a lot, no matter the exterior."

"I wasn't—" Powell started but Athena cut him off.

"I was talking about me, Bran." She shook her head. "I didn't act on it, but clearly I thought of—" she cut off, switching her words. "I could have done terrible things to Pete on Mandy's behalf. I'm no different than you. Certainly, no better."

Powell nodded.

"I'm sorry, Bran. We're more alike than I want to admit. I'm sorry I reacted so badly. You didn't deserve it. And ..." she looked down, tapping her cane against the toe of his shoe, "... I know you thought you were looking out for me."

Hesitantly, Powell's hand reached for hers. As it settled over the hand atop the cane, she felt his relief, guilt, and fear wash over her.

"I'm sorry as well," Powell said." You weren't wrong. I did it for selfish reasons and I should have talked to you about it instead of just reacting."

"I—" she stopped. Athena swallowed hard, almost unable to get the words out. Fear, embarrassment, and anger choked the words in her throat.

"It's okay, Athena. I'm here. Talk to me."

"I need help, Bran. Eight months! So much has happened to me in just eight months and I need help. I think I need to talk to someone."

He nodded. "I support you in all things." Sympathy and encouragement flowed across their hands, telling her much more than his words.

"Friends?"

He squeezed her hand and released it. "Friends."

Athena let her shoulders drop, releasing the tension that had built up in them over the last hour. They had walked while they talked and now it was time to confront new challenges.

As soon as they stepped inside the Senatorial office of Maureen Mitchell, the tension returned. Her strident voice met them as soon as they entered.

"Young woman, I'll have you know I am the head of the Senate Armed Services Committee and I do not have the time to meet every person who demands my time."

She stood at her secretary's desk in the outer office holding a sheaf of paper, drafts of bills. She looked at them over half-eye glasses.

"I only granted this meeting request because Marco Martinez and Richard Dunn are long-time friends."

She turned and walked through her access door to the conference room shared with Jacob Belton, tapping on a cellphone that should never have been in a secure room. She didn't bother to look up as she chided them.

"You have six minutes."

"Ma'am, with all due respect, you have to hear us out today," Athena said. At her nod, Powell closed and secured the conference room door.

"Excuse me, I need to take this call outside before we discuss anything," Mitchell said, angrily waving the phone.

"No, ma'am. I need you to hear us out first," Athena insisted.

Mitchell glared at her. She was not used to taking orders from anyone.

"Senator, we need your help." Before Mitchell could launch another verbal assault, Athena pushed on. "Jacob Belton is a white supremacist, a neo-Nazi, and a terrorist threat to the nation in ways you don't know."

"Oh honey, I know," Mitchell said archly.

Athena blinked.

Mitchell finally looked up from her phone, her piercing blue eyes meeting Athena's.

"You know? Wait, which part?" Athena asked, surprise coloring her voice.

"Young lady, I'm from Missouri, where the Klan is alive and well. I know a damned white supremacist when I smell one."

Athena blinked hard and glanced at Powell.

"And what else do you know?" he asked.

Mitchell gave a cold smile. "As I said, I am the chair of the Senate Armed Services Committee and, as such, I'm in the information business. I receive intelligence reports from CIA and the FBI. Regrettably, the CIA—" Her derisive glance at Powell said she knew he worked from them. "—and the FBI lack your specific talents."

"And?"

"And what, girl? Marco called me himself. I know the score. I may not like him much anymore or your group, and I certainly think it's against God's law, but this is politics—and that is my house. Sometimes you have to understand when the enemy of your enemy is your friend. You have what I need and need what I have. Out with it already."

Athena was speechless and it showed.

Mitchell laughed, true mirth showing on her face.

"Child, I've been in politics longer than you've been alive. You should have seen the strange bedfellows the Cold War made."

"In that case, I need you, and that phone," Athena pointed to the corner coat closet, "to, uh, hide? Stand quietly and discreetly in the closet so I've got a witness to the next meeting. You're the person with the most credibility for what I hope happens next."

"That's all?" Mitchell's expertly drawn eyebrow arched and she gave a small smile.

"If you could record it, that'd be great too."

"Done."

Athena's eye narrowed. "Why are you helping with this?"

Mitchell smiled a genuine smile that crinkled the corners of her eyes. "As you said in our earlier meeting, you have a long time left in this job. I have the rest of my career to fight you and your heathens as I see fit. But right now, Jacob Belton's evil machinations are a greater and more timely threat." A veil of anger rolled across the senator's face. "How we keep getting these fucking clowns elected, I'll never know."

Athena nodded once. "Thank you."

"Besides, I like a worthy adversary. These political goons have no soul. I'll enjoy sparring with you in the future, young woman."

Mitchell rose and walked to the darkened space with all the dignity of a queen. Athena suspected she would lord this over Limitless Logistics one day, and Athena specifically, when she wanted the favor returned in years to come. In that respect, politics was no different from organized crime, though politicians usually had better manners and didn't work such late hours.

Mitchell nestled into the coat closet and closed the door, leaving about a one-inch crack for her to see, listen, and record through.

"You ready for this next meeting, Bran?" Athena asked.

He gave a one shoulder shrug, his face an impassive mask. "I'm ready for all eventualities." And then his face dissolved into a grin.

A chill ran through Athena and she shivered. She looked at him, considering. "Okay, Bran," she said simply. She settled herself in the chair to the right of the head and checked the time. They had two minutes to spare.

From his access door to the conference room, Congressman Belton entered precisely one minute late. He gave her his trademark bright grin and offered his hand, automatically taking the chair at the head of the table.

"Hello, Ms. Hall, a pleasure to see you again so soon." He gave her the customary Pantheon shake.

"And do you know my colleague, Brandon Powell?"

"Don't think I've had the pleasure, Mr. Powell," Belton said, reaching for Powell's hand and shaking it firmly.

"My apologies for not getting up," Athena said in her most charming voice. "This cane is just the worst." She allowed a hint of her Carolina drawl to seep in for effect.

Belton reacted with broadening of his smile. “No worries at all, my dear. Now, how may I help you?”

“Mr. Powell, if you would secure the door?” Athena asked and forced her eyes to keep from flicking to the darkened corner where Mitchell should now be recording the conversation.

“Now, what would the second in command at Limitless Logistics have to discuss with me?” Belton’s toothy smile was still in place, but Athena saw his eyes go flat. He’s suspicious, she thought.

For the barest second, Athena considered easing into the conversation, but subtly had never been her style. She went for his throat.

“The FBI, CIA, and other members of the intelligence community have evidence indicating you are the head of a U.S.-based terror plot responsible for the Montgomery bombing, and another attack to be conducted in the very near future.”

“Yes,” Belton said, his plastic smile holding.

Athena leaned back slightly, eyes wide. “Excuse me?”

“Yes, I am aware they have information that points to me. I have no idea where it comes from, but do you really think a United States Congressman would head an attack on his own people?”

“Congressman Belton, did you order an attack on the Rosa Parks Museum?”

“Valerie, what do you think my job as a congressman entails?” He dodged the question, but Athena could see the images of the bombing planning meetings forming in Belton’s mind.

Athena said, “Why don’t you tell me.”

“My job is to balance their needs with the needs of America as a whole. I can’t ask for all funds to be funneled into my district or my state. While it would certainly help my constituents,” he placed a hand on his chest, “it would leave other Americans lacking. And I must say, these attacks show that Americans have indeed been lacking. Lacking a strong military. Strong institutions like yours have failed to defend America from her enemies, foreign and domestic. And to do that we need funding.”

"Limitless Logistics certainly needs funding, when some people," Athena kept her eyes on Belton, "seem determined to take it away."

"Exactly!" Belton leaned back in his chair and smiled. "Valerie, America has been in long, protracted wars on foreign soil for ungrateful, ignorant thugs, and America's enthusiasm wanes. Think of it—with Cold War-era funding and with support from the House and Senate, Limitless could break through its limits and become more than just a logistics company."

Athena smiled briefly. "Yes, I know Marco has been ... hindered by the budget and spotty political support. I would certainly like to see Limitless take on a more expeditionary role."

He regarded her over his steepled fingers. "Yes. I have nudged certain, um, patriotic individuals and organizations, let's say, into actions that, while morally ambiguous, are designed to build a stronger America." A curious smile creased Belton's face. "Limitless and the Pantheon could be a big part in that."

Athena rocked back. She saw then more of the imagery Ares had seen, including the bomb makers. She saw and heard things that she could testify to.

"Why? Why would you do that? Why would we?"

"Americans don't support the military when it fights on foreign soil. It's exciting for the first few months, I suppose, but support ebbs and money flees when the bodies pile up and a fresh disaster floods the news cycle. An attack on American soil by perceived foreign jihadist terrorists elicits a certain reaction. One which brings funding to the military."

Athena swallowed hard. He didn't even have the grace to look ashamed. "And the white supremacists? The neo-Nazis?"

"The alt-right is shockingly well organized. When I told them they could frame a bunch of hajjis and turn America's hatred on them, they were eager to throw their full support behind me. They are quite powerful and popular in my district, and as you know, I'm but a servant of my people." He watched her expression. "Valerie, I'm going to make you a deal," he tapped the table with a single finger. "Here and now."

Athena squirmed.

"You keep this to yourself, you and your pet spook at the door." He waved vaguely at Powell. "I will guarantee Limitless Logistics is funded to a level that allows you to expand operations into a civilian logistics side and a combat company—a PMC—for discreet operations. Think, Valerie. You can be the CEO of your own private military contractor, first among equals, if you please, when those fat indefinite delivery-indefinite quantity contracts are doled out. I'm sure you'd run it better than that Marco fellow. You certainly seem like a better candidate than Mr. Martinez."

He spit out Marco's name like it was dirty.

"And with you at the helm, Limitless Logistics could be truly limitless. Think of the lives you could save with a combat branch! Then you can expand into civilian logistic services in a space no other log company can match. Think of how you could help those in need of organ transport for emergency surgeries, flood relief, even ultra-secret direct-action missions. You name it."

Athena took a deep breath. In her few months at Limitless, she had wondered why Marco had never worked to find and integrate civilian Jumpers. She knew, now that Zeus's rampant myopia had kept them from even considering the possibility of organizations like *Vmeste*, their Russian logistics counterpart. From what they had learned from *Svoboda*, a more combat oriented group that was against the Russian government, *Vmeste* wasn't allowed guns. She leaned back in her chair, fighting to keep her face blank.

"We live in an uncertain world, Valerie," Belton said. "You may not be quite old enough to remember the Cold War or the fall of the Soviet Union, but I assure you that I do. Russia is rising again, and China is not far behind. Think of how many unknown Chinamen must have your abilities? Do you really want those little yellow bastards to outnumber you?"

Athena nodded slightly, doing the mental math, and trying to hide her wince. She frowned.

Leaning across the table, he said, "On the other hand, if you don't accept this offer, I will end your organization. I will find a way to make every one of your simulated superheroes appear as felons in the legal system. I know I couldn't hope to keep you incarcerated, but I'll make damn sure you are unable to live in the United States." His finger stabbed into the table again and he leaned back, cool confidence on his face.

Athena looked at her hands, almost at a loss for words. Her eyes flicked to Powell. "You're right, you know, Congressman. Limitless Logistics could be more." She shook her head sadly. "I was an intelligence officer before all this, and I know what we face. Yes, Limitless could be more and do so much more. But I won't sacrifice the soul of the Pantheon and the lives of hundreds of children at the hands of terrorists to achieve it." She stood, unsteadily rising to her feet. Powell closed the distance to stand at her side. "Not tomorrow. Not ever. I have your admission. I think I'll take my chances against your threats."

Belton rose as well. "My dear, you? And the spook? Your word against that of a sitting United States Congressman? And where would you say your information came from, huh? You read my mind?" He gave her a mocking grin. "No, little lady. You and that freak parade wouldn't risk exposure. You have nothing to give other than your word and a fat lot of good that will do you. No one will believe you." He sneered.

"Without proof? That might be true," Athena agreed.

Then, from the closet in the corner, came Maureen Mitchell's distinctive voice. The closet door opened, and she stepped out. "But she has a United States Senator witness and a video recording of your treasonous admissions," Mitchell said. Her unique voice was heaven to Athena's ears as the Senator emerged from the closet, cellphone held high and still recording.

Athena felt a flash of rage radiate from Belton, and he telegraphed the thought before his hand even started to move toward a tiny Beretta .380 Tomcat pistol.

Time slowed to a crawl, and Athena shouted "*Gun!*" as his hand reached to his waistband.

Before Belton could draw, Powell closed the distance between them, grasped Belton's head in both hands, and with a sickening twist broke the congressman's neck. Belton's body slumped to the ground in a heap, his handgun clattering across the floor.

Stunned, Athena stared at the congressman's inert body, then up to Powell. She felt as though time, slowed to an agonizing crawl, raced back up to normal speed.

"Holy shit, Bran ..." Athena's shocked face said the same thing without the words.

He simply smoothed his coat and looked to Mitchell, rooted in place with shock and still recording. Her phone had captured Belton attempting to draw his weapon. She was still pointing the device at Belton on the floor when Powell reached over and touched the red Stop button.

"Do you have anyone who can dispose of ... this, or keep him on ice until later?"

Mitchell recovered quickly. To Athena's shock, she nodded.

"Yes. You'd be surprised." Mitchell shook her head. "For how long?"

Powell glanced at Athena and considered. "Until tomorrow afternoon, at least. We have to mop up all the others before they learn of their boss's demise."

"All right. Can do. But not long thereafter. Evil people decompose faster."

"You know what, though? On second thought, it will be safer if we just take him with us back to Limitless. It's secure, and anyone you get to help you here is going to call The Washington Post the moment they're out of your sight. We have to keep his death a secret for now," Powell said. "You know if the cells find out, they'll spook and get in the wind and we'll never find them all. We'll lose our only best chance to catch them tomorrow."

Mitchell straightened, once again the decorous politician.

"I understand," Mitchell said with a measure of relief. "Ms. Hall, you will owe me for all this."

Athena nodded.

"We have to go. Now." Powell caught her hand.

"Yeah. Yes. Go." Her voice was flat, expressionless.

Powell squeezed her hand. "Need help?" he whispered. "We gotta get back to Limitless."

"What?" Athena could see Powell's face, his worried expression, but for some reason his concern wasn't registering in her mind.

"Do you need my help? Getting up?"

She finally realized what he was asking. She inhaled a lungful of air, only then realizing she'd been holding her breath.

"No. No, let's just go. We have to finish planning."

"We'll get the car later. Hell, they can tow it for all the fucks I give right now. Are you safe to Jump us?"

Athena nodded, dragging in another deep breath. She looked at Powell again, then waggled her fingers in goodbye to Senator Mitchell.

"Thanks," Athena said. "We'll be in touch." She nodded to Powell, reached down to grasp Congressman Belton's hand and they Jumped.

They landed in her living room.

"*Shit*, this isn't where I meant to go! This isn't—" Athena gasped, visibly fraying. Because of how they appeared in Athena's apartment, Jacob Belton had landed on the living room couch. Athena instantly dragged him to the floor and onto a washable throw rug. She didn't want his bodily fluids leaking on her furniture. And she was still hyperventilating.

"Relax, take a breath," Powell said quietly.

Athena took a deep breath, then another. On the third breath Powell realized she wasn't controlling the hyperventilating. She waved at him, panic in her eyes.

"Do it, Bran," she gasped out. "Please. Now."

He looked at her hard. "You sure?"

She sucked in a deep, ragged breath, going pale, and nodding frantically in the affirmative.

Powell stepped in and embraced her, his bare hands snaking up to grasp the wispy curls of hair on the back of her neck.

Calm flowed through the touch like the soft lapping of a cool breeze along her body. She shuddered as she relaxed in his embrace.

The adrenaline that had sustained her after watching a man killed in front of her was overridden by Powell's curious talent, and Athena sagged in his arms. Her head dropped to his shoulder and Powell took her weight as her one-and-a-half functioning legs gave out. He maneuvered them to her loveseat, pulling her to his lap and tucking her head under his chin so that her forehead rested skin-to-skin against his neck.

He let his calm flow over her a moment longer before dimming its effect, afraid the tranquility would send her to sleep.

They still had things to do.

"You killed him," she finally said, her voice even and calm.

"Yes, I did." Powell's answer was carefully neutral.

"Thank you," she said simply, and gratitude echoed along their light touch.

"You're, uh, welcome."

"He was going to shoot me. I saw it, in his head, as he pulled the gun." Her voice had a far-off quality to it.

"Without touching him?"

"It was so strong. I could see it in his mind's eye. He was practically shoving the image at me." Athena's voice was devoid of emotion but Powell felt the chaos starting inside her. "And you stopped him."

"Of course." He looked down at her. "You didn't think I'd let him shoot you, did you?"

Powell felt her emotions surge even as her face was blank and realization hit him. He grabbed her wrist, seeking a pulse.

Athena stared at the wall, as if he didn't exist.

"I dunno," she shrugged against him. "We, well, we had some pretty – strong – words last time we talked. And we're friends again, but I wasn't sure."

The pulse under his fingers raced despite her calm exterior. "Athena, where are you right now?" he asked urgently.

Face still blank, she shook her head and he felt rage, hopelessness, and guilt surging against his touch.

"Athena, listen to me. You're having a panic attack. Another flashback. Something," he said. "Come back to me, Athena."

Powell caught her chin his hands and looked into her eyes. Her gaze was unfocused as she stared at some nightmare he couldn't see. He pulled her in closer, trying to touch as much of her bare skin as he could, pushing calm across once more.

"Athena, are you with me?" he asked, rocking her as he held her to his chest. When she didn't respond he tried to push more of his calming across their bare skin. Her emotions calmed slightly but he could tell she was still deep in the morass of her own mind.

"Athena? Hey, talk to me," Powell wrapped his arms around her back, pulling her in as close as he could.

Athena lay against him, breathing deeply for a moment. He could feel the rise and fall of her chest against his.

Athena took one more deep breath. "I'm here. I'm here, Bran."

He let out a breath he didn't know he'd been holding and hugged her tight to his chest. She hugged him back.

She pushed back and looked him in the eyes. "Thank you."

Powell released her. "Athena, we should get back."

"I know," she said but didn't release him. Her eyes met his again and he inhaled sharply.

"Athena," he said warningly. "I need you to step back a second. I'm not sure I can control—"

Athena ignored him, leaning in to press a kiss to his lips and her hips rocked into him. Powell growled and grabbed her hip. He pulled her hard against him then push her back again, breaking their kiss.

"Athena, we can't. You've got to stop." It pained him to say it.

"We can," she said and leaned in again.

"Can we just get through the current crisis and before we worry about what this is?"

"Okay, that's fine," he told her, his face back to its impassive mask. "I just—" he stopped himself.

Athena caught the change in his expression. "You just what, Bran?" she asked softly.

"I just don't want you to use me," he said quietly.

"What?" Athena asked, genuine surprise in her voice.

"I don't want to be used," he told her. "It's not just the sex. You," he paused thinking of his conversation with Murphy, "you're avoiding the real problem. You use what I can do to slap a bandage over the bigger issue. You need help. You need to face the trauma you've had and work through it. I can't be there to calm you down every time you tip toe up to the edge."

"Oh." Athena's shoulders sagged. He was probably right. What he could do was convenient and that sex was amazing. "I'm sorry, Bran. It's not like that. I don't mean it to be like that."

"Will you get help? Real help?"

Athena caught his hand, letting her emotions flow through to him: caring, respect, and desire.

In return, his shifted from dejection tinged with regret to hope.

"Yes, Bran."

Twenty minutes later they were clean, dressed, and back at Limitless with the remains of Jacob Belton explaining to Marco how their meeting had gone sideways.

CHAPTER 23
AMANDA SQUIRES
1930Z 1530L, 09 AUG

Marco's conference room was filled with nearly the entire company. Marco's executive admin, Anna, was seated in the corner typing a record of the proceedings on a Stentura 8000 court reporting steno machine that she'd purchased brand-new for her first job out of court reporting school in 1993.

"So, let me get this straight," Marco said. "We have until zero-nine tomorrow to find and neutralize five suicide bombers or they will detonate explosive vests amid a sea of school children?"

Ares glanced at Athena, who nodded. "The ringleader is dead." Belton's body lay on a cot in the large cooler Medical used to house sensitive chemicals and medicines. "But his terror plot goes on."

Powell looked at Rich and Damarcus, sent earlier to Langley to extract actionable intel from the CIA's detainees, and then affirmed with a nod.

"The most they could get from our detained individuals is the number of attackers but not where they're coming from. And any overt military or law enforcement presence will send them scurrying back to their spider holes, where we lose them until they decide they want to try again."

"Agreed," Marco said with a grim smile.

Ares scrubbed a hand over the stubble on his chin. Athena judged that if they all lived through the next few days, a generous person might be able to start calling Ares' stubble a beard. Her mouth tightened as she tried to suppress her grin.

"Well, okay, then," Ares said. "Can't catch them at a source, can't catch them if they flush, and we can't make a big noise. Sounds like we've got to grab them in the narrow window between when they get to the National Mall and when they detonate."

"Yes," Marco agreed.

A round of nods went through the room as the Pantheon of Jumpers and their handlers stared at the digital map of the National Mall Ares had projected on the conference screen.

"So, we grab them at the site, then what?" Athena asked. "We're anticipating they have explosive vests. If I remember some intel I had access to before this, ya know, all of eight months ago, the devices will probably have deadman switches."

"Deadman switches?" Mandy asked.

"Mandy, you've seen enough spy movies to know this. They hold the button down, but the circuit doesn't activate unless they release the button. If they get shot, stabbed, die, stumble on a curb, or their finger comes off the button for any reason—kaboom." Athena said, mimicking an explosion with her hands.

"Kaboom," Mandy said. Ares caught her eye and gave her a roguish smile that was in no way diminished by his scruffy beard. Mandy felt butterflies in her stomach as she smiled back.

"So, if we grab them, wherever they are, it's got to be away from people when they get to the other side. Including us."

Silence stretched as they considered the problem. Mandy looked at Marco, seeking something, anything that said he had this well in hand. Marco caught her look and shook his head ruefully.

"Yeah, we aren't looking for suicide missions today, thanks. I want to live long enough to see my girls graduate from college. Even if we crudely just bear hug 'em and Jump 'em out of there, they can still happily blow us and themselves to smithereens wherever we take them."

Mandy leaned into Athena and covered her mouth with her hand.

"I never did know what a smithereen was."

"You can Google it," Athena said.

"Skipping?" Ares asked, looking at Powell.

Powell's face was as impassive as always. "I don't see it. It'll get you away but it won't help you. As soon as you're away they could release the trigger just to mess with your day."

Mandy studied him. Despite his neutral face, Powell seemed relaxed. She sat up straighter, closed her eyes, and reached out mentally for Athena's mental signature. Mandy was surprised to feel Athena was there. Not as strongly as in days before, but she could sense both contentment and a stressed hum emanating from her.

Athena looked at Mandy as if she'd detected her mental caress. Mandy turned to Powell, back to Athena, and gave her a knowing smile. She was rewarded with Athena's subtle flush.

So, you and Powell made up, huh? Mandy asked mentally.

Mandy! Did you peek? Athena's shocked, embarrassed reply came back to her.

Nope. But you're standing within five feet of him, and I can feel your gratification.

Pay attention! Athena said.

Their wordless conversation was in the span of a heartbeat and Mandy dragged her attention back to the discussion at the table. Nonverbal was so much more efficient.

"Yes, as long as you can see the spot ahead and mentally envision yourself there, it works," Ares explained. "I even tried skipping over a slight rise in the road, one I couldn't see over, and it worked but it's, uh, unreliable." He shrugged. "You do it at a run and you're moving at the same speed on the other side. If the level is different ..."

"Like seven-league boots?" Wilson asked with a laugh.

"Uh, yeah, I guess you could think of it like that." Ares scratched his stubbly chin. *I need a legit no-shave chit*, he thought. "Skipping forward, making extra-long strides. Still doesn't solve our problem. Skipping only gets us a bit away from the kids and doesn't help us personally at all. We might as well Jump to the dark side of the Moon. Same-same.

Kids will probably be safe, but we still get dead."

They stared at the map and the rectangle of the National Mall.

"We can stage here so it isn't a long Jump to the Mall that would use too many calories. If a single Jumper ends up near multiple bombers, that might help with the extractions, but we won't be able to identify most of the terrorists from tourists without a scorecard. There isn't anywhere we can go randomly on the Mall that will be guaranteed clear on a Thursday morning. Walkers. Joggers. Hell, families with friggin' strollers. It's late summer. The tourists are still out in droves," Damarcus said.

Mandy squinted at the map. "What if we went up? Ares, could we visualize a point above the Mall?"

"I don't know. Maybe so. What are you getting at, Mandy?"

Something in the way he said her name, almost a verbal caress, made her blush.

"Why can't we Jump them to where we know for sure no one else will be in danger—straight up, or over the Atlantic, release, and immediately return to where we started, or even Point Zero. They go *ka-boom* in open air and we're back here drawing beers in the cafeteria and counting our blessings."

There was stunned silence in the room.

"Holy shit—" Damarcus started.

Ares smacked his hands together. "Reverse sky diving! That's fucking brilliant. It's risky as hell. Momentum and gravity will demand their due, but we don't have to be super high for this to work," Ares said.

He grabbed Mandy in an awkward one arm hug, him standing and her sitting, but the respect, admiration, and wisp of desire that came from his touch overrode any embarrassment.

"There's the small problem of momentum you mentioned," Walker broke in. His brows furrowed and he frowned, adding a decade to his otherwise unlined face.

"True," Marco said. "You'll be slow to arrive at your elevated point because you will start essentially horizontal, but if you don't disengage from the load and Jump back almost instantly, gravity will provide downward momentum that will get paid off when you get back to the surface. We could redefine the term hard landing."

"Tough," Ares agreed, "but not a deal breaker. Certainly, the best we have right now."

Mandy listened as discussion swirled about the best way to grab, Jump, and release without allowing too much momentum.

"Falling from a height never hurt Wile E. Coyote, but it isn't so great for real people," Damarcus quipped.

As they argued tactics, Mandy tested a theory. She discreetly reached out to each of the male Pantheon to see if she could mentally connect with them. Without fail, she was able to sense emotions from each. The stronger her personal bond, the more feeling she could detect. Damarcus even straightened abruptly when she touched his emotions.

He gave a startled look around before launching back into his point without identifying her as his intruder.

"No, fifty feet should be enough. You can easily picture yourself in a building five flights above ground and it's enough distance that they probably detonate before impacting the ground. But it's also enough distance to disentangle yourself," Damarcus continued. "That said, what if the little bastards don't trigger their bombs on us? Dead is dead. They might decide to keep the deadman button pressed until they're back on *terra firma*."

"I think higher," Powell said, "and farther. I like Mandy's idea of out over the ocean. Then they can drop into the Atlantic and blow up the tuna if they want to."

"What about parachuting back?" Rich Dunn asked.

"That doesn't get you away from the explosion nearly fast enough," Powell said.

A murmur of agreement floated among the Pantheon.

Powell voiced other concerns. "We don't know if those vests or whatever are filled with some low-grade explosives—or C4. We definitely don't know if projectiles might be embedded. You need to be high enough and far enough away to keep falling or explosive debris from endangering civilians on the ground. As far as our damaging return momentum goes, fifty feet might as well be five hundred. If you don't stick the landing, either fall is likely to be terminal."

The room again fell quiet while the Jumpers considered their employment choices and their staff considered retraining.

"We also need a central, ah, 'drop point,' if we can get it," Powell said. "The CIA and FBI will need to identify these birds from DNA. That will be easier if they all land in roughly the same area." He shrugged his broad shoulders. "Obviously, they needn't be intact."

After a moment, Athena said, "Teddy Roosevelt."

The group turned to her in mystified silence. Marco finally spoke. "Oh-*kay* ..."

Athena had been tapping her iPhone screen for several minutes and pulled up a section of a map she'd been scrutinizing. She pressed the Airplay icon and the map was projected to the large wall screen.

"Theodore Roosevelt Island. It's a national park smack-dab in the Potomac, so we can close it off no sweat. It's close to the Mall, so it's only a small energy investment to Jump there." She moved her finger around the Google map. "It's about eighty-eight acres and full of trees, so if we Jump in at forty-fifty feet and release, the subjects can blow themselves up in the air with no people around if they want to. If they wait to hit the ground, the explosions and any shrapnel will be absorbed by the trees."

"That's pretty good for dealing with bad guys and the citizens," Ares said. "But what about us? Momentum, right?"

"Yeah, that. We can't reliably predict the momentum of individual Jumpers," Athena said. "So, we figure out a soft landing."

She rose unsteadily from her seat and hobbled over to the large screen, reaching up to make her point.

"We preposition Coast Guard helos from Anacostia and DC Metro PD Harbor Patrol fast boats here—" Athena touched the blue area representing the Potomac. "—just south of Little Island, between the T-R and Arlington Memorial bridges. Even if we're off a little, we still just drop into the river and the cavalry picks us up."

Damarcus said after a beat, "What's our Pantheon public exposure mitigation plan?"

Ares eyed Marco. "We don't have one."

"Sir?" Damarcus asked.

"Nothing we can do about it, Dee," Marco said with a shrug. "We'll be seen no matter what and there's not enough time to come up with other options."

Mandy saw Athena's eyes narrow. *It's going to be okay, Athena,* Mandy thought.

We're about to destroy every shred of secrecy we ever had, Athena thought back. *I know we don't have a lot of choices, but it doesn't mean I'm happy about it.*

I know. I'm just helping you recognize that you're spinning up. Maybe it's time the Pantheon came out of the shadows.

From across the room, Athena's eyes met hers. She returned slow, rueful nod.

Rich Dunn and Wilson Armstrong shuffled in their seats, more agitated by the idea of exposure than the prospect of dropping into the Potomac from an indefinite height. James Lee and Walker McCann both gave Marco hard looks but stayed silent. Damarcus simply nodded his understanding.

"Look," Marco told them firmly, "we've always known Pantheon secrecy was at risk every time we take a mission. It's been close before, but the jig is up. I'll let some of our HASC and SASC members know what to expect when we can, but right now, that's the least of our worries." He looked each of them in the eye. "Over seven hundred children expected on the Mall tomorrow. Teachers. Parents. School buses. I'll trade our privacy for that."

Mandy reached out, touching lightly on his feelings, and getting back sadness and regret, but also determination. Marco had carried the company after Zeus's retirement and he was loathe to alter it so dramatically. Though Zeus had been dead for months, everyone still felt the power of his legacy.

Marco's eyes flicked to Mandy. She regarded his without blinking. He took a single deep breath and nodded.

"Okay. That's a plan. I'll notify SECDEF of the broad strokes and follow up with the granularity in a few hours. Ares, who do you need where?" Marco asked.

"Dee? Rich? What did the interrogations give you for sites?"

"It's the Mall's biggest draws: The Natural History Museum, Air and Space, Museum of African American History, Museum of African Art, and the National Gallery. You might detect a specific objective with some of those," Damarcus said bitterly.

Mandy watched Ares consider the room. She reached out, trying to follow the flow of his emotions as he thought. Their bond was nowhere near the strength of her bond with Marco or Athena, but nearly as strong as it was with Damarcus.

She blinked with surprise. Mandy knew she found Ares attractive, his flirtatious attention flattering, and his presence surprisingly soothing, but for his connection to be on the level of Dee, whom she considered almost a brother, must mean he had a very strong attraction to her, too.

"Rich and Walker, take Natural History. Marco, Air and Space. Wilson, African Art. James, can you cover the National Gallery? Dee, you've got African American History. And Athena, dealer's choice. I'll double down on what's left."

"Air and Space," Athena's answered immediately.

Ares nodded and considered. "I'll double down with Dee on African American History then." He looked to Powell. "Can you liaise with the CIA and FBI?"

"Yes," Powell said with a frown. He hated that he was left out of the attack, but he knew why.

Ares looked at him. "I'm sorry, Powell. There's just not much you can do from the ground."

Ares' eyes caught Mandy's and she shrunk in on herself. He walked to her side and held out a hand, the question in his eyes. Mandy slowly extended her hand, placing it gently in his.

"Where do you want to be, Mandy?" he asked quietly. Respect and support flowed through their contact.

"I—" she halted, shaking her head. "I can't go with you. That will never be who I am." She inhaled sharply at the flutter of fear that shot through her like a wave of nausea.

Hestia, Athena's voice whispered into her mind, *goddess of home and hearth. Hold the family together, Hestia.*

Mandy could see and feel Athena's smile. Mandy smiled up at Ares and closed her eyes.

Reaching out through the room, her mind sought the mental contacts she'd known her whole life and the new ones whose presence had burned so effectively into her mind in recent weeks.

Here, she thought to the group, *here is where I belong. Watching my family, supporting them. Giving them what they need. Warring with them when necessary.*

"Mandy?" Marco's voice came to her ears as well as directly across the mental connections she was forging.

She broadcast the group. *I won't*—she hesitated, fully aware her fear also floated across the bond—*I can't go with you. At least, not yet. I'll stay here and do what I do best: coordination. Keeping the Pantheon family connected. I'll do your real-time battle management and keep you better informed than those cellphones can.*

Some of the Pantheon hadn't been aware of the new connections built by Mandy, Athena, and even Ares, and they were taken aback when it echoed in their heads.

James Lee laughed in glee, but then tried broadcasting on his own.

New skill, who dis?

Every Pantheon in the room heard him and laughed at once, leaving Anna, Joe, and the rest of the staff puzzled about what was evidently going on. Zora slept undisturbed next to Ares' seat.

Ares squeezed her hand and released it. "Perfect, Mandy," he said aloud. His smile was warm and genuine and full of promise.

She looked across the table at Athena, and made her decision.

"Call me Hestia," she said with a gentle smile.

"Can you really thread us all together?" Wilson asked.

Ask again, she said in her head. Mandy held their minds close.

Wilson's brow furrowed in concentration.

Can you all hear me, too?

A round of nods and smiles followed.

"I don't know if you all can each go person-to-person, but if what Athena and I have found out is correct, I think as long as I'm holding the group together, it's like a telephone party line."

"You aren't old enough to know what a party line is," Rich protested with a grin. "But this works for me, Mand—uhm, Hestia." He raised an upright thumb and she returned it with a smile of her own. "You dang kids and your silly names."

Ares nodded. "That's settled then. You have your assignments. We know how we're grabbing, and we have faces to study to know who to grab. Let's spend an hour or two rehearsing the 'block-and-tackle' technique, and we'll all bus over to Theodore Roosevelt Island together to imprint our ingress and water landing zones. Then top off your nutrition and get some rest before tomorrow."

Ares looked around the room and got a thumbs-up from Marco.

"Tomorrow is going to be a big day."

CHAPTER 24
THE PANTHEON MELANGE: PHASE 1
1132Z 0732L, 10 AUG

On the sidewalk in front of the National Gallery of Art on Madison Drive SW, Athena tugged at the waistband of her shorts, pulling them back up to her hips and pretending to study the park map posted in front of her. Across two narrow roads and the National Mall, Marco was sitting on the steps at the foot of the National Air and Space Museum.

Calm down, Athena, he said through Hestia's mental link. *You look fine.* He still marveled at this new capability everyone in the Pantheon had unlocked. It was like everyone was on the same radio channel routed through Hestia's switchboard head.

Athena nodded without looking at him. She strolled slowly, her cane crunching in the gravel at her feet, to the far side of the tourist information building. She wished she or Mandy had the forethought to buy her something other than business clothes and ballgowns.

Ares had directed everyone to blend in with the early summer tourists. The old tank top and shorts Athena wore were several sizes too big and only a tattered belt on its last hole kept her shorts from sliding down to bare her derrière to the summer crowd.

Her eyes darted to Marco as she came around the corner of the building. In chinos, a short-sleeved polo shirt, and boat shoes, he was the picture of comfort in the day's early heat.

I'm fine, Marco, she assured him. She wasn't, but no need to tell him. She felt naked without Powell as a silent shadow behind her.

I count three Metro Police by us, Ares cut in. *What does everyone else got?*

Two at Natural History, Rich Dunn said.

None on foot at the Sculpture Garden, but one marked cruiser at the curb here on Madison and I'm fairly sure someone's in it, James Lee said.

Standby, came Wilson Armstrong's reply with the perception of greater effort on his part. *I'm checking around the corner.*

Athena said, *How are you holding up,* Hestia? *This isn't too much effort? Don't over-torque yourself on this.*

No, I'm good, thanks. It's okay, I think.

Her thoughts were a warm glow in all their minds. Her links to all had gradually strengthened as they had rehearsed the night before.

Easier than yesterday. Ask me again in an hour, Hestia said.

All right team, only a few Metro Police *on foot, but I see two cars set up or around the corner from 14th and Jefferson,* Armstrong told them. *I think they're blocking it off to expedite entry and exit for the bus arrivals later.*

I guess they do that, huh? Ares asked.

Athena made her way from the first Gallery of Art building toward the eastern end of the Mall.

Where you going, Athena? Marco asked.

Jeez, I'm just stretching my legs, Dad! Athena said with a mental smirk. *I'm going to see if they're setting up at 4th and Madison. James, Ares, Dee? You want to check your zones?*

A chorus of agreement bounced back and a perception of movement. A few minutes later there was a general agreement that Metro Police were barricading the one-way roads bracketing the Mall between 3rd Street and 14th, including the feeder streets at 12th, 9th, 7th, and 4th.

Looks like you're right, Wilson, Ares said.

Time stretched on as the sun rose higher, making the warm early morning air grow sultry. The roadblock of vehicular traffic didn't deter the typically large number of runners, joggers, and random Yoga and Tai Chi practitioners, and the Mall area crawled with humanity.

Athena made her slow way back to 7th and Madison, her sweaty hand slipping occasionally on the grip of her cane. As Athena crunched along the National Mall's pathway, she bumped into a man walking with his family.

"Sorry," she said and held out her free hand. Noting the familiar blue backpack he carried bearing a white name embroidered on a blue field that read CHEN, she smiled. "Air Force Academy?"

The man was her height, with short black hair cut in a perfect regulation haircut. He smiled. "Carl, Class of '06, out of Horny 18."

She rolled her eyes but smiled. "Ath—uhm, Val, 2010 UNC ROTC, out of Detachment 590," she said with her hand out.

He took it, giving the firm but not crushing handshake of a truly confident man. "Bomber driver, so I've got social skills now," he said with a laugh. His eyes darted to the two small girls skipping circles around him and an exasperated woman.

Athena gave a chuckle. "I'm—" She paused only briefly. "—an intel officer these days, so I think I have fewer social skills now. Sorry for bumping into you."

Carl released her hand with a friendly grin. "Don't worry about it, it happens. Especially as crowded as it is today."

Athena swallowed hard and nodded. "Yeah, it's filling up." She forced a smile to her face. "Well, sorry again, and have a great day."

She waggled her fingers at the two kids and nodded to the man's wife. She watched them walk off, consumed with the happiness of a family vacation, before resuming her pacing.

Athena paused across the road from Marco, leaning against a tree. Pushing up against the sky was the Washington Monument, the upper half of the white obelisk just glistening in the sun as it rose. Athena watched tourists, more numerous now than an hour ago, streaming across the grassy Mall.

"How are we going to protect all these people?" she whispered to herself, afraid to voice her fears across the link. Ares' plan was good, the best they had, but there were so many ways things could go wrong.

"Follow the plan, trust your team, and do what's right, Athena," a voice came from behind her.

"Bran?" Athena said as she turned.

Powell stood behind her, a hesitant smile on his face. "I have a team up and running back at work," he said. "I know there's not much I can do, but I wanted to support you."

He slipped a small bag off his shoulder and held it out. Inside, she found an assortment of candies, IV bags, and sugary sodas.

"I know most guys give flowers when they're making up with," he hesitated slightly. "Well, with female superhero friends, I thought this might be more useful."

"Oh, Bran ..." Athena said and melted into his embrace.

Athena? Hestia's hesitant voice came across in a tightly focused link she was starting to recognize as their personal connection.

Relieved Hestia hadn't said anything across to the group, Athena replied, *I'm fine. Brandon's here.*

"You're talking to them now, aren't you?" Powell asked. When she looked confused, he said, "You get a look in your eyes."

"Just Mandy right now, but yeah." She nodded to Powell and let a hint of laughter flow across her personal link to Mandy. He brought me a bouquet of candy and IVs.

You're a lucky woman, Valerie Hall, Hestia said.

Athena was relieved when she didn't feel even an ounce of jealousy in the response. *I think I am.*

Athena released Powell from her hug. "Just a few more minutes."

"I know. I came up via the Metro to Federal Center and walked from there. I can see the barricades and a few buses lining up."

Athena nodded. *Powell's here,* she told the group. *He says there are buses lining up. It's almost go time.*

The link thrummed with nervous anticipation.

I knew I liked that man, Marco said through the group.

Minutes ticked by.

First school buses rolling in now, Armstrong announced.

I've got a large charter bus passing the barricade at 4th and Madison, Lee replied.

"Gotta go," Athena told Powell. "It's time."

CHAPTER 25
THE PANTHEON MELANGE: PHASE 2
1303Z 0903L, 10 AUG

Big yellow Blue Bird school buses flowed past Athena and Powell, blocking their view of Marco.

Athena wrinkled her nose. "I don't like this, Bran."

"I know, it's blocking our line of sight to Air and Space." He took her hand. "Let's see if we can cut between them next time there's a break."

From his place at the National Museum of African American History and Culture at the western end of the Mall, Ares watched the first bus roll past the Metro Police barriers at Constitution Avenue and 14th Street and go south to make the left onto Jefferson Drive SW. His eyes scanned his assigned area to locate his assigned terrorist.

Years of experience and training guided his actions as he sought anyone out of place among the early morning throng of tourists. His man's face was front and center in Ares' mind, overlaid on every passing face for identification.

They looked at women as well as men, against the idea that a male terror bomber might be dressed in women's clothing.

Middle-aged men in cargo shorts carried toddlers. Harried mothers wore backpacks with tweens just old enough to be rolling their eyes in the middle of the morning. Twenty-somethings, Ares' age but without the weight of his life, cavorted and snapped pictures for social media.

His eyes scanned them all as he sought his targets: Young. White. Male. Wearing a jacket or hoodie on a sultry late summer morning. Ares' eyes flitted from group to group as he listened to Hestia's mental livestream.

Two from the south, Armstrong announced. *Disregard. One's taking his sweatshirt off now. No bomb vest.*

His was just one of many callouts of possibles being made since the 0900 hour passed eleven minutes ago. The young man dropped the sweatshirt to the soft grass and sprinted for a bright orange Frisbee tossed by his friend.

Another possible here, standby, said Armstrong broadcast.

Tension and worry radiated across the link. Athena frowned as she and Powell made their slow way across Madison, now clogged with buses. Her leg ached as she walked, and even putting more weight on her cane didn't abate the throb. No one mentioned it, but the growing pain from Athena's leg wound was caught in the link, affecting everyone associated.

Ares strode along the south side of the building, closest to the Washington Monument as he could be. He discreetly patted the 9mm Sig Sauer M18 tucked carefully along his back.

Given Limitless Logistics' extensive collection of handguns, he suspected he could have asked for a Dirty Harry revolver and gotten it, but he stuck with the weapon with which he'd trained, the military's version of the Sig P320 MHS.

Team, a possible, my location. Mid-twenties male, jacket, hands in pockets. Moving to intercept. Wilson Armstrong's "voice" was clipped but precise as it came across their link, and it was colored with a tinge of fear and anticipation.

Correction. He's early 30s, beard, shaved head. Still in a hoodie with hand in pockets and walking to the crowd.

The suspect then turned 360 degrees and Armstrong's mental facial recognition resounded across the link.

Tally ho! Positive ID, I say again, positive ID. Moving to intercept. The whole Pantheon could feel his energy across the link as he sprinted toward his target. Year of training in the gym carried Wilson, now pushing middle-age, across the Mall in an easy lope.

Ares, I hope this fucking works! Wilson yelled across the bond.

Get you some, shipmate! MPD and Coast Guard confirmed on location for pickup. Ares yelled back.

There was a feeling of exertion then a break. At the same time on the Mall, Ares saw Armstrong's form blur two people into one, and then the mass vanished. Armstrong's fear burned through the link as the mental image separated, becoming two figures, then one.

Release-release-release! came Armstrong's triumphant cry. Then only a moment later, *I'm okay, not blown up or anything! My guy was so shocked I think he held down his deadman button right until he raised his arms to break his fall from about maybe forty feet. Then his device went off when he hit the trees. I'm in the water right where I planned it. DC MPD boats are approaching, but I'm close enough to walk to the shore. I'm all right, y'all. I'm all right. Imma recover for a few minutes and then come back on station.*

For a moment the link went silent, then a chorus of mental cheers filled the link with joy.

Hestia? Ares asked. He could feel the faint thrum of the link, deep in his mind.

I'm here, she responded. *I ... I didn't think I'd feel that so ... closely!*

The link suddenly flared to life. More jubilation, unease, delight, and fear flared across the lines.

Whoa. Okay, everyone calm down. I'm not sure I can hold it! Hestia cried.

Ares let his breath out in a huff and nodded at Damarcus, who stood across the crowd from him.

The link's energy subsided before adrenaline spiked into the group again. Just then Wilson Armstrong appeared back in his previous stakeout position, dripping wet to the skin.

I'm back from the dead and ready to party, y'all! he announced. *Who's got next?*

From her vantage point across from the Air and Space Museum, Athena's eyes darted among the buses, seeking anyone dressed too warmly for a sultry May morning. Her eyes made brief contact with Marco as he scanned the crowd from his side as well.

Contact—Natural History! I'm approaching from 12th Street, Rich Dunn's voice called along the link.

I'm closer, at the pedicab stand right in front, Walker McCann called. Then he walked right up to the suspect and tapped him on the shoulder.

"I'm sorry, sir, but do you know what time the museum opens?" The man turned around and McCann grabbed his hand through the hood, compressing and securing the terrorist's thumb onto the deadman button.

Contact, Jumping! Walker grunted out and disappeared.

"Walker has one," Athena echoed for Powell.

Ares whirled around east a moment later as he heard Damarcus call.

Dark hair, jeans, light blue hoodie, African American Art Museum behind Smithsonian Castle off Independence.

Fortunately, the Museum and the Castle were both temporarily closed, and the civilian traffic back there was extremely light.

Ares could feel Dunn at the Natural History Museum break off and dash across the Mall toward Independence as Damarcus edged toward his suspect. Ares could feel the nervous anticipation as their exertion bled into the link. He desperately wanted to run toward them and help, but he stayed at his assigned post and scanned for more terrorists.

Athena ignored the physical sensations playing along Hestia's link as she and Powell approached the now stopped buses. "Let's cross here, Bran. We might not get a better shot."

The Mall was now a strange mix of the oblivious. Tourists going about their day while others looked around in confusion, hands going for their smartphones or walking and running toward their destinations. Just another nice day in Washington.

Rich Dunn's world shrank as he sprinted to close the distance and his focus narrowed on the image of the man Damarcus had identified. Dunn was only vaguely aware of Damarcus approaching from the other side, also at a dead run.

Everyone connected to Mandy's link felt the curious time dilation of adrenaline as two Jumps executed near simultaneously.

Contact, Jumping! Dunn heard Damarcus transmit only a few feet from him. He glimpsed Damarcus, hands outstretched, and his body laid out in a horizontal flying tackle, grab the bomber in a bear hug and instantly Jump, only a fraction of a second before Dunn arrived. His momentum carried him through the open air where Damarcus had grabbed the terrorist and disappeared.

There's a second suspect here—intercepting now! Rich's voice was calm despite the exertion they all felt in the link.

Through the link, Ares felt Rich's hands grabbing the bomber's, clamping down hard, and instantly he Jumped.

Release-release-release—I'm out! Damarcus called. Then, *Coast Guard helo's inbound for me now.*

Can't— was all Rich could say before the entire network felt Rich's connection wink out.

Damarcus reappeared not far from Ares, landing heavily on his stomach, soaking wet.

"Dee?" Ares asked. Around them, tourists could no longer ignore three mysterious disappearances and some started running away from the Mall area. Ares pushed through the streaming tide to get to Damarcus.

Before Damarcus could answer, James Lee chimed in from the National Gallery. *Runner!*

He sent the image of a young man with a square face, tight haircut, and wearing a green nylon Army flight jacket with military-style Oakley sunglasses.

Watch it, James! Ares broadcast as he checked Damarcus for injuries. *If he's spooked, he might blow early!*

"Marco!" Athena yelled as she and Powell pushed through the crowds near the Air and Space Museum.

On top of the growing chaos, Rich's severed connection was like a missing tooth to everyone on the link. Athena swallowed hard, trying to absorb what had happened and fearing the worst.

Rich? Rich! They could all hear Hestia calling and an urgent pressure grew along the link as she sought him.

Hold it, Hestia—hold the connection, Athena called. She shoved a man out of her way as she limped to the bus-lined road, Powell by her side.

There was a sensation of impact and rolling from James Lee then ...

Contact, Jumping!

"Keep looking, Bran," Athena said and closed her eyes, mind reaching out. *Hestia—the link to Rich, you dropped it.*

He's gone, Athena. Rich is just gone!

I know. I'm so sorry, but we need you. We need the link.

Athena's eye flew open as another detonation thundered across the Potomac from the west.

"One left," Powell said.

"Marco!" Athena shouted aloud, catching sight of him across the road. She limped abreast of a big yellow bus. Still unaware of what was going on around them and squealing in delight, a gaggle of children descended to the sidewalk and streamed from the bus.

CHAPTER 26
THE PANTHEON MELANGE: PHASE 3
1314Z 0914L, 10 AUG

At the African American Art Museum, Ares reeled back, his emotions suddenly his own. Without the link, his thoughts echoed inside his own mind.

"You okay, Dee?"

Dee grunted. "Yeah. Knocked the damn wind outta me though."

Ares looked up, suddenly conscious of the crowd growing around them. Some of the passing civilians had seen Damarcus materialize out of nowhere and stopped to gawk. There were plenty of sidewalk sideshows and street artists in DC, especially on a nice day at the National Mall. The onlookers thought Damarcus was one of them and they awaited his next trick.

Curious civilians watched Ares pat Damarcus's shoulder and rise, backing away as he did. Ares heard an excited chatter but couldn't make out anything distinct.

"Four, Dee," Ares said. "We got four."

Damarcus wince and sat up. "We lost any?" he asked.

"Dunno. Maybe Rich. He went offline and we don't know his status right now."

Damarcus was a pro, and he was determined to save more lives before he mourned any lost ones.

"So, what's left?" Ares asked,

Damarcus said, "Air and Space, I think? That's Marco and Athena." His eyes suddenly unfocused. "Link's up."

"Hestia?" Ares asked aloud. "I can't feel it, Dee."

"I think it's just you, me, Marco, and Athena in with Hestia." He shook his head. "It's just us."

Athena felt Hestia's link flicker back to life. Athena sensed the signal was weak, holding only herself, Hestia, Marco, and Damarcus.

Athena swallowed, wondering where the others were.

She hoped they weren't all dead.

Athena saw Marco's head snap to her right and she followed Marco's sightline, seeing a figure in a light blue hoodie sprinting toward them and the large gaggle of schoolkids.

Tally ho—contact front, Air and Space! Marco's voice thundered along the stilted link, overriding the physical pain and loss.

Athena tried to break into a sprint, but staggered and collided with someone standing near the bus. To her surprise, it was Carl Chen, the Air Force officer she'd bounced off earlier. She realized she was closer to the running figure than Marco but her lurching hobble would never reach the bomber in time.

Can't make it, Athena's cried to Marco. *Too far. Kids!*

She waved her arms frantically in the air.

"Back on the bus, get on the bus!"

She shouted and the words flowed along the link as she waved for the children who had exited. She turned to Chen.

"Get them and your family on the bus—*do it now!*" Afraid the terrorist would blow his bomb vest before Marco could reach him, she tried to mitigate the attack's effects by reducing the number of his potential victims.

From her left, Powell scooped three children up in his arms and bounded up the bus's stairs. On her right, Chen dropped his blue Academy bag and started scooping children up as well, following Powell's lead. Once the Chen and his family were in the center isle Powell screamed, "*Everybody down! Everybody get down right now!*"

Time slowed to a crawl once again. Athena could feel time dilation cause the second hand of the clock shudder to a halt. Adrenaline and Hestia's link burned through her.

Athena envisioned the open field in the middle of the grassy Mall and placed both hands flat against the yellow metal.

Kids are on bus—I'm Jumping it out of here!

No, *Athena, it's too much load!* Hestia cried in her mind.

Athena felt the sensation of Marco's hands on the bomber's hands and through Marco's eyes, the man's stunned snarl.

Contact! was Marco's triumphant cry.

Athena Jumped the entire bus—children, Powell, the Air Force officer with his family, and everyone else—onto the grassy middle and western end of the Mall. She staggered against the bus and started slumping to her knees, depleted. It had been a heavy lift but only a few hundred yards, the only reason why Athena didn't check out entirely.

Jumping! Marco called. There was a sensation of physical struggle. *Release-release-release!* Marco called out.

Safe! Athena cried before her vision went black. She clung to the edged of consciousness, vaguely hearing an explosion, distant and distorted.

Safe! Marco's voice shouted in echo along the link. *I'm ... I'm ... on the beach. Helo ...*

Athena took a deep breath, her vision coming back at the center. She felt Powell's hands on her.

"Athena?" Powell's deep voice called through the fog of her thoughts. The most immediate danger was past, and her sense of time sped up to reality.

Marco? Athena's voice called.

Marco! Hestia's anguished voice joined Athena's as they sought Marco.

Beach ... trouble ... came Marco's anguished reply. *Need ... need help* ... his voice trailed off.

Athena grabbed Powell's hands and, digging deep, Jumped them from the bus in the middle of the Mall to the rocky water's edge south of Little Island. When they appeared there, Athena's thoughts faltered. She found Marco laying on the ground, but her exhausted mind couldn't comprehend what she was seeing.

"Jesus, Marco!" Powell released his supporting hold on Athena and she slumped to her knees beside Marco, her hand reaching out for his, now slick with blood.

Marco? Damarcus and Mandy's voices echoed along the link.

Athena swallowed hard as what she saw finally registered and she choked back a sob. A large pool of blood flowed into the Potomac from where Marco's legs had been blown off at about the knees. Along his arms and chest, shrapnel holes oozed blood.

Powell immediately went into action, stripping off his belt and wrapping it tightly around Marco's left leg as a tourniquet. Without speaking, he pulled Athena's backpack from her shoulders to the wet rocks and removed a length of climbing rope that was carried in its side cargo pocket. He cut about seven feet of the line and applied a tourniquet to Marco's right leg.

"I got tangled in his legs," Marco whispered, his full lips gone pale and bloodless. "I kicked away and Jumped," he explained by voice and mind, "but I was late. A fraction of a second, Athena."

The Coast Guard helicopter landed as Powell pulled Marco's shirt apart and put QuikClot compresses on the two most serious shrapnel perforations in Marco's chest. The others didn't appear life threatening. A medic jumped out of the helo.

"We got it from here, sir!" the medic yelled over the roar of the helicopter.

"I'll help you get him in the chopper," Powell yelled back, and they carried Marco a few meters to the aircraft. It immediately lifted off and turned toward Maryland and Walter Reed National Military Medical Center.

"I'm sorry, Marco," Athena sobbed at the receding helicopter. "I'm so sorry!"

Despite two tourniquets, Marco's blood loss had been great. The blood seeping into gauze patches applied to a myriad of shrapnel punctures pulsed to the beat of Marco's slowing heart. Blood continued to flow from the shattered stumps of his legs, coating the helo floor and making it slippery.

It's *gonna be okay, Marco,* Athena broadcast to the link with false brightness in her mind and tears streaming down her cheeks.

Marco's hand was sticky with drying blood and he waved it weakly above his bloody chest as he replied, *Not for me, Athena. But you're right, bonita, it will be okay ... for you.*

Tio *Marco!* Hestia's anguished cry wailed across their link.

Athena could feel Damarcus also reach out through the shared connection and then pull back, heartbreak in his touch. He knew.

It's *okay, mija.* Marco's voice was weak as it whispered across the link. *Tell Mina and the girls I love them and I'm sorry. I love you too, Mandy. You're my third daughter and you know that. Take care of Athena for me, she'll need your help,* he told Mandy. *Tell Powell. Athena will need him* too, Marco whispered.

The Coast Guard helicopter made a tight final turn on a combat approach to Walter Reed. The copilot had radioed ahead and doctors, nurses, and a pristine white gurney waited near the concrete helipad.

Rich is gone. I'm gone, Madam Vicepresidenta, Marco said to Athena from Walter Reed as he was hustled directly into surgery. His warm chocolate eyes sought the clouds outside the aircraft's window, the light already fading from them. *You have the watch now, Athena ...*

No, *Marco!* Athena cried, still grasping his mind. *Not like this.* She felt his grip loosening with every slowing beat of his heart. *I can't, Marco. We need you.*

The succession protocols are in place. You know what Limitless needs, he breathed a shallow breath, his eyes closed. You're going to do great, kid. You are a fierce warrior! Athena, Goddess of War, is a wonderful new name for you. Wear it proudly ...

Marco's mental grip relaxed across the link and Hestia, Athena, and Damarcus felt the last tenuous touch of his mind wink out.

CHAPTER 27
AMANDA 'HESTIA' SQUIRES
1957Z 1557L, 12 AUG

Hestia stared at the ceiling, letting her mind go blank and centering herself. This would be one of the biggest moments in her life.

Unbidden, memories hit her.

The TVs in the Limitless Logistics 24-hour cafeteria had played all hours of the day, showing the aftermath of their actions on a twenty-four-hour news cycle. It had been a raw nerve, one that everyone in the building touched, but no one could bear to turn the TV off either. Even now, a two days later, tears welled in Hestia's eyes as she thought of the first hectic hours after the bombings.

Trying to recall everyone who was still alive.

Trying to find the bodies of the dead, friend and foe.

Trying to assess and treat injuries.

Trying to struggle forward with the physical and emotional toll.

Everyone on the Pantheon team had been left on their own to get back to Limited Logistics as best they could. Damarcus and Ares had arrived on Point Zero only seconds after Hestia had felt Marco's mind wink out. The found her slumped in a chair in Mission Control and eased her onto a couch, brought her cold water, and sat with her.

No one knew what else to do. Other anxious handlers checked on their Pantheon members as they arrived.

Wilson Armstrong had arrived not long after, loudly demanding to speak to Marco and angry that he didn't know Marco was dead.

They had feared the worst for James Lee, who no one had heard from since Hestia's first link dropped.

Athena Jumped in then to the small Point Zero established at the far end of the conference space. It was almost never used because no urgency requiring it had ever cropped up. The conference room phone had rung then and someone, maybe one of the handlers, had the presence of mind to open the line on the speakerphone. Nurse Sarah in the Limitless clinic called to tell them Lee had made a risky direct appearance in the clinic a while ago. He'd Jumped away from the riverbank right in front of Metro PD Harbor Patrol officers racing to rescue him, which left them very confused.

Lee was battered and bruised, Sarah reported, having impacted the concrete-like water of the Potomac from a height and with more momentum than was smart. She said his hip was fractured and they were getting him stabilized for a discreet ride to Walter Reed's emergency department with a cover story for damage control.

"Copy all, Sarah," Athena said, leaning close to the phone to be heard, unaware she was leaving bloody handprints on the table. "Disregard the cover story for now, just get him there," Athena said and locked eyes with Hestia, her head on Ares' lap.

"We'll clean it up later, if need be, but I don't think we're hiding much of anything anymore."

Hestia had calmed down enough to catch Athena's eye again, neither of them sure if Sarah was talking about damage control for James or Limitless Logistics.

"Keep us apprised, please, Sarah," Athena said calmer than her outward appearance showed. "And if you have anyone you can spare, would you please send up half a dozen Nutrium bags and lines. I think we all could use them."

The rest of the Pantheon and all the handlers and other staff crowded into the briefing room, finding seats, and landing heavily in them. The overwhelming satisfaction was well-tempered by the loss of Rich

Dunn, one of the longest-serving members of the Pantheon, and Marco Martinez, their leader and mentor.

But the theme was *A monster came for us and we killed it.*

Athena limped over to Hestia then, directing Ares to set her down in a chair. Hestia, formerly Mandy, having exhausted her anger, shook her head, voice choking in her throat and unable to speak. She held out a hand.

"I'm so sorry, hon," Athena said. At her touch, Athena's love and support flowed into Hestia. "I left Powell at the scene on the island. His people and the FBI gotta big job combing the forest for all that DNA they wanted for identification of the terrorists." She shook her head and grimaced. "Not to mention any unexploded ordnance. They can have all of those jobs."

Hestia could feel Athena's pain, physical and emotional, within the touch. Underneath was an iron resolve. Hestia felt what was coming next and nodded. She watched Athena stand and face the room.

"All right, everyone, quite a moment." Athena's voice carried above the whispers, shouts, and flurry of handlers assessing their Jumpers. Somewhere in the back, Mark, Rich Dunn's handler, had tears running down his cheeks.

Hestia felt something in the room shift as Athena stood, command radiating from her.

"Ryan," Athena pointed at the man. "I need you to get an after-action together: every Pantheon member and their medical status. Call security and lock down the building. No one in our out unless I say so. This is going to blow up and we all know it."

Athena turned to Marco's handler.

"John, I'm so sorry, but we need you now. Go down to Anna and get the house counsel over here stat. Joe, please go get Zora before Ares loses his mind and tears the office apart."

Ryan, John, and Joe departed on their tasks. Athena leaned on the desk and Hestia could feel the physical pain flow through her.

Athena called after them. "And Joe—let's get someone detailed to thaw out the former Congressman Belton, please?" Joe grinned and raised a thumb. She turned back to the room to see a group of upraised faces looking at her for answers. For leadership.

"Okay we're exposed, but not compromised," Athena said.." I have a plan for how we're going to mitigate some of it. And there's going to be some monumental shifts in how Limitless Logistics does business."

Before anyone could reply, the conference room phone rang. Athena hit the speakerphone button. "Limitless Logistics, Pantheon Actual."

"It's Jim Hastings. What happened out there? Where's Marco, Athena?" came the Secretary of Defense's tense voice.

Hestia closed her eyes, fighting down the stab of despair that hit her.

"Mr. Secretary, General Marco Martinez was killed in action this morning, sir," Athena said.

The SECDEF paused. "I am very sorry to hear that. We go back—went back—a long way. I trust you will inform me when any memorial program is planned. I'd like to be an official part of that."

"We will, sir," Athena said.

"Who's in command there? The public clamor over the terror plot seems to be getting overwhelmed by the reporting on those who saved us from it."

Without a moment's hesitation, Athena answered. "I am in command, sir, under our existing succession protocol. We're working up a public affairs plan, but we'll need your support to execute it."

They spent the next few hours planning and coordinating with the Secretary of Defense, a host of lawyers, and the Pantheon. Then everyone waited to see how the world would react to the news of superheroes in their midst.

Things had happened so rapidly that the Pentagon's press conferences had been disjointed at best. At first the Secretary of Defense denied military involvement, pointing to unnamed "federal agents" engaged in a "joint counter-terror effort to thwart an attack by foreign and domestic terrorist cells on U.S. soil."

But cellphone video captured by citizens on the Mall during the attacks clearly showed Ares, Rich, Athena, and Damarcus putting the *habeus grabbus* on terror suspects and then disappearing with them into thin air. Internet sleuths and Reddit detectives soon identified them as active-duty military before noon the second day, and the Secretary of Defense had been forced to acknowledge that "a secret group of elite military members had assisted federal agents."

He had to soft-pedal the CIA involvement on domestic soil.

Social and news media, especially those with hard-right politics, had been shrill that the Secretary of Defense disregarded the Posse Comitatus Act of 1878, which generally forbids police actions by the military on American soil. Internet gumshoes, having already outed Athena, Damarcus, and Ares as military members, dug deeper into their lives. Soon, their full names and employment at Limitless Logistics was public knowledge.

Then a food worker in the Limitless cafeteria leaked the whole Pantheon story to the NBC correspondent covering the Pentagon and national security, and the feces really hit the fan.

Hestia inhaled and looked at the ceiling again, this time careful to keep from looking directly at the extremely bright TV lights that blazed just beyond the curtain in the DOD press room.

"Peace be with you, child," Senator Maureen Mitchell whispered to her and held out a hand.

Hestia eyed the hand skeptically but Mitchell held it steady. One look in her eyes told her that the Senator had nothing to hide. She reached out. Her shoulders sank as she absorbed the support in Mitchell's touch.

Senator Maureen Mitchell, previously a staunch opponent of everything Limitless had to offer, was now its biggest supporter. Those who had thought to come after the Pantheon with torches and pitchforks ready to burn the witches—literally and figuratively—had been met with Mitchell's calm assertions.

"Pray with me?" Mitchell asked, eying the small gold cross on a thin chain around Hestia's neck. She nodded.

"Heavenly Father, we ask your guidance on this day as we seek to use the gifts you given us in your name," Mitchell squeeze Hestia's hand lightly. "We pray for wisdom and guidance as we guide others in this troubling time. Grant us peace as we mourn our friends and the strength to move forward as we honor them. In your Heavenly name, Amen."

"Amen," Hestia said and squeezed the senator's hand lightly.

"Are you ready?" Mitchell asked her. "This is prime time on a Friday and every news agency worth a damn is here. Even several not worth a damn. You are coming to them live in prime time."

Hestia nodded. "They've already seen what the Pantheon can do. Let's just explain it to them."

The Missouri senator nodded. "Very well then." She smiled her warmest. "But just explain to them like they were six-year-olds."

Mitchell turned to the man seated beside her. "Mr. Secretary, we are ready if you are."

At the man's nod, they all walked to a single podium bathed in studio lights. From somewhere a voice announced them. "Senator Maureen Mitchell, Chair of the Senate Armed Services Committee; Secretary of Defense James Hastings; and Ms. Amanda Squires—Chief Executive Officer of Limitless Logistics."

Senator Mitchell kicked it off.

"Ladies and gentlemen, what we witnessed two days ago is nothing short of a miracle," Mitchell began as the SECDEF and Hestia waited calmly beside her. "We're here to provide background on what you and others witnessed. First, despite some internet accounts, nothing was faked. The videos you've seen are real. A group of special individuals, working with and for the Department of Defense, stopped the largest terrorist attack on U.S. soil since 9/11." She gestured to SECDEF. "Secretary Hastings has more on that."

Mitchell took two steps back and Jim Hastings stepped to the microphone.

"Good afternoon. I will read a prepared statement and will not take any questions at this time." Hastings pulled reading glasses from his suit coat pocket and slipped them on his face, arranging his papers. "As many of you know, the Pentagon has always had elite units with special capabilities: SEALs, Army Rangers and Green Berets, Delta Force, and others. The team at Limitless Logistics is no different than any other elite unit except for one minor difference: where SEALs and Rangers are combat focused, Limitless Logistics has been, as the name states, an elite logistics team. They do not engage in combat operations."

The room exploded into shouts and unintelligible questions.

Secretary Hastings simply raised one hand, quieting the rabble.

"Yes, they were part of the team that halted this attack—in fact, they were the entire team of operators. Their actions resulted in the death of five hostile white nationalist individuals before any of them could detonate bomb vests intended to make the attack look like it was made by Islamic extremists. But I stress that the Limitless actions were completely logistically oriented and in self-defense. They rapidly moved hostile individuals wearing suicide vests out of the range of hundreds, perhaps thousands, of endangered and innocent civilians. Very regrettably, due to the special nature of their capabilities, two of their own members were killed in the process."

Hestia swallowed hard, keeping her emotions in check. Everything was moving so fast, but new day, same stuff, she thought. How she ever thought she could stay removed from Pantheon turmoil was still a mystery to her.

"That's all I have for now. We will have more for you in the coming days and weeks." Hastings gestured to Mandy. "Ms. Squires?"

Hestia took one last deep breath and limped up to the podium.

"Good afternoon." She was glad the studio lights washed out most of the people beyond the front row of reporters. "Until last week I was Amanda Squires, but today and going forward, I am Hestia, CEO of Limitless Logistics ..."

A reporter stood and shouted from the front row. "What's your last name?"

She pinned him with a commanding, unblinking stare.

"It's just Hestia," she replied.

The reporter sat back down.

"As has been shown on more cellphone video than we cared to see, Limitless Logistics is comprised of men and women we call the Pantheon. They are able to instantly teleport to and from known locations on Earth."

The room was hushed for a moment and then again exploded in a cacophony of screaming questions. Aides appeared at the ends of each row of reporters with press kits on thumb drives that were quickly distributed down the rows.

"We call it Jumping. We intend to deploy Limitless assets to focus on unclassified humanitarian missions, such as moving food and supplies point-to-point during natural disasters. We will offer instantaneous transport of critical organs for transplants and other rapid commercial transportation services. We expect the operational portfolio to expand as new customer demands are identified."

Tom Drew, a cable network reporter in the back near the pool camera stand, raised a hand holding a digital recorder and shouted out when the din subsided.

"Ms. Hestia—whoever that is or whatever your real name is—some of *our* experts are still reviewing the videos from the Mall and we're told they look faked. Completely made up. Why would the DOD cooperate with a nominally civilian enterprise to put this obvious hoax before the American people, who are smarter than you all apparently think they are?"

Senator Mitchell jumped up. "You are out of order, sir!" she bellowed as only she could.

Hestia raised her hand.

"It's all right, Senator." She shaded her eyes from the TV lights. "You folks in the back row? Please stand and pull your chairs away from Mr. Drew, please, so I can see better."

A dozen reporters stood and made a clear space. Drew knew his network's camera was in the pool and would be trained on him. His face took on a smirk. *This bitch has nothing for me*, he thought.

"You pool cameras on my left—" Hestia pointed to them. "—stay focused up here. You others point at the space in front of Mr. Drew."

It only took a few seconds for the cameramen to respond.

Hestia turned to Hastings. "Mr. Secretary, would you please count backward from three?"

The SECDEF stood and counted. "Three ... two ... *one!*"

Hestia vanished from the dais and appeared only inches from Tom Drew's face. The room went crazy, and Drew was so startled by her appearance and the powerful air displacement that when he reflexively stepped back, he tripped on the TV camera riser and fell on his butt.

A half-dozen TV cameras looked over her shoulders at the man on the floor as Hestia leaned over him.

"Hestia is the goddess of hearth and home. Fitting for a humanitarian-focused company, don't you think?" Hestia said with a smile. "Any other questions?"

Two hours later, Athena, Hestia, Ares, and the rest of the team were holding a restrained celebration of life for Marco Martinez and Rich Dunn in the large conference room and watching a replay of the press availability unspool on cable news. Hestia's Jump from the press room dais to confront Tom Drew was playing over and over on all the cable news channels, in slow motion, and supplemented by numerous cellphone videos shot of the demonstration.

"Classic, Hestia," Athena said with a big grin. "Just classic."

Hestia smiled. "Mean people suck," she said.

On the big-screen TV, the recorded press conference was winding down and Senator Mitchell was back before the microphone, to no one's great surprise.

"Many of you out there have said nasty things and made drastic accusations of the last forty-eight hours. But hear me when I tell you these are good people, doing good work. Like the parable of the Talents, they too have been given talents, special skills, and like the first two servants, they are using their skill in service to our nation. The sin would be for them to keep their gifts locked away."

Senator Mitchell smiled at the cameras.

"On Monday morning, I am introducing a bill that will designate these special people and their skills as specific national security assets," Senator Mitchell promised. "I already have 79 co-sponsors. This will effectively shield Limitless and the Pantheon from frivolous and harassing litigation and legal castigation, among other benefits. We need them, as much as we need our conventional military branches. We need their skills. And I will not allow ignorance or bigotry to hamper them. There are bigger enemies to defend against in the world."

When Mitchell concluded her comments and stepped back, the room exploded into questions again. She nodded to Hestia who, by their previous agreement, Jumped back to Limitless Logistics in full view of the cameras.

"Well done, Madam CEO," Athena said.

"Thanks, Athena." Hestia settled into a chair across from her boss.

Athena muted the television. "Really, though, you did well. You looked confident and strong."

Hestia nodded. "Is all the paperwork done?"

"Yup," Athena said, shoving a stack of papers toward her. "You are officially the CEO of Limitless Logistics, a commercial logistics company with no government contracts as of today."

"And Ares?" she asked.

Athena smiled. "Ares is delighted to be the working boss of a newly formed command that will engage in special military operations at the direction of the SECDEF. 'Ares Tactical' was his name choice." She rolled her eyes. "*Men*," she said with a wince. "Catchy, though."

The two women shared a smile.

"But Ares Tactical's provisos allow it to function only on government direction, of course. We all retain our military affiliations and pay grades because the government paying us under a whole new contract structure would be a cost even our current political supporters might blanche at." Athena shrugged, resigned to looming changes. "We don't have to reinvent that wheel. Uncle Sugar will still pay us separately for mission work, as before when it was just for Limitless."

"And you?" Hestia asked quietly.

"Shell games again," she said with the ghost of a smile on her lips. "I am the CEO of what the public will know as Athena Strategic Logistics, but inside the DOD it will be known as the 467th Logistics Group, based at Joint-Base Anacostia-Bolling. It buys me time to move Ares Tactical and Athena Strategic out of this building and to a secure combined facility outside of DC. Dee has agreed to be my vice commander, not that I gave him much choice, but I can't oversee two companies alone."

"So, my briefing was just the beginning."

"Yes," Athena said. "Limitless Logistics will again be a logistics-focused company. A lot of what Limitless used to do off the rate card will happen now under Ares and Ares Tactical."

"That seems ..." She searched for the right word. "... devious."

Athena shrugged. "No, just classified. But I expect this furor won't die down quickly and it gives a good face while still ensuring our special skills are available to the SECDEF." Athena paused, considering. "Do you think Senator Mitchell will keep her word?"

"Yes. She's going to hold this over you forever, but she'll use every ounce of her considerable political heft to get us covered. She's a big believer now."

Athena nodded.

A silent moment passed between the two women.

"How are you? Really?" Athena asked.

Hestia shrugged and slumped in her chair. "Fine."

"Liar."

"Maybe."

Athena held out her hand. "It gets easier. Not fast. Not without bumps, but eventually the burden is manageable."

Hestia grasped Athena's hand, letting their bond ease some of her pain. She saw memories surface across Athena's mind: Athena, a young girl in a black dress, at her mother's funeral; Athena, an hour ago, wiping tears from her eyes as she investigated Marco's darkened office for the first time as its occupant.

A tap at the door broke their reverie. "Hey, Athena—oh, hi Hestia,"

Hawkins said with a smile as he leaned in. “I have all the paperwork squared away.”

“Thanks.”

“I’m headed down to grab dinner. Either of you want to join me?”

Hestia gave him a smile. “I’d love to join you. Athena?”

“Thanks, but I’m going to finish up a few things first. I’ll be down in a few.”

Even without physical contact, Hestia could feel Athena give her a mental smirk and a shove toward Ares.

CHAPTER 28
VALERIE 'ATHENA' HALL
1548Z 1148L, 15 AUG

Athena stood at the threshold to Marco's office. The warm colors and dark wooden desk, at odds with the sleek, ultra-modern look of the rest of the building, usually exuded an inviting aura. Now the emptiness left an aching void in Athena's heart. The steely composure she'd cloaked herself in for the last few days crumbled and she sunk into the plush leather chair in the lobby for those waiting on a meeting. Athena dropped her head into her hands, golden red hair curtaining across her face to hide the tears she couldn't stop.

She felt a gentle hand on her shoulder and a tissue appeared at the edge of her vision. She looked up to see Anna, Marco's secretary, offering the tissue with one warm brown hand, wrinkled by time. Athena took it wordlessly, surprised by the gesture. Brisk and efficient, Anna wasn't known for her warmth, but Athena saw tears in her eyes as well.

"Thank you, Anna," Athena said with a sniffle. They were quiet a moment as Athena stared at the wall across the hallway, decorated with some modern art piece.

"You were exactly what he was looking for, you know," Anna said quietly as she settled into the chair at her desk again.

"Anna?"

"I know you two had your points of friction, especially at the beginning, but you were what he wanted as a replacement," she gave a genuine smile. "I know he was ready to turn the reins over to Rich when the time came, but I think they were both relieved when you came in. Even if you turned things upside down once a week," she said with a grin.

Athena grinned through her last of her tears. "I guess I did shake things up a bit, didn't I?"

"It's good. We needed it." Anna reached into a desk drawer and withdrew a pristine white envelope. She laid it on her uncluttered desk and pushed it across to Athena.

Athena stared at her, surprised. "What's that?"

"My resignation. It's undated, so you may accept it whenever your mood strikes. An incoming commander has a right to her own staff."

Anna shook her head and neat corkscrew curls swayed with the movement.

"Athena dear, I've been here almost the entire time Limitless has been operating. I've watched the company be bullied by a government who held their secrecy as the ultimate blackmail." Her eyes flicked to the television, displaying four news channels, all of which were replaying news and social media videos from the terror attack. "It may not have been the way Marco would have wanted to introduce the company to the world, but you've ripped the band aid off and we're out there now."

Athena followed her gaze to the television. As if on cue, each station switched to Hestia's statements and interviews from the week before. Two of the stations then played Senator Mitchell's follow-up statement throwing the full support of the HASC and SASC behind Limitless. A mixture of emotions washed over Athena.

"It's a risk," she said quietly.

"Sure, but aren't all things? Think of all the good you and Limitless, all of it, can do now without lurking in the shadows."

Athena nodded. "It's a brave new world, huh?"

She paused and her eyes fell on Anna's resignation. Athena pushed the envelope back to her.

"As my chief executive assistant, I trust you know what I want you to do with this."

Anna gave a small smile and nodded. She turned and dropped the envelope into a small blood-red pouch labeled BURN BAG. Then her tone went business-like.

"You will need to move into Marco's space, you know."

Athena looked over her shoulder to the empty office. "Now?" A stabbing ache lanced through her heart.

"It won't get easier with time. You've ripped one band-aid off. It's time for the next one. It is actually what Marco wanted, after all."

Athena stood, still awkward and unsteady, but she no longer needed the cane. She stared over her shoulder into the large office.

"Just get your bearings today. We can get housekeeping to move your things tomorrow. The daily business of Limitless can keep rolling along on autopilot another few days."

Athena nodded and limped into the office.

She took in the room, heart aching with every photo of Marco's family she saw. Photos of the Limitless team in business suits, uniforms, or their tactical trousers and ubiquitous travel pack lined the walls. Athena realized Marco had loved the Limitless team as much as his own blood.

Athena sat tentatively on the front edge of Marco's chair and her eyes fell on a photo of her, Hestia, and Marco eating lunch in the Limitless cafeteria. It sat side by side with a portrait of his family. The angle of the shot said it was a frame grab taken from a security camera. Athena picked up the photo, realizing it must be the only shot of the three of them he could get without asking for one.

Athena's heart broke all over again as she realized that at some point, he must have specifically asked someone to capture the image, print it, and put it in the silver frame. That he would so treasure what was, by all photographic standards, a crappy shot, spoke to the depths of his love for Athena and Hestia. But she was still just his niece then, still just Mandy. Athena swallowed hard as she cradled the photo in her hands and vowed to keep it.

"General Hall? Athena?" Anna's voice was hesitant over the titles, but it cut through the reverie.

Athena put the photo back next to Marco's family.

"Okay, first, you know better than that. Yes?"

"I'm sorry, Athena, but I needed you to make that decision." Anna smiled warmly, and Athena wondered where her chilly reputation had been born. "I know I said business could wait, but something has come up," Anna said.

"Okay." Athena wiped her eyes with the backs of her hands. She knew she was going to have to be the boss one day. She guessed it was now. "What's up?"

Anna's mouth turned down in a pinched frown. "I think we may have two, uh, candidates."

"Candidates? For what?"

"Security has five individuals downstairs who said they saw, Ms. Squires—uhm—Hestia's interview on TV. They say they think they belong here."

Athena's eyebrows shot up. She knew she should have expected this after Hestia's interview—she'd all but invited it—but given how rare the ability was, she hadn't anticipated five people stepping forward so quickly.

"Where are they?" She rose from Marco's chair and wobbled toward the door.

"They're in Conference Room B, on the first floor."

"Can you pull up a room feed?" Athena asked, thinking quickly.

Anna nodded and pulled up the security camera.

Athena studied the room, still thinking. She smirked and clapped Anna on the shoulder.

"You might as well tune in; I think I've got an idea. Send Joe to the Jump Room and record both locations." She quirked a smile at Anna and eyed her Air Force uniform hanging under its plastic dry-cleaner nightshirt behind her office door.

"I think this first impression has to count for something," Athena said. Anna departed and Athena donned her uniform, then Jumped into Conference Room B.

Athena landed neatly behind the lectern. She dropped her hands loudly onto the wooden top and smiled as every startled pair of eyes snapped to her. The two men standing in one corner looked stunned and scared. A third man standing near the conference table gave her a shallow nod. A woman seated at the table looked fearful but resolute. The last man who lounged against the wall gave her a tentative smile. An unruffled Security officer stood quietly in a corner.

"Good morning and welcome to Limitless Logistics. I'm General Valerie 'Athena' Hall. I understand you are presenting yourself as candidate logistics officers?" She scanned their faces as they nodded. "Very well, then. It's a pleasure to meet you all."

She walked from behind the lectern, approaching the man leaning against the wall with her bare hand outstretched. She held an image of Point Zero securely in her mind as she greeted each of the five people with a firm handshake, taking their mental impressions.

She returned to the front of the room. "Now, if you are the kind of candidate we're seeking, you can follow me," she gave them a wicked grin, "because you know where I'm going. I'll thank the rest of you for your interest and Security will see you out."

She Jumped without another word.

"Hey Joe, you ready to add a couple trainees?" she asked him with a smile once her feet hit the concentric Point Zero circles. She moved off the location into the Jump Room.

"Anna said there were five?"

"Were five, but only two legit ones."

He flashed her a smile that was an impressive twin of hers. "I'll make sure Security escorts the other three out."

"All done," Athena said.

A moment later, the swarthy handsome man who'd nodded at her greeting landed inside the Jump Room. Joe ushered him off Point Zero just as the tall woman who'd sat at the table stumbled in a few seconds behind him. Athena nodded with a smile. "Welcome to Limitless Logistics. We're so glad you're here."

An hour later Athena was introducing the recruits to Hestia. Jaffar al Rayyan, a 22-year-old from Chicago by way of Doha, Qatar, was scared out of his wits by his abilities. Rachel Ng, formerly and unfortunately known as 'Diamond Steele,' a 21-year-old prostitute from Detroit, had used hers to escape her abusive pimp.

"Hestia will be in charge of your training from here, but if you need anything let her or me know. We're here to help you control your abilities and survive their effects, but we're also a family." She looked at Rachel and Jaffar giving both a gentle smile. "We're all broken in some way and it's easier to heal when your family is there to help." She shot Hestia a smile as well and was happy to see it returned.

Athena Jumped back to the corner of waiting room outside of Marco's office where a Point Zero was established.

"How was it, Anna?" Athena was pleasantly surprised when the woman laughed.

"That was a joy to watch," she said, voice brimming with mirth. "Oh, Lord! Those three boys threw an absolute fit when you Jumped out. About lost their collective minds when the other two figured it out and Jumped after you." She wiped her eyes.

"Security have any problems with them?"

"No, they knew they couldn't fake their way in here. I think one had some strong words as he left but they all went fairly quietly."

"Good. Save the video and send a link to the rest of the Pantheon. That will be our candidate briefing and protocol from here on out."

Anna nodded. "One, ah, discreet question, if I may?"

"Shoot."

"The young lady, she's a 'scarlet' woman, is she not?" Anna asked gently.

Athena nodded. "Well, interesting characterization. I guess the bruises and tattoos are something of a giveaway. She's a Pantheon member now, but yes, she was a sex worker and escaped an abusive situation. She is welcome to speak about it to anyone she'd like, but as far as her records will go? There will be nothing regarding her prior occupation. With that in mind, please send their details to DCSA and let's get their backgrounds started."

The Defense Counterintelligence and Security Agency typically performed background investigations for people applying for Executive Branch jobs, but they gave priority to Pantheon backgrounders.

Anna nodded. "Yes, ma'am." She paused, clearly thinking. "We have a few specialists on retainer, would you like for me to arrange a discreet session for her with one of our crisis counselors?"

Athena smiled, glad to see that Anna recognized that they woman was a victim, not a criminal. "Yes, please. Let's have one available and I will mention it to Rachel."

"Any other business for our new trainees?"

"No, I think Hestia has it under control. I would—" she paused, considering. "Please let Hestia know that the crisis counselor is available to her as well."

"Yes, ma'am." Anna gave her a motherly look. "Should I, uhm ... I mean ... for you?"

Athena took a calming breath.

"Yes, Anna. I ..." she swallowed hard. "Sure. I would speak to them as well." She inhaled sharply. "I think I have a few things I need to work out as well."

Anna laid a warm hand on her forearm. Sympathy and pride flowed through the touch. "The first step and all that jazz, my girl."

Athena gave her a smile. "Thank you. I'll be in my office for the next bit, then possibly out as I smooth things over with our liaisons."

Anna nodded and Athena limped into her new office. Marco's office, she thought.

She snagged her cellphone as she settled heavily into the chair, thumbing the phone open and touching the message app. She stared at the phone with her mouth compressed into a thin line.

Hey dork, you around?

She hit send and bit her lip. To her surprise, Brandon Powell's response was almost immediate.

Running, almost home. You need to meet up?

Terse and to the point, she thought, some things never change. A spark of hope ignited in her and she bit her lip again. She did want to meet up, but it needed to be somewhere neutral if she was going to rehash their actions of recent days.

Yeah, I'd like to talk. Do you have somewhere quiet you'd feel comfortable talking? She hit Send. Knowing how paranoid Powell could be, she felt it prudent to offer him his choice of places. Doubtless, he had some secret hole-up that he'd already swept for listening devices.

I'll be out of the shower in ten. Come on over then, you still have the "keys." I know I asked you not to but you have my permission use them right now.

Athena's mouth hung open. She'd expected to meet him at the CIA headquarters. Or at least somewhere neutral.

Yeah, k. See you then.

She re-read the message and a spark of something else ignited at the thought of him in the shower. She bit her lip, pushing the image of water coursing over the hard muscles in his back out of her mind.

Focus.

She needed to have this conversation. To shore up the little bits of their broken trust that had healed while they worked the last few days. But her mind drifted back to an image of him, towel hanging off his hips as he smiled at her over his bathroom sink.

Focus.

She groaned in frustration and checked the clock. Seven more minutes.

Five more minutes.

"Anna, I'm done here for the day and headed out," she called into the outer office.

"Yes, ma'am. Would you," she hesitated, "would you like me to start packing General Martinez's things this afternoon?"

Athena gave her a horrified look. "No. Gods, no." She shook her head. "I'll start on it tomorrow."

"Yes, ma'am." Anna gave her a look steeped in maternal attention. "I contacted the house counselor; your appointment is scheduled for tomorrow morning at ten."

Athena choked back a bitter reply and smiled.

"Thank you, Anna. Truly."

Anna nodded once and turned back to her computer.

Athena checked the clock on her phone. Three minutes. With a nod to Anna, she shuffled out of Marco's office toward the Jump Room. She could have Jumped straight from the office, but she wanted the last few minutes to clear her mind.

She passed their new trainees in the hall, trailing after Joe as he escorted them to in-processing. She gave them a warm smile and a nod. Jaffar gave her a nod of his head and Rachel returned her smile warmly. Athena looked forward to getting their deeper stories later. For now, she knew they were in Joe's capable hands and with Hestia and Ares leading their teams, the daily business of Athena Strategic Logistics could wait.

As soon as ten minutes had gone by, she sent Powell a text. On my way.

He may have given her permission, but she waited until she got his quick reply before she Jumped from the Jump Room directly into his living room.

"Hey, Athena," he said quietly. His damp brown hair was uncombed and stuck out all over.

"Hey, Bran." She leaned on her weight on her good leg. "I just—" she stopped. Athena swallowed hard. "I wanted to tell you that I've had Anna schedule me for therapy. I'm going to get some help."

The tension that had been etched in Powell's body rushed out. "Oh, Athena," he said and scooped her up in a hug.

"I needed you to know. I didn't want you to think that, if anything happens with us, that I'm using you."

He, then held her at arm's length and looked deep into her eyes. "I know things are weird right now. I know you're working through things, but I'm so glad to hear that. I want to fix this. Athena," he pulled her close, "I love you."

Athena's hands went to his face. She didn't have to ask if he was serious, she felt the love through his touch. "I love you too, Bran."

He hugged her tight. "You will get through this. We'll get through this. Together."

She smiled and pulled him in for a kiss.

Later, as they showered together, something nagged at the back of her mind. Something that had itched at her for the last week, but she couldn't put her finger on it.

Together.

Or in Russian, *Vmeste*.

That was it. They had exposed the Pantheon to the world and hadn't heard a single thing from their Russian counterparts.

END.

ACKNOWLEDGMENTS

I'm grateful to **Charlie "Thunder" Goetz, Dr. Katherine "Newt" Pratt, Kevin Pratt**, the pseudonymous **'Angry Staff Officer,'** and **Kelly "KGB" Borukhovich,** my team of beta readers. They provide me with vital proofreading and help poke at the holes in my plot. Thank you for ensuring I balance the fiction with a dose of reality.

My thanks to **Joe Brown** for his insight on canine handling and his fabulous taste in tattoos. And my thanks to **Matt Holmes** for helping me understand HH-60 emergency procedures and a realistic weight for my Pantheon to move.

Thank you to **Carl "Snickers" Chen**, who was my "Murder Me" contest winner/victim. He and I approached it with a clear understanding that, given the content of the book, there was no way I was willing to kill him off. I appreciate his help as we crafted a scene that worked for both of us and emphasized the themes of the novel.

Of course, due to my day job, I have to be careful not cross the streams between the daily grind and chasing down this dream. My thanks to **Chunks** who signed the paperwork, allowing me to dot my i's and cross my t's to do this in my free time.

As always, my thanks to **Daniel Charles Ross** (*Force No One*) who has helped me mature as an author and is a wonderful mentor. Thank you for the patience you show as we turn my drafts into published novels.

I would be remiss if I didn't thank **my Mom**. She doesn't always understand my passions and hobbies, but she has always stood behind me and offered her unwavering support. Whether it was my military career, bodybuilding competition, triathlons, ultra-marathons, or writing, she supported me.

Finally, my thanks to **my husband** who has supported me from the very start of my writing. He was the first person to hear how I wanted to write this novel. He and I hashed out some of the details of my villain while we waited for traffic to clear on Highway 3 from Seward to Heely, Alaska. He has read every story, no matter how terrible, and offered enthusiastic support of my goals. He's supported me through the publication of masters theses, white papers, academic work, and now fiction.

I thank him for his love, understanding, patience, and support; I could not have done it all without him.

KR Paul
Florida Panhandle
September 2020

About the author

KR Paul was born in California but moved to North Carolina as a child. She grew up rock climbing, horseback riding, and writing fan-fiction like lots of 90s kids. Her love of adventure took her into the US Air Force where her love of writing grew.

She has written non-fiction for business, industry, academia, and leadership education. Through it all, she kept her love of writing and continued to write fiction in her free time.

Today, KR still works her military day job but writes short and novel-length fiction when not being an absolute jock or absolute nerd. When not at work, her hobbies include competitive bodybuilding, video gaming, kayaking, cosplay, skydiving, and playing with light sabers.

Her work serves up a blend of powerful action and the vivid world of urban fantasy. She draws from her own life experiences to fuel the emotionally charged, fast-paced plots found in the *Pantheon* series.

For more information on this and other exciting new authors, please see ForcePoseidon.com
reachout@ForcePoseidon.com

EMAIL

WEBSITE

Made in the USA
Las Vegas, NV
09 September 2021

29905534R00174